THE DROWNED ONES

Recent Titles by Sara Fraser from Severn House

THE DROWNED ONES

A Thomas Potts Mystery

Sara Fraser

This first world edition published 2009
in Great Britain and 2010 in the USA by
SEVERN HOUSE PUBLISHERS LTD of
9–15 High Street, Sutton, Surrey, England, SM1 1DF.

British Library Cataloguing in Publication Data

Fraseer, Sara.
   The Drowned Ones. – (A Thomas Potts mystery)
   1. Potts, Thomas (Fictitious character) – Fiction.
   2. Police – England – Redditch – Fiction. 3. Drowning
   victims – Fiction. 4. Detective and mystery stories.
   I. Title II. Series
   823.9'14-dc22

ISBN-13: 978-0-7278-6854-1   (cased)

All Severn House titles are printed on acid-free paper.

Severn House Publishers support The Forest Stewardship Council [FSC],
the leading international forest certification organisation. All our titles that
are printed on Greenpeace-approved FSC-certified paper carry the FSC logo.

Mixed Sources
Product group from well-managed
forests and other controlled sources
www.fsc.org Cert no. SA-COC-1565
© 1996 Forest Stewardship Council
FSC

Typeset by Palimpsest Book Production Ltd.,
Grangemouth, Stirlingshire, Scotland.
Printed and bound in Great Britain by
MPG Books Ltd., Bodmin, Cornwall.

ONE

I t was late at night when the horseman set out on his journey. He made no farewells and avoided the roads where he might meet with other travellers, choosing instead to take little-used track ways across wastelands and woodlands. For several hours he trotted steadily on through the darkness, until with the first greying shades of the eastern horizon signalling the coming of daylight he reached the canal that stretched from Birmingham to Worcester. He moved cautiously along its towpath and breathed a sigh of relief when he finally sighted his destination, the graceful slender spire of St Bartholomew, the Tardebigge Parish Church, standing on top of the hill that sloped down to the canal. There was a stretch of thick woodland close to the church. Dismounting, he led his horse up the slope and deep into the shadowed depths of the trees.

The beast snickered uneasily; he stroked its soft muzzle and spoke soothingly into its ear.

'Be easy, my beauty. We shall hide quietly here until she comes, and then I'll do the business and be rid of her forever.'

TWO

I t was Mothering Sunday and by long-hallowed tradition young servant women and apprentices were being freed from their bondage for the day so that they might visit their families.

At John Daws' isolated farm his two serving girls had risen hours before dawn to complete their many arduous chores, and now, just after sunrise, they waited in the kitchen dressed in their fineries, while in the bedroom above their heads their master roused from his drunken slumber grunting and coughing.

'Just hark to him! If ever I heard a churchyard cough that's it.' Rosie Brent giggled.

'Well I just hope that he lasts out 'til Michaelmas because the way things are, we'll certain sure not be able to find another place afore then.' Martha Standard was under-sized, dark and sallow featured, in sharp contrast to blonde-haired, red-cheeked, strapping Rosie.

'It udden't bother me if he was to fall down dead this very minute,' Rosie grinned. 'Because after today I'll not give a bugger about this job.'

Martha stared in surprise. 'What d'you mean, Rosie?'

The clumping of heavy boots sounded from the stairs and Rosie put her finger to her lips. 'Shush now! I'll tell you later.'

John Daws came into the room, features haggard and unshaven, croaking hoarsely. 'For pity's sake, 'ull one o' you lazy mares get off your arse and get me a jug o' cider. I'm feeling like death warmed up.'

'And you'm bloody well looking like it, as well,' Rosie retorted. 'And it's your own fault, so don't expect any pity from me.'

Daws slumped down on to the bench facing them and laid his head on his arms, groaning. 'Don't go on at me, Rosie. Can't you see how badly I am?'

She rose and left the room to reappear a few seconds later with a cider-filled earthenware jug. 'Here you are, you silly old sod. Take a sup o' this and you'll be as right as rain.'

He snatched the jug and slurped greedily for long seconds, the glottal in his scrawny throat bobbing rapidly up and down. Then he slammed the empty jug on to the table and belched resoundingly. 'That's it! John Daws is his own man again!'

'Yes, and John Daws is going to be on his own from this very moment,' Rosie declared forcefully. 'Come on, Martha, time's a-wasting and our mams am waiting.'

'What about me breakfast?' Daws demanded.

'It's on the bloody dresser there.' Rosie pointed to the platter of cheese and onions, and the cottage loaf.

'Well, what about me dinner, and me supper?'

This time Rosie pointed to the kitchen range where a large iron pot was hanging on its chain above the fire. 'There's a stew in there which come noontime 'ull be done to a turn. And before you asks, the answer's yes! We'se done all the bloody chores and seen to the beasts.

They'll be as right as rain 'til tomorrow. So you can sit here and drink yourself stupid.'

'If you aren't back here by when I rises tomorrow morning, then you needn't bother coming back at all.' Daws scowled. 'I don't pay you good wages to go off gallivanting on my time.'

'Oh, we'll be back, Master, honest we shall,' Martha promised timidly, but Rosie only laughed at him.

'We aren't got no more time to waste listening to you blethering on.' She took her friend's arm and pulled her from the house.

As they walked away from the farmyard Martha looked up into Rosie's face with awed admiration. 'Oh, Rosie, I don't know how you dares to talk to him like you does.'

The taller girl preened and boasted. 'From this day on I'll talk to any man in whichever way I chooses, Martha. Especially that tight-arsed old bugger back there.'

'Now come on, Rosie. He aren't that bad a master. I've worked for some who're a lot worser than him.'

'That's as maybe,' Rosie conceded graciously. 'But I'm finished drudging for him or any other bloody master. Because after today, I'll be living like a high-born lady with me own house and servants, and maybe me own carriage and pair as well.'

'You never will?' Martha sounded doubtful.

'Oh yes I shall, because come nightfall I'll be a married woman.'

'Married?' Martha gasped in stunned shock. 'Who to? Is it to that bloke you been sneaking out to meet in secret? I saw you with him. But who is he, Rosie? What's his name?'

'I've had a lot of blokes come courting me, so it might be him you saw, or it might not. You'll find out soon enough after I'm wed.' Rosie smiled with satisfaction, enjoying prolonging the mystery of her suitor. 'And you'll be real jealous because he's a proper gentleman, so he is. Look at this betrothal ring what he's give me.'

She held up her left hand to display a silver ring. Then pulled up her skirt to disclose gold-embroidered pink silk stockings tied at her knees with fashionable rosette garters. 'And he give me these. They'm real silk and so am the garters. He says all the high-born ladies and the actresses in London am wearing these.'

'Ohhh! They'm lovely! They must have cost a fortune.' Envy gleamed in Martha's eyes. 'But how does he know what the high-born London ladies and actresses wear? Does he live there?'

'No, but he's been there a lot of times. He travels all over the country.'

'Well, where am you getting wed? Has you had the banns called?'

'No need for them. We'm getting wed by special licence in the Tardebigge church, and then he's taking me to show me the fine house he's bought for us to live in.'

'But what about your mam? Aren't you coming to visit her?'

'I can't today, can I?' Rosie displayed a momentary uneasy guilt. 'But you can tell her that I'll come to see her tomorrow for definite.'

'But what about our Mothers' Day posies?' Martha asked plaintively. 'You said you'd fashion the posies. You knows I'm no good at it. You promised!'

Rosie hissed with impatience, but then softened when she saw her friend's forlorn expression. 'And so I did, and I needs to make a special posy for me wedding as well don't I? Come on, we'll find some blossoms down the bottom field.'

For several minutes the two girls roamed across the broad greensward gathering the early flowerings of sweep's brush, the tiny white petals of whitlow grass, the yellow blooms of coltsfoot, and pink-tinged daisies.

Rosie skilfully fashioned three elaborate posies and handed two to her friend. 'There you are, Martha, that's yourn and give this 'un to me mam from me. Now I got to go. Next time you sees me I'll be a fine lady and riding in me own carriage and pair.'

She hurried away leaving her friend still struggling to fully digest this amazing turn of events.

THREE

Monday March 26th, 1827

Dusk had long fallen over the scattered hamlet of Upper Bentley when Martha Standard summoned all her courage and told her employer, ''Tis no use you trying to stop me, Master, I've got to go and see how Widow Brent's faring. I needs to know if Rosie's been to see her.'

John Daws' haggard, unshaven face scowled furiously. 'I'se treated that ungrateful bitch like a fond feyther, so I has, and this is how she repays me! Buggering off wi' a bloody fancy-man and leaving us to manage the house and stock on our ownsomes!

And I'se got the sowing o' me wheat and beans to see to as well. The bloody bitch couldn't have picked a worse time to bugger off!'

Daws fell silent, breathing hard with temper, fists spasmodically clenching and unclenching.

Martha wrapped a shawl about her shoulders and moved to the outer door. 'I'll be as quick as I can, Master.'

'If that bloody mare's at her mam's house then you tell her from me that if her ever dares show her face here again I'll kick her bloody arse straight off my land.'

'I will!' Martha agreed and went out into the darkness, hurrying through the winding lanes to the isolated cottage of the Widow Brent.

In sight of the tumbledown building she saw the lighted candle set in the lower window and her excitement rose. 'Perhaps that's the guide candle for Rosie and she's here now!'

She ran to the cottage door and knocked loudly.

From inside a woman shouted. 'Thank God! I've been worried half to death about where you might have got to.'

The door was flung open and the welcoming smile on the Widow Brent's careworn features abruptly metamorphosed into a scowl of disappointment. 'Oh, it's you, is it? I thought it was my Rosie come at last. Have you word of her?'

'No, Connie!' Martha shook her head. 'I thought she'd have been here long since.'

Widow Brent's face twisted with anxiety. 'I've been worried to death waiting here for her. Something bad's happened to her, I know it has!'

'No, she'll be alright,' Martha hastened to reassure the other woman. 'Her and her husband am most likely having a bit of a honeymoon. They'll come to see you when it's done with.'

The older woman shook her head. 'Last week I seen a lone magpie three mornings on the trot, Martha, and each time it took wing and flew away afore I could salute it. That's a certain sure sign of sorrow to come, that is. Something bad has happened to my Rosie, I just knows it has. Something evil has befell her!'

As the woman voiced her fears a sudden rainstorm hammered down across the land, and some miles to the north the last trailing tendrils and blossoms of a disintegrating posy of wild meadow flowers slowly sank beneath the storm-lashed surface of the canal at Tardebigge.

FOUR

Redditch Town, the major population settlement of the Tardebigge Parish, was centred on a plateau at the northern end of the 'Ridgeway', a long, high north–south hill spine along which were strung the town's satellite villages of Headless Cross, Crabbs Cross, Astwood Bank and Webheath. Although set in a landscape of farms and woodlands it was a town of industry and commerce, rapidly establishing itself as the world centre for the manufacture of needles and fish hooks, which employed the vast majority of its inhabitants in myriad mills and workshops.

It was the ringing of the mill bells summoning the workers to their daily grinding toil that woke Thomas Potts, Constable of Tardebigge Parish, and he turned on his back in the narrow cot to lie savouring the peaceful atmosphere. No rasping snores, no strident voice, no cries of outrage or thumping of stick on floorboard sounded this morning from his mother's room next door.

He smiled contentedly, and silently prayed. 'Dear Lord, please let her remain in Birmingham for a little while longer.'

He rose from his bed, snatched up a strip of towelling and hurried downstairs, nightshirt flying up around his bony knees, the long tassel of his nightcap bouncing upon his narrow shoulders.

Out in the spike-crowned high-walled rear yard he laid aside his clothing and went first to use the doorless privy situated in one corner. Afterwards he crossed to the pump in the opposite corner and furiously cranked its long handle, bending low, twisting his torso, stretching his limbs under the spurting jets, gasping as the icy-cold water soaked his head, body and legs. Then he snatched up the towelling and scrubbed himself dry until his skin tingled and glowed with friction-created warmth.

As he bent to lift his discarded nightclothes a small black cat plummeted down from the top of the wall and came hurrying, tail erect, to rub against his leg, purring.

'Good morning, Bathsheba.' Tom smiled and stroked his pet's glossy coat. 'We've got salt fish for breakfast, you like that don't you?'

The cat miaowed as if in agreement.

Tom drew on his night-shirt and went back indoors to prepare their meal.

The morning air was chill beneath clear skies but Connie Brent was sweating with pain as she limped with heartfelt relief into the broad triangular open green which was the hub of Redditch Town.

She accosted a passer by. 'I wants to see a constable.'

Without breaking stride the man laughed and winked broadly. 'That's more than I wants to do, my wench.'

She stared after him in bewildered chagrin, but then a second man who had seen what had happened took pity on her.

'Look down there, my duck.' He nodded towards a two-storeyed crenellated building at the eastern point of the triangle. 'See that little castle? Well that's the lock-up where the constable lives. His name's Tom Potts and he's a rare lanky, gangly bugger so you can't mistake him.'

The jangling of the bells died away, the great iron-studded door creaked open, and Connie Brent found herself staring upwards into the dark eyes of the tallest man she had ever met.

'Bugger me, but you'm as long and skinny as a hop pole!'

Tom Potts smiled in wry amusement. 'Not quite so tall or skinny, I believe, Ma'am. Now what can I do for you?'

'Be you Tom Potts the constable?'

'I am, Ma'am.'

Widow Brent's careworn features crumpled with grief and rasping sobs tore from her throat, mangling the words she choked out. 'It's me daughter; something bad has happened to her!'

Concerned by her distress, Tom took her arm. 'Will you come in and sit down, Ma'am. And when you're sufficiently recovered you can tell me everything.'

He drew her through the arched entrance into the gloomy central passageway walled by closed cell doors, at the far end of which was a smaller door which opened onto the rear yard. The only daylight came from the arrow slits that flanked both doors.

'We'll go up to my living quarters, Ma'am, where you'll be more comfortable.'

She followed him to the far end of the passageway where a steep narrow staircase led up to the two large rooms on the top floor.

Upstairs he seated Widow Brent on a chair and listened patiently

to her tearful account of how she had spent the whole of the previous
two days at Tardebigge seeking for news of her daughter.

'. . . and there warn't no wedding took place at the church, and
nobody has seen hide nor hair of my Rosie, not at the wharfs nor
anywheres along the canal path on both sides of the tunnel. What
am I to do now, Master Potts? What am I to do?'

Sympathise though he did with her distress, Tom could not help
but feel that this was the all too familiar story of just another
runaway serving girl.

'There now, Ma'am, try not to upset yourself so. She's undoubtedly merely become tired of working the farms and gone to seek her
fortune elsewhere.' He patted her hand reassuringly. 'I very often have
parents coming to me with such concerns as your own, but every time
all eventually turns out to be well with their child.'

'Not this time it won't.' She wailed despairingly, and went on
to tell him about the magpies she had seen.

Tom experienced a familiar irritation at this credence so many
people gave to ancient and discredited superstition, and was forced
to bite back his impatient dismissal of her fears. Instead he promised her, 'You shall rest here for a while and take some breakfast
with me, Ma'am, and then I'll go directly to Daws' farm and talk
with Martha Standard. After that I'll speak with our Town Crier
and make arrangements to have your daughter's description cried
around the parish, and the offer of reward to anyone who can bring
information as to her present whereabouts.'

'But I'm on parish relief. I've no money to pay for the Crier or
the reward!' the widow wailed miserably.

Feeling guiltily ashamed for his earlier irritation, Tom told her
impulsively, 'You're not to worry your head about that, Mrs Brent;
I'll take responsibility for the payments.'

'Oh, God bless you, Sir! You'm a true Christian soul, so you am.
Bless your kind, good heart! Thank you! Thank you!' The woman
poured out heartfelt gratitude, while Tom sat wondering ruefully
how in his present and customary state of financial impoverishment
he was going to find the wherewithal even to pay the Crier, never
mind the promised reward for information.

FIVE

The north-western point of the green was the start of the long, steep decline of Fish Hill, which fell away northwards, and at the very top of the hill stood the imposing 'Red House', the residence of Joseph Blackwell Esq.

Joseph Blackwell Esq. was Clerk to the Magistrates, Select Vestry Clerk, Senior Overseer to the Poor, part-time coroner for the entire Needle District, and the de facto head and director of the parish constabulary.

Small in stature, with deeply lined pale features and pedantic mannerisms, he was physically insignificant, which caused many new acquaintances to underestimate his potency and think him unimportant. In reality however Joseph Blackwell Esq. was a very powerful and influential figure locally, who often likened himself to the spider lurking in the centre of his own widespread web. Trained in the law, exceptionally shrewd and hard-bitten, he was the custodian of many secrets concerning the ruling aristocracy and master manufacturers of the Needle District.

Now in the early afternoon, sitting behind his desk in the large, book-lined study, hands clasped on his narrow chest, chin resting on steepled forefingers, he listened intently to Tom Potts' report on the earlier meetings with the Widow Brent and Martha Standard. When Tom had finished Blackwell frowned and snapped curtly.

'Damn it all, Master Potts, this is quite plainly just another case of a young serving wench tiring of her situation and running off! How can you even consider for one moment asking the Vestry to pay for the Crier and a reward? Damn it all, sir, if the parish was to go to the expense of searching for every silly flibbertigibbet who runs away from her situation, then the parish would be bankrupt in very short order.' He shook his head in emphatic negation. 'The answer is no!'

The vivid mental image of Widow Brent's distressed, careworn features impelled Tom to persist. 'Well, sir, would it be possible for the Vestry to advance me sufficient money personally to pay for the Crier and reward, and I'll make repayment to them from my future fees?'

The older man expelled a noisy snort of derision. 'The Select Vestry are the governing forum of this parish, Master Potts, not moneylenders or pawnbrokers. It is impossible for them to loan you money for this purpose.'

Once again he shook his head in emphatic negation, then said in a more conciliatory tone, 'However, I have no objection to you enquiring of any carriers, coachmen, drovers or other travellers if they have encountered a young woman answering to Rose Brent's description. With the proviso of course that these enquiries do not take precedence over your current duties, which I'm sure you're eager to be about.'

Blackwell lifted his quill pen, opened the ledger on the desk before him and bent his head over its pages.

'I bid you good day, Master Potts.'

Knowing from past experience the futility of arguing further, Tom bowed and left the room.

Out on the roadway he stood for some moments gazing north-wards down the long steep Fish Hill and across the broad fecund valley of the River Arrow. His mind was still troubled by the memory of the Widow Brent's torment.

'I can't leave it here and do nothing to help that poor old soul,' he said to himself.

He fingered the outlines of the hunter watch in the fob pocket of his waistcoat. The watch had been his father's and its solid silver casing was ornately etched with his father's name. Turning on his heels he walked quickly towards the south-western point of the green on which stood the small chapel of St Stephen adjoining the central crossroads of the town. At the crossroads he turned westwards down the hill and passed by the tall Unicorn Inn and the rows of terraced cottages until he reached a doorway surmounted by three gilt balls. The rat-featured, shabbily dressed man standing just inside that open doorway greeted him with a snag-toothed smile.

'Well now, Constable Potts, have you come to seek the services of everybody's kind uncle yet again?'

Tom sighed sadly. 'Indeed I have, Master Benton.' He pulled the watch from its fob and proffered it to the man. 'Can you advance me something on it?'

'Certainly I can,' Benton assured. 'I'm always willing to oblige a trustworthy customer. Shall we say four shillings at ten percent weekly interest? Those are our usual terms are they not, Constable Potts?'

Tom nodded wryly. 'Indeed they are, Master Benton.'

With the silver coins in his pocket, Tom retraced his steps as far as the crossroads and halted there for a few moments, mentally debating the division of his meagre funds.

'Four cryings at sixpence. The other two shillings to be given as reward to Rose Brent's discoverer, but to be paid only when I've personally confirmed that it's a true identity and not a gammon.'

At this hour of the day, with the vast majority of the population at their workplaces, the town centre was quiet with few people abroad and Tom was surprised to hear the ringing of a brass hand bell and the stentorian shout.

'Oyez, oyez, oyez, William Willmott Esq., surveyor of this parish, demands that all those listed for amending the highway shall report at the Bordesley tollgate at noon on Saturday the thirty-first day of this present month, bringing their allotted tools. Anyone failing to attend will be summoned to appear before the magistrates.

'Henry Cobbs Esq., fishmonger of this parish, wishes to inform his valued customers that he has received a fresh consignment of the finest quality smoked haddock, salted cod and herrings.

'Thomas Mence Esq., postmaster of this parish, requests that all who wish to remit postals, packages or parcels upon Friday's mail coach, to deliver to the Post Office down Littleworth the said postals, packages and parcels this very day . . . God save the King.'

Tom walked towards the owner of the stentorian voice, Jimmy Grier the Town Crier, resplendent in his ostrich-plumed tricorn hat, scarlet waistcoat, green tailcoat, yellow breeches, white stockings and silver-buckled shoes.

'You're in fine voice today, Jimmy.'

'If I am it's the only bloody thing that is fine. Me rheumatics is killing me, and me head feels like it's bursting, and me guts is aching like buggery,' the bent-bodied, elderly man complained bitterly.

'Well, are you able to add another cry to your list?' Tom asked.

'Only if I gets paid in advance, because me pockets be empty and me throat is as dry as an old maid's quim. If I don't get to wet me whistle a bit sharpish, I'll not be able to cry another word.'

Tom handed Grier two shillings and he brightened immediately.

'Four days' cries you wants, I take it.'

'Yes please, starting today and finishing Sunday.'

Grier screwed his rheumy eyes fast shut. 'Give it to me.'

Tom related the message he wanted spread, as always marvelling at this old man's talent for being able to remember any instructions, no matter how detailed, after one repetition.

Grier nodded and rang the hand bell. 'Oyez, oyez, oyez. A reward is offered to any person knowing the present whereabouts of Rose Brent, a yellow-haired young woman standing more than five feet high, and of robust build. Last seen on Sunday last in the hamlet of Upper Bentley, wearing a brown dress, green chequered shawl, black bonnet, pink stockings, rosette garters and black boots. The said reward to be paid on application to Constable Potts at the lock-up. God save the King.'

He grinned toothlessly at Tom. 'Does that fit the bill?'

Tom grinned back. 'As always, Jimmy. Many thanks. I'll bid you good day now.'

He had only walked on a few paces when his name was shouted.

'Thomas! I been looking all over for you.'

Tom, knowing why the other man had sought him out, swallowed hard to counter the sudden dryness of his throat.

'Good morning, Josiah. What can I do for you?'

Josiah Danks, ruddy-featured, burly-shouldered, five foot ten inches of tough, veteran Royal Marine, and currently head game-keeper to the Earl of Plymouth, could strike fear into the most hardened poacher.

Tom, gentle-hearted, weakly bodied, timidly pacifistic by nature, was fighting desperately against the urge to turn and run.

Danks halted and scowled. 'Our Amy is soon coming back from visiting her auntie. Now she'll reach her nineteen years next month, and what I wants to know is if you be intending her to become an old maid?'

Tom shook his head and emphatically declared, 'Of course I'm not! It's my dearest wish to marry Amy.'

'How old be you now, Thomas?' Danks immediately answered his own rhetorical question. 'Thirty-four years by my reckoning. Does you intend to be in your dotage afore you makes me a granddad?'

'No, that's not what I want, Josiah,' Tom answered with total sincerity. 'I love and honour Amy with all my heart, and she knows it very well. But how can I ruin her life by marrying her at this time, and dragging her down into a state of wretched poverty? My only income is the miserable fees I get for constable's duties. There are more than enough days when I can barely fill my own stomach with food, never mind feed and clothe a wife and children.'

Dank's harsh tone modulated. 'Listen, Thomas, I knows very well that Lord Aston has got you over a barrel. I knows that he's forcing you to stay on as constable against your own wishes, and it's no fault of yourn that you'm in this sorry state o' rags not riches.

I knows as well that you treats our Amy with kindness and respect and that she's in no danger of you ever dishonouring her. But me and Missus Danks wants to see her settled down wi' a husband, home and kids of her own; and you'm the chap above all others that we both most wishes with all our hearts to be the father of our grandkids.'

He reached out and, smiling kindly, patted Tom's shoulder. 'But I'm feared that you'll lose her to another, Thomas, unless you weds her quick. Because there's no shortage of young chaps in these parts whom be setting their caps for her, and there's a couple of 'um that she seems very partial to. So you look sharp and ask her to wed you and get them banns called, that's my advice to you, as your true friend and wish-to-be pa-in-law.' He about-turned and marched smartly away.

Tom sighed despondently. Pretty, flirty Amy Danks was the love of his life. He wished with all his heart to marry her, and sometimes she also appeared to want their marriage. But, as he had told her father, he dreaded dragging her down to share his poverty and being forced to watch her suffering the terrible hardships that such poverty inevitably brought with it.

'We and our children, if we had any, would all spend our lives as parish paupers. How can I even think of sentencing Amy to such a miserable existence?' he asked himself sadly. 'I can't ask her to wait for me in the vain hope that by a miracle my fortunes will improve sufficiently for me to give her a good life . . .'

SIX

Midday, Tuesday April 3rd

Tom was standing by the stocks and pillory which flanked the front door of the lock-up when the horseman rode up to him and demanded gruffly, 'You there! The lanky 'un! Can I take it that you'm the constable?'

Tom lifted his yard-long, crown-topped red, blue and gold painted truncheon 'This is my staff of office.'

'Master Cooke, the Wharf Superintendent at Tardebigge, asks that you come straight away to the Plymouth Arms to speak with him. He says it's an urgent matter. You can ride pillion wi' me.'

'What's the problem?' Tom queried.

'It's summat to do wi' the tunnel Leggers.' The rider scowled. 'When there's any trouble on the bloody canal it's nigh on always summat to do wi' them bastards!'

Tom's stomach lurched and he thought miserably, 'I wish I hadn't got out of my bed this morning! The last thing I need right now is trouble with the Leggers.'

The half-mile-long Tardebigge canal tunnel curved deep beneath the hill that was topped by St Bartholomew's church. To save time and money the engineers had not continued the towpath through the tunnel, which meant that the barges' tow horses had to be unharnessed at one entrance and taken over the hill to be reharnessed at the other end. The barges were propelled through the tunnel by human muscle power in a process known as legging. A plank was laid across the bows of the vessel and a man would lie on each end of it, then thrusting their feet against the walls of the tunnels would propel the barge along. Three people were needed for this task: one on the rudder and the two men on the plank. A boatman might perhaps have his wife with him but he would still need assistance to get the barge through the stretch of dripping, evil-smelling darkness.

To meet this demand there had come into existence a group of men known as the Leggers who lived in crudely built shanties on either side of the tunnel and who, for a few pence, would leg the barge through it. When legging a barge it was essential to synchronize the thrusting of the legs, otherwise the barge would be forced off course and would crash into one side or the other. When this happened the plank and Leggers would be sent flying and were all too often crushed between the barge and the walls or trapped beneath the barge and drowned. In the thirty years during and after its construction twenty-three men had met their deaths inside the tunnel and more than fifty had been crippled for life, resulting in the widespread belief that the tunnel was both cursed and ghost haunted.

But it was neither curses nor ghosts that concerned Tom during his painfully bouncy pillion ride towards Tardebigge. His dread was the possibility that he might be forced into a violent confrontation with the notorious Leggers.

They were the outcasts of the parish. Shunned by all the respectable inhabitants as being shiftless ne'er-do-wells, notorious for their drunken, violent propensities; and since there were taverns at each end of the tunnel neighbouring the western Old Wharf and the eastern New Wharf, those propensities were constantly refuelled.

The Plymouth Arms Inn stood on the hillside above the western canal tunnel entrance and the New Wharf adjoining it. Once the fine three-storeyed residence of a country gentleman, it had evolved into a select coaching inn, catering mainly for the numerous visitors to the nearby Hewell Grange, seat of the Earl of Plymouth, and those among the canal company's high-ranking employees and passengers who could afford the expense. A little distance further down the sloping road, the Cherry Tree tavern serviced the bargees and the low-ranking canal workers.

Tom's carrier halted his mount on the road out of sight of the Plymouth Arms and told his passenger, 'You must get off here because I'm turning back.'

Tom gingerly levered himself backwards over the horse's rump to the ground and with a sigh of relief stood rubbing his sore thighs and buttocks.

'Why do you turn back here?' Tom asked.

'For the good o' me 'ealth,' the man grunted and, pulling his mount's head around, kicked it into a fast canter back the way they had come.

'For the good of me 'ealth.' Tom repeated the words and smiled in wry amusement. 'Perhaps he's a reformed drunkard and doesn't want to risk going near an inn.'

He walked on down the hedge- and tree-lined roadway and as he moved into the bend of the road the wind carried the sounds of harsh shouting and shattering windows to his ears. Sudden apprehension filled him, and his pace abruptly slowed.

He rounded the bend and his mouth dried with fear as he saw the seething crowd of raggedly dressed, shaggy-haired men and women on the wide gravelled forecourt of the Plymouth Arms.

'Oh my God! What am I to do?' Tom stood as if paralyzed, his only bodily motion the trembling of his hands.

'Send that thieving bastard out here, Master Cooke, or we'll bring this place down around your ears,' the short, thickset man leading the mob bellowed threateningly.

'He's not here,' a man's voice shouted from the house. 'How many more times must I tell you?'

'You'm a fuckin' liar,' the mob's leader bawled. 'You'se had your chance, so now we'll break the door in and string the bugger up ourselves.'

'I'm warning you, I've guns here, and I'll use them if I have to,' the man inside shouted.

The mob's leader only laughed derisively, and pointed at the door. 'Smash it in, lads.'

Howling like ravening beasts, his followers hurled a volley of stones and brickbats at the steep-gabled, three-storeyed building, while another group ran forwards with a long heavy wooden pole and smashed it like a battering ram against the porticoed door, which shuddered under the impact but still held firm.

A gun blasted from the upper storey, pellet shot exploding the gravel in all directions, and the leading ram bearer fell to roll over and over, clutching his bleeding legs and screaming, 'I'm murdered! I'm murdered!'

The shock stunned the crowd into a motionless silence, which was broken by the man inside shouting defiantly, 'I've more guns ready loaded, and I'll use them!'

A frisson of uncertainty passed through the onlookers, and some of them began to edge backwards away from the building. Then the sudden appearance of another figure started all heads turning.

The screams of the wounded man had propelled Tom forwards at an ungainly, jelly-legged trot, waving his truncheon above his head, shouting words distorted by his fear-parched throat and lips.

'Stop this! I command you in the King's name to stop this!'

Tom came to halt between the crowd and the building, some yards distant from the group now surrounding the wounded man, and shouted, 'I'm Thomas Potts, constable of this parish, and I command you in the King's name to disperse, or I'll arrest you. Disperse now!'

No one moved or made answer and his eyes went from face to face to be met with either sullen glares or jeering grins. Still racked with fear, he was momentarily unable to decide what to do next, and could only stand dumbly staring at them.

The leader came striding towards Tom, who swallowed hard, and screwed up all his resolve.

'I'm arresting you in the King's name, for being the ringleader of this riot.' Try though he might to keep his voice steady, he could not prevent its nervous stuttering.

An aggressive scowl twisted the other man's dirty, heavily stubbled features. 'You'm arresting me? You'm arresting Jacky Whittaker?' he demanded incredulously. 'You and whose army, you long streak o' piss?'

He turned from side to side addressing the crowd. 'Did you hear that, lads? This long streak o' piss says he's going to arrest me! Just look at him, will you. I've seen more meat on a fuckin' piece o' string!'

Jeering laughter and catcalling erupted from among the onlookers, and Whittaker stepped up to Tom, standing on tiptoes to thrust his face so close that his gin-laden breath gusted into Tom's nostrils.

'If you wants to arrest somebody in the King's name, then arrest that bugger inside there, who's just done his best to murder one of us. Because you aren't got a cat in Hell's chance of taking me in.'

Every atom of Tom's being was clamorous with the desire to escape from this threatening violence and seek a place of safety. But he stubbornly refused to surrender to that clamouring.

He coughed to clear the choking sensation in his throat, and repeated, 'I'm arresting you in the King's name, Master Whittaker.'

Whittaker grinned derisively, stepped back a pace and shouted, 'Take him down, boys!'

Heavy bodies crashed into Tom's back and side, bringing him thudding to the ground. Brutal hands clamped his arms, legs and throat. Struggling desperately, he was lifted bodily and carried away, a din of exultant bawling filling his ears, punches and kicks thumping into his body.

'Chuck the bugger over the bridge!'

The shout was taken up by a score of voices.

'Over the bridge! Over the bridge! Over the bridge!'

'Noooo! I can't swim! I can't swim!' Tom howled in anguish.

He hurtled through the air, tumbling head over heels to impact into chill water.

The air slammed from his lungs, he plummeted beneath the scummy surface of the canal, terror blotting all else from his mind.

Once, twice, three, four times, arms and legs frantically flailing, his head momentarily broke the surface and he tried to drag in breath as he reached the weed-thick bank, but only sucked in muddy water, choked and sank again. Terrible agony racked his chest, a black cloud enveloped him and he lost consciousness and sank down.

The swirling mud-churned surface of the water stilled and smoothed.

'Fuckin' hell! I reckon he's drownded!' a man shouted in sudden alarm. 'If he has, then we could be hanged for murder!'

The raucous laughter and jeering abruptly quietened.

'It warn't nothing to do wi' me! I never chucked him in!' another man hastily disclaimed.

'Nor me neither! Nor me! Nor me! Nor me!' several voices reiterated.

'I'm off!' Someone turned and ran, immediately followed by others in the crowd.

A well-dressed man came running out of the Plymouth Arms and down the slope to the towpath, shouting, 'Some of you carry that shot man to the doctor. You lot there, come and help me.'

He lowered himself into the canal, drew a deep breath and dipped down beneath the surface, reappearing with his arms wrapped around Tom's muddied, weed-festooned head and shoulders.

Those who had followed him hastened to drag the limp body out of the water.

'Empty that butt and fetch it over here!' the rescuer instructed as he levered himself on to the bank and stood with water streaming from his hair and clothes, staring hard at Tom's apparently lifeless grey-blue face. 'Get a bloody move on, damn you!'

When the barrel was brought to him he tipped it on to its side. 'Now help me turn this fellow over and lay him across the barrel. I want his stomach to be on the middle.'

Tom was turned, lifted and placed, bent double, over the barrel, his head and shoulders flopped against the ground on one side and his feet and knees on the opposite side.

'You two take his feet, you two take his arms,' the rescuer commanded. 'Now I want you to start rolling him backwards and forwards, but don't take his weight. His guts have got to be pressing down onto the barrel. Get on with it!'

The four men obeyed, pushing and pulling, rolling the barrel backwards and forwards, Tom's stomach and lower chest being rhythmically compressed by his own weight as he too travelled over the barrel.

The onlookers shouted excitedly as water gushed from Tom's mouth.

When the water ceased to spill out, the rescuer issued fresh instructions, and eager hands stripped Tom's clothing and rubbed hard all over his skin in desperate endeavour to restore warmth and life to his clammy flesh.

'He's bloody dead!' a man declared. 'Look at his chest! He aren't taking any breath in, is he?'

'Let me through.' The rescuer knelt to press his ear against Tom's chest. 'He's still alive, his heart's beating strongly.'

'Then why aren't he breathing if he's living?' someone queried doubtfully.

'Here you am, Master Cooke, pour a drop of this into his mouth.' Jacky Whittaker came pushing his way through the cluster around Tom's body to proffer a flask of gin.

Cooke carefully dribbled a little of the spirit between Tom's purpled lips.

Tom's entire body jerked and the sound of choked coughing erupted from deep within his chest.

'That's it!' Cooke exclaimed delightedly, and heaved Tom on to his side, repeatedly clapping him hard between the shoulders. 'That's it, my bucko, get it all out!' Strings of mucus oozed and dangled from Tom's gaping mouth as he coughed and struggled to draw in wheezing half-strangled breaths.

Slowly Tom's coughing ceased, and his breathing became easier. He rolled on to his back and lay staring dazedly up at the sky.

Martin Cooke scowled at Jacky Whittaker. 'You'll find yourself paying a heavy price for trying to murder a constable.'

'Murder? Me? Don't talk so sarft, Master Cooke,' Whittaker scoffed. 'All he got was a ducking, and I warn't able to see who it was that chucked him over the bridge.' He winked at the other men. 'How about you lads? Does any of you know who laid hands on the constable?'

'Yeah, it was them strangers who's fucked off. I doubt we'll be seeing any of them again in a hurry,' one man answered and the others hastened to agree.

'Ahr, it was them lot.'

Whittaker turned back to Cooke. 'If I was in your shoes, Master, I'd be worrying meself about shooting poor Billy Jones, like you did. That looked very much like you was trying to murder him.'

'Don't talk rubbish, man!' Cooke angrily rebutted, and was about to say more when one of the onlookers suddenly called out.

'Fuckin' 'ell! Look there!'

Two yards from where Tom had been dragged out of the canal, a mud-covered, weed-festooned body was floating face downwards in the filthy water, only part of its back visible.

The crowd left Tom and lined the bank to stare at the corpse.

It was only now that full awareness was returning to Tom. His body was shivering uncontrollably, and every breath he took sent pain lancing through his lungs. Mortified at the realization of his nakedness he rolled over and forced himself on to his knees, scrabbling for his clothes.

The men's attention was focussed on the floating body and they ignored Tom as he struggled to dress in his soaking garments.

'One of you go and fetch a boathook, and pull that floater in,' Martin Cooke ordered, then came over to Tom. 'How are you feeling, Constable? You'd best come with me to my quarters and get dry.'

'That's very kind of you, sir,' Tom accepted gratefully. 'May I know your name?'

'I'm Martin Cooke, Wharf Superintendent for the Birmingham and Worcester Canal Company. It was I who sent for you to come here when this lot started playing up.'

He proffered his hand and helped Tom to rise unsteadily to his feet. A wave of giddy faintness swept over Tom and he swayed violently.

The other man put his arm around Tom's waist. 'Lean upon me.'

The giddiness receded and Tom experienced a flush of shame at his physical weakness.

'Thank you for your kindness, sir, but I'm able to walk by myself.' Then he realized in dismay: 'I've lost my constable's staff! Lord Aston will dock my fees to pay for a new one.'

The two men were slowly making their way up the slope leading on to the bridge when Jacky Whittaker shouted after them.

'Master Cooke, you'd best take a look at this floater. It's a bloody woman.'

An unbidden image of Widow Brent's anxious, careworn features rose instantly in Tom's mind, and dread struck through him. He followed Cooke back down to the towpath, his thoughts on the description of the missing Rose Brent.

'Yellow-haired, blue-eyed. Just over five feet tall. Robust build . . . brown dress, green-chequered shawl . . . black bonnet and boots. Pink stockings.'

The dead woman was lying on her back, her face and neck swollen, discoloured and the flesh torn in parts by the ravaging of eels and fish.

Tom crouched by her side and gently wiped mud from her face and hair, confirming that she was blonde. He pushed open her eyelids and saw the glassy blue irises. She had no bonnet, shawl, stockings or boots but her dress was brown, and he estimated her height to be more than five feet and her build robust.

Tom sighed sadly. 'I do believe that this woman is named Rose Brent. She went missing during Sunday last. I've been having her description cried in the Redditch neighbourhood.'

'Well, by the look of her swelling and the eels' feedings she's been in the cut for about a week.' Jacky Whittaker said. 'I reckon she was tangled in the weeds and when you was thrashing about in the water you loosened the weeds' grip on her, and the gas in her belly brought her up. It usually takes four or five days for a drowned 'un to blow up enough wi' the gas to bring 'um up to the top again.'

'I 'opes you aren't kettle-stomached, Gaffer,' another man told Tom with relish. 'Because this 'ull be a midnight crossroads job, won't it, if her's killed herself. You'll be having to drive a stake through her heart when she's put under the crossroads, won't you? I've a mind to come and see you do that.'

Tom was greatly disturbed at that likelihood and he snapped at the man. 'Hold your tongue! We don't know if she is a suicide. The poor girl could have stumbled and fallen by accident into the water.'

'Ahr, perhaps you might be right, Gaffer.' The man's face displayed his disappointment. 'But we'se found a young wench in the cut afore now. She'd been babbied, her had.'

'Do they still follow that practice here?' Martin Cooke asked curiously. 'Burying a suicide on a crossroads at midnight with a stake through the heart?'

'Oh yes!' Tom replied, disgust throbbing in his tone. 'My Lord Aston holds fast to the belief that a suicide must be given the midnight crossroads burial with the stake through the heart to prevent the corporeal body from rising from the dead. He claims it's to satisfy the simpletons who believe that the constant passage of feet across the grave dissipates the unquiet spirit little by little, preventing it returning to haunt.'

'Have you carried one out?' Cooke asked.

'No, thank God!' Tom answered forcefully. 'And I hope and pray that I'm never called upon to do so. It's a practice that should have no place in this modern world. It belongs to the Dark Ages, and should have remained in them.'

He gently touched the dead girl's face. 'I'll not be driving any stake through this poor girl's heart. Not if Aston and another twenty like him were to order me to do so.'

'Good for you,' Cooke congratulated warmly. 'Now what's to be done with her?'

'Firstly I need to have her moved to the Redditch lock-up and have her identity confirmed. After that there must be a post-mortem examination and coroner's inquest.' The image of Widow Brent's face flooded Tom's mind, and he murmured sadly, 'God have mercy on her poor mother.'

'My carter will bear the girl to the lock-up,' Cooke offered.

'Thank you very much, sir.' Tom was only now taking full note of his benefactor's physical attributes.

He looked to be in his late twenties, with ruggedly handsome features topped by thick black curly hair. Broad-shouldered, shorter than Tom but still well above average height, Martin Cooke was a fine example of masculinity.

He smiled, showing strong white teeth. 'Will you now come and dry yourself by my fire, Master Potts, and take a drink with me?'

Tom opened his mouth to gladly accept the invitation, but again the unbidden image of Widow Brent came before his eyes, and he regretfully declined.

'Many thanks, Master Cooke, but it's urgent that I get this poor girl carried to Redditch, and then go for her mother.'

'Another time then, perhaps.' Cooke shook Tom's hand warmly. 'I'm delighted to have made your acquaintance, sir. I shan't forget the courageous way in which you came to my aid against that mob. But after this finding there'll be no more trouble from them.'

'Why were they rioting?' Tom asked curiously.

'They were after a man known as Irish Joe, who they claim had stolen money from them. But he's been gone from here for days now.'

'Can you identify the men who actually threw me over the bridge?' Tom queried.

Cooke regretfully shook his head. 'I fear not, Constable. In all the hubbub it was difficult to single out faces.'

Inwardly Tom felt relief that he had found an excuse not to risk another confrontation with the Leggers. 'Oh well, if that's the case then it's pointless for me to question them. I shall merely consider it to be a misfortunate happening and let it pass.'

'But if I can ever be of any other service to you, then do not hesitate to call on me for it.' The other man smiled.

Tom grimaced ruefully. 'Might I ask then that you have enquiry made for my constable's staff, Master Cooke? It will cost me a pretty penny to replace it, I fear.'

'That enquiry shall begin immediately,' Cooke asserted, and with that final exchange the two men parted.

SEVEN

Morning, Thursday April 5th

The elderly Doctor Cuthbert Price was palsied, with a rocking head, shaking hands, and failing eyesight. Because of his physical condition his medical practice had dwindled to virtually nothing and he had been reduced to genteel poverty. But his fine mind was still clear and his senses of taste and smell still acute.

It was for this reason that his old friend Joseph Blackwell tried to help him earn a little money by carrying out any post-mortems required by the parish.

He greeted Tom warmly at the door of his home in the village of Alvechurch, some three miles northwards from Redditch.

'I'm very happy that you are to assist me today, Master Potts. What transport do I have?'

'Master Blackwell's pony and trap, sir, with myself for coachman, and as always I'm greatly honoured to be of assistance to you.' Tom smiled and bowed, for he both liked and respected this old man.

'Excellent!' Price chuckled, his ill-fitting ivory false teeth rattling in his almost lipless mouth. 'So let us proceed without delay, Master Potts, and earn ourselves a little spending money. I take it that our subject has been identified?'

'Yes, sir,' Tom confirmed. 'Master Blackwell loaned me the trap and I brought her mother over to view the girl. It was pitiful to see the poor woman's grief. She is totally distraught.'

He took the other man's medical chest and strapped it on to the carrier of the trap where he had already secured his own bag of what he termed his investigation kit. He then helped Price to clamber up on to the seat of the trap.

As the trap's iron-bound wheels crunched over the gravelled turn-pike road the two men chatted amiably.

'You will of course do the dissecting today, Master Potts; you have the eye and hand for such work. What a great pity it is that you were unable to complete your final medical studies after your poor father's untimely death. I always thought that he should have left the army and set up in private practice; he was such a very fine surgeon.'

'He was indeed, sir.' Tom was gratified to hear his father praised. 'But he loved being a military surgeon, and wanted me to follow in his footsteps and enter the army when I was fully qualified.'

'You were his apprentice from a very early age, were you not?'

'Indeed I was.' Tom smiled wryly. 'At the age when other boys were still playing with their spinning tops, I was studying medical tracts, and walking the wards with my father. Sometimes even assisting him in operating on or dissecting poor dead soldiers.'

'Do you not feel that fate has dealt with you very harshly by taking your father and inflicting poverty upon you while you were still such a young man?'

'There are the odd moments when I feel a sense of self-pity,'

Tom admitted somewhat shamefacedly. 'But then I look around me at the sufferings and dreadful poverty of others and realize how much I have to be truly thankful for. I've good health and sufficient spare time to study the various subjects I'm interested in. Plus I still possess my father's collection of books and his medical journals.' He paused and after a momentary reflection went on. 'And believe it or not, although I earn only meagre fees as a constable, I'm increasingly finding satisfaction in carrying out some of the duties that the post entails.' He grinned wryly. 'Even though certain of those duties actually terrify me.'

'As they would me.' Price chuckled, and then asked, 'This woman, I presume she drowned in that accursed tunnel at Tardebigge?'

'That's more than likely,' Tom agreed. 'It's small wonder that the more superstitious people in these parts believe it's haunted. It's taken so many lives and caused so much suffering.'

'Indeed it has, but should we give any weight to superstitions?' Price smiled grimly. 'Tell me, Master Potts, do you believe in ghosts and hauntings and potent curses?'

Tom pondered briefly before answering tentatively. 'I've never knowingly seen a ghost, but I've had some strange experiences occur in my life, and been told by people, whose probity I don't doubt, about the strange happenings that they've experienced. So, like William Shakespeare's Prince of Denmark, I do believe that there are more things in heaven and earth than are dreamt of in our philosophy.'

'Neatly answered, Master Potts.' Price chuckled appreciatively.

A mile from Redditch centre they came to the closed Bordesley tollgate and were forced to halt and ring its bell.

A tiny, misshapen-bodied old crone with a huge floppy mob cap on her head came hobbling on two sticks from the Toll Keeper's small cottage, calling hoarsely, 'Doctor Price, this is well met. I needs your help.'

Price squinted at her through his pince-nez glasses. 'What ails you, Granny Lock?'

'It's that bloody useless husband o' mine. He's eating so much and getting so bloody fat he can't hardly walk, and I'm having to do all the work around here. It'll be the death o' me, so it 'ull.'

'What would you have me do, Granny Lock?' Price smiled with amusement.

'Stop the bugger eating. Get some of the bloody fat off him.' As she spoke her nose and chin almost touched before her toothless mouth, and her red-rimmed eyes glared like smouldering coals in her withered, weather-beaten face.

'The heath pea, Granny Lock.' Price told her. 'Also known as the bitter vetch. It's a herb found growing in the hedgerows. Do you know of it?'

'No! But I knows somebody who 'ull know of it. What does I do with it?'

'Crush and steep it in hot water, then when the water cools, pour some of it into your husband's drink. Once he's drunk it, he'll forget to eat for days on end. He'll soon be as thin as a rake.'

'I'll do that.' The old crone hobbled to the trap, took both sticks into her one hand and held the other out towards Tom.

'One horse carriage, so that's a sixpenny toll to pay, Master.'

'But I've already paid toll when I came through hardly an hour since,' Tom protested. 'And I'm carrying out official parish business.'

'And I'm carrying out official turnpike business. So pay up, or you can sit here 'til bloody Doomsday, for all I cares.' She scowled.

Price chuckled throatily, and put in, 'When are you going to pay me my fee for the consultation, Granny Lock? Which just so happens to amount to sixpence.'

'When that fat useless bugger of an husband o' mine gets to be as thin as a rake, and not a moment afore,' she retorted.

Tom rummaged through his pockets and found just enough coins to pay her. As she pocketed the money he thought ruefully: 'There goes my supper.'

EIGHT

Covered by a sheet of canvas, the corpse of Rose Brent lay face uppermost on a trestled table beneath a hastily erected awning in the rear yard of the lock-up. Close at hand a row of large and small glass and earthenware pots were lined up on the ground, and another trestle table bore a microscope, a box of glass slides, quill pens, inkwell and note paper.

'I thought that this would be the best place for us to work in, sir,' Tom explained. 'We've the benefits of untrammelled daylight, the water pump close to hand, and all is made ready.'

'And the further benefit that should Blackwell come to view the proceedings we shan't have to listen to his grumblings about us stinking out the inside of the lock-up, shall we?' Price chuckled.

'Dear friend though he is, I must confess that his constant carping about his kettle stomach gets on my nerves at times.'

Tom drew off the canvas sheet and his companion bent low, squinting through a pince-nez at the girl's swollen discoloured features.

'I've cleansed and examined her thoroughly for wounds, suspicious contusions and broken bones, but found nothing to indicate that she was killed by a weapon,' Tom informed. 'Which leaves the possibilities of death by drowning, poison, suffocation, strangulation or natural causes.'

Price straightened. 'Which do you think is the most likely in this case?'

Tom shook his head. 'I've no idea. She told her friend that she was going to meet a man who had promised to marry her, but didn't tell his name or anything about him except that he was a gentleman who was going to buy her a fine house and her own carriage. Of course the man might not have even existed. She could have been merely telling a pack of lies to make her friend jealous. But I'm troubled by the disappearance of her silver ring, and the garters and stockings. Shoes can fall off easily; shawls and bonnets can be carried away by the movements of the canal waters. But I don't think that rings, garters or stockings can be stripped off by any canal water movements. I think it would need human hands to do that.'

'Yes indeed, but those hands were perhaps the girl's own,' Price concurred. 'However, let us set to work now, Master Potts.'

Tom took up a scalpel, and in his mind asked the dead girl for pardon for what he was about to do to her corpse.

Drawing a long deep breath, focussing all his concentration, he began the task. He cut a V-shaped incision in the front of the neck and continued the long cut from the base of the neck to the pubis, making a deliberate detour around the navel, which because of its tough tissues was hard to cut through and very difficult to sew up afterwards. Slimy bloody fluids oozed from the parted tissues, and the foul stench of decaying flesh filled his nostrils.

Next he slid the exposed stomach clear of the other intestinal organs and manoeuvred it over a large earthenware pot, then cut it open with scissors and drained its contents into the container before detaching the entire stomach completely and placing it in another pot. He excised and separated into more pots the small and large intestines, heart, liver, kidneys, lungs, and finally the larynx from the neck.

'I congratulate you, Master Potts.' Price told him. 'That was neatly and speedily done; I couldn't have performed it better myself.'

'Thank you very much, sir.' Tom felt inordinately gratified at the praise.

He went to the pump and worked its handle, washing the blood, slime and filth from his hands and arms, and ducking his head under the spouting jets to cool and refresh his heated senses.

While Tom dried himself on a strip of coarse towelling his companion lifted the larynx and, after careful examination, declared 'The hyoid bone is intact and there is no blood infused in the tissues, so I'm confident that strangulation was not the cause of death.'

Price next turned his attention to the pots holding the organs.

'There are no weeds or algae in the stomach or oesophagus, Master Potts, but there is mud and water, of course. Were the hands clenched in cadaveric spasm?'

'No, sir.'

'That's a pity, because it is the surest indication of death by simple drowning, is it not?'

With Tom's assistance the old man spent several hours examining, dissecting, testing the organs, and at last sighed despairingly.

'This poor soul was pregnant, Master Potts. But I confess that I cannot state with absolute certainty what has caused this death. None of her organs appear to be diseased; there are no traces of poison or of bodily injury, and her lungs are not as ballooned as I would normally expect to find in a drowned subject. Of course the length of time she was in the water makes any diagnosis much more uncertain. I think that we'd best assume she died from drowning, and in kindness to her mother, attribute it to accident, not suicide.'

A strong sense of unease struck unaccountably through Tom. Despite his respect for the old man's expertise and depth of knowledgeable experience, a small voice in his mind repeated vehemently over and over again: 'He's wrong! He's wrong! He's wrong!'

But before he could voice any opinion, the other man said wearily, 'I'm feeling very tired, Master Potts, and I'd like to go home immediately. Perhaps you'll be kind enough to tidy her up after you've taken me back.'

'I'll be glad to, sir,' Tom agreed, then frowned worriedly. 'But I've no money left to pay the tolls.'

'I'll pay.' Price swayed as if bodily weak. 'But kindly get me home now, Master Potts.'

*   *   *

Dusk was approaching when Tom returned to the lock-up and crowds of weary, begrimed men, women and children were spilling out from the mills and factories after their long hours of grinding labour. As he passed some shouted mockingly after him.

'There goes that lanky bollocks!'

'Nearly drownded himself in a puddle, didn't he?'

'He's long and skinny enough to have stood up in it!'

Tom ignored their gibes, long accustomed now to the general unpopularity engendered by holding the post of Parish Constable.

Back in the lock-up he lit a lantern and went to the rear yard. He stood for some time looking down at the dead girl and the sense of uneasiness evoked by Doctor Price's verdict stirred ever more strongly within his mind.

Driven by an overwhelming compulsion he spent the next hour delicately shaving thin slivers of tissue from the insides of the various organs. Placing the slivers in individual small pots he covered them with sulphuric acid, stirring the mixture with a glass rod to quicken the dissolving of the tissues. Then he replaced the organs back into the body cavity, sewed up the gaping wound, washed the cold dead flesh clean, and wrapped her in the sheet.

Until sleep came he spent the hours poring over his father's medical journals. At dawn he rose from bed and hurried to check the small pots of acid. Finding that the slivers of flesh had completely dissolved he instantly prepared slides from the mixture and sat studying them intently under the microscope.

After repeated re-examinations of the slides he finally felt confident enough to go and make his report to Joseph Blackwell, carrying the microscope and slides with him.

Blackwell was at his study desk when Tom faced him and declared without preamble, 'Sir, I'm convinced that Rose Brent was already dead when she went into the canal. So she couldn't have committed suicide or fell in by accident, as Doctor Price believes.'

Tom stood nervously awaiting an angry challenge followed by contemptuous dismissal from the other man. But to his surprise Blackwell made no immediate reply, only bent his head, seemingly deep in thought. Then after lengthy moments he stared hard at Tom and questioned curtly, 'What evidence have you to back up that statement, Master Potts?'

'Diatoms, sir! Or rather the lack of diatoms within the organs. Please examine the slides,' Tom requested.

The other man shook his head. 'It's no use me doing that; I wouldn't know what I was looking at. Explain to me what these diatoms might be? I don't recall hearing of them before.'

'They're microscopic organisms which are found in natural waters, such as the river and lakes which feed this canal. When a creature dies by drowning these diatoms are drawn deep into the body by the frantic efforts to draw breath, and while the blood still circulates they find their way into the various bodily organs, even into the bone marrow. They can be detected by dissolving the tissue in a mineral acid because they have acid resistant silica shells, which survive to show up under the microscope.

'If the creature is already dead when entering the water, few or none of them are to be found in the body because there is no forceful intake of breath to pull them into its depths. Which is why I'm confident that this poor girl was already dead when she entered the water.'

'How have you come by this particular knowledge of these diatoms, Master Potts?' Blackwell demanded.

'Initially my father taught me about them. He experimented with drowning rats in both fresh and salt waters, and following his death I continued to make those same experiments.'

'And humans? How many human specimens have you studied?'

'Err well . . . well . . . err . . .' Tom became hesitant. 'Actually this poor girl is the first opportunity I've had to examine a human specimen. But a couple of years ago I had the opportunity to examine some drowned sheep.'

'Drowned sheep and rats! A solitary human specimen!' Blackwell exclaimed, frowning. 'By God, Master Potts, you're presenting me with precious little evidence of your vast expertise in the matter of drowned human beings. Particularly when I contrast your experience in these matters with that of my friend Doctor Price.'

'I well realize that Doctor Price has vast experience and knowledge, sir, and that compared to him I am merely an apprentice,' Tom agreed ruefully. 'But my father's journals contain several minutely detailed findings from human cases of drowning, and I'm anxious to present my theory to Doctor Price for his consideration.'

Blackwell pondered for some moments, then asked, 'So what do you say has killed her, and how did she come to be in the canal?'

'I think that the cause of death might have been suffocation. Coupled with the fact that her intimate clothing is missing, I can't help but suspect that there was foul play involved. But I've no idea about the motive for killing her. She was pregnant, so a charge of bastardry might have been looming over some man; but a silver ring she was wearing has disappeared, so perhaps it could have been robbery.' Tom hesitated momentarily, then suggested, 'I think that we should drain and search the canal channel for a distance each side of where she was found, to see if there might be any discoveries which might aid the investigation.'

Again Blackwell sombrely considered what he had heard and Tom waited apprehensively for a severe rebuff.

'By God, Master Potts, your vivid imagination never ceases to astound me!' Blackwell scowled. 'How do you think my Lord Aston will receive this fanciful theory of yours? And how will he receive your suggestion that the canal traffic should be brought to a standstill while the channel is drained?'

Tom's heart sank, and he offered tentatively. 'Perhaps not gladly, sir.'

'And my friend Doctor Price, do you not think that he will be mortally offended by this imputation that he has made the wrong diagnosis? And with justification, when he is so vastly more experienced and knowledgeable in performing post-mortems than yourself.'

'Of course he is, sir. I fully accept that fact. But in this case—'

As Tom spoke a knock sounded on the room door and Blackwell's manservant's voice called, 'There's a gentleman come to call, sir, who says it is of the utmost urgency that he speak with you.'

Blackwell lifted his hand to silence Tom. 'Very well. Show him in.'

To Tom's surprise it was Martin Cooke who entered, introduced himself and after apologizing to Blackwell for disturbing him, went on.

'The reason for my coming here is most urgent, sir. I regretfully have to inform you that early this morning one of our Leggers was found dead, floating in the Tardebigge canal tunnel.'

Blackwell's thin lips pursed irritably. 'But why should informing me be a matter of such urgency, Master Cooke? It is not a rare happening to have Legger scum drowning in your tunnel.'

Cooke's eyes flashed with resentment at the sneer, and he retorted, 'Yes, Master Blackwell, it is not an infrequent occurrence. But this man was known as Irish Joe, and he was the one whom the Leggers were seeking to lynch a few days since. Perhaps they have succeeded in their purpose.'

'Perhaps they have indeed.' Blackwell's thin lips curved in a mirthless smile as he turned to Tom. 'There now, Master Potts; it appears that you may now have a genuine case of possible foul play to investigate. So let me hear no more of that other fanciful theory we were talking of. The coroner's inquest on Rose Brent will be held on Monday and the verdict will be accidental death by drowning.' To Cooke he said pleasantly, 'Constable Potts will accompany you back to the canal, sir, and do his best endeavours to investigate this matter. I bid you both good day.'

Outside as Cooke released his horse's reins from the hitching ring he told Tom, 'I've good news for you, Master Potts. I have your constable's staff in my office. My clerk spotted it among some nettles by the roadside. It looks none the worse for wear.'

'Thank you very much.' Tom breathed a sigh of relief, and admitted ruefully, 'I have to confess that going about my duties without having it in hand to bolster my authority, I've been feeling sadly powerless. Not to mention the worry of trying to find the wherewithal to pay for a new one.'

NINE

Late afternoon, Friday April 6th

The coach and pair driven by Richard Humphries came to a standstill on the narrow roadway outside the arched tunnel entrance of the huge needle mill at the bottom of the long steep Fish Hill.

'All off now, if you please, gentlemen, and make your own way up the hill. You can board again at the top of it if you so choose,' Humphries directed the all-male passengers seated on top of the coach, then descended from the driver's seat and opened the coach door.

'Will you ladies and gentlemen step down, if you please? This hill's too much of a drag for me horses. They won't reach the top wi' all you lot pulling 'um back.'

The first passenger to emerge was a youngish man, fashionably dressed in a blue coat, check trousers, embroidered waistcoat, fine white linen and a wide-brimmed slouch hat. Next a pretty young blonde-haired girl exited and her blue eyes dancing with mischievous amusement teased the coachman.

'Master Humphries, you shock me! I would have thought that a man of your strength and stature could have pulled the passengers, coach and horses up the hill all by yourself.'

'Don't you be so saucy, Amy Danks. You aren't yet too old for me to put you over me knee and spank your bum.' He leered mock-salaciously. 'And I'd enjoy doing it, as well.'

'I'll tell your wife that when I meet her next.' Amy giggled.

'Don't you dare! Because then it'll be me who gets a spanking from her.' He chuckled, and turned to speak to the remaining inside passengers. 'Widow Potts, Master Bromley, be so kind as to step down now.'

'If you dare to move an inch, Charles Bromley, I'll break my cane over your head!' a strident, high-pitched voice threatened. 'We've paid our fares and this villain must carry us to our rightful destination.' The voice rose to an angry shriek. 'And that destination is the yard of the Unicorn Inn, Redditch, in the Parish of Tardebigge, Worcestershire.'

Humphries sighed resignedly. 'Now, Widow Potts, you know very well that it's long established custom for passengers on my coach to walk to the top of the Fish Hill. To save the horses from overstraining their hearts.'

'It's very true what Master Humphries says, my dear,' a man's mellifluous tones quavered nervously.

'Hold your noise, Bromley!' the Widow Potts screeched furiously. 'I'll be the judge of truth here!'

'Come now, Ma'am, will you please step down?' Humphries leaned forwards so that his ruddy features were framed in the coach door, to be instantly confronted eyeball to eyeball by the sweaty, crimson-hued, balloon-like features of the woman whose gross body wallowed across almost the entire rear-facing seat. Her foul spittle-flecked breath gusted against his face and he recoiled, clutching his nose.

'Ah-ha! There now! Do you see this, everyone? He's raising his fist against me!' Widow Potts screeched. 'This vile brute is offering violence towards me. I'm a poor defenceless woman, and he lusts to beat me like he beats his poor pathetic, crushed-down slave of a wife. He's a beast! A bully! A danger to womankind!

'If you were a man, Bromley, you'd thrash him to within an inch of his life. You'd call him out, sir! You'd challenge him to a duel to the death! He is threatening your betrothed wife-to-be and terrifying her! How can you just sit there and do nothing to defend my honour and my life?'

Shrinking into his corner of the opposite seat, the small, pot-bellied, middle-aged proprietor of Bromley's Stationery Emporium for All Articles of Stationery, Rare and Antique Books and New Literature removed his crumpled top hat and mopped his sweaty pink bald pate with a grubby handkerchief. Magnified eyes blinking rapidly though bulbous-lensed spectacles, lisping through slipping bone false teeth, he pleaded frantically, 'I beg of you to calm yourself, my dearest Gertrude. I'm sure that Master Humphries offers no threat to you. He is a gentleman.'

'A gentleman? A gentleman?' Widow Potts' hanging jowls swung from side to side as she shook her head in disbelief. 'Are you a simpleton, Bromley? Are you such a thick-headed country bumpkin that you cannot recognize what constitutes a gentleman? My dear lamented late husband was a gentleman born and bred, Bromley. Truly a noble man, for whom I still grieve from the very bottom of my heart every minute of the night and day.

'This ruffian standing here threatening me! This wife beater! This brute beast! He is nothing but a jumped-up cart driver! If you were man enough to reach up and touch the very soles of my dearly beloved, grievously lamented husband's shoes, then you would have sprung to protect me from this cart driver's insults and violence. You would have demanded vengeance and inflicted injury or death, or both, upon him.'

Sucking her lips noisily she sat glowering at her fiancé, who coughed and fidgeted and tried to look everywhere but at the object of his affections.

The dismounted passengers had stood watching the clash, some with enjoyment, others looking disgruntled.

'If this was my coach I'd yank her out by the scruff of her neck,' one of the latter group declared.

'How would you find the scruff when it's buried beneath such a mountain of fat? You'd only lose your fingers in it,' another man sallied, and there was general laughter, but Amy Danks angrily turned on the joker.

'You should be ashamed of yourself jeering at an old woman. It's not her fault that she's so fat.'

'How dare you call me fat, Amy Danks?' Widow Potts shrieked indignantly. 'I've a mind to box your ears for you! You ignorant, saucy little bitch!'

Amy flushed with indignation. 'Well if that's the thanks I get, I'll not take your part any longer, Widow Potts.' She slung her sack bag over her shoulder and flounced away up the hill, and the male inside passenger hurried after her.

'May I accompany you, young lady? I'm in need of further directions when we reach the top, and I can carry your bag for you.'

Amy slowed her pace and when he caught her up she asked, 'Directions? What sort of directions are you needing?'

'To a livery stable where I can hire a horse. I have to go to the Hewell Grange.' He smiled, displaying good teeth. 'It belongs to my relative.'

Amy's blue eyes sparkled impishly. 'Your relative? You surely can't mean the Earl?'

'Indeed I do mean the Earl. I'm his cousin, twice removed.' He swept off his slouch hat and bowed courteously. 'Permit me to introduce myself. I am Eugene Sinclair. I heard the lady call you Amy Danks; is that Mrs or Miss?'

'It's Miss.'

'That surprises me, Miss Danks; I would have thought that a young lady of such beauty would be long since married.'

Although he was not conventionally handsome, Amy found the man very attractive. He was blond haired, with striking steel-blue eyes. Powerfully built, with regular sun-tanned features, tuneful educated accents, and the clothing and bearing of a gentleman.

She handed him the sack bag, and as they walked on side by side she couldn't resist flirting a little with him.

'I've had many offers of marriage, Master Sinclair, but I've yet to meet my Sir Galahad.'

'Then you must come to the next ball at the Grange. I'm sure that there will be a suitable Sir Galahad among the young bloods who flock there on such occasions.'

'I've been to many balls at the Grange. But I've not seen anyone suited for me.' Amy waited with amused anticipation for his reaction.

He could not completely hide the surprise he felt. 'You've been to many balls at the Grange, you say?'

'Oh yes,' she replied airily. 'My father's one of the Earl's game-keepers, and me and my sisters used to go and look through the windows to see all the fine ladies and gentlemen at their dancing, including yourself, sir. You stay at the Grange very often, don't you, and if I remember rightly, you spend a lot of time in the Earl's library, sorting through the books and doing a lot of writing. That's when you're not out riding around the parish, which I've seen you doing many times.'

He nodded. 'That I do, Miss Danks. But I don't recall ever having seen you at the Grange.'

'Well you couldn't be expected to notice a servant's child; and since I started work I live away from my father's cottage most of the time.'

'Your work, Miss Danks? What might that be?'

'I'm a barmaid and general dogsbody at the Fox and Goose. It's that tavern on the south side of the green, about halfway down the market place. Have you ever been there?'

'No, but now I've met you, Miss Danks, I shall most certainly patronize that establishment.'

'Well you'll find a very select custom there, Master Sinclair. We get all the rich needle masters coming into our best parlour. Very high and mighty they act as well. You'll feel very much at your ease in their company, I'm sure.'

He chuckled knowingly. 'You may continue to tease me all that you wish when I come to visit the Fox and Goose, Miss Danks, because I'm daring to hope that you and I shall become good friends.'

'That remains to be seen, Master Sinclair. But it might well be possible.'

When they reached the top of the hill Amy took back the bag and told him, 'If you turn right at the crossroads by the chapel there you'll see the Unicorn Inn. John Mence is the landlord, and he keeps a couple of horses for hire. I'm sure that you'll find his terms reasonable.'

'It's been a pleasure to meet you, Miss Danks.' He swept off his hat and bowed. 'And you may expect to see me very soon in the Fox and Goose.'

'Goodbye, Master Sinclair.' Amy smiled radiantly and walked away across the green.

He stood watching, savouring the graceful sway of her shapely body. Visualizing how she would smell and taste and feel laying naked and helpless beneath him. He ran his tongue over his full lips and promised, 'Oh yes, little Amy Danks, I shall most definitely be coming to call on you.'

An idea suddenly came to him, and once again he hurried after her.

'Miss Danks, wait a moment please.'

She halted and turned.

'Do you intend going on to your father's house now, Miss Danks?'

'I may be. Why do you ask?' A coquettish smile curved her moist shapely lips.

'Well, since I'm going to hire a horse, allow me to offer you a ride there. I'm sure you've ridden pillion before, and it's better to ride three miles than walk them carrying that bag, is it not?'

'Perhaps it is, but I don't have to walk three miles, Master Sinclair. My father doesn't live near the Grange. Our house is on Mount Pleasant, only half a mile from here.'

'Well, in that case will you do me the honour of allowing me to walk there with you and to carry your bag?'

'I shan't be going to see my family until tomorrow, and I'll be leaving my bag in my room at the Fox and Goose.'

He reached forward and took the bag from her. 'Then I insist on carrying your bag to the Fox and Goose, Miss Danks. I beg you not to break my heart by refusing me this honour.'

Amy giggled delightedly, and knowing how envious her female workmates would be to see her being squired by such a fine gentleman, she could not resist such a temptation.

'Very well, sir. You may carry my bag to the door, but then you must go away and leave me in peace.'

'I promise I will, Miss Danks. But I can't promise not to come and take refreshment in your tavern at some time in the very near future.'

Again she giggled, and told him, 'That will gladden the heart of my master, Tommy Fowkes. He loves to have gentlemen drinking in his pub.'

They walked on side by side, and Amy's eyes danced with delight as she saw the faces suddenly appear staring out from various windows of the Fox and Goose.

At the bottom of the Fish Hill the stalemate dragged on. Widow Potts would not alight from the coach. Richard Humphries would not drive on until she did so. Charles Bromley remained trapped in his corner seat. The outside passengers still clustered as spectators, while in the adjoining needle mill many others were peering curiously through the grimy window panes.

A large covered wagon pulled up behind the coach and its driver shouted to Humphries, 'Move on, damn you! You're blocking my way into the mill.'

'I aren't moving an inch until this bloody woman shifts her fat arse,' Humphries bawled, and the wagon driver jumped down on to the road and came to confront him.

'I've got a load o' steel wire on board, and if my master has to wait any longer for it he'll have my guts for garters. So bloody well shift, or I'll be having *your* guts for garters.'

The beefy-bodied Humphries raised his meaty fists threateningly. 'Not you, nor another dozen like you could have my guts for garters. So just sod off!'

A stocky ageing man came out from the arched mill entrance and challenged angrily, 'What are you trying to do here, Dicky Humphries? Bring my works to a standstill? I needs that wire right away or I'll be losing production else. Now fuckin' move afore I gets my men out to move you.'

Irascible, self-made Samuel Thomas spoke and dressed like the rural labourer he once was. He favoured a rustic smock, broad-brimmed slouch hat, leather breeches and hob-nailed boots, in contrast to his fellow fashionably clad, top-hatted needle masters.

Following this direct intervention by one of the richest and most powerful needle masters in the industry, Humphries realized that he was facing greater odds than he could defeat.

'This aren't my fault, Master Thomas. It's all this bloody woman's fault. My horses can't get up the hill with her inside. Her's too bloody weighty for only two of them to pull wi'out doing themselves an injury.'

'Why aren't you got a full team on then?' Thomas queried.

'Because he's too mean and greedy to run a full team!' Widow Potts' strident screech sounded. 'He's trying to do the run on the cheap, like he always does. The beast would rather kill these poor horses than harness a full team to make their work easier. Cruel, vile swine that he is! If you were only half a man, Bromley, you'd thrash him into an inch of his life. Why won't you protect me?'

'Now please calm yourself, my dear. I beg of you!' Bromley bleated pleadingly.

'My two leaders got tangled up with a barrow when I went into Brummagem this morning, and were brought down, and took some bad cuts. I've left them up there to be treated. I'd have had a full team on else,' Humphries explained to Samuel Thomas. 'But I've now got to journey on to Evesham. I can harness up me two spares once I get to me yard, but if these two has to drag my present loading up the hill they'll not be fit to continue, so I'm going to have to pay through the nose to rent more beasts from somewhere. Do you see the problem I'm faced with, Master Thomas? I can't afford to lose so much money, times being as hard as they be.'

'Fair enough.' The needle master nodded, and came to the coach door to face the Widow Potts. 'Do you recognize me, Ma'am?'

'I might, but then again I might not!' she snapped petulantly.

'If you will get down, Ma'am, and let this coach be moved, I'll make arrangement to have you taken up the hill and to your very doorstep. Will that suit?'

She screwed her lips and sucked noisily on them for some seconds, before grudgingly accepting. 'It might.' Only to add almost instantly, 'But then again, it might not!'

Yet another large wagon came to a halt behind the blocking vehicles, its driver and his mate shouting for the way to be cleared.

Samuel Thomas lost patience and growled, 'I'll tell you what, Ma'am. If you don't shift yourself, then I'll get my men to shift you.'

'If anybody dares to lay a finger on me, I'll have my son lock them up. He's the Parish Constable,' Widow Potts shrieked furiously, her puce complexion turning to an almost black hue.

Thomas coloured bright red and roared equally furiously, 'And I'm the bloody Head Vestryman in this parish, and so I'm one o' your bloody son's masters, and he'll do whatever me and the Vestry tells him to do . . . And that won't be to lock up any of my men for shifting your arse out of this bloody coach, my lady!'

'Agghhh!' Widow Potts screamed loudly and slumped sideways with eyes closed as if in a faint, breath snorting heavily through her nose.

'Oh my God, she's having a heart attack!' Charles Bromley shouted in dismay. 'It's well known that she has a weak heart! You've killed her!'

'Have I hell as like!' Thomas denied heatedly, but nevertheless stared at the comatose woman with some concern, and urged her, 'Come now, Ma'am, rouse yourself.'

The widow showed no reaction, and the needle master cursed beneath his breath, then stepped back from the coach and told the waggoner, 'Unhitch your team and harness 'um to the coach, and draw the bloody thing up the hill.' He turned to Humphries. 'When you gets up on the green, fetch Doctor Laylor to have a look at her. Tell him I'll pay his bill.'

Inside the coach Widow Potts' snorting breath quickened its noisy tempo, and her lips quirked momentarily with a grin of triumph.

TEN

'**N**ot a pretty sight, is he, Master Potts?' Martin Cooke grimaced. 'The bugger was ugly enough in life, God only knows. But he's a damn sight uglier in death.'

'Irish Joe' was naked, laid flat on his back on top of a work bench in one of the wharf's outbuildings.

Tom stood staring thoughtfully down at the muddied features of the dead man, whose lips were drawn back in a rictus snarl displaying blackened snags of broken decayed teeth.

'One thing I will give him credit for though.' Cooke smiled grimly. 'He don't stink half so bad now as he did when he was alive.'

'His clothes?' Tom wondered aloud. 'Where are they?'

'The Leggers took them and his clogs, when they pulled him out of the canal,' Cooke explained. 'It's an established custom when one of them dies to divide his possessions up between themselves. Then they each put a few pence in the pot to give to the widow or family of the dear departed. None of them put any pence in the pot this time, however. They said that his clothes didn't cover what he thieved from them, so they'd be damned if they'd throw good money after bad.'

'Did Irish Joe leave a lawful widow hereabouts?'

'God only knows. These shanty women are usually shared around freely among the Leggers!' Cooke shrugged.

Tom bent and scrutinized the mottled discoloured flesh, turning the body over and back again, but could discover no obvious signs of inflicted wounds or broken bones.

'I'll have to move him down to the lock-up, Master Cooke, so that there can be a proper post-mortem examination made.'

'My carter will take him there for you tomorrow morning. He's had practice in it, has he not?'

Tom thanked him, and requested politely, 'Will you permit me to make enquiries of your wharf people and the Leggers? I'll try not to keep them from their work for too long.'

'Of course,' Cooke readily assented. 'But you'll do better if you question the Leggers before they push any barges through, because once they've got a few pence in their pockets they addle their brains with rot-gut gin in double-quick time.'

Over the next hours Tom had ample proof of that assertion and his questioning of drunken Leggers and their sluttish drabs bore no fruit as to Irish Joe's whereabouts before his death. Neither could the more sober wharf employees or their womenfolk give him any information.

The night was dark and rain was falling when Tom decided to abandon the task and return to Redditch. He left the shelter of the huddled buildings and shanties adjoining the wharf, turned up his coat collar, bent his head against the driving rain and started out to trudge the three miles back to the lock-up. He had covered only a score of yards when he heard a voice calling him from his rear. He stopped and swung about as a dark swathed figure came up to him.

'What do you want with me?' Nervous at being accosted by someone the darkness rendered unrecognizable, Tom tensed, gripping his staff with both hands.

'Just a few words is all I wants with you, that's all.'

It was a woman's voice, speaking in a broad Irish brogue, and Tom's tension eased.

'I'm listening.' He stared hard at her, but her head was covered with a shawl and he couldn't see her features.

'It's about Joe, him that they pulled outta the water. I might know something about him. I might know why he was dead in the water.'

Tom experienced a surge of anticipation. 'Then please tell me what you know, Ma'am.'

'What's in it for me?' she demanded.

Tom thought quickly. 'I'm sure that if your information is useful to me, we'll be able to come to an arrangement regarding recompense.'

'What the fokk do youse mean by that?' she demanded suspiciously. 'What the fokk is recompense?'

'It's a payment,' he told her. 'If you can tell me something which enables me to understand what happened to him, then you may well receive a payment for that information. So what is it that you want to tell me?'

She hesitated for a few moments, and Tom urged, 'I promise you, Ma'am, that if your information is useful, I shall make sure that you receive payment.'

'Alright then, but swear on the Cross that you'll not peach on me. It'll be curtains for me if anyone was to find out I've been talking to you.'

'You have my word on it, Ma'am,' Tom promised sincerely.

'Alright then, I'll tell you. D'you recall that dead girl who was pulled outta the water on the day that you was chucked in?'

'I do,' Tom confirmed.

'Well, about a week afore that day Joe was well pissed one night, and he was telling me that he knew something that was going to keep him and me in clover for the rest of our days. He was rambling on about some girl and a rich fella that we both knew well, who he'd seen her with a couple o' times afore. He told me that he'd seen this fella taking her into the wood on the hill down from the church that very night, and that afterwards he saw them having a shouting match down by the cut—'

'Tessy, where the fuckin' 'ell am you?' A man's harsh bellow came from the Leggers' shanties and a lantern's beam pierced the darkness. 'Get back in here now, or I'll knock three bells o' shit outta you, you Paddy bitch!'

'Oh, Jaysus! That's Jacky Whittaker! I can't be seen with you! I'll give you the fella's name when you pay me for it,' the woman hissed and fled into the darkness, leaving Tom staring after her in frustration.

'Tessy, I knows where you'm hiding, you bitch!' The harsh bellow came again and the lantern beam moved nearer to Tom.

The rain abruptly beat down with redoubled fury, and fearing that he would be discovered, Tom turned and resumed the trudge towards Redditch, his excitement rising as he thought about the possible connotations of what this woman might have to tell.

'Tessy!' Her name echoed repeatedly in his thoughts. 'Tessy! What am I going to learn from you, Tessy?'

ELEVEN

Saturday April 7th

Tom woke in the darkness and automatically sat up in his narrow cot and stretched out for his tinder box on top of the bedside chest. Still half fuddled with sleep, he used the flint and steel to kindle a flame in the tinder and light the candle, then reached for his hunter watch, which he customarily hung on the cot post. Only to remember that the watch was still at the pawnbroker's.

'Dear God, what time is it? Wearily pushing the bedclothes aside he got up to open and look out of the diamond-paned window, and saw the first pale of dawn on the black horizon.

He began to dress, his thoughts busy with the many tasks he must try to complete on this market day.

'Serve the notices to appear on Monday to the Coroner's jurymen. Take delivery of Irish Joe's corpse. Check the market sellers' licences. Check on that stray sheep at the cattle pound. Serve that summons for assault on Nellie and Israel Govier. Try and find time to get up to the wharves to see if I can talk to Tessy again . . .' He grinned ruefully. 'And, most urgent of all, go and beg Grocer Groby and Baker Scambler to let me have some provisions on tick.'

The lock-up bells jangled loudly and Tom wondered who could be calling so early. Shielding the candle flame with his hand, he hastened downstairs, shouting, 'I'm coming, I'm coming.'

The noisy jangling was increasing in force and tempo as he pulled the door open.

'Thomas! Thomas! Oh, thank God I've found you!' Charles Bromley gasped in relief. 'Where the devil where you yesterday? I spent hours ringing the bells.'

'I was away on my duties and didn't return until a late hour,' Tom explained with a sinking heart.

'Well never mind it, you're here now. As you see, your sainted mother and myself are safely returned from our travels, and I can plainly see that you are delighted to welcome us home.'

Tom managed a wan smile. 'Indeed I'm happy to see you safely home again, Master Bromley.'

'Tut tut! Thomas! Have I not repeatedly requested you to call me Papa?' Bromley reproved sternly. 'Your dearest Mamma and myself have been betrothed for five months now. Do you not agree that it's time that all formalities of address were done away with between myself and my betrothed's only child, to whom I'll soon be standing in the proud position of Pater Familias?'

'Where's my mother?' Tom evaded making an answer and peered out across the dark green.

'She has a room at the Unicorn Inn. Obviously it wouldn't have been seemly for her to stay un-chaperoned at my house. Before I parted from her she instructed me to tell you that you must fetch her from the inn after she has breakfasted. She said on no account were you to call for her before the noon o'clock. She was so exhausted from the journey that she must enjoy a long rest before she can be moved.'

'Can be moved?' Tom queried.

'Exactly so, Thomas.' Bromley's bone false teeth clicked loudly. 'You know very well that she will require transport. She surely cannot walk such a distance, and then of course there is also her baggage. And she also asked me to remind you to bring your purse with you. John Mence charges high prices for bed and board. You wouldn't credit how much our dinner cost us; I do believe that fellow is more of a grasping shylock than even his brother.'

'Dear God!' Tom muttered despairingly. 'Did neither of you have money to pay for your dinner even?'

Bromley shook his head and explained mournfully, 'It was the fault of our coach fares, Thomas. They cost every last penny I possessed.'

Tom could only nod. 'Very well, Master Bromley. I'll go for my mother later this morning.' He stepped back inside and began to close the door.

'Thomas! Thomas! Wait a moment, I beg of you,' Bromley panted frantically. 'I must warn you that your dearest Mamma was not in her usual sweetness of humour when I parted from her last night. You must approach her with care, my boy, and tread very softly.'

'Thank you, Master Bromley; I most certainly will do my utmost to do just that.'

Tom pushed the door firmly closed. Resentment burned within him, but then he decided that he couldn't really lay all the blame on the couple. Knowing that they were returning shortly, he accepted that he should have made arrangements to have his mother let into the lock-up if he were absent from it. Back upstairs he sat down on a stool and began taking a depressing mental inventory of whatever bedding, furnishings and personal possessions he could pawn to pay his mother and Charles Bromley's bill at the Unicorn Inn.

TWELVE

In the private parlour of the Fox and Goose Amy Danks was relating her adventures in Birmingham to the rapt audience seated around a table strewn with the remnants of a hearty breakfast.

'And one night my auntie and uncle took me to see the Soho works all lit up as bright as the sun with gas lamps, and there was some houses round about that were all lit with gas lamps as well. It was like a miracle to see them. But then we had to walk past the gasworks where they make the gas and it didn't half stink.'

Landlord Tommy Fowkes' fat red cheeks ballooned and he blew out a gust of derision. 'Bloody Brummagem! Everything stinks up there!'

'Don't you dare say that, you cheeky bugger!' His equally fat red-faced wife rounded on him furiously. 'I was born in Brummagem, and me mam afore me, and me granny afore her! And I'se smelled worser stinks in bloody Redditch than I ever did in Brummagem!'

'If you has then it's because you brought 'um here with you!' he riposted.

Their fat, red-faced daughter Lily intervened. 'Oh shurrup, the pair of you. I wants to listen to Amy's stories, not to your bletherings.'

Her parents subsided into an aggrieved silence.

'We went to a theatre one night – oh, it was wonderful. Like a palace, it was. I've never seen anything so marvellous! It put the Grange in the shade, I'll tell you.' Amy's blue eyes shone and her rosy cheeks glowed. 'And in the intervals we ate oysters and drank black stout and port wine, just like the gentry was doing in the boxes. And I was getting a lot of attention from the young gentlemen, I can tell you."

'What was happening on the stage?' Lily's expression was wistful. 'I'd love to go and see something on a proper stage in a proper theatre, so I would.'

'All sorts happened,' Amy replied. 'There was singing, and dancing, and a play, and some performing bears. It was wonderful!'

Old Benny the Potman poked his head around the door and with a large dew-drop quivering on the tip of his long nose announced lugubriously, 'You'm wanted in the tap room, Gaffer. Maisie says there's a bloke moaning about the porter. Reckons it's bin watered down, so he does.'

Fowkes rose to his feet. 'Moaning about my porter, is he? Reckons it's watered down, does he? I'll kick the cheeky bugger's arse right through the door.'

'And I'll help you do it.' Mrs Fowkes followed her husband through the door, leaving the two girls at the table.

Lily lowered her voice conspiratorially. 'What about the chaps, Amy? Did you meet any nice chaps up in Brummagem?'

Amy smiled with satisfaction. 'Dozens!'

'Did you meet him up there? That one who walked you to the door yesterday?'

Amy shook her head. 'No, I met him on the coach.'

'What's his name?'

'Eugene Sinclair, and he's a very fine gentleman. He's a cousin of the Earl, and when he comes here he lives in Hewell Grange.'

'Who're you talking about, Amy?' a pretty, buxom young girl asked as she came through the door.

'That's for us to know and for you to find out, Maisie Lock,' Lily Fowkes snapped irritably. 'What's you come poking your nose in for? You'm supposed to be working.'

'And I has been, while all the time you still been a-laying in your stink-pit and stuffing your guts in here, you fat cow!' Maisie Lock retorted, and asked again, 'Who're you talking about, Amy?'

Amy explained, and could not resist mischievously gilding the lily somewhat.

'And he's begged you to go to the next ball at the Grange with him!' Maisie exclaimed, and envy gleamed in her eyes. 'You'm a lucky bugger, you am, Amy Danks. When I saw him coming across the green with you, I thought you was just showing him the way to the pub. But instead of that you was getting off with him.'

Lily Fowkes had sat seething with anger and now attacked. 'How dare you say that? She warn't getting off with him at all! You knows very well that Amy's already got Tom Potts for a sweetheart, and she aren't going to go with anybody else. She aren't desperate to get a man like you am, you jealous cow!'

'Tom Potts?' There was the hint of a sneer in Maisie's tone. 'He aren't got two ha'pennies to rub together, and his old ma is a bloody horror. If I was in Amy's place I know who I'd choose to wed between this new gentleman and Tom Potts, and it 'uddn't be the one wi' no gold in his pockets, and a rotten miserable bitch for a ma.'

'I'll thank you to let me do my own choosing, Maisie Lock!' Amy reproved sharply. 'And the same goes for you, Lily Fowkes!' She got up from the table. 'I'm going to go and see me family; I'll be back before noon.'

'And I've got to take some stuff down to me granny's,' Maisie announced, then sneered openly at Lily. 'So until we gets back that means that you got to do a bit o' work for a change, Fat Arse!'

'Are you going to go and see Tom Potts, and let him know that you're back, Amy?' Lily asked. 'He'll be really upset if you don't.'

Amy's blue eyes sparkled impishly. 'There's one thing you need to know, Lily my dear, and that's that you must never be seen to chase after a man. You always have to make him think that he's chasing after you. Tom Potts will soon find out that I'm back, I don't doubt, and then he'll come chasing after me.'

Amy and Maisie left the Fox and Goose together, walking side by side towards the central crossroads. As they passed the walled chapel and graveyard of St Stephen Maisie whispered urgently, 'Look there, Amy. That dandy standing by the chapel gate. Aren't he the one who walked you back across the green yesterday? He's bloody good-looking, aren't he, you lucky cow.'

Even as she spoke Eugene Sinclair moved from the gateway to meet them, calling, 'Miss Danks, this is a happy encounter. I was hoping that I might see you.'

The girls halted and the man reached them, removing his top hat and bowing courteously.

'Whatever would you want to see me for, Master Sinclair?' Amy dimpled coquettishly, flattered by the pursuit of this fashionably dressed fine gentleman, and at the same time hugely savouring Maisie's patent envy.

'Why, to bask in the sunlight of your beauty, Miss Danks. Whatever else?' He chuckled. 'And I will openly confess that I've been waiting here since dawn for just such an opportunity.'

Piqued that he had not even glanced at her, Maisie Lock asked him tartly, 'Why wait out here, Master, when you only had to step into our pub to see her?'

'Maisie, don't be so rude to the gentleman,' Amy reproved sharply.

The girl tossed her head and spluttered indignantly. 'Well, that's all he had to do, warn't it? Just step into our pub.'

Ignoring Maisie, Sinclair explained. 'I was returning the horse I hired yesterday, Miss Danks, and since you had told me that you were going to see your family this morning, could not resist waiting here for the chance that I might catch a glimpse of you. I didn't call into the Fox and Goose because I thought that the landlord might object to having one of your admirers disturbing you at your work. If I have caused you any embarrassment by waiting here, I beg of you to forgive me for it.'

'You've done nothing that needs any forgiveness from me, Master Sinclair.' Amy's imp of mischief impelled her provocatively to tease Maisie. 'And yes, I'm going now to see my family, and shall be very glad of your company on the walk to my home.'

Sinclair bowed gallantly. 'And I shall be the happiest man in the world now that you have done me the honour of permitting me to escort you there, Miss Danks.'

'Tarra, Maisie, I'll see you later.' Amy smiled brilliantly at her friend, who tossed her head and stormed away, muttering furiously.

Tom Potts came trudging from the lock-up en route to the pawn-shop with a blanket-wrapped bundle slung over his shoulder. He saw the two girls and the man standing some forty yards ahead of him and, recognizing Amy, his heart thudded with elation.

'She's back safe and sound! Thank you God! Thank you!'

He quickened his pace to come within shouting distance, but then saw Maisie Lock hurry away, and Amy walk on side by side with the man, who offered his arm for Amy to rest her hand upon. Even at this distance he could see that they were smiling and talking animatedly together. His elation plummeted, his pace slowed.

'She has a new admirer.' Dread overwhelmed him. 'And he looks like a dandyish sort of fellow.'

'While you bear the appearance of an elongated scarecrow!' a voice jeered within his mind.

'Why in hell's name did I not take the trouble to shave and tidy myself, instead of coming out looking like a scavenger, and a damned scruffy one at that!' he castigated himself savagely. 'Perhaps it's just as well that Amy didn't see me to compare me with that dandy.'

Amy and her escort disappeared around the corner of the cross-roads, and Tom trudged glumly on, trying to steel himself for whatever heartaches might be in store.

THIRTEEN

'When are you going to get up and do some work, you lazy useless hound?' Granny Lock demanded angrily. 'You knows well that it going to be busy today, what with the market and all.'

'Get up? How can I?' Old Gaffer Lock questioned plaintively. 'I aren't got strength to move more than to roll over and have a piss in me pot. I'm wasting away to nothing. I'm just skin and bone.' He rubbed his massive belly, and groaned. 'Me guts is killing me and I aren't been able to get a mouthful down me neck for bloody days, has I?' He glared accusingly at his wife. 'I 'udden't put it past you to have poisoned me, you spiteful old bitch! I saw you put summat in my beer, didn't I?'

'Poison you! Poison you!' she screeched. 'I wish I had poisoned you, you useless idle sod. I wish I'd ha' poisoned you afore I ever met you.'

'God Almighty! Are you two at it again?' Maisie Lock came into the tiny single-storeyed cottage. 'Whose fault is it this time?'

Both old people began to shout accusations of blame, and then the tollgate bell added its strident janglings to the discordant cacophony.

'I'll go,' Maisie told them, and putting down the sack she held went outside shouting, 'Leave the bloody bell alone, will you? I'm here, aren't I!'

The horseman released the bell rope, and his dark eyes appreciatively examined the oncoming girl's shapely figure as he asked, 'Who might you be, pretty girl? What's your name?'

Maisie's initial instinct was to tell him to mind his own business, but then she came closer and realized what an attractive man he was, lean-bodied, sun-tanned face, the unshaven black stubble around his mouth emphasizing the whiteness of his teeth.

She took in his wide-brimmed hat, multi-caped tweed riding coat, the large leather shield badge tied around his upper right arm, and already well aware of his profession, smiled flirtatiously.

'You tell me who and what you am first.'

'I think that you can tell from my voice that I'm a Welshman.' He grinned. 'And that you know very well already from my badge that I'm a drover. You can plainly see by what's following me that I'm in a large way of business, as well.'

He pointed back along the winding road which led to Alvechurch where another horseman was leading a mooing, grunting herd of long-horned black cattle. Other men on foot, dogs at their heels, flanked the beasts, swinging long whippy staffs and continuously calling out, emitting a noise which was neither shouting, crying nor singing, but a noise which was peculiar to itself and which carried far and wide across the surrounding countryside.

'They'm making a terrible din,' Maisie observed disparagingly.

'It has a purpose, pretty girl,' the drover explained. 'It's to warn any farmers who've got loose stock to gather them in, because if the beasts get drawn into the herd it's the devil of a job to separate them from it.'

'And from what I'se heard tell about you Taffys there's many the time you don't even try to separate them from it,' Maisie accused.

He threw back his head and laughed long and loud. 'There's truth in what you say, pretty girl. But you may ask anyone along the droving roads about Daniel Wynne, and they'll all tell you that I'm an honest man, and have always separated the strays from my herds.'

'I believe you, though thousands mightn't,' Maisie riposted cheekily.

'Well then, now you accept that I'm an honest man, tell me your name.'

'It's Maisie. Maisie Lock. And my granddad, Gaffer Lock, is the toll keeper on this gate.'

'And you're his assistant.'

'No I'm not!' she denied indignantly. 'I wouldn't spend my days and nights doing a thankless rotten job like this 'un. I work in a fine lively pub, where all the needle masters and the gentry come to do their business, and we sometimes have fiddlers playing, and singers, and sometimes even conjurors doing turns.'

'And what's the name of this pub of yours? I'd like to come and see you there, and treat you to a drink.'

'It's the Fox and Goose on the south side of the green. You can't miss it.' Maisie was relishing the prospect of showing Amy Danks that she too could attract handsome, gentlemanly admirers.

'I know it well enough, and I'll be seeing you there, Miss Maisie Lock, and very soon. But for now can you open the gate and let my beasts pass through?'

'How many, Master Wynne?' Granny Lock came hobbling to query.

'Hello Granny Lock,' Daniel Wynne greeted her with a smile. 'I see that you're as beautiful as ever. You still must be drinking from the Holy Well of Eternal Youth.'

'And I see that you'm still as silver-tongued as ever, you Taffy bugger!' she scolded, but her rheumy eyes held a warmth that belied her sharp tone as she told the girl, 'Now don't you pay no attention whatever to what this Taffy bugger tells you, our Maisie. He uses that silver tongue of his just to get daft-yedded wenches to lift their skirts for him, and when he's had what he wants from 'um, then he's gone. He's the ruination of women, so he is. A bloody heart-breaker!'

The Welshman laughed, shaking his head. 'Don't believe your grandmother, Miss Maisie. It's myself that has had my heart broken all too many times. Especially by this beautiful lady.'

'How many beasts do you want to pass through?' the old crone demanded.

'Just six. I'm putting the rest to grass at Gibbon's place up towards the Beoley Cross, so they won't be passing through your gate, will they?'

'Are you going to take 'um up town yourself?'

'I am, and one of my men will go with me.'

'Will he be riding?'

'No, he's on foot.'

'Right then, that'll be tuppence for the cattle, and four pence for you and your horse. Your man can pass for free.'

'Tuppence for my beasts?' Wynne protested indignantly. 'At all the other gates I use the toll rate is four pence a score. So that's a penny for five, and that extra beast shouldn't count for toll. And another thing, the other gates only charge three pence for a horseman.'

'Then you must use them gates instead if you so chooses.' The old crone cackled with glee at his reaction. 'But they won't lead you up to Redditch Green, 'ull they?'

'You're robbing me!' Wynne declared bluntly. 'And I'm of a mind to refuse to be robbed.'

Granny Lock was obdurate. 'Then you can turn round and piss off back the way you'se come. Because until I gets your tolls in me hand, you aren't coming through my gate. The Turnpike Trust has set the prices to charge, and I has to obey 'um because they'm my masters, not you!'

By now the oncoming herd was almost on them, enveloping them in a cacophonous wave of sound, and Daniel Wynne surrendered.

'Here, you old witch, take your blood money!' He handed coins to Granny Lock, who cackled with delight and crowed triumphantly to Maisie.

'Let this be a lesson to you, my duck. Never let any sweet-tongued man put one over on you. What we've got atween our ears can always best that wormy thing that they got dangling down atween their bloody shanks!'

FOURTEEN

Tom returned from the pawnbroker's to find the canal company cart carrying Irish Joe's tarpaulin-wrapped corpse waiting outside the lock-up, and a black-clad clergyman standing beside it. Tom was pleased to see the clergyman, with whom he shared a warm friendship.

'Will you wait while I get this fellow inside before we talk, John?'

John Clayton, Curate of St Stephen's chapel, was tall, powerfully built and strikingly ugly in features, but when he smiled he radiated good fellowship and charm.

'Get the door open, Tom, and I'll have this poor soul inside in a jiffy.'

The carter stood open-mouthed with amazement when Clayton lifted the long tarpaulin bundle in his arms as if it were weightless and carried it through the door.

'Where do you want him?'

'On the trestle table out in the yard, if you please, John.'

Although Tom had witnessed his friend performing great feats of strength before, he still marvelled at this casual display of muscular power.

With the corpse settled beneath the overhanging awning, Clayton asked, 'Where do you have Rose Brent?'

'She's in the end cell nearest the yard. She's coffined and ready to be moved.' Tom could not suppress a slight grimace, and an edge entered his tone. 'The verdict is to be given as accidental death by drowning.'

'I know, Blackwell sent for me yesterday afternoon. I'm to conduct the burial on Wednesday morning.' Clayton paused and stared questioningly into Tom's face. 'Is something troubling you about the verdict? I thought I saw a change in your expression, or was it merely my imagination?'

Tom drew a deep breath. 'It's the diatoms, John, or rather the lack of them, that's troubling me greatly.'

'Diatoms?' Clayton shook his head. 'What in hell's name are they?'

Tom explained at length, and when he finally lapsed into silence could not stop himself fidgeting uncomfortably as he waited for his friend's reception of this novel and outlandish-sounding theory.

Clayton's ugly features were creased in a thoughtful frown. After long moments he said quietly, 'After talking to Blackwell, I went to see Widow Brent that evening, and told her that the verdict was to be accidental death by drowning. I know that I wasn't acting according to the letter of the law by telling her a verdict had been decided upon before the inquest was actually held. But I was hoping it would bring her some comfort to know that her daughter was not a suicide, nor a victim of violence.'

He paused, shaking his head before going on slowly. 'Widow Brent's reaction was not how I expected it would be. She gripped my hands as tightly as she was able, and asserted with great passion that Rose could never have drowned by accident because she had been born with her head covered by the caul. The poor old woman insisted on bringing me into her cottage to witness for myself that she still had her daughter's caul in her possession. She keeps it carefully wrapped up in paper, and strangely enough the membrane appears to be as smooth and fresh as the day it was cut away from Rose's head. Widow Brent vehemently insisted that Rose must have died by other means than drowning, and that someone else must have been responsible for her daughter's death.'

An uneasy smile touched Clayton's lips and he spread his arms wide. 'Now I know that the superstition is still widely believed that any person born with a caul can never die by drowning so long as the caul is kept safe and whole in their possession, but surely a highly educated and intelligent man such as yourself, Tom, cannot give it any credence.'

'Of course I give no credence to the caul superstition.' Tom shook his head firmly. 'But I'm still convinced that Rose Brent did not die by drowning; and there is a strong possibility that she was killed and dumped into the canal after her death. I intend to investigate the case fully, no matter how long it takes me to do so.'

'Speaking as your friend, Tom, I think that you should give this matter much more thought,' Clayton warned gravely. 'On the basis of your father's journals, and your own limited experiments, you're claiming that the presence or absence in the body of these diatoms – whatever they might be – are the proof that Rose Brent was murdered. By making this claim you're also in effect saying that Doctor Price is wrong in his diagnosis. Ergo, he is incompetent!

'Let me remind you that Cuthbert Price is not only the bosom friend of Joseph Blackwell, but was also until his retirement the personal medical consultant of the Earl of Plymouth of Hewell Grange, the Lord Goodricke of Studley Castle, my Lord Aston himself and many of the needle masters.

'Let me remind you also that the verdict on Rose Brent's death has already been decided upon by Blackwell and Lord Aston, and the jury will as always follow their direction. Blackwell and Aston might well regard your rejection of this verdict as being a direct challenge to their authority, and then it will be "God help you!" Because no one else will lift a finger to support you. You'll be standing completely alone, my friend. I tell you frankly, my own material poverty is such that I dare not risk being dismissed by Lord Aston for supporting you, not with having my sisters to maintain as I do now.'

He reached out to enclose Tom's bony shoulders with his huge hands and shook him gently.

'I beg of you, Tom, let this matter lay. Accept the verdict of accidental drowning. You already have more than enough difficulties to contend with in your life, without creating a damned sight more. These diatoms you speak of might well exist. But the import of their presence or absence in bodily tissues will never be accepted as proof of anything, except for the fact of their mere existence. Take my advice, Tom, and put all thoughts of challenging this verdict from your mind . . . Now I must go, so I bid you a good day, my friend.'

Left alone with the tarpaulin-swathed corpse of Irish Joe, self-doubt flooded into Tom's mind.

'Diatoms! Whatever they might be?' The dismissive tones of John Clayton reverberated in his ears.

By nature timid and pacifistic, he dreaded the prospect that a man he admired greatly, Joseph Blackwell, who had supported him during the times when the whole district had mocked and jeered at him, might now turn against him.

'Perhaps Doctor Price *is* correct in his diagnosis. He is vastly experienced compared to me. Maybe I am indulging in wild fancies. After all, what proof do I have that my father was right, that diatoms act within the body in such a manner? Only my own experiments. So am I merely acting out of conceit? Creating theories to suit my own fancies? Theories based on minute little creatures that can only be seen under a damned microscope! Why don't I just accept that the verdict is accidental death by drowning, and that's an end to it!'

He fetched his staff from upstairs and left the lock-up, resolved to give no more thought to Rose Brent's death. Yet try though he might to dismiss the vivid image of the girl's dead mud-streaked face from his thoughts, he knew that he would find no peace of mind until he had discovered the truth of what had happened to her.

At this hour of the morning the market vendors were still taking their posts and setting out their wares along the south side of the chapel wall and green. There were stalls and barrows laden with vegetables, poultry, rabbits, cloth, crockery, pots and pans, interspersed with the baskets of the trinket and button hawkers, peg makers and cheese makers, egg and butter wives, quack nostrum sellers, herbalists, caged songbird dealers, broadsheet and patter criers, and the authorized beggars.

Tom moved along the line checking the marketing permits and licences to trade of the stall holders and the other vendors. As he passed by the Fox and Goose he couldn't help but stare longingly at its windows and doorway, wondering if Amy Danks was inside. He wanted to enter the pub and ask for her, but with the memory of her walking, smiling and talking with the dandy painfully fresh in his mind, he was nervous at how she might greet him.

'Anyway, I've far too much work to do today, to be able to spend time running after Amy,' he excused his own timidity. 'Perhaps I'll have opportunity to call on her later.'

'Good morning to you, Master Constable Potts. By the miserable look on your face you're obviously in need o' my services. Sit you down on Jemmy the Toothpuller's throne and I'll have that bad bugger out from your jaw afore you can say "Jack Robinson".'

The Toothpuller was tall and skinny bodied, lank greasy ringlets hanging down around his swarthy pockmarked face. His upper body was festooned with long bandoliers of blackened rotten teeth, and strings of the same were wrapped around and dangling from his crumpled top hat.

'I'm the right man to release you from your agonies. There's no tooth ever been able to resist my arts. I've pulled the fangs of wolves and lions and sabre-toothed tigers. And when I was soldiering in India the Rajahs used to beg me to come and pull the tusks from their elephants.'

He gestured towards the large wooden armchair with its myriad fixed leather restraining straps.

'These straps are only for show, Master Constable Potts. They holds the scaredy cats still so they don't wriggle too much and rupture themselves. A man of your calibre only needs to sit down and open his mouth wide, and the tooth is out so quick that you won't feel not a pang of discomfort. You won't even know that it's gone until I holds it up before your eyes.'

Tom shook his head and smiled. 'I don't need your services today, thank you, Jemmy. My teeth are sound. I scrub them twice a day with fresh birch twigs, and three times a week I polish them with Newton's Restorative Tooth Powder.'

The Toothpuller opened his mouth wide and ruefully tapped his toothless gums. 'Just as I did meself, until I took the scurvy when I was serving with Lord Nelson aboard the *Victory* and all me teeth fell out in the course of one night. But you needn't worry if you should take the scurvy and all your teeth drop out. Because I can plug new teeth back into the holes. Just you take a look at these.'

From the canvas bag slung from his shoulder he brought out a small bundle in a pink-coloured wrapping, which when he opened it metamorphosed into a badly soiled and torn silk stocking. He reached down inside it and brought out a handful of white human teeth.

'I got these a few months since. Fresh pulled from a young woman who was pulled out of the river at Bewdley, God rest her soul. Real beauties, aren't they, and I've been saving them for just the right customer. Not a hole, nor crack, nor blemish on them. Just imagine how fine they'll look when plugged into some lucky bugger's jaws.'

Tom's heartbeat quickened as he stared at the pink silk. 'The young woman who drowned, is that one of her stockings?'

The other man shrugged. 'I dunno, the teeth was wrapped in it when I got 'um. It was all above board. I bought 'um from the Bewdley Poorhouse. The young wench warn't known thereabouts, you see. So they couldn't give a name to her, and nobody come to claim her, even though the Vestry had notices put in the Brummagem and Worcester news sheets. So after a few weeks her was buried by the parish, and they sold me her teeth to set against the burial and funeral costs, because her hadn't got a brass farthing on her, or anything else worth selling.'

'How was she drowned? Was it an accident?'

'Nobody knows. Her was found washed up on a weir. But her was well rotted by then so they couldn't tell much about her, except that her was pregnant. Perhaps the bloke who babbied her had left her in the lurch and she topped herself? But anyways the Bewdley Vestry give her a Christian burial out o' kindness.'

'When was she found? What was the date?' Tom's heart was

pounding now as he considered the similarities between what had happened to Rose Brent and this unknown girl.

'Well, I bought these at the end o' November, but I disremember the exact date. Her had been buried by then, o' course. But her must have drowned late on in the October, I should reckon.'

'Thank you, Jemmy.' Tom walked on, his head bent, his thoughts in a tumult.

'Can there really be any connection between the two? Was the girl wearing pink silk stockings and a silver betrothal ring like Rose Brent? Where might she have come from? If she has family then surely they would have been making enquiries for her themselves, and studying the notices in the newspapers?'

He experienced a flash of despair.

'The Severn rises in mid-Wales. She could have been swept down river from any point along it, and if she was already rotting badly when pulled out she might have been in the water for weeks.'

He came to a decision. 'I should go to Bewdley myself and talk to the people there who saw her body. It's about forty miles' round trip. Best part of two days on foot, but maybe I can get the loan of a horse?'

A shiver of apprehension coursed through his body. 'What will Joseph Blackwell have to say when I tell him I must go to Bewdley?'

It was shortly before noon when Tom was admitted to Joseph Blackwell's study, where with some trepidation he requested to be allowed to go to Bewdley, and explained the reason why.

Joseph Blackwell's pallid features frowned incredulously. 'You want to go to Bewdley because of a pink silk stocking and some teeth which you think may be connected with the drowning of Rose Brent?

'I cannot believe that I'm hearing this, Potts! Pray tell me now which of your assistant constables are to carry out the duties of your office while you're strolling to Bewdley and back? Because John Hollis is presently confined to his cottage, labouring under yet another of his fits of lunacy, and Charles Bromley is about as much use in upholding and enforcing the law as a turd is for slicing cheese!

'Quite apart from these unfortunate facts is the other fact that I expressly bade you to accept the verdict of accidental death on Rose Brent, and here you are defying my order! Challenging my authority! Have you gone mad like your friend Hollis?'

Tom momentarily quailed before this onslaught, but stubbornly fought down his apprehension and related his brief encounter with Tessy the Irishwoman.

'So I'm convinced, sir, that she has information that will throw fresh light on the deaths of Rose Brent, and of Irish Joe.' He paused, drew a long breath and summoning all his resolve blurted, 'Just as I'm convinced that there will be an absence of diatoms in Irish Joe's body to prove that he also was dead before he was put into the canal.'

He waited tensely, hands locked behind his back, fingers nervously kneading, as Blackwell pursed his thin lips, steepled his fingers and sank his chin upon them, eyes fixed on the open ledger on the desk before him.

After what seemed to Tom to be an endless stretch of time, Blackwell sighed heavily, placed his hands on the desk and fixed a stern gaze on Tom's face.

'I fully acknowledge, Potts, that whether through your own abilities, or by sheer luck, you have enjoyed some success in apprehending criminals. Therefore, with the strict proviso that it will not impinge upon your normal duties, if this Irish trollop gives you valid information then I shall allow you to further investigate the deaths of Brent and the Legger, and also to go to Bewdley.

'But be warned! If you make a laughing stock of yourself then I shall not shield you from the wrath of my Lord Aston, who as you well know is very willing to render your own existence a veritable Purgatory.'

Tom exhaled in relief. 'Thank you very much, sir.'

He turned to leave, but Blackwell halted him brusquely. 'Hold hard, Potts.'

'Is there something more, sir?' Tom queried anxiously.

Despite the frown on Blackwell's face, there was a suspicion of amusement glinting in his eyes.

'Indeed there is.' Blackwell took a cashbox from the desk drawer and counted out some coins. 'Here is an advance on the payment of the fees you're owed by the parish. I would advise you to redeem your watch and other possessions from Judas Benton's clutches, before the excessive interest that that vulture demands causes you to fall into bankruptcy. Also you might consider clearing your slates at Baker Scambler's and Grocer Groby's, as well as paying your mother and Charles Bromley's bill at the Unicorn Inn.'

Tom flushed bright red with embarrassment, as Blackwell continued. 'You may borrow my horse and trap to transfer your mother and her baggage from the Unicorn to the lock-up. You'd best hurry to do that, Potts, because I know that she is waiting very impatiently for you. I bid you good day.'

'Thank you, sir. I'll go there immediately.'

Still red in the face, Tom exited, marvelling yet again at the breadth of the information network to which his employer had access.

Blackwell stared at the freshly closed door and emitted a long drawn-out throaty chuckle. 'My God, Thomas Potts, I truly believe that you are the finest sniffer-out of evil doings that the Lord ever put breath into, and as long as I live I shall do my utmost endeavours to retain you as the constable of Tardebigge Parish. No matter how much you dislike the post!'

FIFTEEN

The grandfather clock chimed the hour of noon and Amy Danks told her mother and siblings, 'I'm going to have to go back to work.'

'Oh, your dad 'ull be so vexed that he's missed you,' her mother exclaimed. 'Can't you wait a while longer? He might be back soon.'

Amy shook her head regretfully. 'I can't bide any longer, Mam, it'll be getting really busy now, what with it being a Mart Day and all. Tell me dad to come down and see me tonight if he can, and failing that I'll try and come up for an hour tomorrow afternoon.'

She left the cottage, waving back to the woman and children clustered at the door, and walked up through the woodland towards the Mount Pleasant road which sloped gently downwards to Redditch some half a mile distant.

From his concealed vantage point close to the roadway the horseman sighed with relief that his vigil had ended. He waited for the girl to step on to the road and begin walking towards the town, then kneed his horse to a trot and went after her.

Amy heard the iron-shod hooves on the gravel, looked back, and could not repress a smile of satisfied vanity.

Eugene Sinclair came alongside and reined his mount back to match the speed of her steps.

'This is a very pleasant surprise, Miss Amy.' He lifted his top hat and bowed low from the saddle.

'Is it really such a surprise for you, Master Sinclair?' she asked teasingly.

He laughed delightedly, and admitted, 'Of course it isn't. I've been skulking about here in hopes of seeing you again. But I'll wager that you know this very well.'

'I know that it's as well for you that me dad didn't see you hiding in the bushes or he might have taken you for a poacher else, and then you'd have been in hot water. Me dad is not a man who hesitates to shoot poachers, or any other undesirables who he thinks might be up to no good.'

'Well now, if I'd suffered a charge of buckshot up my backside, then I would have counted it a price well worth paying to set my eyes on you once more, Miss Amy.'

'Mercy me! What a gallant knight you are.' She giggled.

'Come,' he invited, patting the broad rump of the horse. 'Ride pillion with me. Let me have the pleasure of knowing that I've saved you from walking on this damnably laid gravel. Your feet are far too dainty for such a rough hard paving.'

Amy hesitated for a moment or two, then the thought of how jealous her workmates would be upon seeing her so romantically escorted back to the inn sparked her imp of mischievousness.

'Very well, Master Sinclair. I accept your offer.'

SIXTEEN

'God Almighty! What's this vile stink? Why have you let this place get so filthy, you wretched, idle beast?'

Widow Potts' furious screeching carried far beyond the confines of the lock-up, causing passers-by to stop in their tracks to wonder what was happening.

Tom, bent low and panting under the weight of his mother's massive wooden trunk, halted halfway up the stairs to explain.

'It's only a poor dead girl, Mother, and she certainly doesn't smell that bad.' Then he added tentatively, 'And there's another poor dead fellow out in the yard. But he's well wrapped and not smelling too badly either.'

'Dead girl? Dead fellow? Oh God!' Widow Potts screamed piercingly, dropped her walking sticks and, clutching both hands to her heart, slumped back against the rear wall next to the stairs. 'The unnatural swine has turned body-snatcher! Save me, Lord! Save me from this evil animal, I beg you! I'm too young to die!'

The passers-by hastened to cluster and stare with avid curiosity through the open front door.

Unable to turn in the narrow stairwell because of the size of the trunk on his back, Tom could only struggle on upwards, gasping desperately.

'Please, Mother, compose yourself. I will explain everything.'

'Save me! Kind people, save me! He means to murder me!' Widow Potts begged piteously, stretching out her pudgy be-ringed hands towards the audience at the door.

'I'm come, my love. What's the matter?' Charles Bromley pushed through the crowd and came through the doorway in a sweaty panic.

'He's brought me into a charnel house, Bromley! He means to murder me! I know he does! Vile, wicked, unnatural beast of a son that he is.'

The onlookers clapped and cheered, laughing uproariously.

Tom set down the trunk in his mother's room and hurried back downstairs.

Charles Bromley's magnified eyes glared accusingly through bulbous lenses.

'Explain yourself, sir,' he demanded furiously. 'Why in Heaven's name are you terrifying your lady mother so?'

'Yeah, why be you a-doing this, you cruel, wicked, unnatural son?' one of the spectators shouted facetiously.

'Somebody fetch a constable! There's murders being done here!'another howled, and immediately the rest starting bawling in unison.

'Murder! Murder! Fetch a constable! Murder! Murder! Fetch a constable!'

Charles Bromley stretched his arms as far as he could reach around the torso of his fiancée, which was to the sides of her shoulders, and shouted at Tom. 'I defy you, sir! You shall not harm a single hair of my love, while I still have life enough in my body to protect her.'

Tom could only shake his head and mutter wearily, 'Dear God, give me strength!'

He went to the front door and slammed and bolted it shut.

The audience jeered and catcalled, but deprived of their entertainment very soon drifted away.

When all was quiet Tom stalked back along the corridor to face the glares of the betrothed couple. Summoning all his patience, he explained the whole story.

'The man and girl are here because we have to perform post-mortems. The girl's has been done and she'll be handed over to her family for burial on Wednesday morning. The man's post-mortem will be performed on Monday morning, and then he also will be taken away for burial as soon as possible.

'I'm sorry if the smell discommodes you, Mother, but sadly that is an unavoidable accompaniment of death.

'Onions?' Charles Bromley questioned. 'Do they have raw onions in their mouth? That is the only salutary preventative against corpse stink.'

Tom could only shrug helplessly. 'No, they don't, because I don't accept that belief. But I've wrapped the poor girl in tarred cloth and put a deal of herbs in the coffin to overlay the smell.'

'Faugh!' Widow Potts blew a raspberry of derision. 'It's very plain that you've neglected to do what's right and proper, you fool! If you had half the sense of a gnat, you would have pushed a raw onion into her mouth, and sewed her lips together to keep it firm in place. Then she wouldn't be stinking the place out like she is! You're useless! Absolutely useless!'

For a brief moment Tom fantasized about pushing a raw onion into his mother's mouth, and sewing it in situ. But not wishing to prolong this conversation he told them politely, 'Please excuse me, I must go about my duties. There are provisions in the larder and a jug of fresh cider should you need them.'

'How I thirst for a pot of fragrant green tea, such as I used to enjoy when your father was alive,' Widow Potts whined plaintively, then sneered. 'But of course, your father was a gentleman who enjoyed much success in his honourable profession. Which enabled him to provide properly for his family and to purchase little luxuries such as the finest green tea. Unlike his useless pauper of a son.'

With her scathing words echoing in his ears, Tom took a battered leather satchel from its hanging peg, shouldered his crowned staff and left the pair.

Outside he drew long breaths of the clean fresh air deep into his lungs, and struggled to dispel the angry resentment that his mother invariably managed to provoke in him.

'She's old and ailing in health. I have to accept this, and not allow myself to become so riled up against her.'

He checked the contents of the satchel, sorting through the warrants for the Goviers and the coroner's jurymen summonses as he walked through the market, which was now becoming thronged by domestic servants shopping for their employers and white-aproned, mob-capped housewives trailing children at their skirts. These were the early shoppers, but numbers would rapidly increase when the mills and factories released their workers. The dealing and selling would continue late into the evening hours and become hectic when the bargain hunters came hurrying in search of any perishables which the vendors needed to sell quickly and more cheaply before those particular commodities began to rot.

As Tom passed the Fox and Goose its landlord Thomas Fowkes was standing in the doorway, hands rubbing his massive belly, his eyes lustfully dwelling on the breasts and hips of the more attractive women.

The dislike between Tom and Fowkes was mutual, but nevertheless Tom could not resist the overwhelming impulse to go to the other man and enquire, 'Has Amy returned yet from Birmingham, Master Fowkes?'

Rudely keeping his gaze roving among the women, Fowkes grunted an assent.

'Might I have a word with her, please?'

Still refusing to look at Tom, Fowkes shook his head. 'Her's otherwise engaged just now.'

Stung by this blatant display of ill-manners, Tom protested. 'But I only wish to say a welcome back to her. It won't take more than a moment.'

Fowkes glanced towards the crossroads, grinned in satisfaction, and looked Tom fully in the face.

'Oh, alright then, Constable, have it your way. Look up there. Her's coming back now.'

He jerked his thumb towards the crossroads and Tom turned to see a horse approaching at a slow walk. Dismay struck through him when he realized that the woman riding sideways pillion on the beast with her arms wrapped around the horseman's waist, was Amy.

'That chap is Eugene Sinclair, and he's a relative of the Earl himself. He's a real dandy, aren't he? Look at the quality of his cloth and linen. Young Amy's certainly being courted by a better class o' sweetheart these days, aren't her just!' Fowkes was taking malicious pleasure in Tom's patent discomfiture. 'I reckon that if her plays her cards right she could end up marrying him. She won't be the first pretty tavern wench to snare herself a fine gentleman. But I expect that you knows that already, don't you, Master Potts?'

Acutely aware that the other man was deliberately taunting him into voicing a heated reply, Tom's own self-respect made him determined to deny the innkeeper that pleasure, and he answered levelly, 'Indeed I do, Master Fowkes, and he's a very fine fellow from all accounts. I'm sure that he will behave honourably towards Amy.'

Fowkes grimaced uncertainly. This was not the reaction he had expected to provoke. But before he could formulate another cutting gibe, Eugene Sinclair reined in the horse in front of them, and with effortless ease lowered Amy to the ground.

'Why, Thomas, have you been waiting for me? What was it you wanted?' Amy Danks could not resist playing the minx, even though she was truly pleased to see Tom again. 'This is Constable Potts, and a friend of my father's, Master Sinclair, he's like another uncle to me, aren't you, Thomas?'

'I am honoured to make your acquaintance, Constable Potts.' Sinclair bowed in the saddle.

With both shock and jealousy rending him, it was all that Tom could do to keep up a façade of equable courtesy, as he returned the bow.

'The honour is mine, sir.' He turned to Amy, and managed to force a smile. 'I hope I find you well and happy, Amy? Did you enjoy your stay in Birmingham?'

Despite her deep affection for Tom, Amy's vanity was sorely piqued by him not displaying any visible signs of shock at her words, nor any resentment or jealousy towards Eugene Sinclair, and she was suddenly driven by momentary spitefulness.

'Of course I did, because I was greatly admired in Brummagem; and the sooner I go back there the happier I shall be,' she snapped irritably, then smiled coyly at Eugene Sinclair. 'Thank you for escorting me back here, Master Sinclair, I'm looking forward very much to talking with you again. But now I must go to my work.' She bobbed a curtsey and ran into the inn.

'I must leave you also, gentlemen.' Sinclair saluted them with his riding crop and trotted away.

'Like an uncle to her, are you, Constable Potts? Well I must say I thought that young Amy saw you in a different light to that.' The innkeeper's fat red face exuded spiteful satisfaction. 'But that's the trouble wi' these modern-day wenches, aren't it? They'm too flighty-yedded and free and easy. Not sensible and biddable like they used to be when me and you was young men.'

Tom was mentally reeling from the shock of Amy's apparent

change in attitude toward him, but his stubborn pride would not allow him to display any dismay or hurt in front of Fowkes.

'I must go about my duties, Master Fowkes. Good day to you.' Tom walked quickly from the inn, his mind in a torment of painful confusion.

SEVENTEEN

Dusk was falling and Martin Cooke was directing the unloading of a barge at the Tardebigge New Wharf when Daniel Wynne rode into its large enclosed yard, closely followed by a man on foot leading a long-horned cow by its roped nose.

Cooke went to greet the newcomers. 'Good to see you, Cousin Daniel, only I expected you to be here sooner. All goes well, I hope?'

The drover dismounted and the pair shook hands.

'All's well, Cousin. I'd have been here sooner, but one of your damned Redditch butchers insisted on haggling over the price of his beasts for hours.' Wynne chuckled wryly. 'My God! We Welsh drovers are always accused of being tighter with our money than bloody shylocks, but compared to Joshua Vincent we're spend-thrifts. I swear it's easier to draw blood from a stone than to draw money from that bugger's pocket.'

Cooke moved to examine the black cow standing docile at the side of its shaggy-haired, bearded, huge-built handler and remarked disparagingly, 'The beast looks a bit on the bony side. Have you been driving it hard? Or is it older and tougher than Methuselah?'

Daniel Wynne chuckled. 'You know well that I never drive my herds above two miles to the hour, and pay a fortune for good grass for them. She might be getting old but she's pure Welsh Black stock, and calved only three months past. Should you choose to pasture her I reckon there's another six or seven months of milking left in her; and I guarantee when she's brought to the slaughter her meat will be succulent enough.'

'What's the asking price?'

'Six pounds and eighteen shillings, Cousin, and if I'm making more than a six-pence profit from it, then may God strike me dead this instant. I'm only letting you have it so dirt cheap because you're my favourite kinsman.'

'And you owe me more than a favour or two, don't you, my bucko?' A slight edge of hostility had entered Cooke's tone.

Wynne spread his arms and smilingly beseeched, 'And have I not done my very best of late to repay those favours, my dearest cousin?'

There was a brief pause, then Cooke smiled ironically. 'Only under duress, my dearest cousin.'

Their eyes locked and a palpable tension developed between the two kinsmen.

The cow's huge handler shouted something in the Welsh language.

'What in hell's name is he saying in that barbaric tongue of yours?' Cooke demanded. 'It's about time that you ignorant bloody Taffys learned to speak the King's English.'

'Well that's where the problem lies, my dearest cousin.' Daniel Wynne grinned. 'We ignorant Taffys are too ignorant to be capable of learning the King's English. But don't you risk telling Shanko Mawr there that he's an ignorant bloody Taffy. He could break both our backs with one hand if he lost his temper.'

After a moment Cooke laughed, and the tension between them dissolved.

'Shanko wants to know how long he has got to stand here like a spare prick at a wedding?' Wynne translated.

'He can put it in the paddock behind that timber stack over there.' Cooke pointed.

Wynne took a small jemmy from his saddlebags and gave it to Shanko Mawr. As the three men passed through the paddock gate Tom Potts appeared in the yard and hurried to catch up with them.

'Hello Master Potts, it's good to see you. Do you bring me news of Irish Joe's post-mortem?' Cooke smiled in welcome.

'It's to take place on Monday morning, Master Cooke. I'll let you know of any developments,' Tom told him.

'This is my cousin, Daniel Wynne; he's just delivered this fine beast to me.'

Tom bowed. 'I'm honoured to make your acquaintance, Master Wynne.'

'And I yours, sir,' Wynne returned the salutation.

'Master Potts is our parish constable, Daniel. He's investigating the death of one of the Leggers.'

'Is he now?' Wynne stared appraisingly at Tom. 'Is there something suspicious about the man's death, Master Potts?'

Tom shrugged. 'I'll know more after the post-mortem, Master Wynne. At present I can't really voice any opinion.'

Shanko Mawr spoke to Wynne, who replied in the Welsh tongue, then explained to his companions.

'Shanko's going to fell the beast, so that I can take its shoes off. It would be best if you both moved away a little distance.'

When they did, Shanko Mawr stepped up to the cow, simultaneously grabbing its muzzle with his left hand, its right horn with his right hand, placing his boot firmly against the cow's right foreleg and, twisting its muzzle upwards, forced the horn down. The beast bellowed in fear and pain and thudded over onto its side, hitting the ground with such impact that the right horn buried itself into the earth. Shanko Mawr hurled himself down across the beast's neck while Wynne used the rope to lash the animal's kicking legs together, then jemmied off the small bi-plated iron shoes from its hooves.

Tom was amazed at the strength and dexterity that the huge drover had displayed, and voiced his admiration as the rope was unlashed and the cow struggled upright once more.

'This is the first time I've ever seen men wrestle and hold a cow down, Master Wynne. You're both exceptionally strong.'

'My part in it is more to do with technique than bodily strength. Shanko is the Hercules here, not me,' Wynne replied. Then he added with a touch of vanity, 'But yes, I am strong. As several who've tried to cheat me have found out to their cost.'

'It's also the first time that I've seen a shod cow,' Tom said.

'We have to shoe all our cattle for the drove. Their hooves are not tough enough to travel long distances over rough terrain and gravelled roads.'

'It's time to eat, gentlemen,' Martin Cooke put in. 'You'll take supper with me in the Plymouth Arms, of course, Cousin Daniel. You're very welcome to join us, Master Potts.'

'I regret that I can't at this time,' Tom demurred. 'I'm here on official business.'

'On official business?' Cooke's eyebrows arched questioningly.

'Yes, I want to talk to one of the Legger women, an Irishwoman named Tessy. Do you know her?'

'What surname does she have?' Cooke was frowning thoughtfully.

Tom shook his head. 'I don't know. I only spoke with her very briefly, and truth to tell I didn't even get a clear view of her face, what with the foul weather and the darkness.'

'That's a pity.' Cooke smiled sympathetically. 'A description might have helped me to identify her. The trouble is, you see, Master

Potts, these Legger sluts come and go all the time, and are vagabonds and jail trash every one of them. Has this one been thieving poultry, picking pockets or brawling in the taverns?'

'Not that I know of. She said that she had information which might throw some light on the deaths of Rose Brent and Irish Joe.'

'Did she now?' Cooke chuckled. 'And I'll wager that she also said she must be well paid for that information.'

'She did indeed,' Tom conceded wryly.

'Well, speaking from my own experience of the Legger sluts, I wouldn't pay her a ha'penny. Because all she'll give you is a farrago of lies.' Cooke was contemptuously dismissive.

Daniel Wynne had been listening intently, and now he laughed. 'For an extra ha'penny she'll most likely offer you a night in her bed and a share of her fleas and lice as well, Master Potts.'

He turned and spoke rapidly to Shanko Mawr, who nodded and walked away.

'I've sent him to the Cherry Tree for his supper,' Wynne explained. 'It'll be a liquid one, no doubt. Shanko's powerfully fond of the drink.'

'How will he make himself understood?' Tom queried. 'I doubt that anyone in the Cherry Tree speaks the Welsh tongue.'

'Oh, don't you worry about Shanko, Master Potts. He speaks the English tongue as well as any Englishman when he needs must use it, and what's more he can read and write it as well.' He chuckled and winked. 'Which is more than a great many Englishmen can do.'

The three men walked in company to the forecourt of the Plymouth Arms where they chatted about the droving of cattle for a time before parting with mutual protestations of good will.

Tom made his way through the deepening murk to the stretch of muddied, litter-strewn waste ground where a cluster of crudely built shanties housed the Leggers. He met with a man coming from the shanties whom he recognised as Shanko Mawr. But the Welshman ignored his greeting and passed without any acknowledgement or even a glance in his direction.

A pack of mangy dogs came rushing, barking furiously, but turned and ran yelping when Tom brandished his staff at them. Smoke trailed from a few of the shanties' brick chimneys and here and there the wavering gleams of firelight showed through cracks in the shutters. In the network of narrow alleyways between the buildings the air was thick with the stenches of excreta, urine and rotting waste, and Tom's boots slid upon thick layers of slimy mud.

He rapped on a door with his staff. 'Is anyone within?'

'Who's asking?' a hoarse whispery voice answered.

'Thomas Potts, Constable of Tardebigge Parish.'

'Have you got any pongo wi' you?'

'No, I haven't.'

'Then you can just fuck off.'

'At least open the door and have a word with me,' Tom requested, as he took what few coins he had from his pocket and rattled them noisily in his hand. 'I'm ready to pay for useful information.'

'Just fuck off. I'll not tell no fuckin' constable nothing.'

Tom knocked again but no answer came from within and he decided nothing more could be gained from this shanty.

For many more minutes he searched the fetid encampment, rapping on the doors of the shanties, but no one answered from inside any of them.

'They'll all be at the Cherry Tree,' he told himself finally. 'Perhaps I should go there directly.'

He began to retrace his steps and noted one isolated shanty which had been in darkness before but now had light gleaming through cracked shutters.

'Somebody's come home by the looks of it.'

He made his way to it and rapped the door. 'Is there anyone within?'

This time a deep rough voice replied, 'What's you want?'

'I'm looking for someone. Can I come in and speak to you?' Tom rattled the coins again. 'I'll make it worth your while for any information you can give me.'

'Tell me what you wants to know?'

'The whereabouts of the Irishwoman, Tessy?'

He waited for a reply, but none came.

He stood for long moments, undecided as to what he should do next. Then he heard behind him a heavy rasping of breath, and a splashing of feet on mud. He turned, and a crushing weight thudded against the side of his head, sending him colliding with the wall and toppling senseless to the ground.

EIGHTEEN

Sunday 8th April

All across England the bells of cathedrals, churches and chapels were summoning the faithful to morning worship. In Redditch the solitary bell of St Stephen's chapel gave tongue while the Reverend John Clayton stood at the chapel gateway to greet his flock.

As always John Clayton drew ironic amusement from the fact that although he constantly sermonized that all humankind were spiritually equal in the eyes of God, here at the House of God the physical inequality of humankind was blatantly demonstrated. Only the richer and socially better-placed inhabitants were buried in the St Stephen's chapel graveyard. The poor and lowly were banished to their final resting places down in the valley stretching northwards from the bottom of the Fish Hill. Buried half a mile from the town in the Old Monks graveyard adjoining the grassy mounds which once had been the Cistercian Abbey of Bordesley.

Each Sabbath day when the weather was fine the rich and powerful Hemmings, Bartleets, Milwards, Taylors, Cresswells and their ilk alighted from their carriages at the St Stephen's gate and paraded grandly around the chapel forecourt. Ostentatiously greeting and talking with their social peers often for an hour or more until, led by the most important family present on that particular occasion, they would enter and take their cushioned seats in their own rented pews at the front of the chapel.

The poorer, humbler worshippers waited respectfully in the roadway outside the chapel yard, not daring to enter until their 'betters' were ensconced within the building itself. Only then would they file inside and sit on the narrow wooden benches at the rear of the chapel, with only the very boldest among them risking an exchange of brief muted whispers with their friends and acquaintances.

For Thomas Fowkes, Sunday mornings were a source of immense gratification and self-pride. As the bell tolled he would swagger towards the chapel, dressed in his finest broadcloth and linen. Following dutifully behind him would be his wife and daughter clad in the most ornate gowns and bonnets that the town's dress-makers and milliners could produce, while his servants Amy Danks and Maisie Lock, wearing their Sunday best, brought up the rear of the small procession.

This familial Sabbath parade had been instituted by Fowkes the previous year, when he had been chosen by the Chapel Vestry to join the select grouping of the Chapel Wardens, an appointment which catapulted him to sit in conclave and administer the affairs of the Chapel with such local luminaries as the Hemmings, Bartleets, Cresswells, Milwards, Taylors, etc. An appointment which in his own eyes had raised Thomas Fowkes to his rightfully deserved pos-ition among the very highest of the parish – indeed perhaps even the County – Genteel Society. An added boost to his self-esteem was that as a Chapel Warden he had been permitted to rent one of the smaller, humbler transept pews and adorn it with his own brass nameplate. It was unfortunate that because of their abundance of flesh only he and his wife could manage to squeeze into its confined space, but he lived in hopes that some day a larger side pew, or even one of the prestigious centre pews, would become available for rent. In the meantime his daughter would have to remain seated among the poor and humble.

'But why can't I come and walk in the yard with you and Ma, Pa?' Lily Fowkes pouted resentfully. 'Why do I have to stand outside here every Sunday wi' the bloody serving wenches!'

'Because I tells you to.' Tommy Fowkes scowled threateningly. 'And if you don't like it, then you can lump it.'

'But all the other young ladies am peacocking it inside the yard, so why can't I? I'm wearing as fine a finery as them stuck-up little cows!'

'You knows very well why you has to stay with the girls, so stop pestering your Pa about it, you ungrateful little wretch!' her mother scolded.

The couple passed through the gate, preening proudly as John Clayton acknowledged their coming, leaving their daughter scarlet-faced with furious resentment.

'This is bloody awful this is! It makes me feel small being stuck out here among the roughs and scruffs!'

'Well take comfort from that feeling, Lily,' Maisie Lock baited. 'Because it's the nearest you'm ever going to come to being nice and small and slim like me and Amy.'

'Now don't start quarrelling, you two,' Amy reproved them. 'Let's see if we can choose which of the stuck-up little cows is wearing this week's daftest hat. Like that bloody silly turban Charlotte Milward's got on. What does she think she looks like?'

She pointed at a particularly grotesque article of millinery, and all three of them giggled.

'Begging your pardon, sir, but if you'm Parson Clayton, can I please speak to you?'

'I am indeed Reverend Clayton, and of course you may speak to me, my dear.' John Clayton smiled kindly down at the small, sallow-featured young woman.

She bobbed a curtsey. 'Me name's Martha Standard, sir, and I'm come to speak for Widow Brent. Only she can't come herself today, because she's feeling very poorly.'

'Well I'm sorry to hear that. You must tell her that I shall pray for her. Now how can I help you, my dear?'

'Well she . . . well, we both of us really wants to know what's happening with poor Rosie? Rosie was my best friend, you see, and losing her has been a sore grief for me as well as for her mam.'

John Clayton nodded sympathetically. 'I'm truly sorry for your loss, my dear. Well now, what is to happen to Rosie is that tomorrow morning there will be a Coroner's Inquest and the medical gentlemen will give their evidence as to the cause of her death, and after they have . . .'

Martha Standard stood, eyes wide, listening intently to his mellow voice, her mouth slightly open and the tip of her tongue protruding between her lips.

Eugene Sinclair reined in his mount to a trot and, standing up in his stirrups, moved around the edges of the crowd on the roadway scanning faces, questioning silently. 'Now where are you, my pretty little Amy? Where are you?'

Martin Cooke and Daniel Wynne trotted side by side down the Front Hill, along the Evesham Street, and came to the centre of the crossroads.

'Should you not attend the service, Cousin Daniel? John Clayton preaches a powerful sermon.' Cooke smiled grimly. 'You may find that his words will help you to keep your baser instincts under control during this present drove.'

Daniel Wynne grinned broadly. 'I fear that no amount of sermons will ever serve to keep my baser instincts under control, Cousin. As you know full well from your own past experiences, they are hereditary in our family.'

'Perhaps so, but at least I pray to the Lord for the strength to curb my share of the inheritance.' Cooke held out his hand. 'Goodbye for the present, Cousin Daniel. Give my best regards to Olwen and the children.'

'And give mine to Edwina.' Wynne winked and added teasingly, 'It's always been a source of wonder to me that such a high-born woman ever chose to wed such a low-born ruffian as you. I'm not surprised that she prefers to spend her days in that damned fine mansion house of yours, rather than be here with you and mixing with all the riffraff. It's because you come from Welsh trade stock that she's always refused to meet any of our family, isn't it? Serves you right for marrying into a family of English snobs!'

'She's not a snob,' Cooke protested heatedly. 'And the reason that none of our family have been invited to my home is because my wife is currently rather unwell and safeguards her privacy on the advice of the medical gentlemen.'

'Calm down, Cousin, I'm only ribbing you.' Wynne chuckled and they parted company.

'Thank you, Parson Clayton, sir. Thank you ever so much. I shall tell Widow Brent every word that you've told me,' Martha Standard thanked John Clayton when he had done speaking.

'Good, and tell her also that God will somehow bring her comfort. Goodbye for now, my dear.' John Clayton walked away from the gateway.

Martha Standard bobbed a farewell curtsey and scurried home-wards, her head bent, all her attention focussed on trying to store the information Clayton had imparted to her.

'Ohhh!' she cried out in shock as she bumped heavily into a horse, stared dazedly up at its rider, then furrowed her brow uncertainly.

'Watch where you're going, girl, you could have brought my horse down,' the rider chided her, and trotted quickly on.

Martha Standard stood motionless, bemused, grappling with the memory this fleeting encounter had brought swirling up from the depths of her mind.

'It's him! No. It can't be! But it is! It's him that I saw wi' Rosie them times! No! No, it can't be. But is it? Is it him? I must make sure!'

She looked wildly about her, desperately seeking for the horseman. But he had gone from her sight, and the crowd was now moving toward the gate hemming her in on all sides.

As the fleeting moments lengthened Martha's doubts inexorably mounted and strengthened, until finally she accepted the situation.

'It's just me being over-fanciful, aren't it? There could be a hundred blokes in this parish who might put me in mind that I knew their faces. I'm just letting me fancies run away with me, that's all. I'm seeing things that aren't really there. That bloke couldn't be Rosie's sweetheart.'

But the horseman's memory had also been fired by this brief encounter. 'Was that little bitch Rose Brent's workmate? What was her name now? Martha? Martha Standard? Yes, that's it! How much did Rose tell her about me, I wonder? Has she recognized me? She looked very hard at me, that's for sure. But how can I be certain that I've got the right girl?' He scowled in sudden fury. 'Jesus Christ! Will this run of stinking bad luck never end?'

NINETEEN

Late Afternoon, Monday 9th April

As the horse-drawn barge came into dock the flour-dusted miller standing on the Stoke Prior Wharf held up his watch and tapped its face, bellowing furiously.

'What bloody day does you call this? I've been waiting for me delivery since eight o' the clock bloody Sunday morning!'

''Tis no fault o' mine, Gaffer!' the bargee bellowed back. 'I had a delivery at the Tardebigge New Wharf on Saturday and had to stay there until Sunday afternoon to get me lading bill altered, because the warehouse clerk at Brummagem Basin had made a fuck-up. And then last night summat went wrong in the Tardebigge engine house and 'til it was pumping again I couldn't pass through the lock flight for lack o' water. So it's no use you blaggardin' me for being late coming.'

He shouted to his horse boy. 'Give him a hand to unload his stuff.'

The miller and boy untied the stay ropes and started to draw back the canvas sheet which covered the cargo of grain-filled sacks in the bows of the barge.

The miller suddenly stopped motionless, and exclaimed in shock, 'Bloody hell! What the fuck have you brought me?'

The bargee left the rudder and came forward. He too came to a sudden halt.

'Bugger me! Where did that come from? What is it?'

Gagged, trussed hand and foot, sacking wrapped tightly around his face and head, unable to move and hardly to draw breath because of the weight of the sacks of grain which all but buried him, Tom could only silently thank his God for this rescue.

'Could be a beast o' some sort,' the miller offered doubtfully.

'Is it dead?' the boy questioned nervously.

'Go and get that stuff off so we can see what it is,' the miller told him.

'Not me,' the boy refused flatly. 'What if it bites me?'

'Come out o' the way!' The bargee irritably pushed past them and stepped down to Tom's side.

He bent and tentatively kneaded the sacking with his hands. 'It feels like a yed!'

Tom nodded in eager agreement.

'Fuckin' 'ell! It's alive!' The bargee yelped in fright and jumped back. 'It bloody well moved! I felt it shifting!'

The interchange between the three had drawn other men and boys to the barge side.

'Look there, what's that?' One man pointed. 'Just there, look. Pick it up, it won't bite you.'

The bargee moved where the man directed and extracted Tom's painted crowned staff which was squeezed between two sacks.

'That's a bloody beadle's stick, that is,' the miller declared.

'No it aren't, it's a constable's,' another man contradicted.

Tom summoned all his strength, struggling to move his head and shoulders, trying desperately to shout, but only able to emit barely audible grunts.

'Gerrout o' me way, the lot o' you! Bloody nancies that you are!' The man who had spotted the staff scoffed contemptuously and, climbing on board, went to Tom and forcibly tugged and pulled at the tight-swathed sacking until it came free and revealed Tom's head.

The discovery brought loud shouts of shock and surprise.

'Get some water, quick,' the rescuer ordered, and quickly heaved the imprisoning grain sacks aside, untied Tom's gag and bondage, and said to him, 'I reckon your mouth 'ull be as dry as burnt tinder, so don't go trying to say anything until you've took some water. You won't make any sense else.'

Tom groaned in distress as blood pumped freely once again through constricted veins and arteries into cramped, deadened muscles, bringing with it agonizing shooting pains.

His rescuer held a mug of water to his lips. 'Take it slow now. Just sip it at first, and wash your mouth out.'

'Hark at him!' the miller jeered. 'Does you think you'm a bloody doctor, Chalky White?'

'Not a bit of it,' Chalky retorted angrily. 'But back in the war when you was sitting on your fat arse safe here at home, I was fighting the Froggies all across Spain and Portugal, and I've seen what thirst can do to men. If you drinks quick and heavy when you'm dry as a bone, then you can do yourself damage. So just shut your mouth, Fatty, afore I shuts it for you.'

Tom gratefully sipped the musty water, feeling it moisten and soothe the sorely parched mucous flesh of his tongue, cheeks and throat. The initial agonizing shooting pains in his limbs gradually subsided into bearable aches, as did the painful lump on the side of his head.

'Who am you?' Chalky asked.

Tom told him, and the information evoked a chorus of surprise from the listeners.

'Who did this to you?'

Tom could only shake his head. 'I've no idea. I was passing through the Leggers' shanties by the Tardebigge New Wharf on Saturday night, and somebody came from behind and hit me.'

There were voluble exchanges among the listeners.

With Chalky's helping hand he rose to his feet, and a wave of giddiness caused him to wait until it passed before asking, 'What day is it, and where am I?'

'You're at Stoke Prior Wharf, three and odd miles from Tardebigge, and it's Monday afternoon.'

'Oh my God!' Tom muttered in dismay and felt for his watch, but the fob pocket was empty, as were his other pockets of the few coins he had possessed. He scrabbled at his chest and breathed a sigh of relief to find that the key to the lock-up's front door was still beneath his shirt hanging from the ribbon tied around his neck.

'I've been robbed of my watch and money.'

'Then it's more fool you for being in that rats' nest by yourself on a dark night,' the miller observed sourly. 'You aren't the first bloke to be bludged by Legger scum, nor won't be the last.'

'Well, at least they had the goodness to leave you your staff, and your titfer.' Chalky grinned and pointed down to the top hat which Tom had been lying on. 'So you can still go to the Lord Mayor's Ball.'

Seeing the flattened hat, Tom now took stock of his clothing, and grimaced. It was thick with stinking excremental mud.

With gallows humour he remarked wryly, 'Somehow I've the notion that I'll not be made very welcome in any such Select Assembly in my present condition. Unless it's a Scavengers' Ball, of course.'

The men laughed and Chalky told him warmly, 'I likes your style, Master Potts; and you'll be made very welcome in Chalky White's washhouse, should you care to clean yourself up a bit.'

'I would indeed, Master White, and many thanks to you for the invitation,' Tom accepted with alacrity.

The two men walked to the isolated cottage on the outskirts of the widespread hamlet, and when they reached it Tom spent time washing his body and clothing at the washhouse pump, and restoring some shape to his hat. As he finished the task his host brought out a blanket.

'Put this round yourself, Master Potts. You can hang out your things by the fire, and share a jug of ale and a bite to ate wi' me while they'm drying.'

Tom was greatly touched by this further kindness and, stomach rumbling with hunger, was more than happy to accept.

They sat facing each other across the rough-fashioned wooden table in the spotlessly clean, sparsely furnished room. The fragrant scents of the bunches of dried herbs hanging on the whitewashed walls mingled with the scents of burning apple wood, and the onions, cheese and fresh bread they ate.

After they had finished their food and were sharing a jug of ale and pipe of tobacco, Chalky White related his story.

'This dwelling was left to me missus by her old granddad. It's been lonely for me since me missus died because me daughters am both wed now and got homes and families of their own, and me son's long since gone for a soldier. That was me own fault really, him going for a soldier. Because I used to fill his yed full o' tall stories about me own soldiering days and he couldn't rest content until he'd gone and followed the drum himself.'

'Where is he now?' Tom was truly interested, having already taken a strong liking to this new acquaintance.

The other man's eyes clouded with sadness. 'He's dead and gone, I fear. He warn't no letter writer and nor be I, but a few years ago I did get a letter writ for him by a comrade to tell me that their regiment was being sent out to the West African coast, the bloody Bight o' Benin. Well Master Potts, you knows the old rhyme don't you? "Beware and take care o' the Bight o' Benin / There's just one comes out, of twenty goes in . . ." Then a couple o' years past I heard tell that the regiment had been all but wiped out by the fevers and the battles with the Tozers, and that my boy was almost certain dead and his mates with him.'

Tears misted his eyes. 'It's not knowing the how or why he died that rips me up, Master Potts. The not knowing the how or why is the worst part of it.'

Without warning the image of the grieving face of Rose Brent's mother filled Tom's mind, confronting him with her dreadful sorrow, and he found himself silently vowing, 'I'll find out how and why your daughter died, ma'am. I swear on my dear father's grave that I'll never give up the quest until I know the truth of it!'

Impelled by his desperate need to speak of it, Tom began to talk in lengthy detail about Rose Brent's death, and how he could never bring himself to accept the verdict of the coroner's court. He also explained how the Irishwoman Tessy had told him she had information that could possibly solve the mystery.

When he fell silent once more his companion said thoughtfully, 'I know Irish Tessy well. She's a sharp one, and always has an eye for the main chance. But speaking of Rose Brent wearing a brown dress, plaid shawl and black bonnet – I see'd a yellow-haired wench who was matching that. If I recalls rightly it was last Mothering Sunday as well.

'I works on the lock maintenance all along the canal from Tardebigge to the Worcester Basin. Well there was some repairs needed doing on the number one lock up by the Tardebigge engine house, and it being the Sabbath it meant that there 'uddn't be a deal o' traffic to get in me way. So while I was doing the job I see'd this wench coming along, and fine-looking piece o' goods she was, if you gets my meaning. That's why I took note of her. She must have come back and forrards past my workplace half a dozen times. So I asked her very civil if her was looking for some-body.' He chuckled wryly. 'But all her told me was to mind me own fuckin' business else when her husband come she'd set him on me. The cheeky cow!'

'And did you see her husband come?'

'Not 'til gone nightfall. I was packing me tools up to go back home and they come past arm in arm heading in the direction of the tunnel. They was having a row and making a racket, that's how I noted 'um.'

'Can you describe the man?' Tom asked eagerly.

White shook his head. 'No, it was too dark and he had his back to me. I only knew it was them because I could hear her voice plain. She was a loud mouth, alright.'

Tom philosophically accepted the disappointment of not having any description of his quarry. 'Ah well, it can't be helped. But if you should ever hear anything which might give some indication of who the man is, I'd be most grateful if you'd tell me. And of course if there's any talk of who might have bludged me.'

'Oh I will, you may count on it,' White assured.

'While I think of it, can you give me a full description of Irish Tessy?' Tom requested, and listened intently, stowing all to memory as the other man complied.

Hanging close to the fire Tom's clothes were now half-dried, and he rose and started to dress.

'I must be leaving, Master White. I can't put off facing whatever is waiting for me in Redditch any longer. My heartfelt thanks for all your kindness.'

The other man stood and proffered his hand. 'I reckon we're friends enough for first names now, aren't we, Tom?'

'Indeed we are, Chalky!' Tom responded with a firm handshake. 'And I hope that some day soon I'll have the opportunity of returning your splendid hospitality.'

The night sky was clear, and Tom's seven-mile journey back to Redditch was lit by the first-quarter moon and vast canopy of stars. As he neared the town his apprehensions deepened and his mood depressed.

'What's Blackwell going to say about me missing Irish Joe's post-mortem? What's he going to say about me being bludged? When the word gets out about that, I'm going to be a laughing stock yet again. What will Amy think when she hears everybody laughing and jeering at me for the umpteenth time? Will she be driven even closer to that dandy? Will she despise me utterly now? And my father's watch? I'd have sooner lost every other thing I possess rather than that.'

The town's streets were quiet and still with only an occasional gleam of light showing from a window. The lock-up was in complete darkness and Tom experienced sharp pangs of guilt that his mother had been left alone there since Saturday with two dead bodies.

'I can't just open the door and walk in. Suppose she wakes and hears me moving about, she might well imagine that the dead are risen and be frightened. I'd best rouse her first.'

He tugged repeatedly on the iron bell pull, shouting loudly, 'There's no need for you to be alarmed, Mother, it's me, Tom.'

Above his head the window casement opened and from it appeared a silhouetted, night-capped head bellowing angrily, 'Hell and tarnation, Tom Potts, leave off them fuckin' bells 'ull you! I'se only just got to sleep, and here's you fetching me from me bed. Why can't you come home at a proper time, like decent folks does?'

'Dear God!' Tom gaped up in surprise at the Town Crier, old Jimmy Grier. 'What are you doing here? Where's my mother?'

'I'm here on the orders of Joey Blackwell. And your mam's spending your money fast and loose, my bucko. Her's living like the gentry. Tucked up as snug as a bug in a rug in the best room of the Unicorn.' The old man cackled gleefully. 'And you'm going to have to pay me for me time as well, so I hope you've got plenty o' rhino in your pockets. And for another thing, Joey Blackwell is going to have your guts for garters when he gets a-hold o' you. I 'udden't want to be in your shoes, Tom Potts, not for all the tea in China! The news is all over the town that you was press-ganged aboard a bloody barge. They'm saying that when you was found you thought you was on a Man-o-War and you told 'um there'd been a terrible storm and the waves had made you sea-sick.'

'Oh my God!' Tom felt as if his shoulders were sagging under the weight of his woes, and shaking his head he told Grier despondently, 'In all truth, Jimmy, I'm starting to wonder if this is not truly the worst weekend of my entire life!'

TWENTY

Tuesday morning, 10th April

Tom was forcing his way through murky shadowed depths, dim human forms constantly rising before him, holding their hands out to him in supplication, beseeching his help with pitiful cries, only to drift further and further away as he struggled to reach them, and finally disappearing from his sight leaving only their muted wails of despair lingering in his ears.

'Wake up, 'ull you! This bloody porridge is getting cold! Wake up!'

Tom started from sleep, a hand shaking his shoulder, Jimmy Grier's voice rasping in his ears.

'Wake up! I'm fed up of standing here wi' your bloody break-fast. Wake up!'

Tom sat up in the narrow cot, rubbing his eyes to clear his sight and struggling to marshal his sleep-fuddled senses.

'It's well past seven o' the clock, you lazy lump. I been trying to wake you for bloody ages,' the old man complained irritably. 'I've got work waiting for me, and can't be doing wi' waiting here all bloody morning for you to bloody stir yourself and crawl out of your stink-pit. I don't get paid for poncing around the parish like bloody Lord Muck on the bloody King's business like you does, Tom Potts. I has to toil for me daily bread. Now get this grub down your neck.' He thrust the bowl of porridge and a large pewter spoon into Tom's hands.

'I'm off now. Don't forget that you owes me two shillings for me having to sleep here and guard them stiffs for the last two nights.'

Tom had to call out his thanks for the breakfast to the old man's clumping footsteps on the stairs.

He stirred the lumpy, tepid oatmeal and absently spooned it into his mouth, while his thoughts centred on the other news Grier had told him the previous night.

Widow Potts had awoken early on Sunday morning, and finding Tom's cot had not been slept in and the outer doors were locked, had proceeded to shriek and howl from her bedroom window that her wicked son had run off and abandoned her in a charnel house of the risen dead. As usual in Redditch a crowd of spectators had quickly gathered, and the more malicious among them had loudly urged her to save herself by jumping out of the window, promising to catch her in a neckerchief.

Someone had run to tell Joseph Blackwell what was happening, and he had come with his manservant. Blackwell had his own key to the lock-up, and once he was inside and had calmed Widow Potts, then the crowd had grown bored, and dispersed. Widow Potts then insisted that Blackwell had her transported in his trap to the Unicorn, where she still remained.

Noticeable by his absence from all these proceedings was the Widow Potts' betrothed, Charles Bromley.

'Do I blame him for staying away?' Tom asked himself. 'No!'

Jimmy Grier had told him that the post-mortem on Irish Joe had been carried out on Monday morning by Cuthbert Price, assisted by Theobald Vaughn, the local apothecary and druggist, and they had judged that the man had died by drowning. The coroner's inquest later that same day brought in the same verdict.

'Theobald Vaughn!' Tom tutted disparagingly. He had had previous dealings with the aged apothecary, who was virtually senile, desperately short-sighted, and perennially drink-sodden. 'I'm going to do my own tests on Irish Joe.'

Even as he made that decision the lock-up bells jangled loudly. Tom put the porridge bowl aside, went through to his mother's room and peeped cautiously through the casement window to see it was Joseph Blackwell's manservant who was at the front door.

Tom opened the window and leaned out. 'Has your master sent you?'

'Yes, Jimmy Grier come to tell him you'm here, and he says that he wants to talk wi' you real urgent. And if I was you, I'd come post-haste, because he's spitting blood and feathers, so he is.' The man grinned with spiteful pleasure. 'I 'udden't want to be in your shoes, Constable Potts. Not for—'

'All the tea in China!' Tom ironically finished the sentence for him. 'Tell him I'll come as soon as possible.'

He threw off his night-shirt and, naked, took his father's medical chest and hurried down to the cell where the shrouded corpse of Irish Joe lay in a cheap, crudely made coffin. Outside the cell he set out small jars in a row, using a charcoal pencil to mark each jar's individual identity, and half-filling each with mineral acid. Then knowing what awaited him he plugged his nostrils with small balls of vinegar-dampened bread and entered the cell.

The stench of rotting flesh permeated the confined space, and thickened to a fetid miasma as Tom levered the lid of the coffin off and propped it to one side.

Driven by the harsh necessity to make haste he used a scalpel to cut through the shroud, and the stitches in the cold flesh. The dissected organs had been replaced in the cavity in a slimy, stinking jumble and because of the poor light in the cell Tom was forced to lift them out and carry them into the central passage for identification. As he had done with Rose Brent, Tom carefully cut tissue from each putrid organ and placed the slivers of flesh into the allotted jar of mineral acid.

Once this task was done, he left everything laying as it was and rushed out to work the pump in the rear yard, gasping and shivering as he poured buckets of cold water over his head and body, swilling and scrubbing the lingering tendrils of corpse stench from his hair and skin.

He hurtled back upstairs, dragged on his shirt, breeches and boots and left the lock-up at a run.

His ungainly, lolloping progress across the green attracted the attention of the man and girls who were talking together in the chapel yard.

'Damn me, Miss Amy, but your friend Thomas Potts presents a most peculiar sight, does he not?' There was the suggestion of a sneer in Eugene Sinclair's tone. 'Can the lock-up be on fire, do you think? Or perhaps he's engaged in a hot-foot hue and cry? That must be why he's behaving like a half-naked, demented creature.'

'Have you heard what they'm saying about him, Master Sinclair? A chap in the dairy told me first thing this morning.' Maisie Lock seized the opportunity to score off Amy. 'They'm saying that Potts is the first chap in history who was daft enough to let himself be press-ganged on to a barge in Tardebigge. And they'm saying that when he was found in the barge he thought that he was on the ocean in a Man-o-War. He wouldn't believe them when they told him that he was only in Stoke Prior on the canal, and he said that couldn't be because he'd felt the boat tossing about on the waves.'

She laughed with a spiteful satisfaction. 'I honestly don't know what you could ever have seen in him, Amy, to take him for your sweetheart, and him being a pauper to boot.'

Amy was being torn inwardly by battling emotions. Her first reactions on seeing Tom's hatless, coatless, clumsy dash across the green had been intense relief that he was safe and well, followed by intense embarrassment that he could be presenting such a demeaning spectacle. Now it was furious anger that was gaining the dominance, and she rounded on Maisie. 'Don't you dare tell such lies about me, Maisie Lock! You know full well that Tom Potts was never my sweetheart, but only a close neighbour that me family befriended. I'm not like you, Maisie Lock. I don't have to flutter me eyes at anything wearing breeches. I've always got dozens of fine-looking chaps chasing after me, wanting to be my sweetheart!' She gathered her long skirts in her hands and ran back to the Fox and Goose.

Tom was oblivious to any attention he was attracting. Panting heavily he reached the Red House and bent over, hands on knees, until he regained breath.

He straightened and reached for the lion-head brass knocker, but even as his fingers touched it the door opened and Joseph Blackwell beckoned him to enter.

'Where the Devil have you been, Potts? I do not take kindly to being kept waiting by any underling.'

In the study Blackwell seated himself at his desk and pointed to a chair.

'Sit down, Potts, and when you have composed your thoughts, give me the full account of what happened to you.'

Tom tried to disregard the flutters of apprehension in his stomach that the expectation of being subjected to the withering scorn and censure of this man always created.

He marshalled his thoughts and related all that he could remember of the various incidents, adding no embellishments, making no excuses, offering no theories.

While Tom was speaking the other man at times made rapid jottings in a small ledger.

When Tom fell silent Blackwell frowned severely at him.

'I'll say nothing about your half-clothed, unshaven, totally disreputable appearance even though it confirms what I've already begun to hear. The jeers indicate that you are once again become a laughingstock throughout the parish. People are saying that you are providing the Leggers with the best sport they've enjoyed for years and that you have become their proprietorial village idiot. That Redditch has poor mad "King William" as its resident figure of mockery and the Tardebigge Canal Company now has you. The whole parish is relishing the sport the Leggers are enjoying at your expense. General opinion has it that you are grievously over-matched in this particular contest.'

The biting sarcasm struck deep into Tom, and he felt the burning of shame. Then his stubborn resolve hardened, and he asserted doggedly, 'There are many instances in history, sir, when even the most grievously over-matched have finally triumphed over all opposition.'

Blackwell stared speculatively at the notes in the ledger for several moments, then challenged, 'Have you prepared the microscope slides yet?'

'The slides, sir?' Tom was instantly wary.

'Come now, Constable.' A wintry smile curved Blackwell's thin lips. 'I know you too well to believe that you've accepted the verdicts of Doctor Price and my own Coroner's jury on the cause of death of Irish Joe.'

Tom knew that any attempted evasions would serve no purpose, and admitted flatly, 'I've begun preparing the slides, and come tomorrow morning they should be ready for examination.'

Blackwell scowled. 'And this woman, Tessy? Are you still intending to question her?'

'Ah well, in for a penny, in for a pound!' Tom thought resignedly, and confirmed, 'That's my intention, sir.'

Blackwell resumed his speculative scrutiny of the jottings in the ledger.

Tom waited for the verbal storm to break over him . . . and waited . . . and waited. His inner tension became increasingly unbearable, until at last he was driven to break the silence.

'Well, sir?'

Blackwell looked up, frowning bleakly, but lurking deep in his eyes was a twinkle of warmth.

'Fortunately for you, Constable Potts, my Lord Aston is presently absent from the parish, and will be so for an undetermined time. In the meantime make sure that your normal duties are properly attended to, so that he will have nothing further to complain of on his return.

'Now the Vestry has agreed that since it is most unlikely that we shall be able to discover his "Place of Settlement" the parish will bear the expense of this Irish Joe to be buried together with Rose Brent in the paupers' section of the Old Monks graveyard. The carrier, George Jolly, has been hired to take both coffins there. You will deliver them over to Parson Clayton at nine o'clock on Wednesday morning.

'In the matter of your proposed investigations, I want to hear no more of them. Concentrate instead on discovering who it is among the damned Leggers that has made such a dismal fool of you! Good day, Constable Potts.'

Head bent deep in thought Tom left the Red House and walked past the row of shops and tenements which ran along the western side of the green facing the front of St Stephen's chapel.

There were a few loungers, others going about their various concerns and a horse and cart creaking past. Standing in the doorway of the baker's shop was its proprietor, Charles Scambler, a young man who regarded himself as being the leading 'wag' of the town. He saw Tom approaching and shouted loudly, 'Here he comes, my Lords, Ladies and gentlemen, our town's own "Jolly Tar". Captain Thomas Potts, of His Majesty's Barge, the *Leggers' Delight*. Pipe all hands to quarters, Bosun!'

All heads turned in Tom's direction, and raucous jeers sounded.

'Jolly Tar? He looks more like the fuckin' "Shipwrecked Mariner" to me!'

'No, he's the bloody shipwreck itself!'

'No he aren't! He's the last rat to leave the sinking ship!'

Each succeeding sally was greeted with hooting laughter and applause.

Knowing that if he showed any reaction to these provocations it would merely add to his tormentors' enjoyment, Tom could only hold his head high and walk on with as much dignity as he could muster.

He reached the central crossroads and halted indecisively. 'Should I go now to the Unicorn and see my mother? But when she sees me in my present state she'll only berate me for looking like a tramp, and shaming her.'

A horseman reined in beside him. 'Hello, Master Potts. I trust you're fully recovered from your long voyage?'

Tom forced a smile. 'Indeed I am, Master Wynne. The sea airs were most salubrious.'

The Welshman's white teeth shone. 'I like your sense of humour, Master Potts.'

'Well, in this case I have to laugh, because otherwise I fear that I'd weep about what happened to me,' Tom confessed ruefully.

'My cousin Martin and I have been wondering if you have any idea about the identity of the footpad who bludged you?' Wynne queried. 'Martin has told his men to listen out for any talk of it, by the way.'

'No, I've not a notion of who it was,' Tom answered, then remarked, 'I thought that you would have been droving your herd far from here by now.'

'Normally I would have been, but some unexpected opportunities for profitable business have come my way locally and the grazing is good, so I shall possibly remain hereabouts for another week or so.' Wynne winked roguishly. 'I find that the ale in Tardebigge Parish is much to my taste, as are the pretty girls who serve it. In fact I'm on my way to ogle a couple of them now. Will you join me for a glass or two?'

'I'd like to very much, but unfortunately I've a deal of neglected duties to attend to,' Tom demurred. 'Another time, however.'

'I'll look forward to it, Master Potts.' Wynne touched his hat brim in a farewell salute and cantered away down the Market Place.

Tom stayed watching as the Welshman dismounted outside the Fox and Goose, tied his horse to a wall hitching ring, and entered the inn.

The image of Amy's smiling face rose up in Tom's mind, and he murmured glumly, 'What can I offer you, Amy, compared to all these dashing bloods who come flocking to ogle you?'

Unwilling to further lower his depressed spirits by going to face his mother's scornful spite, he cut back across the green and returned to the lock-up.

TWENTY-ONE

Wednesday 11th April

After brief hours of restless, broken sleep Tom rose before dawn and shaved by candlelight, painfully nicking his throat and cheeks several times with the cut-throat razor. He held a towel to the blood-seeping wounds and vowed wryly, 'I swear that if I'm ever wealthy enough, I'll only ever be shaved by a professional barber for the rest of my days.'

He breakfasted on bread and milk, sharing the meal with his cat, Bathsheba, then took the candle and went downstairs to the cell where Irish Joe was ensconced.

One by one he lifted the small glass jars which contained the acid and flesh and held them before the wavering flame, screwing up his eyes to examine their swirling contents.

The acid had done its work, and the slivers of tissue had been liquefied.

Tom carried the jars back up to his room and laid them out together with the thin glass slides and microscope on the small table before the window. He paced about the room, waiting impatiently for sunrise to bring the full daylight he needed to be able to prepare and examine the slide specimens.

Across the parish others who had endured restless broken hours of sleep were also waiting for the sunrise.

In this hovel a woman sat cradling in her arms the child who had died in the night, mourning her loss with bitter tears. In that hovel a weary father roused his weary wife and children from their beds of rags and straw, cursing the needle masters who paid them such a miserable pittance in return for their ceaseless gruelling toil.

In this fine house a woman paced the floor, fervently begging God that the child quickening in her womb would be the son her husband so desperately craved, and not yet another unwanted girl. In that fine house a man sat with head in hands knowing that all his wealth, all his property, all his worldly success, were power-less to protect him from the cancerous tumours that had invaded his body.

In the attic bedroom of the Fox and Goose Amy Danks lay awake in the bed she shared with the snoring Maisie Lock, asking herself over and over again, 'What shall I do? What shall I do?'

In another room in the south of the parish a man lay awake in bed telling himself, 'I need to be certain sure that it was Rose Brent's workmate I bumped into. If it is her, then she's bound to be at the funeral . . .'

TWENTY-TWO

Tom experienced a sense of exultant satisfaction as he completed the examination of the final slide beneath the microscope.

'Too few diatoms in the entire series! He was already dead when dumped into the canal. That proves it! There's a killer – or killers – at work here!'

He jumped to his feet and began to pace backwards and forwards in the confined space of his room, his brain throbbing with questions for which he had no answer.

'Are these two deaths connected? What about the girl found at Bewdley? Is she another connection? How were they killed? Why were they killed?'

The jangling doorbells brought him to a dismayed standstill.

'Oh my God! It must be nine o'clock, and I haven't sewn Irish Joe back up!'

He flung the casement open and leaned out, calling, 'I'll be down shortly.'

'You need to be quicker than that; I've only managed to sneak out for a couple of ticks,' Amy Danks called back.

'Amy!' He was completely taken aback at this totally unexpected visitation. 'What are you doing here?'

'I'm waiting for you to open this door.' She smiled.

'What time is it?'

'It's just past nine o'clock.'

'Oh m-my God!' he stuttered in dismay, as from the corner of his eye he noticed a horse and cart approaching and the tall figure of John Clayton striding beside it in company with two women clad in shabby mourning cloaks and black ribboned bonnets.

Her smile faltered. 'You don't seem very pleased to see me, Tom?'

'Oh, I am.' He was frantically trying to regain his composure.

'So then? Are you coming down to let me in, or what?' Her smile had disappeared.

'I can't! Not at this time anyway.'

'Why not?' she challenged.

'There's something very urgent I have to do,' he offered lamely. 'Perhaps we can talk later?'

Her blue eyes flamed with sudden temper. 'I risk a row off my boss for sneaking out to come and see you, and this is how you treat me? No, we'll not be talking later. In fact we'll not be talking ever again!' She tossed her head angrily and ran back towards the Fox and Goose.

'Oh, Amy, I fear we're truly star-crossed, you and I.' Tom shook his head in despair as he dragged the sheet from his bed and ran back downstairs.

The doorbells jangled and Tom apologized to the dead man's waxen grey face. 'I'm sorry, Irish Joe, but I've not got the time to sew you up again. So here's a nice clean sheet instead to cover you decently.'

He quickly wrapped the sheet around the corpse, hiding the long gaping post-mortem gash, then rushed to unlock the front door.

After the exchange of greetings Tom gently advised Widow Brent and Martha Standard: 'Because of the length of time that poor Rose has been dead, perhaps it might be better that you do not view her. Reverend Clayton can do so and will be able to confirm to you that she is most decently and properly laid in her coffin.'

'That'll be for the best, Connie.' Martha Standard put her arms around the tragic-faced older woman. 'Let's you and me remember Rosie like she was, all fresh and bonny and full o' life.'

Widow Brent held out a small paper-wrapped package and pleaded, 'Put this into my baby's coffin, Parson. It's her caul, and if her aren't buried with it then her won't never rest easy in her grave. She'll rise and come back to search for it, that's the Gospel truth, that is.'

'I'll put it in her coffin, my dear. She'll rest easy, I do assure you. Now wait here while I go to see her.' Clayton took the package and followed Tom into the lock-up.

'I have to look and see that it's Irish Joe as well, Tom.' He smiled and joked grimly. 'Even though I'm fully aware that you haven't sold him to an anatomist, our damned Vestrymen demand that I check that you're not giving me a box full of earth to bury.'

The viewing of the two corpses took only seconds and while Tom was screwing the coffin lids down Clayton went to call the carrier.

'Master Jolly, will you be good enough to come and help us bring the coffins out?'

While Widow Brent and Martha Standard held the horse's head, the three men carried the coffins from the cells and loaded them onto the cart.

'Begging your pardon, Parson, but which one is my daughter?' Widow Brent asked timidly.

'She's in here, my dear.' Clayton laid his hand on the crudely made box.

The two women laid small posies of wild flowers on its lid, and then the old woman enquired, 'And who's the poor soul in this other one?'

'He's a Legger who was drowned in the Tardebigge Tunnel. An Irishman, I believe.'

'And there's no one come here to say a goodbye to him?'

'No.' Clayton shook his head regretfully. 'Sadly we know of no kinfolk or friends of his.'

'I know that my Rosie, bless her good heart, 'udden't want to see the poor friendless soul without a single petal on his grave. She'd want him to share her flowers.' Widow Brent moved one of the posies on to Irish Joe's coffin.

The simple kindliness of the gesture moved Tom deeply, and he asked the old woman, 'Will you permit me, ma'am, to accompany you to the graveyard and pay my last respects to your daughter by your side?'

Tears streaked down her withered cheeks, sobs choked her voice and she could only nod her assent.

With John Clayton going before the cart, George Jolly leading the horse, and Tom and the two women bringing up the rear the small cortège moved slowly towards the Fish Hill along the roadway skirting the rear of the chapel. Before they had gone many paces Tom became aware that Widow Brent was limping, and he and Martha Standard each took one of the old woman's arms, supporting her weight to help her walk more easily.

No mourning bell tolled. No solemn procession of bannered mutes and carriages followed a hearse laden with costly wreaths being drawn by black-plumed, glossy groomed horses. But as always when death was passing, no matter how poor and humble the cortège, men removed their hats and stood in silent respect, women hushed their children, bobbed curtseys and bowed their heads.

In the chapel graveyard from a hidden vantage point behind an ornate tombstone the man staring at the small figure of Martha Standard asked himself worriedly, 'What am I going to do about you, Martha Standard? Will it be a question of your neck or mine, I wonder?'

TWENTY-THREE

The old gravedigger, Hector Smout, was waiting at the gate of the neglected, ragged-hedged cemetery and when he saw the small doleful procession approaching along the narrow lane he hobbled to meet it.

'G'mornin' to you, Parson.' He doffed his battered slouch hat.

'Good morning, Master Smout, is everything prepared?' Clayton asked.

'O' course it is!' Smout asserted indignantly. 'When has it never not been?'

'I mean no offence, Master Smout.' Clayton hastened to placate the old man. 'You've always done your work perfectly, I know that very well. Now if you please, we shall need your further assistance to lower the coffins because as you can see there are only three of we men come here today.'

Smout scowled in disgust, shaking his head and muttering beneath his breath, but then his rheumy eyes moved to Widow Brent's grief-ravaged face. His demeanour softened, and he stated gruffly, 'I knowed Connie here, when we was both young 'uns, didn't I, Connie? And there was a time when we meant a deal to each other. Weren't that so, Connie?'

The old woman nodded. 'That were so, Hector.'

'Well I'm very sorry for this trouble that's come on you, Connie. And I shall do all that I can to help lay your child proper and respectful into her last resting place. And though I says it meself, I'se done as neat and sweet a piece o' digging it as you'll find in the length and breadth o' this land. It's fit for a king to lie in, so it is.'

He beckoned them all to follow and hobbled back to the gate.

The four men carried Irish Joe's coffin inside the cemetery, while the women remained by the cart.

As they entered, John Clayton saw the two widely separated mounds of earth and questioned in a whisper, 'What's this, Master Smout? Is there another burial to come today?'

'Well if there is, nobody's told me about it,' Smout grunted.

'The Vestry has ordered these two to be pauper burials. That means they go into the common grave, as you well know.'

'O' course I well knows, and the man can be put in wi' them we buried last week. But because of me and her mam being old friends, so to speak, I thought it 'ud be a comfort to Connie if her girl could be laid to her rest in that 'un over there. There's only one o' the old monks a-laying in it, and Rose 'ull be safe with him. Not like wi' some o' the evil buggers in the common pit. God only knows what badness they gets up to wi' each other.'

A note of asperity entered Clayton's tone. 'Master Smout, you are talking of dead people laid in consecrated ground. So have done with this nonsense. It might well be construed as sacrilege.'

'Some might call it nonsense, but they are them who aren't seen what I've seen, and aren't heard what I've heard, come the dark night and the witching hour when I've been here all alone a-watching and a-listening,' the old man hissed.

'That's enough, Master Smout! Say nothing more!' Clayton snapped, and the old man scowled and lapsed into a sullen silence.

Listening to this whispered exchange, Tom could not help but think that if the clergy could preach of eternal life, and the dead rising from the grave on the Day of Judgement, then Hector Smout had an equal right to express his beliefs.

When the men had lowered the two coffins into their respective graves John Clayton took position midway between them and said quietly, 'I assume that Irish Joe is of the Catholic faith, but I'll stand here so that my prayers may carry over him, as they will carry over Rose. But it's more fitting that the ladies are at Rosie's graveside. The remainder of you may stand where you wish.'

The three men exchanged glances and by unspoken accord moved to stand with the women.

Clayton declaimed sonorously, 'Man that is born of a woman hath but a short time to live, and is full of misery. He cometh up and is cut down like a flower; he fleeth as it were a shadow, and never continueth in one stay . . .'

A racking sob shook Connie Brent's frail body, and Martha

Standard tearfully wrapped her arms about the old woman and drew her close.

Pity for them whelmed over Tom, and in his mind he vowed impassionedly, 'From this moment forward my foremost concern will be to discover the truth about Rose Brent's death, and bring her killer to justice!'

'. . . In the midst of life we are in death: of whom may we seek for succour, but of Thee, O Lord . . .'

'As soon as these burials are done, I'll go to the canal and find the Irishwoman, Tessy,' Tom decided.

'. . . Thou knowest, Lord, the secrets of our hearts; shut not thy merciful ears to our prayer, but spare us, Lord most holy . . .'

When the opening prayer ended, Tom joined with the others in casting handfuls of earth down upon the coffins of both Rose Brent and Irish Joe while John Clayton intoned a second prayer.

'We therefore commit their bodies to the earth, ashes to ashes, dust to dust; in sure and certain hope of the Resurrection to eternal life through our Lord Jesus Christ . . .'

'Instead of Resurrection to eternal life, why couldn't you first let this poor girl spend a little more time with her loved ones upon this earth?' Tom suddenly found himself fiercely questioning God. 'Why couldn't you show some mercy to her poor mother, instead of bringing such terrible grief down upon her?'

But even as he asked the questions, he accepted the absolute futility of voicing them.

The shortened burial service was over and John Clayton gently ushered the sobbing women from the cemetery, and asked George Jolly, 'If I pay you for your trouble, Master Jolly, can you give these ladies a ride back to their homes on your cart? I fear that it's a very arduous walk for Widow Brent to make at this particular time.'

The carrier shook his head as if in refusal, and Clayton frowned, but Jolly lifted his hand to forestall any words from the clergyman.

'I want no payment, Parson. I'll carry them home because I'm a Christian, and do it gladly.'

Tom watched pityingly as the cart creaked away with the women clasped weeping in each other's arms.

From inside the cemetery the dull thumping of clods of earth on to a coffin marked where Hector Smout was filling up the graves.

'Where do you go now, Tom?' Clayton enquired. 'I can offer you some refreshment at my house.'

Driven by his need to set about discovering the truth of Rose Brent's death, Tom thanked him, but refused.

'I need to go up to the Tardebigge Wharf without further delay, John.' Then he frowned as the unwelcome thought of his mother intruded. 'But before that I'll have to move Mother back into the lock-up, because if she stays at the Unicorn any longer, we'll both find ourselves in the Debtors' Prison.'

TWENTY-FOUR

'I'll tell you frankly, Master Potts, that if you hadn't come for her, then I'd have had to put her out onto the street this very day.' John Mence, landlord of the Unicorn Inn, regarded Tom with some sympathy. 'She's a most contrary woman to deal with. My servants were threatening to leave, if she didn't go.'

'I'm truly sorry if she's been causing problems for you, Master Mence.' Tom's apology was issued at the very moment he could clearly hear his mother's strident shrieking as she berated some unfortunate serving girl. 'I'll settle the account and then move her directly.'

When the other man presented him with the bill, Tom inwardly shuddered, and mentally selected the items he would be taking to the pawn shop to replenish his now emptied pockets.

'I'll have my man carry her baggage to the lock-up, Master Potts.' Mence grinned. 'You'll be needing both of your hands to convey your mother back there, I don't doubt.'

'Indeed I shall.' Tom nodded ruefully.

'So there you are, you wretch!' Widow Potts stumped heavily into the room, her sweaty face purple with temper. 'Why has God punished me so unjustly? Why has he given me such a vicious monster for a son? Why did you abandon me? What have I done to deserve such heartless cruelty?'

Tom looked down into her pig-like, fat-puffed eyes and for the thousandth time silently asked his dead father, 'Why did you ever marry this woman, Father? How did you manage to bear so patiently the years of misery she gave you?'

'Well?' Her shrieking filled his ears. 'Answer me, curse you! You've been off whoring and drinking again, haven't you, you filthy beast! Leaving me in this disgraceful slum hovel, where I've been sorely mistreated and insulted! You should have protected me, you worthless waster!'

The vivid memory of his beloved father on his death bed begging him to care for her as a dutiful son enabled Tom to draw a deep breath, take her arm and gently lead her from the inn.

'Come now, Mother, let's get you home.'

'Home? Home? It's not my home you're forcing me back to. It's a foul charnel house, and the dwelling place of evildoers! It's not my home!'

Fortunately for Tom's ears, the sheer effort it cost Widow Potts to carry her gross billows of heavy flesh forced her very quickly to use all her breath solely to move one leg after the other.

Another hour had passed and Tom had got his mother back into her room, prepared food and drink for her, and settled her comfortably.

'I must go now, Mother. I've things to attend to.' He took up his staff and left the lock-up with her complaints of being deserted echoing in his ears.

Although the prospect of once again venturing into the midst of the Leggers was not a pleasant one, still the escape from his mother's diatribes lightened Tom's spirits, and he set out for the Tardebigge Canal in good heart.

It was an hour later, when he breasted the hill by Tardebigge Church and was walking down the slope to the New Wharf, that apprehension struck through Tom, quickening his heartbeat, shortening his breath, slowing his pace.

'What might I be walking into here? What might they end up doing to me this time?'

For a few moments the urge to turn and walk back to Redditch assailed him, but he deliberately evoked the visual image of the grieving face of Widow Brent.

'No, I'll not fail you, you poor soul. I'm going to find who killed your daughter no matter what it may cost me.'

He screwed up his determination and picked up the pace again.

'Watch out, lads, here's the stowaway come!'

'Where am you sailing to this time, Shipmate?'

The raucous shouts of wharf workers greeted Tom's entry into the New Wharf yard.

'Warn that Brummie bargee he'll be carrying extra cargo for free if he don't take care.'

'Ahrr! Tell him to make the lanky bugger work his passage this time!'

Tom ignored them and went to knock on the door of Martin Cooke's office, which was opened by a bespectacled, inky-fingered clerk who with a broad grin announced, 'If you're looking to book a berth for a sea passage, I can't help you. This aren't an ocean-going shipping office.'

'I've come to see Mr Cooke,' Tom told him.

'The boss aren't here.'

'Where can I find him, please?'

'Gawd knows! He might be anywhere between the Worcester and Birmingham Basins. He's a bit of a traveller, like you are.'

The man's sneering attitude was starting to rile Tom, but he maintained his politeness. 'When is Mr Cooke expected back?'

'That's hard to say. He's doing lock and wharf inspections. Sometimes he's gone for a couple of days. Sometimes for a week or more. Now I've got work to do, even if you might not have any, so bugger off!'

The man slammed the door in Tom's face.

For an instant or two Tom lusted to smash the door open, drag the clerk out and hurl him bodily into the canal. Then his ironic sense of humour asserted itself.

'I'd best not risk it. On past experience it could well be him who chucks me into the canal!'

A group of Leggers were lounging near to the tunnel mouth and Tom asked them, 'The Irishwoman, Tessy, where can I find her?'

'Fuck knows!' One of them shrugged, and then the entire group turned their backs on him.

Realizing the futility of any further attempt to question them or anyone else in the yard, Tom left. Back on the road he stood indecisively for some moments, then on impulse went down to the Cherry Tree tavern.

It was a long, single-storeyed thatched building, shabby and tumbledown in appearance, and as Tom approached there were no sounds emanating from it. But as he pushed open its door and ducked his head to pass under the low lintel he heard a woman's laughter.

The room was gloomy and fuggy with coal smoke and the fumes of stale beer. Tom straightened and his top hat hit the low ceiling rafters and fell off. As he stooped to lift it from the sticky dirty layers of sawdust which smothered the floor a woman's voice exclaimed in surprise.

'Tom Potts? What are you doing here?'

He looked to where the solitary occupants of the room were seated at a table by the window and in equal surprise exclaimed, 'Maisie Lock! It's you!'

'Well it was me, the last time I looked at meself.' She laughed.

'Come and join us, Master Potts. What will you have to drink?'
Daniel Wynne's white teeth gleamed in a welcoming smile.

Still shocked by this totally unexpected encounter, Tom moved
closer to the couple, shaking his head.

'No, I thank you, Master Wynne. I'm here on duty.'

'And what duty might that be?' the Welshman asked.

'I'm looking for someone. An Irishwoman named Tessy.'

'Oh yes, you've spoken of her before, if I remember rightly.'
Wynne nodded, and quipped to Maisie Lock, 'She's the baggage
Master Potts was looking for just before he went on his voyage.
She must be a real beauty because the failure to find her made him
so distressed that it drove him to face the perils of the deep on a
leaky canal barge.'

Maisie screamed with laughter.

Tom reddened with embarrassment, and in an attempt to hide it,
flustered 'Is anyone else here? Of course I can see there's no one
else in this room, but I mean the landlord, or one of his helpers
perhaps?'

'I'm Terry Wilkes, and I'm the landlord here.' A man came from
the shadowed door behind the counter-shielded row of barrels on
the far side of the room. 'What d'you want with me?'

'I'm looking for one of the Legger women. She's the Irishwoman
named Tessy.'

'Not any more, she aren't a Legger woman. Did a runner, her
did. Days since. But if Jacky Whittaker ever gets his hands on her,
her won't never be running nowhere never again, the cheeky mare
won't.' The landlord chortled with amusement.

'Why so?' Tom queried.

'Because he'd had a good night's winnings at cards and her did
a runner wi' 'em when he was laying pissed out of his yed. Took
a full bottle o' best rum that he'd just bought; and his tobacco and
his spare shirt and britches as well, the cheeky mare did. You won't
be seeing her in these parts ever again, that's for sure. Not if she
wants to keep her yed on top of her shoulders.'

Tom recognized that the man was speaking truthfully, and frustration coursed through him. Tessy had been the only lead he had
to a possible identification of Rose Brent's lover.

'Now then, Tom Potts, am you seeking another sweetheart? Is
that why you wants to find this Tessy?' Maisie Lock grinned provocatively. 'You just wait 'til I tells Amy. She's already vexed with you
as it is. She'll most probably take up with one of the chaps who'm
chasing after her when she hears about this.'

His patience strained to breaking point by intense frustration, Tom snapped curtly, 'You may tell Miss Danks whatever silly tittle-tattle you choose to, girl. Good day to you, Master Wynne.'

Outside in the cool fresh air Tom immediately regretted his momentary outburst and thought despondently, 'As though things weren't already bad enough between me and Amy, I've gone and put my foot in it yet again.'

Shoulders bowed he walked slowly up the slope. When he reached the wall overlooking the tunnel entrance he stopped and, leaning his elbows upon the parapet, gazed down at the dark waters beneath.

'It's not good. With Tessy gone I've no other lead to follow except to go to Bewdley as soon as I can and make enquiries there. Meanwhile Rose Brent will lie unavenged in her grave, and what's worse is that her killer might even now be preying on some other poor wretched girl!'

With a dispirited sigh he pushed himself upright and walked on.

In the gloom of the Cherry Tree tavern Daniel Wynne pulled Maisie Lock close and kissed her passionately, his fingers moving expertly to undo buttons, untie laces and loosen clothes so that his hands could explore and fondle soft warm skin, firm breasts, erect nipples . . .

TWENTY-FIVE

Bewdley Poorhouse
Noon, Friday 13th April

At the locked gate of the Bewdley Poorhouse a short, pot-bellied man came in answer to Tom's calling, and stood facing him through the bars.

'I'm Thomas Potts, Constable of the Parish of Tardebigge. Am I addressing Master Amos Barry, keeper of the Bewdley Poorhouse?'

'You are,' the man grunted.

'I'm come to enquire about an unidentified young woman who was drowned and buried here by order of the Vestry in November last.'

'A young drowned wench, buried hereabouts sometime in November last year d'you say?' Amos Barry noisily sucked his teeth and scratched his grey-stubbled chin, then queried suspiciously, 'What might be your interest in her, Master Potts?'

'Anything you can tell me about her, Master Barry.'

Barry shook his head. 'You aren't took my meaning. What I wants to know is why you're asking me about such a woman? You being a constable and all. Was she wanted for some crime or other? Pinched something, had she? Like money or jewels or suchlike?'

Tom hesitated, suspecting that this man before him might well have removed valuables from the girl's corpse for his own gain. He answered cautiously, 'I've no reason to believe that she'd stolen anything of value, and I'm not here to investigate any sort of thievery. Also I haven't got the slightest interest in recovering any valuables she might have had with her. The finder of any such articles is welcome to keep them. I seek only for some information.'

Tom paused momentarily, searching the other's man's face for any reaction to this assurance, and thinking he saw a favourable indication went on, 'Because a short while ago another young woman was taken from the canal at Tardebigge Parish, and she was wearing only her gown and a petticoat. But when last seen alive she had on a bonnet, shawl, stockings, garters and boots. I'm curious as to why she was lacking all those articles when pulled from the canal. I'm also curious to discover if the young woman pulled from the river here was also lacking her clothing. I'd like to know how she was dressed when she was pulled from the river.'

Amos Barry stood mulling over what he had heard, sucking his teeth, scratching his chin. Then he smiled grimly. 'You're thinking that the young woman in the Tardebigge canal might have come to her death by foul means, aren't you?'

Tom saw no point in denial, and admitted immediately, 'I am, Master Barry.'

'Well, the woman here was pregnant, but her was too battered by the river and the length o' time her had been in the water to rightly know whether it was by foul means or not she'd come to be in it. But her still had her bonnet hanging from her neck, and her gown and petticoats on her. Stockings as well, and a pair o' garters, but only one shoe.'

'The stockings and garters, Master Barry, what were they like?' Tom questioned eagerly.

'The women who laid her out said that they was all made o' silk. Pink silk, if I remembers rightly. And the garters was them fancy ones with rosettes. But the trouble was that bumping along the river for a good many miles like she must have done had torn everything up so bad that nothing was worth saving to sell on. That's why we had to sell her teeth to put towards the cost of burying her.'

For the first time a gleam of pity entered the poorhouse master's eyes. 'I've wondered a few times since who she might have been, and if her's got parents or kin wondering where and what's become of her.' He shrugged. 'Ahhr well, her's at peace now at any rate. I've got to attend to me duties, Master Potts. So I'll wish you a safe journey back to Tardebigge.'

'Thank you very much for your help, Master Barry,' Tom told him sincerely, because what he had heard had left him elated.

He was walking away when his name was shouted, and he turned to see the poorhouse master waving him to come back.

'Hold fast, Master Potts. I've just remembered something else.'

He hurried into the house and came back within seconds holding something that he handed to Tom.

'We found this on that wench. It was tied inside her bodice. You can take it with you if you want.'

Tom examined the article, which was a small wooden spoon ornately carved along its entire bowl and handle with intricate designs. It struck a chord in his memory, and he murmured, 'Is this what is known as a "love spoon"?'

'That's it,' Barry confirmed. 'It's what the Welshmen give to their sweethearts. The bloke carves it for her and gives it her for a keepsake.'

'She might have been a Welshwoman then, made pregnant by a Welshman?' Tom wondered aloud.

'She could have been. The river rises a good distance into Taffy land. The poor wench might have fallen in anywhere along its length. Goodbye now, Master Potts.'

Tom walked away from the gate, staring down at the love spoon in his hand, the memory of finding the Welshman Daniel Wynne and Maisie Lock together coming vividly into his mind.

'I wonder if Wynne has given you a love spoon, Maisie Lock? Or a pair of pink silk stockings?'

Tom shook his head impatiently and asked himself a further question. 'Why should I even be wondering whether or not Daniel Wynne has given Maisie Lock either a bloody love spoon or a pair of stockings? What the hell have either of them got to do with Bewdley?'

TWENTY-SIX

Afternoon, Sunday 15th April

'I'll have to be getting back, Mam. Tommy Fowkes will be wondering where I've got to else; and I'd best not try his temper too much by being late back to me work again today,' Amy Danks said.

The older woman shook her head and smiled wryly. 'He's too soft with you by far. I wish I'd had a boss as easy-going as him when I was a young wench. I don't know how you gets away wi' playing him up like you do. You and that young hoyden, Maisie Lock, are a right pair.'

'Phew! Men are easy to handle if a girl knows how to butter them up.' Amy smiled confidently and kissed her mother's cheek. 'Tarra now, and tell me Dad I'll see him next Sunday.'

'Wait while I put me bonnet on and I'll walk a bit of the way back with you.'

'No, don't bother. The kids will be wanting their supper as soon as they comes in, so you'd best get it ready for them.' And before her mother could say anything more, she had gone through the door.

She hurried towards the Mount Pleasant turnpike and smiled with satisfaction when she saw the man standing by his horse, discreetly within the roadside trees.

Eugene Sinclair emerged from the shielding trees and came to meet her, frowning questioningly. 'I've been waiting here for hours, Amy. What have you been doing in there?'

Her petulance flared instantly. 'What business is it of yours what I've been doing in my own home? I didn't ask you to wait here, did I?'

She turned from him and walked quickly down the long sloping road towards Redditch.

His fists clenched, his eyes reddened with rage, and his mouth opened to shout after her. But the angry words were not voiced as he controlled himself.

'Let her play her silly games for the time being,' he thought to himself. 'My turn will come soon enough to play my own game.'

He mounted his horse and kicked it into a gallop, riding at reckless speed to overtake and dismount to block her way.

'I'm so sorry, Miss Amy. Please don't be angry with me. It's just that I become so anxious when I don't see you. I become so frightened that you no longer want anything to do with me, that I lose all sense and speak without thought. Please forgive me. I beg you to forgive me.'

'Humphh!' She tossed her head indignantly and walked around him.

Twice more he was forced to gallop after her before, with a smile of satisfaction tugging at the corners of her mouth, she deigned to stand still and listen to his pleas for forgiveness.

'Oh, very well then. This time I'll forgive you. But remember in future that I'm not a woman who can be spoken to like that.'

'I'll remember, my dear. I swear it!' he assured her vehemently. Then he requested humbly, 'Will you permit me to escort you back to the inn?'

'Oh very well, if you must,' she conceded with an outward show of reluctance, but inwardly glowing with her sense of dominance over this fine Gentleman Dandy. 'But I've no wish to ride pillion. I want to walk today.'

'Your wish is my command.' He bowed with a flourish.

She eyed him archly. 'Take care, Master Sinclair; I might make a wish that you'll find it hard to accept as a command.'

'Then try me,' he challenged. 'Make a wish that you think I'll find it hard to accept as my command.'

'Then stay quiet while I think of one,' she replied, and they walked on in silence until they reached the central crossroads of the green, where Amy came to a halt and faced him.

'Well, Miss Amy? Do you have that wish for me?' He smiled.

She returned the smile, and her eyes danced with mischievous humour. 'Indeed I do, Master Sinclair. I wish you to present me to your cousin and his wife as a lady that you consider to be your friend and equal.'

'Present you to the Earl and Lady Harriet?' He was momentarily shocked, then threw back his head and roared with laughter.

Amy's smile suddenly metamorphosed into a piqued grimace and she snapped curtly, 'There now, that's put the cat among your pigeons, hasn't it, Master Sinclair? I'm really just a lowly servant girl to you, aren't I?'

His laughter stilled, and there was a calculating gleam in his eyes. He shook his head and told her with measured emphasis,

'Indeed you are no such creature in my eyes, Miss Amy. I shall be delighted to present you to my cousin and his wife upon their return to Hewell Grange, whenever that may be. But we must use the intervening time to equip you with the correct clothing so that you will do yourself and your family honour on such an august occasion.'

He fumbled in his saddlebags and pulled out a small paper-wrapped package, which he pressed into her hand.

'Now pray do me the honour of accepting this small token of my deep regard for you. You may open it when you're back in your room. It is the beginning of your new wardrobe. Goodbye for now, Miss Amy.'

Smiling broadly he bowed, mounted and rode away.

Amy stared uncertainly after him, feeling simultaneously disturbed yet excited by what he had said and done.

Too curious to wait until she went back to her room, she tore open the paper, and gasped with delight as the ultra-fashionable pink silk stockings cascaded shimmering across her fingers.

TWENTY-SEVEN

Friday 20th April

As Martin Cooke drove his horse and trap into the carriageway of his secluded hillside home on the border of Tardebigge Parish he experienced the all too familiar sense of depression creeping over him despite the fine sunset and the pleasant warmth of the evening air. The old half-timbered house, its fabric shrouded by thick ancient ivy, surrounded by overgrown lawns, weed-choked flowerbeds and shrubberies, radiated an air of neglect and decay. Despite the thickening shadows of dusk no lights shone from its mullioned windows, no smoke curled from its tall chimneys. Forcing down the powerful desire to turn and go back the way he had come, he steered the horse to the ruinous stable block at the rear of the building and halted.

A middle-aged, dour-featured woman clad in sombre black mourning clothes came from the house and he greeted her politely.

'I hope you are well, Mrs Chesney. How is my wife?'

'Somewhat disturbed, sir, and she's taken to her bed again. She was in the drawing room this morning and thought that she saw a man staring at her through a gap in the curtains.'

'And was there a man there?' Cooke asked.

'No, sir. When I heard her screaming I immediately went outside to check. There was no one.'

'You're sure of that?' he pressed for confirmation.

'Of course I am.' Her expression was impassive, but resentment flickered in her pale eyes.

Cooke noted that flickering, and was quick to mollify her. 'I should not have asked that last question, Mrs Chesney. I know that I can trust you implicitly.'

She gave a single curt nod of her head to acknowledge acceptance of his apology.

'I think that from now on it will be best for us to keep the gates chained and padlocked, Mrs Chesney. You'll find the usual provisions in the trap, and also the French cognac that you requested. I'll go and speak to my wife.'

Cooke went into the curtain-shadowed darkness of the house, and as its musty damp smell enveloped him his depression deepened. He fumbled his way up the broad staircase, and hissed savagely, 'Satan's curse on the day that I ever met you, Edwina! And let his curse be on me also for having chosen you to be my wedded wife!'

TWENTY-EIGHT

Sunday 22nd April

Tom cut the large loaf of bread on the tray into slices and spread them thickly with salted butter. He sniffed the jug of milk to check that it had not turned sour, added the jug to the tray, then carried it to the open cell door.

'Here's your breakfast, Sean, and the bread and milk are fresh. The cart will be here shortly, and it's a fine clear morning so you'll have an enjoyable journey.'

The cell stank of unwashed flesh and filthy rags, and Tom could only feel relief that this morning he'd be moving its present occupants – an Irishman, his wife and three small children – into the neighbouring parish of Bromsgrove.

'Good man yourself, Master Potts.' The burly, sandy-haired Irishman grinned. 'It's always a pleasure to spend a night in your fine establishment. Is that not so, Roisin? Haven't I always said the same about this place?'

'So he has, Master Potts. There's never a truer word he's spoken,' his slatternly, fat-bodied wife happily confirmed as she took the tray from Tom's hands and began to feed her small mop-headed children their meal.

Tom chuckled with ironic amusement. This was the third time since he had become constable that Sean Macafferty had passed through the lock-up en route for deportation to his native parish of birth in Ireland. Tom couldn't help but feel a sneaking sense of admiration for the way in which men like Macafferty utilized the savage Law of Settlement to their own advantage.

Tom heartily disliked as a constable having to enforce that law, which was that the Right of Settlement – the right to receive parish Poor Relief – was confined to those who were born within the parish boundaries. A man or woman could work and live respectably, sometimes for many years, in a particular parish, but if misfortune came upon them and reduced them to penury and want they could not obtain any help or relief from that same parish, but would be removed back to their parish of birth, by force if necessary.

Tom had witnessed himself how when trade was good the local masters and employers encouraged people to come to Tardebigge Parish and supply whatever skilled or unskilled labour was needed. But the moment trade slackened, or accident, disease or age incapacitated these incomers, then to avoid having to give them any Poor Relief the Vestry ordered that they must be evicted from the parish. A Vagrant Pass would be issued by two Justices and the paupers and their families, escorted by a constable, would be carried in a cart to the parish boundary to be handed over to the constable and cart of the neighbouring parish, and so transported onwards across boundary after boundary until they reached their birth parish.

Sean Macafferty however was not an incomer seeking lawful employment, but a life-long professional beggar, who regarded the Vagrant Pass as one of the rightful perks of his chosen calling. Whenever arrested for vagrancy he would produce certificates and letters issued by the Priest and Vestry of his native parish stating that he was an honest labourer seeking employment, who had fallen into poverty and unemployment through no fault of his own. A Vagrant Pass for repatriation to Ireland would be issued by the Justices in his place of arrest and he and his family would then embark upon a comparatively easy few weeks of free cart travel, plus food and shelter in lock-ups. A short break in Ireland, and back he would come to mainland Britain to begin begging again.

The jangling bells announced the arrival of George Jolly with his horse and cart and Tom went to speak with him.

The carrier appeared to be disgruntled, and Tom remarked, 'You're not looking happy this morning, Master Jolly.'

'With bloody good reason.' Jolly's weather-beaten features glowered. 'One of them bloody Morteson sluts from Silver Street is threatening to lay bastardry charges against my youngest lad, if he don't get the banns called. So I expect you'll be bringing the magistrate's warrant to my house afore this week's done.'

'You don't want him to marry the girl then?'

'O' course I don't! He's just a daft young sod who reckons he loves her, bloody fool that he is! Her's a bloody pauper from the worst slum in the parish. Them bloody Mortesons has never had a pot to piss in. I've forbid him to marry her, and that's that! Let her bring the bloody charge and be damned to her.'

'If he weds her then you'll have a grandchild. Surely that is something to be happy about,' Tom argued. 'I know the Mortesons are poor, but they're good-living people. It's not the father's fault that he's too infirm to get regular work. The daughters both have work, do they not?'

'As bloody washer girls!' Jolly snorted contemptuously. 'Earning a few measly pence a week! I knows from experience how slum rats like the Mortesons feather their nests by marrying into families of successful men of business like what I am. Then they cadge their bread for the rest o' their miserable lives from that same successful man.' He shook his head and declared vehemently. 'I won't let my son ruin his life by wedding that wench. Let the magistrates issue the Affiliation Order against him if they wish. I'll wait and see if the babby is feeble and likely to die soon. If it is then I'll pay the half-crown a week maintenance for a while. But if the babby thrives, then it'll be cheaper in the long run for me to pay the ten pounds lump sum for the full release from the order, and sign the little bastard over to the parish.'

Tom knew both of the young people in question, and sincerely pitied their plight. But he also knew that it was futile for him to argue further in favour of the wedding. The right of a father to enforce absolute rule over his wife and children was sacrosanct and unchallenged in both law and custom.

'Please God take pity on that poor girl and her unborn child,' he prayed silently.

'Are we ready to make a move, your honours?' Sean Macafferty came grinning broadly from the lock-up shepherding his family before him. 'Look at that fine cart we're to ride in, my darlings. Jaysus, we'll be feeling like Lords and Ladies riding in our own coach, won't we just?'

'Me and your missus and kids 'ull no doubt be feeling like that, Paddy, but you'll be walking behind my cart, not riding on it. My old mare is too frail to be carrying a great useless, lazy lump like you in such luxury,' Jolly told him jocularly.

The Irishman laughed. 'Ah well, it's a lovely sunny day, is it not, and a bit of pedestrian exercise will do me no harm at all. It'll give me an appetite for the fine dinner I'll be enjoying in the next lock-up tonight. But I might get to feeling a bit lonely walking all by meself.'

'You won't be lonely, Sean, I'll be walking beside you.' Tom smiled.

The small procession set off at a leisurely pace and were turning into the long street leading south from the central crossroads when they were accosted by the shabbily clad, rat-featured pawnbroker, Judas Benton.

'Might I have a private word with you, Master Potts? I'll not detain you more than a few seconds.'

The two men walked a little distance from the cart and Benton asked, 'Have I offended you, Master Potts? Do you think me to be an untrustworthy fellow?'

Tom stared in puzzlement. 'Why do you ask me such a question, Master Benton?'

The other man kneaded his hands together as if he were washing them. 'Well, the day before yesterday I visited with my cousin, Ephraim Billings, who has a pawn shop in Worcester. We do a deal of business between us.'

'So?' Tom was still puzzled.

'Well, we were going through his stock, and much to my surprise I found this article there.'

He pulled a silver hunter watch from his pocket and held it up dangling from its chain in front of Tom's eyes.

The watch slowly turned to display the ornate etching on its case and Tom gasped in shock.

Judas Benton's fanged teeth showed in a satisfied snarl. 'It's your father's watch, I believe, Master Potts. Which you've pawned with me before, have you not?'

'Indeed I have, Master Benton.' Tom nodded, his heart thudding with excitement.

'Then why did you not deposit it with me this time? Have I not always been fair and honest in my dealings with you?'

'Because it was bludged from me in the Leggers' shanty town on the Tardebigge canal on the night of Saturday the seventh day of this month.'

Benton's features creased in alarm. 'I didn't know that this was bludged from you, Master Potts! My cousin can verify that yesterday I paid the ticket money and the interest on it to redeem it from him. I hope that I'm not going to lose my money over this?'

'Of course not.' Tom shook his head impatiently. 'I shall repay you in full, Master Benton. But what did your cousin tell you about whoever pawned it?'

'Only that it was a woman, and she brought it to him on Thursday last.'

'What about her? What was her name? What address did she give?' Tom fired questions. 'For your cousin's good, Master Benton, you'd best tell me whatever you can of her.'

Benton's manner became cringingly apologetic. 'There are many men in my line of business who don't press for names and addresses, Master Potts. I regret to say that my cousin is not so careful in his dealings as I am. He doesn't keep his books in such strictly detailed order as I do. And you'll appreciate, I'm sure, that many people who come to pawn their goods don't give their proper names and addresses anyway.'

'Well what can you tell me about her?' Tom pressed relentlessly. 'What did she look like? How old was she? Had she the speech of a gentlewoman or a scullery maid?'

'He told me that she was a youngish, rough-looking drab, and had the Irish brogue in her speech. In fact, now I come to think of it, I remember he said that she told him her name was Bridie Quinn, and the watch was given her by a gentleman as payment for the comfort she'd given him.' Benton's voice trailed off haltingly and his eyes were wary as he waited for Tom's reaction to that final sentence.

Tom smiled grimly. 'Let me assure you, Master Benton, that I am not that gentleman.'

'The thought never entered my mind, Master Potts, I swear to

you on my honour!' the other man insisted emphatically, and proffered the watch. 'Here you are, Master Potts. Take your watch back,
and settle the debt with me at your own convenience. Of course
there will be no further interest on the advance chargeable to your
good self, and there's no great hurry for you to settle our account.
I know that I can have full confidence in you as to the repayment
of the debt.'

Tom was thinking hard about what he had heard. From the
description of her the woman could well be the missing Tessy. But
could it be she who had bludged him? Or could she in her turn
have stolen the watch from the bludger?

The words of the landlord of the Cherry Tree tavern came back
to him, about Tessy running away having stolen Jacky Whittaker's
possessions.

'Is that what happened?' Tom considered. 'Did Jacky Whittaker
bludge me, and Tessy stole my watch from him with the rest of his
things? Is Whittaker the bludger?'

'Take the watch, Master Potts, I insist!' Benton urged and pressed
the timepiece into Tom's hand. 'I wish you a good day and a safe
journey.'

He hurried away so quickly that Tom could only call after him.
'Many thanks, Master Benton. I'll settle with you as soon as
possible.'

When Tom rejoined his companions George Jolly asked him curiously, 'I saw that shylock bugger showing you that watch. Has he
just sold it to you?'

'Why do you ask me that?' Tom queried.

'Well, if you remember, I got burgled by them bloody Rippling
Boys last year didn't I? And one of the things I lost was a timepiece.'

Tom took the watch from his pocket and showed it to the carrier.
'It's not yours, Master Jolly, I do assure you. It was left to me by
my father.'

'Oh, you had to pop it, did you, to get a few o' the readies?'
Jolly grinned sarcastically. 'Empty pockets! That's the trouble o'
being such an upright and law-abiding constable, aren't it?'

'It certainly is, Master Jolly,' Tom agreed ironically. 'Now let's
get on our way.'

The boundary with Bromsgrove Parish ran through the tiny hamlet
of Finstal, a mile to the west of the Tardebigge canal wharves, and
as Tom walked down the slope leading past the Plymouth Arms
and the Cherry Tree tavern a nervous tension gripped him.

'If we run into Jacky Whittaker now, what shall I do? Will I place him under arrest and take him in for questioning on suspicion of bludging me? What if he puts up a struggle? They say that he's a very tough customer. A savage, vicious brawler.'

He felt his mouth drying and his throat tightening at the prospect of a violent confrontation with a man of such formidable reputation.

The cart creaked past the Plymouth Arms, the entrance gates of the New Wharf, a row of cottages, a couple of single cottages, and finally the Cherry Tree tavern, and although there were many sounds of voices no one was met with on the roadway.

As the Cherry Tree receded in the distance Tom could not restrain a heartfelt sigh of relief, followed immediately by a burning sense of shame at his own self-perceived cowardliness.

'Dear God! I'm not worthy to be known as my father's son! He was a brave man who stood his ground against any odds. While I tremble with fear at any prospect of trouble. Shame on me for being such a coward!'

TWENTY-NINE

In the extensive walled yard at the rear of the Cherry Tree excited men, women and children were clustered around a yard-deep, plank-lined, broad-squared pit from which the ground sloped sharply upwards to form a natural amphitheatre. In one corner of this pit shrilly squeaking rats were packed together in a heap of squirming terror, frantically clawing over each other's bodies in vain efforts to escape from the attack of a small terrier dog.

The dog burrowed its nose into the heap and emerged with a squealing rat between its fangs, which it shook fiercely as blood spurted to splash across planking already strewn with the wriggling, twitching bodies of rats.

'Let it drop, Tinker! Let the bugger drop!' Eugene Sinclair bawled angrily.

Standing by his side Martin Cooke frowned anxiously and shouted to the acting timekeeper and referee, landlord Terry Wilkes.

'Time's up, is it not?'

'No it aren't, Master Cooke, there's twenty seconds to go.'

'Drop it, Tinker! Goddamn and blast you! Drop it!' Sinclair bellowed and hurled his riding whip at the terrier.

The animal tossed the rat aside and again burrowed its head into the heap of rats to pull out seconds later with yet another rat between its teeth.

'Five, four, three, two, one! Time's up!' Wilkes rang the brass bell he carried. 'Time's up!'

A man jumped down into the ring and snatched up the barking, struggling terrier into his arms.

Martin Cooke's face tensed unhappily as he counted the bloodied and broken rats on the floor.

Eugene Sinclair crowed exultantly as he made the count. 'Eleven! Well done, Tinker! There now, Cooke, did I not tell you that my little dog was a champion ratter! You were foolish to bet so much money against him.'

Cooke shook his head and blurted desperately, 'Your dog hasn't made the full sum of kills. There are three of those rats still living!'

Sinclair smiled confidently. 'Then I call upon the referee to give his judgement on them. Are you willing to accept his verdict?'

Martin Cooke hesitated momentarily, then grudgingly accepted. 'Very well. Master Wilkes verdict will be acceptable to me.'

The landlord jumped down into the pit and picked up the disputed bloody-furred bodies one by one, feeling them with his fingers, examining them closely.

After a pause he declared, 'There's this 'un here still got life in it. These other two am dead. The twitching is just the last muscle action. There's no life left in 'um.'

'Then that makes a score of ten within one and a half minutes.' Sinclair laughed triumphantly. 'I've won our wager, have I not, Master Cooke?'

'Yes.' Cooke nodded glumly.

Sinclair turned to the onlookers and shouted boastfully, 'Did I not say that my little Tinker is the finest ratter in the parish, bar none? Here's the proof of it.'

'Best ratter in the parish? You'm having a laugh, aren't you, my fine gennulman?' Jacky Whittaker pushed through the crowd scoffing derisively. 'Your dog's a bloody duffer at killing.'

'Then put your own dog up against mine, whatever your name is,' Sinclair challenged.

'My dog!' the half-drunk Whittaker laughed. 'I aren't got no need for a dog. I'm Jacky Whittaker, I am; and I do me own killings of rats. I'm the champion ratter o' the fuckin' parish, I am. You ask anybody hereabouts if that aren't so.'

Shouts of assent sounded from the onlookers.

Sinclair instantly scented an opportunity for further profit and challenged, 'Then make a match of it against my dog, Whittaker. London Rat Pit Rules to apply, and Master Wilkes here to be the timekeeper, referee and final judge. Each contestant to have five separate minute runs in turn at the rats, and only dead ones to count as scored. Any that still have life in them being disqualified. But you can only use your mouth and not take any rats into your hands, or use any other part of your body other than your teeth to kill them with.'

He turned and addressed the onlookers, 'I'll take bets at even odds on this match from anyone here. Master Wilkes to act as stake-holder.'

'If you rates that fuckin' useless mongrel so high, then give odds against me. Or haven't you got that much faith in your prize puppy dog?' Whittaker challenged in his turn.

Sinclair grinned confidently. 'Alright. To demonstrate my faith in my dog I'm prepared to give odds of two to one against you. So, have you got money to back yourself with? Or are you merely a blowhard?'

Whittaker didn't hesitate. 'Oh yes, I've got money alright. I'll back meself for three sovs.'

He held the gold coins high for all to see, then handed them to Terry Wilkes, who bit hard on them and declared, 'These sovereigns am true coin of the realm. Master Whittaker is a true sportsman. Is there anybody else who wants to make a wager?'

The onlookers cheered vociferously and now the Leggers amongst them clamoured eagerly around Wilkes.

'I'll lay a shilling on Jacky.'

'Here's a florin on Jacky.'

'Fuck the expense, here's a half-sov on Jacky.'

'Hold on, hold on, damn your eyes!' Wilkes protested angrily. 'Give me a chance to write the bets down, will you?'

As more and more money was bet on Whittaker, Sinclair tauntingly baited Martin Cooke.

'Why are you not betting on your Legger, Cooke? I'm giving exceptionally generous odds. Is your appetite for gaming deserting you? Have you perhaps decided that you've already lost too much through your poor judgement of a dog?'

Cooke's eyes hardened with resentment and after a momentary hesitation he took the bait. 'I'll lay fifty guineas on Whittaker. Or is that too heavy for you to accept, since you're giving such generous odds?'

Sinclair smiled with satisfaction. 'Too heavy for me? I think not, Cooke. I was expecting a gentleman of your gaming calibre to wager more than such a paltry sum. Particularly since you are already in so deep.'

Cooke's eyes glinted with resentful anger and, unable to restrain himself, he spat out, 'Then make it two hundred guineas, sir. Or is that still too paltry a sum for you?'

Sinclair smiled and bowed. 'I'm more than happy to accept the wager, sir; and of course no money will be passed on through Wilkes. After all, we are both gentlemen, are we not, and can settle the final reckoning between us at some mutually satisfactory time.'

The Bromsgrove constable and cart had been waiting for the Redditch party at the parish boundary and the handover of the vagrant family was quickly made.

'So long now, Master Potts. No doubt we'll be meeting again and renewing our cordial relationship.' Sean Macafferty grinned and held out his hand.

'No doubt we will, Master Macafferty,' Tom conceded wryly, and shook the other man's hand in farewell.

Tom took his seat by the side of George Jolly and the cart creaked slowly back toward Redditch.

When the Cherry Tree tavern came into view tense apprehension again gripped Tom, but this time he grimly refused to surrender to it, and vowed silently, 'I'll not shame your name this time, Father.'

Tom knew that in law he could demand assistance from any bystanders to make an arrest, and that if those bystanders refused to aid him, they were subject to being punished by fines and imprisonment.

'I'll call on Jolly to help me to arrest Whittaker,' he decided, and told his companion, 'You may have a prisoner to carry to Redditch, Master Jolly. I'll begin the search for him at the Cherry Tree. I'll make sure that you get paid for your assistance to me in bringing him back to the lock-up.'

'Who might he be?' the carrier asked.

'The man who I think bludged me on the Saturday before last.'

'What's his name?' Jolly frowned in concern.

'Jacky Whittaker.'

'Oh no!' Jolly refused emphatically. 'Look, Master Potts, I'm not a coward, but tackling the likes of Whittaker and his Legging mates is too much to ask from me. What's going to happen to my family if I'm crippled or kicked to death by those bastards; or if

I'm put in jail for not aiding you? All my missus and kids will ever get from the Parish is a few pence of relief, or a ticket to the Poorhouse.'

The refusal put Tom into a quandary.

'You don't have to face Whittaker now,' a voice whispered persuasively in his mind. 'Why risk your neck when you've no actual proof that he did bludge you? Be sensible. Just stay on the cart and ride on through. If later on you get absolute proof that Whittaker did bludge you, then you can summon the Yeomanry to help you arrest him. Do it the easy way, and keep yourself safe. Be sensible and go straight back to Redditch.'

The temptation to heed that persuasive voice was overwhelming, and for a few moments Tom wavered. Then the sharp visual images of two faces arose in his mind. The faces of his father, and Amy Danks.

'How can I shame my father's memory and live with myself, or expect Amy ever to love and respect me, if I play the coward now?'

He drew several long deep breaths, struggling to gather courage, to steel himself for whatever might lie ahead. But the prospect of a woman and children being left bereft of a husband and father through Tom's own actions was too much for him to even contemplate. So he told the carrier, 'It's alright, Master Jolly. I'm not going to call upon you for any assistance. You may drop me off here, and go on back to Redditch; and don't worry because no matter what might happen to me, no one will ever find out that you knew of my intentions. You can say that I merely asked you to drop me off here.'

The other man gusted a loud sigh of relief, and halted the cart. Then frowned worriedly, and urged, 'Why don't you come back to Redditch wi' me, and then if you still wants to go after Whittaker get the magistrates to swear in some Special Constables, or call out some of the Yeomanry to help you arrest the bugger.'

Again Tom was sorely tempted to take that advice, but still his own stubborn refusal to surrender to his self-perceived cowardice asserted its dominance.

'You go on now, Master Jolly. I'll be perfectly alright. I'm sure of that.'

He slapped the horse's rump and set it into motion, then stood at the roadside gazing longingly after the cart, wishing with all his heart that he was still seated upon it. He summoned his resolve and headed towards the Cherry Tree tavern, and as he neared the building heard the tumult of excited voices sounding from its rear yard.

A youth carrying a covered basket came running from the wharf towards the tavern. As he neared him Tom shouted, 'What's going on in the yard?'

'A ratting match atween Jacky Whittaker and a gennulman's dog,' the youth panted excitedly. 'I been sent to fetch these fresh rats because they both been killing summat amazing like. It's the best match I'se ever seen in me life!'

Tom followed the youth through the rear gate of the yard and halted to study the scene before him, his exceptional height giving him an unobstructed view over the heads of the noisy crowd. He noted firstly Eugene Sinclair and Martin Cooke standing together on the edge of the pit. Next he saw Jacky Whittaker, stripped to the waist and surrounded by his gang, one of whom was using a piece of rag to clean and staunch the blood seeping from the numerous rat bites on Whittaker's face, neck and torso.

Across the pit from Whittaker two men were tending to the yapping struggling terrier, which was also bleeding from many bites. In the pit itself Terry Wilkes was carefully examining the dead and wounded rats strewn across the plank flooring. While in one corner a much diminished heap of small furry bodies still writhed and squeaked in shrill terror.

The crowd made way for the basket-carrying youth to get to the pit side, and he emptied his basket on to the floor of the pit.

The crowd cheered resoundingly as the falling rats thumped down, scurrying about in terror, their shrill squeaking sounding strangely like the cries of new-born children. The spectators lining the pit top crouched to slam their fists in rhythmic unison against its wooden walling, shouting, 'Run! Run! Run! Run!'

The fresh rats swarmed to the existing heap, trying to burrow deep into its shelter, clawing desperately to gain entrance into its promised haven.

'Shurrup! Shurrup!' Terry Wilkes bellowed as he finished his task and rose to his feet. 'The count for Tinker on his fifth and final run is six dead, and four still with life in 'um. That makes the total of fifty-one dead 'uns scored so far for Master Sinclair's dog. Hand me the bag.'

A blood-dripping sack bag already heavy with dead and dying rats was passed to him, and he collected the latest casualties and dumped them into the sack. Then clambered out of the pit and announced, 'It's Jacky Whittaker's turn for his final run now. So when you're ready, Jacky, you can get stuck into them fresh buggers.' He grinned broadly. 'They've still got a bit o' shit on 'um because we aren't had time to give 'um a wash. But I know that you won't mind the taste of it.'

'O' course he won't,' a wag shouted. 'He's been eating shit all his life!'

Whittaker glowered at the man, and threatened. 'When I gets done wi' you, Simmy Bennett, you won't be able to eat any shit at all, and not even take a sup o' piss.'

Bennett's features creased in alarm and he spluttered, 'There's no call for that, Jacky. I was only having a laugh wi' you. I didn't mean nothing by it.'

Uncertain as to his best course of action Tom moved slowly around the top of the slope behind the crowd, then came to a halt as his shocked gaze fell upon two young women positioned midway down the opposite slope.

Dressed in their Sunday bonnets and fineries, Amy Danks and Maisie Lock stood arm in arm, faces glowing with excitement, all their attention centred on the pit below.

The crowd roared as Jacky Whittaker allowed his wrists to be secured behind his back by a strip of canvas and then jumped down into the pit.

'Your score is thirty-nine dead 'uns, Jacky,' Terry Wilkes shouted. 'You needs to kill a baker's dozen to win the match.'

Some of the crowd chanted, 'Thirteen! Thirteen! Thirteen! Unlucky! Unlucky! Unlucky!'

Others chorused encouragement to their champion.

'Easy! Easy! Easy! Jacky can do it! Easy! Easy! Easy!'

A supporter held a bottle of gin to Whittaker's lips and he took several swigs of the spirit, swilling it around his mouth and spitting it out on to the heap of rats, bellowing, 'This 'ull make the buggers taste a bit sweeter!'

His supporters laughed and applauded uproariously.

Whittaker went down on to his knees in front of the heaped rats and Wilkes shouted, 'Mind you wait for the bell, Jacky.'

'Then fuckin' ring it, 'ull you!' Whittaker bawled.

'Stand by!' Wilkes lifted the bell and counted. 'Five, four, three, two, one. Time!'

The bell-clapper clanged, the crowd roared, Whittaker's face plunged into the writhing heap of fur and his mouth clamped on a squealing rat. With a jerk of his head he hurled the creature on to the floor at the side of his knee, bent sideways to clamp its skull between his teeth and savagely crunch and crush the thin bones. The entire sequence unfolded with an amazing rapidity.

Rat after rat turned in desperate terror to fight. Biting savagely, burying their razor sharp teeth into the man's face, neck, torso, at times two, three, four furry bodies hanging simultaneously from Whittaker's bleeding flesh. Rat after rat met its bloody death.

The crowd became a seething, heaving, howling, screaming entity.

From deep within Tom's being the tribal instinct of humankind kindled. An atavistic excitement irresistibly took hold of him as he watched this deadly age-old battle between man and vermin, and without conscious volition he started shouting in concert with the crowd, shouting for Whittaker to assert man's ordained dominance over all other life forms on this earth.

The bell rang, and it took the combined efforts of two strong men to drag the kill-crazed Jacky Whittaker back from the slaughter ground, and to force the release of a skull-crushed rat from between his clenched teeth.

'Order! Order! Let's have some order here! Order! Let's have order!' Terry Wilkes' repeated stentorian commands took effect and the raving crowd gradually quietened.

Wilkes got down into the pit and one by one picked up the newly dead rats, holding the limp, bloody furred bodies aloft, then tossing them aside as he shouted the count. 'One. Two. Three. Four.'

The crowd cheered at each number.

'Seven. Eight. Nine!'

Tom could not stop himself from joining in their plaudits, which became a frenzied roaring as the count reached its final tally and Wilkes announced, 'Ten. Eleven. Twelllvvve! That makes a total score of fifty-one dead 'uns. Jacky Whittaker draws the match!'

Eugene Sinclair smiled ruefully. 'By God, Cooke, that ratting beast of yours has cost me a pretty penny in winnings.'

Cooke's tension was evident in his eyes. 'It was a damned close run, Sinclair.'

'Master Wilkes?' Sinclair shouted.

'Yes, sir.'

The man came to him and Sinclair handed him a purse heavy with coin.

'Pay out my bets, if you please, Master Wilkes. I'll settle with you afterwards.'

'Very well, sir.'

Sinclair turned back to Martin Cooke. 'Our last wager is void, of course, Cooke. As for our previous wagers, I believe they now total somewhere around six hundred guineas. Of course, since we are both gentlemen I am confident that you will make tally and payment to me in the very near future.'

'Of course,' Cooke assented. His smile resembled more of a grimace of despair.

Sinclair frowned across the pit to where the bloodied, sweating Jacky Whittaker was standing swigging from a bottle of gin, glorying in the plaudits of his supporters.

'Do you wield any influence, or have any real degree of control over that animal across there, Cooke?'

A wary glint entered Cooke's eyes, but he only shrugged carelessly. 'As much influence or control as any casual employer of such a brute could wield, I suppose.'

The crowd were dispersing, and still at the top of the slope Tom was beset with conflicting urges, the strongest of which was to go across and speak to Amy Danks. The other two urges battling for dominance were bravery and cowardice. One to attempt to arrest Jacky Whittaker without further delay, the other to make no attempt to arrest Jacky Whittaker and to leave this place without further delay.

He saw Eugene Sinclair go to the two young women. Amy greeted the man with a radiant smile, linked arms with him and the trio went back up the slope and into the tavern.

Dejection created a tight knot in Tom's stomach. 'I've really lost her, haven't I? She's found herself another sweetheart.'

Next he saw Jacky Whittaker leave his gang of supporters and go to talk with Martin Cooke.

Tom drew a long deep breath, and rallied his determination. 'I'll take Whittaker in now while he's with Martin Cooke. If he and his mates kick up then Cooke will certainly give me aid. He's a gentleman and knows where his duty lies.'

Shouldering his staff like a musket Tom crossed the rapidly emptying slopes to confront Whittaker, inwardly marvelling at how calmly resolute he was feeling now that the die had been cast.

He confronted the man and told him in a firm voice, 'Jacky Whittaker, I'm taking you into my custody, in the King's name!'

Whittaker gaped in astonishment. 'What the fuck for? What's I done?'

Martin Cooke also was taken aback with surprise. 'What's this about, Master Potts?'

'I've good reason to believe that Whittaker is the man who struck me down from behind and robbed me in the Leggers' settlement during the evening of Saturday the seventh day of this present month.'

'I did no such thing!' Whittaker bellowed in denial. 'I never laid a fuckin' finger on you! Youse got the wrong bloke!'

'Hold your tongue!' Tom snapped curtly. 'You'll have your chance to speak when I bring you before the magistrates. I'm arresting you in the King's name, Whittaker, so you'd best come quietly.'

Martin Cooke's brow was deeply furrowed, and there was a gleam of dismay in his eyes.

'I'll be fucked if I'll come quiet, you long streak o' piss!' Whittaker bawled in furious anger. 'How many times must I tell you that it warn't me who fuckin' bludged you that night! It warn't me!'

Cooke suddenly moved to intervene, shouting harshly, 'Hold your tongue, damn you, Whittaker!'

The man quietened, but still hissed curses and denials beneath his breath.

'Hear me for a moment, I beg of you, Master Potts,' Cooke requested. 'Would you please confirm that we are talking of the evening of Saturday the seventh day of this month?'

'Indeed we are, Master Cooke.' A wild elation was coursing through Tom as he realized that all fear had left him. His entire being was centred on achieving one single objective: the successful arrest of Jacky Whittaker.

'Are you sure of this particular date?' Cooke pressed.

'Yes, Master Cooke. I'm completely sure! I would stake my own life on it!' Tom declared positively.

The other man shook his head, and with apparent regret told Tom, 'Well, that being the case, Master Potts, I have to tell you that it definitely could not be Whittaker who robbed you. Damned foul rogue he might well be, but on that particular day he was away from here in my company from morning until late at night. Most of the evening we spent journeying along the towpath from the Diglis Basin at Worcester and didn't arrive back at the New Wharf until long past midnight.'

'He was with you?' Surprise struck Tom, to be overlaid instantly by a mixture of puzzlement and suspicion. 'Can you be absolutely sure of the date?'

'Yes, of course.' Cooke nodded, then demanded indignantly, 'Do you doubt my word, Master Potts? What reason could I possibly have to lie?'

Tom paused to choose his words carefully, before stating quietly, 'I do not question your probity, Master Cooke. But I most certainly doubt the accuracy of your recollection. If you will think again,

I'm sure that you will recall that on that particular evening I met with yourself and your cousin, Master Wynne, in the paddock beyond the wharf yard. We stood together and watched Master Wynne and his man, Shanko, wrestle a cow to the ground and remove the iron plates from its hooves. Come now, Master Cooke. Think on what I tell you. Surely you must remember it now?'

They stared with silent challenge into each other's eyes, and as the seconds passed Tom's determination became iron-set that no matter what troubles might come out of his present course of action, he would not deviate from it by a single iota.

It was Martin Cooke who gave way. He reddened and blurted out in chagrin, 'Goddamn, my memory has become like a sieve these last few months! You have the right of it, Master Potts. I do now recollect our meeting on that evening. I must beg your pardon for any confusion I may have caused. It was totally unintentional, I do assure you.'

'It's of no matter, sir.' Tom bowed. 'But now, with your leave, I shall take this man into custody for further questioning.'

'You'm taking me nowhere!' Whittaker growled threateningly. 'It warn't me that bludged you! I warn't nowhere near the shanties that night.'

Tom measured the distance between himself and the other man, shifted his grip on the staff and prepared to swing it.

Cooke hastily intervened. 'Go quietly with the constable, Whittaker. You'll only be making things worse for yourself if you don't.'

Whittaker glared sullenly at Cooke, who hardened his tone to a harsh command.

'Do as I say. Go quietly with the constable, or I'll call my own men in to aid him.'

For a brief while it seemed that Whittaker would defy Cooke. But finally he shrugged, and told Tom, 'Alright, I'll come quiet with you. But on one condition.'

'And what's that?' Tom asked.

'That I'll not be shackled and dragged along like some slave. Instead I'll walk side by side with you like a freeborn Englishman.'

'That's satisfactory to me,' Tom agreed. 'So now say goodbye to your friends, and we'll be on our way. Walking side by side.'

There were tense moments as Whittaker went to say farewell to his gang, who glowered at Tom, shouting foul epithets and seeming eager to prevent the arrest. But Whittaker returned to him and the pair of them walked away from the rear of the yard side by side.

As they passed by the tavern windows the sounds of loud enjoyment, ribald laughter and bawdy singing came clearly to Tom's
ears, and anguish lanced through him as he thought of Amy and
Eugene Sinclair making merry together within those dingy walls.

'Dear God,' he begged silently. 'Don't let any harm come to
Amy. Please protect her, and don't let that man bring on her any
sadness or shame.'

They journeyed in silence until the outlying buildings of Redditch
came into view and Whittaker suddenly came to a halt, complaining
aggrievedly, 'You'm wrong, you know! It warn't me that bludged
you. Just what makes you so sure it was me?'

Tom's heartbeat quickened, adrenaline pulsing through him as
he nervously readied himself for trouble. Striving to keep his voice
level and his manner calm and confident, he answered, 'I've good
reason to believe so, Whittaker. But the magistrates will decide on
the evidence.'

'What evidence?' Whittaker scowled.

'You'll hear it on Tuesday when you come up before the bench.
And don't be stupid enough to try to escape now, because should
you manage to get away from me, there'll be a hue and cry called.
You'll be hunted down like a mad dog.'

Whittaker's stained, broken teeth bared in a savage grin. 'By
fuck, but you'm a windy bugger! I can see that you'm shaking in
your boots. But you've no call to be feared because I aren't going
to bust your head and run off. So let's get on, shall we? I'm looking
forward to having a nice lie down, and enjoying a smoke and a
flagon o' gin in the peace and comfort o' me own little cell.'

He patted his pockets, causing the coins within them to chink
together, and winked slyly. 'I takes it that you'll not object to sending
out for a drink and smoke for me, Constable. Afore his trial it's a
prisoner's right if he's got the rhino to be able to buy himself all
the pongo and pipes of bacca that he wants.'

'Of course it is, and I'll make sure that you get whatever you
want in that way,' Tom confirmed readily, filled with relief that he
was not going to have to fight with this formidable opponent.

'Let's make haste then,' Whittaker chuckled genially. 'I'm getting
bloody thirsty.'

It was only much later during the dark silent hours of his sleepless
night that Tom's troubled thoughts of Amy Danks were intruded
upon by the memory of Martin Cooke's intervention.

Tom concentrated hard, marshalling the verbal and visual

memories of what had occurred during those moments. Mentally examining them over and over again, and ultimately concluding, 'He deliberately lied!'

At first Tom was reluctant to accept his own conclusion.

'No! I must be mistaken. Martin Cooke is a gentleman. An honourable man. In fact it can justifiably be said that I owe him my very life. How can I believe that he would deliberately lie to protect scum like Whittaker?'

But struggle though he might to reject the unwelcome conclusion, slowly and inexorably it strengthened and took hold as total conviction. Bringing with it an inescapable companion: suspicion.

'Why did he lie? Why should he need to protect Jacky Whittaker?'

THIRTY

Monday 23rd April

'We rode back in a carriage and pair, just like real Ladies. And we was as drunk as bloody Lords as well, wasn't we, Amy?' Maisie Lock sought confirmation from her friend. 'And we didn't have to spend a ha-penny. Amy's new sweet-heart paid for everything. He's a real gentleman, so he is. It's plain to see that he's mad in love with her.'

Across the back-parlour breakfast table Amy Danks preened with satisfaction, but mock-scolded, 'Oh do give over, will you, Maisie. How many times must I tell you that Master Sinclair isn't my sweet-heart? We're just friends, that's all.'

'Well now, my girl.' Tommy Fowkes gave his avuncular smile. 'Judging from the attentions that Master Sinclair is paying you – and there aren't nothing hole in the corner about 'um – I should say that he's got honourable intentions towards you.'

'Don't talk so sarft, Pa.' Lily Fowkes could not restrain a jealousy-fuelled outburst. 'How can a fine high-born gentleman like Master Sinclair have any honourable intentions towards a low-born pub skivvy? All he wants is to have his wicked way with her. That's plain to see for anyone with a bit of common sense.' She added a final withering comment, 'Which you all seems to be lacking this morning.'

'Who are you calling a low-born skivvy, Lily Fowkes?' Amy challenged indignantly. 'I'll have you know that my family is every bit as well-born as you Fowkes lot. We're good yeomen stock, we are. My Dad is the head keeper to the Earl, and the gentry talks to him like he's an equal, and begs him for advice. Not like they barks at your dad as if he's a dog.'

All three girls began to furiously shout and scream at each other at the tops of their voices.

'Girls! Girls! Just quieten yourselves down, 'ull you?' Tommy Fowkes intervened sharply. But was totally ignored.

'What's going on here?' Mrs Fowkes burst into the room. 'You'm making enough racket to raise the dead! Now shurrup! SHURRUP I say!'

Her strident bellowing brought an instant hush, the girls knowing well that, unlike her husband, the formidable Gertrude Fowkes was more than ready to take a stick to their backs should they defy her commands.

She glared at Amy and growled. 'There's some stuff come for you, but I'm beggared to know if I should give it you now, the way you'm playing up.'

Amy artfully displayed contriteness. 'I'm ever so sorry, Mistress. I shouldn't have got all het up like I did. I'm really sorry. Truly I am. It was only for a minute though.'

'You'd better start behaving like a Lady all the time, my wench. A fine gentleman like Master Sinclair won't marry you else, will he?' The older woman's tone was softer now, and her eyes held a gleam of admiration.

'He won't be marrying me anyway, Mistress.' Amy tried to look sad. 'He's never even hinted at wanting to marry me. Him and me will only ever stay as friends.'

'I don't think that's the case, girl.' Mrs Fowkes chuckled richly, and called out. 'Benjiman, you old shank o' bone! Bring that stuff in here, and shift yourself a bit quick for a change.'

Old Benny the potman entered, the ever-present long dewdrop dangling from his nose.

The girls emitted a unified gasp of shock when they saw the three huge pineapples he carried in his arms.

'Look at this lot!' Mrs Fowkes exclaimed admiringly. 'Wi'out a doubt they been raised in the Earl's hothouse up at the Grange, because there's no bloody pineapples grows outside in these parts in April, or any other bloody month o' the year.'

'Who brought 'um, Mam? They're not really for Amy are they?' Lily Fowkes demanded.

'One of the footmen from the Grange brung 'um, not two minutes since. And he said I was to tell Miss Amy Danks that they'm a token of gratitude from Eugene Sinclair, Esquire, for her honouring him with her company yesterday.'

'Didn't he send any message to me?' Maisie Lock scowled with pique.

'No he bloody well didn't,' Mrs Fowkes snorted disparagingly. 'It's no use you looking as if you'se just swallowed a dog's turd, Maisie Lock. It's always been very plain to those like me with the wisdom to see it that Eugene Sinclair, Esquire, aren't got no eyes for any other woman but our Amy here.'

She beamed at Amy's flushed face and sparkling eyes with a virtually maternal pride. 'And so he should fancy her. She's the prettiest young wench in the whole of this parish. In the whole of the county even. I'll take my oath on it.'

Across the green in the lock-up Tom Potts had been pacing restlessly up and down the central passageway of the cells for more than an hour, furiously debating with himself.

'Shall I go across there? Or shan't I? I want to know that Amy's safe and well. It's nothing more than my obligation as a friend to her family.'

A cynical voice from the depths of his mind immediately challenged that last averment. 'Oh no! That's not the real reason you want to see Amy, is it?'

After a moment's hesitation Tom ruefully admitted, 'No it's not. I want to see her because I love her; and I hate the fact that it looks as if I've lost her to that damned dandy. But if I go to the pub and ask for her she might send me away with a flea in my ear.'

'When am I going to get me breakfast? I'm fuckin' clemmed! Me belly thinks me throat's been cut!' Jacky Whittaker shouted aggrievedly through the open hatch of his cell door.

Tom halted, and exclaimed, 'Oh my God! I'd clean forgotten that the larder's empty!'

'And so am I! And unless you wants to open this bloody door and find me laying here dead of starvation, then you'd best get me some decent grub. It's a prisoner's right to be well fed three times a day, and not on pigs' swill neither.'

Tom could not suppress the sense of relieved satisfaction. Now he had a valid official reason to go across to the Fox and Goose. Tommy Fowkes had a contract with the Vestry to feed prisoners in the lock-up if because of pressing duties the constable was not free to prepare their food.

'What pressing duty do I have to carry out at this very hour?' Tom sought to think of one.

'Thomassss? Thomassss? Where are you?' Widow Potts' angry shrieks echoed from the upper floor. 'Where's my breakfast? Do you intend to starve me to death, you hound of Hell? Come here and face me, I dare you!'

'I do believe that at this moment, discretion is the better part of valour,' Tom decided wryly and, hatless and coatless, fled through the front door.

In the back parlour of the Fox and Goose there was a hubbub of excited speculation as to when and where Eugene Sinclair would ask Amy to marry him.

'I hope you'll be holding your wedding breakfast here, my duck?' Tommy Fowkes was already measuring his potential profit.

'Of course she'll be holding it here,' his wife declared positively. 'After her being like a daughter to us for all these years, it's only right and proper that she does.'

Lily Fowkes' fat red face radiated bitter jealousy, as she sneered, 'Well, her can't hold it in that dirty, poky hole her own family lives in, can her?'

Maisie Lock instantly sprang to her friend's defence. 'Eugene Sinclair, Esquire, won't care if they holds their wedding breakfast in a bloody pigsty, so long as he gets wed to Amy. He told me as much himself only yesterday.' She smiled with steely eyes at Lily, and added sweetly, 'But of course you wouldn't have heard him say that, would you, Lily dear? Seeing as how he didn't invite you to keep company with him, like he begged me and Amy to.'

Before Lily could think of a suitably cutting rejoinder, Old Benny shambled into the room and announced lugubriously, 'The constable's come, and he says it's very urgent.'

'What's very urgent?' Tommy Fowkes frowned.

'I dunno. He never told me,' Benny mumbled over his shoulder as he exited.

'Bugger bloody Potts! Why does he have to come bothering me when I'm at me breakfast?' Fowkes scowled, and began gruntingly to raise his fat bulk.

'No, Master, you sit and finish your breakfast. I'll go and see what he wants.' Amy sprang to her feet and ran out.

'There she goes again,' Lily accused angrily. 'Playing fast and loose wi' that poor Tom Potts' affections! I do believe that she'll not be satisfied until every pair o' britches in the parish is chasing after her. Shame on her!'

'And I do believe that you'll not be satisfied until you manage to get just any pair o' britches chasing after you, Lily dear. But that'll be a long time coming, won't it? If ever!' Maisie Lock smiled spitefully.

'Oh, Tom, why aren't you dressed?' Amy chided angrily as she entered the passageway and came to stand, frowning, directly in front of him. 'You haven't shaved, or even combed your hair, have you? No wonder folks make mock of you like they do.'

The familiar churning of his stomach whenever he met this girl assailed Tom, and he could only mumble miserably, 'It was urgent that I came immediately, Amy.'

'Well what is it you want?' she snapped.

'I need two breakfasts sent over to the lock-up. One for a prisoner, the other for my mother. I need to carry out an urgent duty and don't have time to prepare any food for them both.'

'Alright, I'll see to it right away.' She nodded, and then hesitated, staring at him searchingly. Despite her annoyance at his unkempt appearance she could not help but feel a deep concern for his obvious unhappiness. 'Are you alright, Tom? Is there something else that you might want to say to me?'

In his mind impassioned words kindled and fired. He wanted desperately to tell her how much he loved her. To beg her to wait for him until his fortunes bettered and he could offer her marriage and financial security. Once, twice, three times the words formed on his tongue, but each time the ever-present harsh judge that dwelt in the depths of his mind forbade him to voice these passionate pleas.

'You would bring her down with you to spend a lifetime of poverty, distress, hardship and ruin. You cannot do such a wicked thing to someone whom you profess to love so dearly.'

'Well? Is there something you want to say to me?' she demanded.

He could only shake his head and murmur despondently, 'No, Amy. Not at this time. I'll bid you a good day.'

He turned from her and with bent head and slouched shoulders walked quickly out of the front door.

Amy followed to stand in the doorway and with troubled eyes watch his tall lanky figure until it disappeared into the lock-up. She shook her head as her emotions swirled confusedly and asked herself over and over again: 'Who is it that I truly want? Who is it?'

THIRTY-ONE

I t was mid-morning and Tom, now clothed and shaven, stood in front of Joseph Blackwell's study desk waiting for his seated employer's reaction to what Tom had reported.

Chin on his steepled forefingers, the older man mused silently for a time, then began to speak in measured tones.

'An unknown Irishwoman pawns your father's watch in Worcester. This Irishwoman's physical description fits that of a trollop who dwelt among the Leggers of the Tardebigge Tunnel until, it is claimed, she absconded with the belongings of the man known as Jacky Whittaker. You conclude that among those belongings was your father's watch. You take this as the proof therefore that Whittaker is the man who assaulted and robbed you during the evening of Saturday the seventh of April, and you propose to bring him before the magistrates on this charge.'

Blackwell shook his head bemusedly. 'I cannot believe that I'm hearing this, Master Potts. How can you possibly delude yourself into believing that my Lord Aston will accept this evidence?'

'There's something else, sir,' Tom persisted doggedly. 'I don't know for what reason he did so, but I also believe that Martin Cooke attempted to give Jacky Whittaker a false alibi for the evening in question.'

'Pray do tell me about that. I'm sure that it will fully enlighten me,' Blackwell invited in a sarcastic tone.

Tom related the incident, and observed to finish, 'I strongly suspect that Cooke has ulterior motivations for trying to protect Whittaker.'

Blackwell expelled a derisive snort. 'Suspicion, no matter how strong, is not proof!'

'I know that, sir,' Tom conceded. 'But I'm confident that given time I can obtain the proof of what I suspect.'

'Unfortunately the tally of your suspicions grows ever lengthier by the day; and your obtaining any proof appears to be ever more unlikely.' Blackwell emitted a dry chuckle. 'According to you there are an abundance of murders, robberies and ulterior motivations, but you've yet to discover any tangible evidence concerning them.'

'Oh come now, sir!' Tom protested indignantly. 'There is most certainly tangible evidence of my being assaulted and robbed.'

'But no tangible evidence as to the identity of the perpetrator,' Blackwell riposted. 'Just as there is no evidence which can be accepted by a court as to whether Rose Brent and Irish Joe were dead before they were dropped into the canal.'

'No!' Tom accepted reluctantly.

Blackwell frowned sternly, and his tone brooked no protest. But his eyes held warmth. 'You have acted too hastily, Master Potts, and consequently will have to release Whittaker this very hour.'

Tom nodded glumly. 'Very well, sir.'

'Don't be concerned about any complaint of unlawful arrest being levied against you.' The hint of a smile twitched Blackwell's thin, pallid lips. 'I shall ensure that none will get a hearing from anyone in authority.'

'I much appreciate your assurance on that score, sir,' Tom thanked him stiffly.

'I trust that you do.' Blackwell's manner became almost jocular. 'Now go about your normal duties, Constable. Should you have any time to spare from them, I would suggest that you continue to spend it in pursuing any lines of enquiry which might result in tangible evidence of murder, robbery and ulterior motivation.'

Blackwell paused, then stated with deliberate emphasis, 'Bring me true quality of such evidence, Constable Potts, and I will not hesitate in acting upon it. Now I bid you good day, and good hunting!'

Tom left the Red House vowing determinedly to himself: 'It's plain that Blackwell accepts that I'm right in my suspicions of murder. I'll get the evidence for it. Come hell or high water, I'll get it!'

Tom unlocked the cell door and told Jacky Whittaker, 'You're free to go.'

'Letting me out, am you? Well, I'm real disappointed, I am. I was looking forwards to seeing you make a cunt of yourself in front of the magistrates,' Whittaker jeered.

As he finished speaking Widow Potts' strident shriek sounded from upstairs.

'Thomassss! Is that you back again, you unnatural whelp? You grievous excuse for a son! Get up here this instant. My commode's overflowing and stinking the place out. Why couldn't you empty it before you went gallivanting off doing God only knows what?'

Whittaker roared with delighted laughter and bellowed, 'Emptying women's shit buckets! That's all you'm good for, aren't it, Potts? Wait 'til I tells me mates that your mam makes you empty her shit bucket and wipe her arse for her. You should have been born a wench, you bloody great nancy-boy!'

The sneering gibe struck home, but Tom kept his face impassive and, pointing towards the front entrance, said quietly, 'Just go now, Whittaker. You and I will no doubt have dealings with each other again.'

'Oh yes we shall.' Whittaker's tone became threatening. 'Because I'm going to lay a complaint before the magistrates that you've unlawfully locked up an innocent man. We'll see what they has to say about that, shan't we?'

'Indeed we shall.' Tom nodded and forced himself to smile pleasantly. 'Now are you going, Master Whittaker? Or do you choose to remain here on a voluntary basis, and to pay the parish for your bed and board?'

'Thomasssss! Thomassss! Get up here, will you? Dear God, did ever another poor pitiful creature in this world suffer as I am suffering?'

Tom shuddered inwardly as the shrieking dinned in his ears.

Whittaker hastily pushed past Tom and hurried out of the lock-up, shouting back over his shoulder as he went, 'I'm off out of here, nancy-boy. I can't stand her rattle for another second. If I was you I'd throttle the old cow.'

'If only you would, Whittaker.' Tom sighed longingly, and was about to make his reluctant way up to his mother's room, when the bells summoned him to the front entrance.

He was surprised to find Chalky White standing there. 'What brings you here, Chalky?'

'Well, that's a fine welcome!' White chuckled wryly.

'Oh, forgive me! It's only my surprise at seeing you,' Tom hastened to apologize. 'But it's very good to see you again, and you're most welcome. Now please come in and take some refreshment.'

White held up his hand in demurral. 'No thank you, Tom, I can't stay. I have to get back to Tardebigge Wharf as quick as I can. The reason I've called is to tell you that I've seen Irish Tessy.'

'Where? When?' Tom's heartbeat quickened excitedly.

'In Worcester, just coming up to midnight on Friday last. I caught a glimpse of her talking to a bloke outside a pub called the Horn and Trumpet. It's close by the market down the street called the

Shambles. The Shambles is where the whores ply their trade. I didn't risk hanging about to see more because it's not a safe place for a respectable man to be in at that hour on a dark night.'

'Are you sure it was her if you only had a glimpse?' Tom queried.

'Oh yes, I'm pretty sure,' White said confidently. 'Although it was only a glimpse I've always had a good memory for faces, and I remember thinking that she looked quite respectable. She was wearing a cloak and bonnet instead of showing her bare tits off like she does when she's on the razzle on the canal.'

'Then that's good enough for me,' Tom accepted. 'The Horn and Trumpet, close by the market in the Shambles. I'll find my way there easily enough.'

'Well if you go there late at night, you'd best take a posse of constables with you. Or a brace of loaded pistols, because there's them there who'd cut your throat for fun,' the other man advised dryly, then despite all Tom's entreaties to stay and have something to eat and drink, he took his leave.

Tom stood in the doorway thinking hard as to how and when he could get to Worcester.

'Of course, I'll have to talk with Blackwell and get his leave to go there.'

'Thomassss? Thomassss? Where are you, you cruel beast? God's curse on you for abandoning me!'

Widow Potts' strident shrieks caused a passerby to shout jeeringly, 'Now then, you cruel beast, what's you a-doing to your poor old ma? Has you chucked her down the privy?'

'If only.' Tom sighed inwardly, and shouted aloud. 'Be easy, Mother, I'm coming. I'm coming directly.'

THIRTY-TWO

Evening, Monday 23rd April

As darkness fell Daniel Wynne and the landowner reined in their mounts and watched as the men on foot and their dogs drove the herd of cattle into the hedged pasture on the outskirts of Worcester city.

Daniel Wynne informed his companion, 'This will be a two-night stay for the cattle and my men, Master Windthrop. I have to go on in advance tonight for reasons of business. Shall we call it ten shillings for your grass?'

The bluff-featured, beefy-bodied farmer pursed his lips thoughtfully, then countered, 'Add a shilling each for your men to take shelter in my barn, and six shillings for my food for you all, and the bargain is made.'

Wynne laughed, and counter-offered, 'Make it sixpence each for my men. Because your barn is extra draughty and they reckoned that the last time they slept in it they were shivering all night long.'

'Taken,' Windthrop agreed, and both men spat onto the palms of their right hands and leaned from the saddle to clap them together with a resounding impact.

Windthrop pointed towards a large bull. 'That's a fine beast, Master Wynne; if the price is right I might be interested in taking it off your hands.'

Wynne shook his head. 'Sorry, but you're too late. It was promised last month and the price agreed. It's going to Redditch Town for a May Day bull baiting.'

Windthrop's expression soured. 'Bloody Redditch! The last time I was there, I hadn't been in a pub above five minutes, and was just starting to enjoy a sup of ale, when one of those bloody needle pointers picked a fight with me. It's a blessing that they all die young from doing that work, aren't it? They're worse than wild beasts, so they are. Drunken, evil savages, the lot of them! I was lucky to come away from there with my life, I reckon.'

The three drovers secured the gate of the paddock. Wynne beckoned Shanko Mawr to come to him, and when he did so said in Welsh, 'You three will be sleeping in the barn. Master Windthrop will be sending food to you. Have you arranged the watch keeping?'

The huge man nodded, and asked in his turn, 'Where will you be sleeping and eating this night?'

'That's none of your business,' Wynne snapped curtly. 'The servant doesn't question his master.'

The big man scowled and gritted out, 'I'm not questioning as a servant. I'm speaking as the brother of your wife.'

'And speaking as your master, I'm telling you to keep your nose out of my affairs.' Wynne's face reddened with anger. 'What I choose to do is no concern of yours. Keep that in mind if you want to continue in my service. Because you know well that without my protection you'd be living in want and misery.'

The other man seemed unperturbed by the implied threat and

snarled, 'And without me to do your dirty work, you wouldn't be lording it for much longer over anybody. You'd be dangling from a gallows if I told what I know.'

Wynne smiled savagely. 'And you'd be dangling by the side of me, wouldn't you, my bucko?' He turned his horse and said in English to the farmer, 'Shall we go to your house, Master Windthrop? I've a powerful appetite for some food and drink.'

'And you shall have it directly, Master Wynne.'

The two horsemen kicked their horses into motion and cantered away.

Shanko Mawr glowered after them, teeth bared like a savage wolf, his hands spasmodically clenching into massive fists.

Daniel Wynne had eaten and drunk well when a few hours later he took his leave of his host and rode into the city outskirts. The houses were dark and silent beneath the light of the quarter moon, and only the occasional barking of a watchdog carried through the still night air. Wynne halted outside a small cottage and looked about him, then satisfied that he was unobserved went to the cottage door and rapped a staccato signal on its knocker. A woman's voice called softly from inside.

'Who's there?'

'It's Daniel Wynne, of course.' He frowned. 'Who else would you be expecting?'

'Perhaps I might be expecting somebody who doesn't lie to me all the time, and leave me here to starve.' Her voice held anger.

'Oh come on now, honey, don't be vexed with me. It was urgent business that held me up. But I'm back now like I promised, and I've brought you a fine gift as well.'

'And what might that be?' she challenged.

'It's a beautiful love spoon that I've carved with my own hands. It's a true token to show that I'm wanting to marry you.'

'A bloody love spoon? I can't eat nor wear a bloody love spoon, can I!' she scoffed derisively.

Wynne grinned and, taking coins from his pocket, rattled them loudly.

There was a lengthy pause before the woman opened the door and with a throaty chuckle extended her hands to him. 'Come in quick. I don't want me new neighbours to have cause for gossip.'

He stepped inside, pushing the door closed with his foot, pulling her into his arms, kissing her passionately, his hands greedily searching her full-breasted naked body.

In the dark shadows beneath the eaves of a nearby cottage Shanko Mawr cursed sibilantly beneath his breath in murderous rage.

THIRTY-THREE

Worcester City
Morning, Saturday 28th April

Standing beneath the porticoed entrance of his opulent home, the Alderman, Sir Marcus Cassel, scanned the letter, then stared keenly at the rain-bedraggled figure on the steps below him.

'In this letter my old friend, Blackwell, states that he holds you in high regard, Constable Potts. Are you indeed the relentless bloodhound that he claims you to be?'

'I'm most gratified to hear that Master Blackwell has such regard for me, sir,' Tom replied with somewhat mixed feelings. 'But I'm most certainly not a canine.'

Cassel frowned and asked. 'What is it I can do to aid you?'

'I'm seeking a young woman that I need to question concerning certain deaths which I believe to be murders. I've had information that she may be here in Worcester frequenting a tavern, the Horn and Trumpet, situated in the Shambles. I'm hoping that you may give me permission to talk with your constables to find out if they know of her present whereabouts.'

The Alderman nodded confidently. 'My constables keep a very close eye on every house of ill repute in this city, and the thieves and strumpets who frequent such stinking hell holes.'

He paused and scrutinized Tom's soaked clothing, then instructed, 'Go round to the stables and you'll see the kitchen door. Tell my cook that she is to let you dry yourself at the fire, and that she is to give you a breakfast. My manservant will bring you a note to take to my Head Constable, Henry Vickery.' He gestured in dismissal and went back into the house.

After trudging for almost seven hours through chill wind and driving rain on an empty stomach the prospect of food and warmth sent Tom gratefully hurrying to the rear of the house.

Two hours later in the small, stone-built watch house of the city constables, florid-faced, shrewd-eyed, burly-bodied Henry Vickery took out a ledger from the wall cupboard, opened it and requested politely, 'Be so kind as to give me that description again, if you please, Master Potts.'

Tom repeated the description of Irish Tessy that Chalky White had given him.

'She stands under five in height. In form is full-breasted and well-shaped. She has brown hair and eyes, and her nose is flat from breaking. She speaks with the Irish brogue, and at times has called herself Bridie Quinn. When my informant saw her outside the Horn and Trumpet she looked to be wearing a dark cloak and bonnet, but because of the lack of light he couldn't describe her clothing more fully. However, he knows her well so the physical description can be trusted.'

'If that's the case then I believe we have her here. Take a look at this one's description.' Vickery proffered the ledger, his finger pointing to an entry. 'She first came to our notice twelve days ago. A couple of my lads questioned her because she was loitering among the whores and bully boys in the Shambles. You see we keep a close watch out for any new-come suspicious characters and enter their physical details as soon as we spot them. This one gave her name as Bridie Quinn, and swore she'd just come over from Sligo to seek for honest work. There was no wanted notice out for her, so until Wednesday last we had no real reason to pull her in.'

Tom read the neat handwriting and his hopes rose. Bridie Quinn, the name given by the Irishwoman who had pawned his watch with Ephraim Billings. The same Irishwoman that Tom was certain was Irish Tessy.

'Can I question her straight away, Master Vickery?'

'You can't question her, Master Potts.'

'Why so?' Tom was puzzled. 'From what you said I assumed that you took her into custody on Wednesday.'

His companion nodded. 'Oh yes. We have her in custody alright.' Then added immediately, 'But she'll be of no use to you, I fear. She's laying in the cellar beneath our feet, as dead as the proverbial door-knocker. Come and take a look at her.'

Vickery lit a lantern and led Tom along a passage and down a narrow flight of stone steps into the dark, dank coal cellar.

The dead woman covered by a blanket was laid on a trestle table next to the heap of coal beneath the chute.

'She was found just after dawn on Wednesday last hanging from a tree branch down by the river at the rear of the cathedral. Take a close look, Master Potts; she fits the description of the woman you're looking for without any doubt.'

He pulled the blanket off the naked corpse and shone the lantern light upon the pallid mottled flesh, reciting quietly, 'Youngish in age, with brown hair, brown eyes, flat nose, big tits, well-shaped body, standing under five feet in height. Her clothes, shoes and bonnet are under the table here and there are no bloodstains or any damage to them. There will be a post-mortem and inquest of course, but it's plain to see that there are no suspicious injuries to suggest anything other than suicide. She's not the first unfortunate creature to hang herself down by the river, not by a long chalk, and she most certainly won't be the last.'

Tom stared at the swollen pallid face, noting the darkly cyanosed lips, slightly protruding tongue, and the deep ligature mark on her neck which followed the line of the lower jaw and disappeared upwards behind her ears. He was forced to accept that she fitted the description of Irish Tessy, and sighed with feelings of both pity for the woman and frustration that his only promising line of enquiry was now irrevocably blocked.

'Are you satisfied that this is the woman you were seeking, Master Potts?' Vickery asked.

'I believe I am, Master Vickery.' Tom nodded, and briefly placed his hand on the dead woman's forehead. 'May God rest this poor creature's soul. To take her own life in this way she must have felt that there was no one in the entire world who loved or cared for her.'

'Well, judging from what we found tied inside her bodice she'd had somebody who cared for her at some time or other.' Vickery bent and rummaged among the heap of clothing, then straightened and held an object toward Tom.

'Do you know what this is, Master Potts?'

Tom drew in a sharp intake of breath, as vivid memories sparked of Amos Barry at the Bewdley Poorhouse and another possible suicide who'd had such an article tied inside her bodice.

'It's a love spoon, Master Vickery. It's a traditional love token that Welshmen carve and give to their sweethearts.'

'Well recognized, Master Potts.' Vickery applauded. 'There's precious few people hereabouts could identify it for what it is. Most would think it's just another fancy spoon.'

Tom's thoughts were racing. 'The market in the Shambles, cattle are dealt there, are they not?'

'Oh yes, and all other types of livestock.'

'So drovers come frequently?'

'Of course. How are the livestock to get here else?'

'And some of these drovers would be Welshmen, would they not?'

'Of course.' Vickery's florid face displayed puzzlement as to why he was being asked these rhetorical questions.

Tom was battling to control his rampaging mental images, in which for no good reason two faces and two names dominated. Daniel Wynne and Maisie Lock, sitting intimately together in the Cherry Tree tavern!

He suddenly became conscious of Henry Vickery's puzzled stare, and it was as if a bucket of freezing water had been thrown into his face, shocking him back to reality. He sobered abruptly and was able to apologize with an outward composure.

'Forgive my asking such needless questions, Master Vickery; I was quite carried away by a sudden wild notion that occurred to me.'

'And what might that notion be?' The other man was instantly interested.

'It was the love spoon. I began to imagine the possibility that it could have been a Welsh drover who gave it to her, and that she's killed herself because he has perhaps very recently cast her aside. She might even have come here knowing that he would be bringing cattle to the Shambles market during this present month.'

Vickery mulled over this for some moments, and acknowledged, 'It's as likely a theory as any other, Master Potts.'

'And as unlikely as any other theory ever to be proven,' Tom accepted wryly, then on impulse questioned, 'Has a Welsh drover by name of Daniel Wynne ever come to your notice? He's a handsome, gentlemanly type of man.'

'Daniel Wynne? Daniel Wynne?' Vickery murmured thoughtfully, and nodded in satisfaction as remembrance came to him. 'Yes, I recall meeting with him about eighteen months past, and as you say he's a handsome fellow. One of his men, a veritable giant, created a ruckus in the Horn and Trumpet and it took five of my constables to overpower him, and they were all hardy fellows well used to dealing with trouble.

'That same night Daniel Wynne came here to the watch house and insisted on fully compensating my men for their blood and bruises, and paying for the damage in the tavern. Then he insisted on presenting me with a very generous donation to be distributed to my favourite charities. What was I to do, Master Potts?'

He paused and Tom, realizing what was expected from him, immediately offered, 'Well, Master Vickery, I have to say that if

I'd been in your position on that occasion I would have released
the man into the care of his master and not bothered to trouble the
magistrates about the incident. A mere ruckus in a house of ill
repute is far too minor a matter on which to waste the magistrates'
valuable time. Particularly since all damage to people and property
had been well compensated for.'

'Exactly so, Master Potts.' Vickery smiled warmly. 'Those were
my sentiments entirely.'

Tom bowed. 'All that remains for me to do now, Master Vickery,
is to thank you most sincerely for your help, and to take my leave.'

Vickery walked with him to the street door, asking casually,
'Have you ever seen the giant I spoke of? I believe they call him
Shanko Mawr, or some such outlandish name.'

'I have indeed,' Tom replied. 'And his strength is truly phenom-
enal.'

'I'll say.' Vickery's tone held awe. 'At one point in the fight
he grabbed my strongest man in his arms, and nigh on squeezed
the life from him. The other lads managed to batter the bugger to
the ground, but my man was completely senseless by then. He told
us afterwards that he wasn't able to draw a single gasp of breath
into his body, he was being crushed so tightly.'

Tom grinned ruefully. 'If Shanko Mawr grabbed me in such a
grip he'd break my frail body in two, I fear.'

They shook hands and Tom set out on the trudge of over twenty
miles' distance to Redditch dispiritedly asking himself over and over
again, 'What can I do now to discover poor Rose Brent's killer?'

He had covered several weary miles when the memory of Henry
Vickery's words suddenly clamoured in his mind.

*'Grabbed my strongest man in his arms and nigh on squeezed
the life from him . . . My man was completely senseless . . . wasn't
able to draw a single gasp of breath into his body . . . completely
senseless . . . wasn't able to draw a single breath into his body . . .
Nigh on squeezed the life from him . . . squeezed the life from him
. . . squeezed the life from him!'*

Tom came to a halt as previously tentative supposition burgeoned
and hardened into absolute conviction. 'That's how Rose Brent was
killed. She was literally squeezed to death, and so was Irish Joe!'

He paced slowly onwards and with each step was now finding
it increasingly easy to rationalize the other suspicions which he had
previously rejected as figments of his over-active imagination.

'I've seen how strong Shanko Mawr is, and Daniel Wynne as
well. Either of them could squeeze someone to death. And the Welsh

love spoons? The silk stockings? Could Daniel Wynne be the man giving them to the women?

'The bodies in the canal? Wynne knows the canal well and has close connections with it through his kinsman, Martin Cooke.

'In one way and another there are links of a sort between Rose Brent, Irish Joe, Irish Tessy and the dead girl at Bewdley. And is Maisie Lock also linked to the chain? Well in her case I might be ahead of the game this time.'

He felt renewed determination coursing through him as he quickened his pace and strode on towards Redditch.

THIRTY-FOUR

Sunday April 29th

Across the wooded hillsides it seemed that summer had come at last. The sun was high and hot, the fecund scents of woodlands and pastures and the sounds of myriad life forms that dwelled in them filled the gently wafting air. The distant tolling of church bells carried faintly to Martin Cooke's ears as he prowled restlessly through the weed-strewn, neglected flowerbeds, shrubberies and lawns of his isolated house.

'Master Cooke? Master? Where are you?' His housekeeper's harsh voice called from an upstairs window of the house and he moved from behind the shelter of a shrubbery.

'What is it, Mrs Chesney?'

'There's somebody at the gate.'

'Well go and see who it is, damn you!' he shouted angrily.

'I'm in the middle of dosing her,' she retorted dourly. 'You'll have to go yourself.'

'Fuckin' hell!' he cursed furiously and strode around the house and down the gravelled driveway which led to the public road.

Outside the high spiked ironwork gates was a horse and carriage and two top-hatted, soberly dressed men standing staring through the fretwork, one of them furiously jerking at the bell pull from which a long post-suspended wire ran up to the house.

'Goddamn and blast!' Cooke raged inwardly as he recognized one of his callers.

The white-haired, mutton-chop-whiskered elder of the pair

challenged indignantly, 'Why is this gate padlocked, sir? Have you turned my niece's house into a prison now with these spiked walls and gate?'

'Indeed no, Uncle Mackinnon.' Cooke forced himself to smile pleasantly. 'I'm merely keeping tramps and trespassers away from my house.'

'Pray do not address me as Uncle,' Mackinnon snapped. 'I am not your blood kinsman.'

'Very well, if you do not wish me to acknowledge our familial marital ties I shall in future address you solely as Mackinnon. Now may I enquire as to the purpose of your visit, and who this gentleman is?'

'I'm come here to see my niece, and this gentleman is Doctor Robert Stewart of Coventry, my own doctor since many years.'

'I'm honoured to make your acquaintance, sir.' Cooke bowed politely and the other man stiffly returned the salutation.

'I've brought Doctor Stewart here to make a thorough examination of my niece and to diagnose her physical and mental condition,' Mackinnon stated.

'By whose authority?' Cooke asked, again smiling pleasantly.

'Her father's.' Mackinnon produced a sealed letter and brandished it before Cooke's eyes. 'Sadly he and his lady wife, my sister, are too infirm to travel at present, and they have entrusted me with the task.'

Cooke shook his head regretfully. 'I'm truly sorry to hear of their infirmity, but you may return to Coventry and assure them that all is well with Edwina. She tells them this in her letters, so they have no cause for concern. She is merely labouring under a nervous affliction, and is receiving the finest medical treatment and the most tender care that money can provide She's already well on the way to making a full recovery.'

'Well in that case you'll have no objection to myself and Doctor Stewart seeing her, will you?' Mackinnon asserted forcefully. 'I've always been her favourite uncle, so it will greatly cheer her to see me again.'

'I'm sure that seeing you at any other time would indeed greatly cheer her. But my own doctors are most insistent that until she is fully recovered she must not be subjected to any type of excitement whatsoever. Seeing you here so unexpectedly, and being subjected to an examination by a strange doctor, would dangerously excite her and might well bring a relapse in her condition. I can't risk that happening to my dear wife. So with the greatest regret I dare not allow you to disturb her at this time.' With apparent reluctance Cooke sadly shook his head. 'It is out of the question.'

'Goddammit, man! I'm her favourite uncle and have come all this distance on behalf of her parents. I demand to see her,' Mackinnon blustered cholerically, and rattled the thick padlocked chains. 'Unlock these, damn you, and allow me in. This is my niece's house, and you have no right to bar me from entering it!'

'I am her husband, and what was hers is now mine by virtue of marriage. I have every right to bar you from my house if I so choose.' Cooke's eyes reddened with fury but his voice was low and calm. 'I am a reasonable man, Mackinnon, and I can fully appreciate your sincere concern for Edwina's well-being. You may be assured that the very moment my doctors tell me that she is fully recovered, then anyone and every one of her family and friends will be made welcome here. You have my solemn oath on that. Now please excuse me, I must return to my wife. Good day to you, gentlemen.'

He turned on his heels and walked quickly back along the driveway.

The two men watched until he had disappeared into the house, and Mackinnon gusted harshly, 'I've never liked or trusted that bastard from the very moment I first laid my eyes on him. He only married my niece for her money. If I were thirty years younger I'd climb over this damned gate and horsewhip the bugger!'

THIRTY-FIVE

Monday April 30th

The clanging tollgate bell brought Granny Lock hobbling from her cottage, waving her walking stick threateningly.

'Ha' done, will you! I'm here, aren't I? Ha' done afore I puts my stick over your yeds!'

'And how are you, my own May Queen? You're looking as fresh and young as this fine morn,' Daniel Wynne greeted her with a broad smile.

The old crone squinted her eyes to peer at the two horsemen and the black, nose-ringed bull.

'Is that the beast that's going to be baited tomorrow? He's a big bugger, aren't he?'

'He is indeed, my lovely lady, and he's got a fighting heart as big as his body. He's a true Welshman and he'll be breaking the backs of your English bulldogs, and the hearts of their English owners, tomorrow afternoon.'

'It'll take more than a lump of Taffy cowshit to break our Redditch bulldogs' backs.' She cackled with scornful laughter. 'My nephew's dog 'ull have that bugger pinned in two shakes of a ram's tail.'

'And who might your nephew be?' Wynne asked. 'Because I'll offer him good odds if he fancies a wager.'

'He's Ritchie Bint, and his dog's named Gripper.'

'I'll offer you a wager as well, my sweetheart. I'll pay double tolls for this morning if Gripper pins this bull, and if he can't then we pass through for free this morning.'

'But if I lets you pass free now, then how does I know that you'll pay me if you loses?' she demanded suspiciously.

'You can keep this as a surety.' He slipped a ring from the little finger of his left hand and gave it to her. 'This is solid silver. I'll collect it from you when I come back through the gate, after the bull's broke Gripper's back.'

'Ahrr, go on then.' She opened the gate, cackling with laughter. 'You just make sure you'se got money to pay me the double tolls by nightfall tomorrow, or you'll never see this ring again else. Come to think on it, I might just lose it on purpose anyway, just for spite.'

Daniel Wynne laughed also as he moved past and away from her, but following him leading the bull Shanko Mawr scowled and leaned from the saddle to hiss menacingly into the old woman's face.

'That ring belonged to my forebears and if it goes missing it won't be only your nephew's dog that gets its back broke, you old witch.'

She stared after him as he led the bull onwards and her toothless mouth opened to shout an insult, but then the memory of the murderous expression on his face kept her silent.

'Least said, soonest mended,' she told herself nervously. 'He's a bloody lunatic, he is. There's no telling what he might do.'

THIRTY-SIX

Tuesday May 1st

Martha Standard had hardly slept and sat up in her bed before dawn on May Day morning. She shook her young bedmate's shoulder.

Ten-year-old Hattie Manders stirred and groaned in protest.

'You've woke me up, and it's dark still.'

'Does you want to be pretty, or not?' Martha demanded. 'Has you forgot what day it is? We needs to gather the dew at sunrise because that's when it does the business best. So get up and get dressed.'

'I wish me mam hadn't never sent me to work here,' Hattie whined pettishly.

'And I wish she hadn't neither, because you'm neither use nor ornament. Now get up afore I gives you a slap.'

'But I'm still tired,' the girl moaned plaintively, as she rolled from the bed and began to dress.

Martha smiled. 'Has you forgot that it's May Day holiday in Redditch today, and if we gets our tasks done quick the Master's said he'll take us there on his cart. You'd like that, wouldn't you, riding like a lady in a cart? There'll be all sorts of people there, and there'll be fiddlers and dancing and a May Queen chosen.'

'Shall we be able to dance?' Hattie's spirits perked.

'O' course we shall. And don't forget that if you behaves yourself the Master 'ull certain sure let you stay in Redditch with your mam and dad tonight, and come back here tomorrow morning. Come on now.' Martha took the girl's hand and led her downstairs.

'I'm hungry, Martha. Can I have me breakfast?'

'Not yet. We'll do our tasks first, and then have our breakfasts when the Master comes back.'

'Where is he?'

'He'll be in the Tardebigge churchyard washing his goitre.'

'What's that?' The girl was mystified.

'It's that big lump he's got on his neck. The first May dew is like a magic spell, so it is. Me and you can wash our faces in the dew we gathers under the old oak in the bottom pasture, and that'll keep our skins lovely and clear and make us pretty for the whole year. But to get rid of that lump the Master has to gather the dew before sunrise from a young man's grave. He has to pass his hands three times across the grave from head to foot of it, and then rub the dew he's gathered on to his lump and it'll get rid of it.'

'Where will the lump go?'

'Buggered if I know! It's just goes, that's all. Come on, it's getting near to sun up and we needs to be under the oak tree when it rises.'

They exited from the house and hurried hand in hand across the fields, heading for a huge ancient oak tree that stood in solitary splendour.

THIRTY-SEVEN

In the shared bed in the dark attic room of the Fox and Goose Maisie Lock lay with her hands behind her head, a worried frown on her face.

'Will he marry me like he promised?' The question nagged her continuously. 'Will he come back? I shouldn't have let him, should I? I should have made him wait. What if he's put me up the duff, and he don't come back? What'll happen to me then?'

Laying on her side of the bed, her face turned to the wall, Amy Danks was also racked by troubling doubts.

'I'll be nineteen years old in a couple of weeks, and still not wed. Am I fated to be an old maid? There's plenty o' chaps setting their caps at me, but there aren't none of them offering me a wedding ring. Well, none of them who I'd fancy being wed to anyway. I don't want to become a man's skivvy. Working me fingers to the bone all me life; having babbies every year until I'm too old and worn out to breed any more. I want to be a lady, and have a big house, and fine things about me, and servants to be at my beck and call. Eugene Sinclair could give me all those things, couldn't he?

'But what about Tom? Well, I do truly care for him. He's lovely but he keeps on saying that he can't offer me anything except hardship, and that's why he can't marry me yet. Not until his fortunes change. But if they don't change, then what? Could I marry him if he stays poor? I've already had a belly full of hard work and empty pockets! What if that's all he'll ever have to offer? And how could I bear to live under the same roof as that evil old bitch of his mam? Well, I couldn't, and that's the answer to that!'

Grunting with effort, Widow Potts levered her gross body upright in her bed and shrieked, 'Tom? Tom? Where's my breakfast? Are you intending to starve me to death, you wicked wretch? Where's my breakfast?'

'It's here, Mother.' Tom Potts entered his mother's room carrying a loaded wooden tray. 'I've brought you onion porridge, and some fresh-baked bread I've fetched only this minute from Charlie Scambler.'

'And what am I to drink, pray tell me?' she demanded. 'My throat is so cruelly parched and sore with dryness, that I'm hardly able to croak out a word!'

'What I've drunk myself, Mother.' Tom placed the tray on the stool beside the bed. 'A jug of cider, but I've stirred a lump of sugar-cone into yours. I know that you like it sweetened.'

'Sweetened, he says! My God, see what I've come down to. Presented with a breakfast that a beggar would scorn, and having to drink cheap sour cider that tastes of cat's piss,' she grumbled bitterly. 'Your neglect of my necessities is nothing short of scandalous. My only comfort is that your poor father is dead and in his grave, because if he were living he would be heart-broken to witness your foul treatment of me.'

From the surrounding areas came the sounds of the mills and factory bells ringing out to salute the ancient festival of May Day. They proclaimed this day's freedom from gruelling toil for their workers, and for a few moments Tom pictured his mother being forced to join the workers ranks and for once in her life of laziness having to do some hard physical work. His spirits lifted by the brief fanciful interlude he told her pleasantly, 'If you say so, Mother. Now as you know it's May Day holiday and I must be on duty, so you'll see little or nothing of me today. I'll arrange for a cooked dinner to be brought to you later. Is Charles Bromley coming to keep you company?'

'That's none of your business,' she snapped. 'My personal relationships are no concern of yours. And before you go gallivanting and whore-mongering around the parish, my commode needs emptying.'

'As you wish.' He picked up the commode and left the room.

*   *   *

In the dining room at Hewell Grange, Eugene Sinclair sat alone at the huge polished table listlessly toying with the succession of breakfast dishes served to him by the ornately bewigged and liveried footman. Plates of cured ham, coddled eggs, jugged hare, smoked fish, haunch of venison. Pots of scented China tea, Brazilian coffee, bottles of French, Italian and Spanish wines. Nothing could rouse an appetite completely destroyed by the unwelcome news that the butler had greeted him with on his return from his overnight carousing.

'Haven't I more than enough to worry me without the ugly raddled old bitch hounding me so? Goddamn my rotten luck!'

His thoughts turned to Amy Danks, and he sighed ruefully. 'The sweetest little morsel I've met in ages as well. Well, there's nothing else for it. I'm just going to have to chance my arm sooner than I planned to.'

The footman approached with a platter of savoury cold meats, and Sinclair impatiently waved him away. 'I want nothing more.'

The dark-suited, majestically mannered butler came to him next and enquired, 'Might I enquire if Sir will be requiring a horse again today?'

'Yes, I shall, and tell that damned useless stableman that I don't want that broken-winded bag of bones he keeps foisting onto me. I want a decent nag for a change. Tell him to have it ready for me within the hour. And make sure that that fellow whom I've lodged in the servants' quarters is conveyed with his dog to the Pound Meadow in Redditch at two o'clock this afternoon. Send him by carriage because if he's not there on time and in a sober condition, I'll have your guts for garters.'

The butler's face remained impassive. 'Very well, sir. And may I enquire if Sir will be dining here tonight?'

Sinclair shook his head.

The butler made no move to leave, but stood waiting expectantly.

'Goddamn it, man!' Sinclair exclaimed petulantly. 'Why do you hover over me so?'

'Well, sir, if your lady grandmother's party should arrive back here today and enquire as to your whereabouts, what may I tell her?'

'You may tell her that I'm up Jack's arse, hanging from a nail.' Sinclair jumped to his feet and stamped out of the room.

The butler grinned contemptuously and told the footman, 'Well, the slimy turd knows where he rightfully belongs, don't he? I just hope that Jack aren't had a shit for a month or two.'

The footman roared with laughter.

*   *   *

In his office at the Tardebigge New Wharf, Martin Cooke sat at his desk, deep in troubled thought and struggling to steel his nerves.

'There's no other choice left to me. It has to be done, no matter what the risk. I can't keep on putting it off.'

His clerk came in from the yard. 'The men want to know what time they can knock off, Master Cooke? They'm eager to see the bull-baiting.'

'As we all are, Jenkins.' Cooke forced a bluff smile. 'Tell the men that the two coal barges at the Old Wharf must be cleared, and the timber for Worcester Basin loaded onto Simcox's boat. They can knock off then.'

Alone again, Cooke paced restlessly up and down, telling himself over and over again, 'I have to do it. I have to do it.'

THIRTY-EIGHT

After breakfast in the Fox and Goose Tommy Fowkes marshalled his staff in the private parlour, and like a general addressing his troops on the eve of battle exhorted them.

'It's May Day, girls, and as you well know it's one of the best days for business in the whole year. So remember that today you must keep your powder dry, aim steady and keep our colours flying high. Discipline and good order, girls, that's what you needs today. You must keep a cool head under fire, like the Duke of Wellington did at Waterloo. Remember at all times that if you keep steady and firm then victory . . .'

'Bloody hell, Dad, does you think we're soldiers that you must spout such nonsense to us?' Lily Fowkes interrupted indignantly.

'No, we aren't bloody redcoats, Master Fowkes! So just stop talking to us as if we am!' his wife scolded. 'I've got too much work to do to waste a moment longer listening to your daft bletherings.' She stormed from the room muttering angrily to herself.

Amy and Maisie smothered their giggles, while Lily challenged her father.

'What about our holiday? You promised us when we did all that extra work at Easter that we'd have a holiday come May Day. Me and the girls want to go to the May Queen crowning, and have a dance.'

'Go to the May Queen crowning?' Fowkes puffed out his cheeks and snorted derisively. 'Try and get crowned May Queen yourselves more likely!'

'Well, why shouldn't we?' Lily demanded.

'Because you knows very well that the May Queen is always picked from among the needle masters' daughters and them others who've been invited to enter for it. Not from the likes of you lot.'

'Well Amy and Maisie might be low-born scruffs, but you always says that our family has become the equal in rank of any needle master now that you've made your pile of money. So why haven't you made them invite me to enter?' Lily riposted.

The other two girls were smarting with resentment at Lily's description of them, and before Tommy Fowkes could make any reply Amy said sweetly, 'Lily's right, she's the equal in rank of any of the needle masters' daughters. Maisie and me are too low born and scruffy to be elected, even though everybody agrees that we're the two prettiest girls in the parish by a long chalk. But it's not Lily's fault that she's just a little bit too heavy to be invited into the competition for the May Queen, is it, Maisie?'

'No, it's not Lily's fault that she's too fat. It's a real pity for her because she's such a nice, sweet-natured girl.' Maisie smiled sympathetically.

Lily burst into tears and, throwing her long apron back over her face, slumped down on to a chair, her shoulders heaving violently as she sobbed.

'Now look what you've done, Master Fowkes!' Amy accused reproachfully. 'How could you speak so unkind to your own daughter?'

'And all she wanted was what you promised her faithful that she'd have. Just a couple of hours' holiday this May Day, that's all she wanted. Just what we all deserve, that's all,' Maisie added her contribution.

'I've never known you to be so hard-hearted before, as to begrudge us a couple of hours of freedom. Never!' Amy shook her head sorrowfully, and looked near to tears herself.

Tommy Fowkes scowled uneasily, his hanging jowls quivering, eyes flicking guiltily from one to other of the three girls. He drew a long shuddering breath and stamped out of the room, shouting as he went.

'Be damned to you all! Take your bloody holiday then. But if you aren't back here working by six of the clock tonight, I'll bloody well chuck you all out into the gutter!'

Giggling delightedly Amy and Maisie clasped hands and danced around the room, then jointly cuddled and soothed Lily.

'Come on, dearie. Dry your eyes and get your finery on. It's May Day.'

THIRTY-NINE

While clocks throughout the town struck the eleventh hour, Tom Potts examined himself by sections in the cracked wall mirror in his room and decided that he was as neat and well brushed as his threadbare clothing would permit.

'Pity I can't do anything to improve my woeful features and skeletal body,' he murmured in humorous self-deprecation. 'However, it's what the Good Lord decided to bestow on me, and I must do the best I can with it.'

From the roadway below his open window came the noise and laughter of excited children and he moved to lean out and look for them. Dressed in their best clothes, girls and boys of all ages were congregating on the green, some carrying nosegays of wild flowers and garlands of evergreens, others here and there waving flags and one group carrying aloft a two-poled banner bearing the motto: God Bless the Queen of the May. There were also large numbers of adults assembling to watch the proceedings.

Tom smiled with genuine pleasure to see their happy excitement and thought proudly, 'It's the upkeep of our ancient festivals which identifies us, and helps to make us the greatest nation on earth.'

Although Tom recognized and abhorred the many injustices and wrongs that were inflicted upon countless thousands of his fellow countrymen by their own ruling classes, he was nevertheless deeply imbued with patriotism, coupled with an intense pride that in naval, industrial and trading strength England ranked foremost amongst the nations of the earth.

A sudden uproar came from further east along the street and Tom was forced to lean perilously far out of the window to see what was happening. In the roadway outside the Red Lion tavern a circle of men dressed in red shirts and leather waistcoats were surrounding and bellowing encouragement at two savagely brawling combatants.

'God help me!' Tom groaned in dismay and his stomach churned in nervous apprehension. 'It's not yet noon and the Pointers are already fighting drunk. I'll be lucky to end this day in one piece.'

He rammed his top hat low down upon his head, took up his staff and left his room shouting, 'I'll see you later, Mother.'

'I've no wish to see you ever again, you cruel unnatural fiend!' his mother shouted back.

Outside the lock-up Tom was hailed in a friendly manner by a passerby who matched him in height and tripled him in weight.

'Good morning, Constable Potts.

'Good morning Master Groby.'

Tom had much respect for Balthasar Groby, who kept a grocer's shop in the row of buildings facing the front of St Stephen's chapel. Groby was by far the biggest and strongest man in the parish, a fervent Methodist lay preacher who never drank alcohol, smoked tobacco, took snuff or fornicated.

'I see the Pointer lads are getting savage drunk as usual, Constable Potts.'

'Indeed they are, Master Groby, but so long as they're only fighting each other I'm inclined to let them get on with it.'

'Quite so!' Groby agreed emphatically. 'Someday, God willing, they will come to know the truth of Isaiah 5/11 . . . "Woe unto them that rise up early in the morning, that they may follow strong drink; that continue until night till wine inflame them."'

'Amen to that!' It was Tom's turn to emphatically agree.

'A word, Constable? Might I have a word?' Another man approached, small and slender in build, his short-sighted eyes blinking rapidly behind the pince-nez which wobbled alarmingly on his long thin nose.

John Osborne, the master of the Free School erected and endowed by the Earl of Plymouth for the boys of the Tardebigge Parish, was the self-appointed, self-important organizer and director of the May Day rituals.

'Yes, Master Osborne, how can I be of service to you?' Tom enquired.

'The May Day Committee are ready to select the May Queen. I require you to shield the Committee from any dangers.'

Tom stared at the orderly, seemingly happy crowd of adults and children gathered on the green and asked in puzzlement, 'Who among these people are a danger to the Committee?'

'How should I know?' Osborne demanded. 'I'm a schoolmaster, not a constable! It's your responsibility to identify and apprehend the miscreants.'

'I'm confident that should it become necessary Constable Potts will do just that.' Balthasar Groby intervened. 'And for today I've been asked by the Committee to act as the Festival Steward. So there will be two of us keeping order at this gathering if Constable Potts will permit me to assist him.'

'I'm delighted to have you with me, Master Groby.' Tom was genuinely grateful.

The three of them walked across to where a platform of planks and trestles had been erected against the chapel yard wall. The ladies and gentlemen of the Committee were seated on benches upon this makeshift stage, the centrepiece of which was a gilded empty throne. Some distance further north across the green a tall, gaudily decorated, ribbon-streaming Maypole had been set up.

In front of the stage, resplendently uniformed Town Crier Jimmy Grier rang his brass hand bell and bellowed, 'Oyez, Oyez, Oyez. The Honourable Ladies and Gentlemen of the May Day Committee will now select the May Queen and her Handmaidens. Let all young ladies who's been invited come forward and present themselves before the Honourable Ladies and Gentlemen of the May Day Committee. God save the King!'

Several daughters of the parish's socially prominent families stepped out from the crowd. Cheeks glowing, eyes sparkling with excitement, dressed in flowing gowns, feathered bonnets upon their elaborately coiffed hair, they upheld the reputation the locale enjoyed for producing pretty, elegantly clad girls.

'Form a line, young ladies. I must insist that you stand in line,' John Osborne officiously marshalled them. 'When I point to you individually, you must take two steps forward and present yourself to the Honourable Ladies and Gentlemen of the Committee, and state your two most consummate accomplishments. You will then take two steps backward and regain your place in the line. Is that clearly understood by all of you?'

John Osborne pointed at the first girl in the line. She stepped forward and curtseyed gracefully, then straightened to declare, 'I am Miss Rebecca Merry, and I am accomplished in playing the pianoforte and singing.' She stepped back into line.

Osborne's commanding forefinger moved along the line in strictly measured sequence.

'I am Miss Amelia Bartleet, and I am accomplished in the writing of poetry, and the Language of Flowers.'

'I am Miss Letitia Milward, and I am accomplished in playing the harp and fine needlework.'

'I am Miss Sarah Hemming, and I am accomplished in the singing of Italian opera, and in the painting of watercolours.'

Each announcement was received with hand-shielded exchanges of opinion among the Committee, and their nods and smiles of approbation, while the spectators responded with audible gasps and comments of admiration at such evidence of diverse talents.

With the roll call completed John Osborne mounted the stage and solemnly conferred with the Committee. The contestants fidgeted impatiently, eyed each other's gowns and bonnets disparagingly, and exchanged smiles, grimaces and hand signals with their knots of supporters in the crowd.

Osborne left the stage, beckoned Jimmy Grier to him and whispered into the old man's ear, then came to Tom and warned, 'Now you must stand alert for violent protests and disorder, Constable Potts.'

He strutted back up on to the stage leaving Tom somewhat mystified. 'Disorder? Violent protests? This crowd is composed of the respectable, law-abiding people of this parish.'

The brass hand bell rang out.

'Oyez. The Handmaidens of the May Queen are hereby decreed by the Committee to be Miss Sophia Shrimpton, Miss Sarah Hemming, Miss Hepzibah Whitehouse and Miss Letitia Milward. God Save the King!'

'Look at their faces.' Balthasar Groby chuckled. 'They looks like they've found a penny and lost a sovereign.'

The four chosen girls' expressions betrayed shocked resentment that they had been chosen as mere handmaidens, while by contrast the remaining eight girls were displaying varying degrees of hope and confidence that they were to become the May Queen.

From the crowd there sounded isolated voices of protest, and Tom suddenly began to wonder if John Osborne's warning of violence and disorder might contain some substance.

The hand bell rang again.

'Oyez. By the unanimous decision of the Committee the May Queen is decreed to be Miss Rebecca Merry. God save the King!'

There was a unified gasping of surprise from the crowd. A few shouts of disagreement with the choice of Queen rang out from some supporters whose rejected contestants were displaying mortified disbelief, but then a great roar of applause burst from the vast majority of the spectators to drown out the dissenters.

Lily Fowkes reacted with a furious tirade, 'Bugger me! This can't be so! Becca bloody Merry! Her Dad aren't got no property nor nothing. He's always been two steps away from the bloody Poorhouse! If she could enter the competition then why couldn't I? It aren't bloody fair!'

'It is fair. Her uncle's got a needle-scouring shop and is his own master,' Amy defended the result.

'But her mam was only ever a dressmaker's stitching skivvy.' Lily pouted like a petulant child. 'The other wenches are daughters of rich people, like what I am.'

'That's as maybe, but it's a fact that Becca's the best-looking girl by far among that lot. She's a nice sweet girl as well, and can sing like an angel. She deserves to win.' Amy was beginning to lose patience with her friend. 'So just shut up about it, Lily!'

In company with Balthasar Groby at the side of the stage Tom had been surreptitiously glancing at Amy Danks and her friends, and he was enduring a poignant sense of despair and loss.

'She's the only girl I've ever loved, or ever will love,' he accepted sadly, and his despair deepened as the dandyish figure of Eugene Sinclair pushed through the crowd to join the three girls, who greeted him with obvious pleasure. 'But I've lost her, haven't I? How can I compete with that man who has so much to offer her?'

'Why were you not standing in that selection line, Amy?' Sinclair smiled fondly. 'You're prettier by far than any of those girls.'

'Because according to Lily here, Amy and me are only low-born scruffs, and you have to be high-born and rich like she is to get invited to stand for May Queen.' Maisie Lock's voice dripped with sarcastic venom.

'I said nothing of the sort, Maisie Lock!' Lily Fowkes denied angrily.

'Oh yes you did,' Maisie retorted. 'Didn't she, Amy?'

'Let's not quarrel,' Amy pleaded with them. 'Let's enjoy our holiday.' She turned to Sinclair, and her eyes sparked with mischievous humour. 'I've no wish at all to be the May Queen, Eugene. It's satisfaction enough for me to know that I've long been acknowledged to be the prettiest girl in the parish.'

'In my eyes you're the prettiest girl in England.' Sinclair bowed gallantly. 'And I'm ready to fight a duel with any man who denies that fact.'

Glowing with gratified pleasure Amy turned her head to look towards the stage, and her gaze fell upon Tom Potts who was standing looking downwards at the ground seemingly lost in thought. Her smile faltered as she noted his despondent expression.

'Oh, Tom, what's troubling you?' she wondered. 'I hate to see you looking so miserable.'

Directed by John Osborne, Rebecca Merry and the handmaidens removed their bonnets, then went up onto the stage.

The Ladies and Gentlemen of the Committee rose to their feet as Committee Chairman Richard Hemming, the young scion of one of the most powerful needle manufacturers, took Rebecca Merry's hand and placed her on the throne with the handmaidens ranged on each side of her. The crown, a wreath of colourful anemones, was brought for Richard Hemming to place on Rebecca Merry's head.

Jimmy Grier rang his bell and proclaimed, 'Oyez. Oyez. Oyez. Our May Queen is crowned. Let all those present pay her homage. God save our May Queen!'

The Committee men and women bowed and curtseyed, while the spectators applauded uproariously.

Wreaths of white flowers were brought forwards and, to cheers and clapping, Richard Hemming placed them in turn upon the hand-maidens' heads.

All around the outer fringes of the crowd men and women on horseback and sitting in carriages were watching the ceremonies. Two other horsemen were slowly circling the outer fringes searching for a particular face. One of them found what he sought and cantered to tell the second man, 'He's here.' Daniel Wynne pointed. 'Over there with the girls from the Fox.'

Martin Cooke squinted his eyes against the sunlight. 'Where exactly?'

'To your left, in the front there.'

'I have him,' Cooke declared.

'Let's hope that he's in the mood for a gamble today.' Wynne grinned.

'Are you absolutely sure that your bull can't be pinned?' Cooke sought assurance.

'I'll stake my life on it!' Wynne asserted with total confidence. 'Let's get stabled now. I want to spend a little time with my sweet Maisie before the baiting.'

While the crowning was done the profusely sweating John Osborne and his pupil teachers, using their canes to whip the laggards, marshalled the children into the desired processional formation.

A small pony carriage gaily decorated with flowers and evergreens was brought onto the green and to the rear of the formation. Attended by her handmaidens Rebecca Merry was led to it on the arm of Richard Hemming.

Jimmy Grier rang his bell and announced, 'Oyez. The Coronational Procession will proceed past the lock-up, and down to the Big Pool. Then up the Ipsley Street and the Back Hill, round the Duke of York inn and down the Front Hill. Then along the High Street to pass over the crossroads and in front o' the chapel and stop where the Queen will seat herself on her throne again.

'Then the kids will line up to kiss the Queen's hand, and she'll give 'um a sticky bun each. Buns being supplied by Master Timothy Munslow, the sole proprietor of Munslow's Cakes and Sweetmeats Emporium next door to the Fox and Goose over there on the south side of the green. After all the buns have been give out there'll be games and dancing round the Maypole . . . God Save Our May Queen!'

'No! It ought to be "God save all of us" from having to listen to you bletherin' on about Tim Munslow's bloody stale buns, Jimmy Grier!' a disgruntled spectator shouted and was wildly applauded.

Hattie Manders tugged on Martha Standard's hand and pleaded, 'Can we walk in the procession, and kiss the Queen's hand and have a bun?'

Martha smiled down at the child's eager face. 'I can walk in the procession with you, but they won't let me kiss the Queen's hand and have a bun. I'm too old for that.'

Richard Hemming approached Tom. 'My Lord Aston has told me that I may call upon your services, Constable Potts. Will you and Master Groby be so kind as to head the procession and ensure that the way is clear for it? I would do so myself, but I am expected to lead the May Queen's pony.'

Tom was staring so intently at Daniel Wynne and Martin Cooke, who had just joined Eugene Sinclair and the three girls, that he was unaware of Hemming's approach.

'Constable Potts?' Hemming tapped Tom's shoulder.

'Oh! Excuse me, I was lost in thought for a moment,' Tom apologized.

'No matter.' The young man smiled pleasantly and repeated his request.

'Certainly we will,' Tom acceded immediately.

He and Groby took their places and the procession moved off to the applause of the crowd. Directly following Tom and Groby

were the two biggest boys carrying the great emblazoned banner
declaring God Bless the Queen of the May. Then came the long
formations of children with their flags, nosegays, wreaths and
garlands, preceding the four handmaidens and the carriage in which
Rebecca Merry sat regally waving acknowledgement to the plaudits of her May Day subjects.

John Osborne shouted at the top of his voice, 'Sing! Sing! Sing!'
and the massed voices of the children carolled an ancient May Day
ballad in tuneful unison.

> 'We come to remind you of merry May Day,
> And show you our garlands so fresh and so gay.
> We thank our Creator for Springtime and flowers,
> And spend in his service our earliest hours.'

The crowd of onlookers swirled and moved in many directions,
some seeking fresh vantage points along the processional route,
others heading for the taverns, yet others walking towards the
Maypole to await the return of the May Queen.

In the middle of the lines of excited children Martha Standard
and Hattie Manders walked happily singing at the tops of their
voices, glorying in the clapping and cheering of the people they
passed.

Martha suddenly glimpsed one man in the crowd and gasped in
shocked recognition. 'That's him! That's Rosie's sweetheart! I'm
sure that's him!'

She turned her head to stare, craning for a clearer view, but the
children behind her cannoned into her back forcing her onwards
and when she looked again his face was lost among the seething
kaleidoscope of myriad strangers' features.

She walked on, her mind filled with troubling doubts. 'Was it
him? Am I imagining it? Was it? Wasn't it?'

As the procession passed Daniel Wynne and his companions he
drew Maisie Lock aside. 'Let's go somewhere on our own. I've no
wish to be with this lot. I only want to be alone with you.'

'But I can't leave my mates,' she demurred. 'We're going to go
to the dancing. We been looking forwards to it for weeks.'

'You can be with your mates later, can't you?'

'But we'll be working later. We'em only on holiday 'til six
o'clock. Tommy Fowkes says he'll sack us if we aren't back at
work by then.'

'You can still go to the dancing with them. Just come with me for an hour.' A tone of self-pity entered his voice. 'This is a cruel thing to do to a man.'

'A cruel thing?' She was puzzled. 'What d'you mean?'

'Exactly what I say.' He looked crestfallen. 'I've neglected my bull and risked losing a lot of money to spend time with my sweetheart, and she doesn't want to be with me. It's a cruel hard thing to bear.'

Her eyes moistened and she asked tremulously, 'Am I, Daniel? Am I truly your sweetheart?'

'You're truly my one and only sweetheart, and I've brought you the proof of how much I love you,' he huskily assured her. 'What's even more cruel and hard to bear is that you should feel the need to ask me that question. I meant every word that I said to you that night. How can you doubt me after I was so loving and tender with you? I'm beginning to wonder if it's me who should be doubting your love for me.'

Desperately wanting to believe his words, she read his troubled expression and the moist gleam in his dark eyes as visual proof of his love for her.

'I'll see you later at the dancing, girls,' she announced and hurried away hand in hand with Daniel Wynne.

In the loft above the livery stable Maisie Lock and Daniel Wynne lay panting on the soft pile of hay, their naked bodies entwined in the hot sweaty aftermath of passionate loving.

Wynne raised his body and rolled off her. He retrieved his clothes and began to dress.

'What are you doing?' Maisie questioned in surprise.

'What does it look like I'm doing?' He pulled a mock-incredulous face. 'Haven't you seen anybody do this before? It's called getting dressed, and it's what you need to be doing as well.'

'Don't make mock of me, Daniel,' she remonstrated petulantly as she sat up. 'You couldn't wait to pull me clothes off when you dragged me up here, could you, so why are you so eager for me to put them back on now?'

For a brief moment his expression hardened, but then he chuckled and told her, 'Listen, my sweetheart, if I had my way, we'd both stay naked every and all the times that we were on our own. But today I've got a lot of important business to attend to.'

'So business is more important to you than what I am!' She pouted sulkily.

Smiling broadly he shook his head and continued to dress.

'I just asked you a question, didn't I?' Her voice became shrewish in tone.

Wynne pulled on his coat and took a small paper-wrapped packet from the pocket, which he held down in front of her eyes.

'You see this, my girl? This is why I do business, and why business is important to me.'

'What's it got to do wi' me how important your business is? I don't care a fig about your bloody business.' She shrugged her shoulders with pretended indifference.

'Well I do believe that you'll care about what's in this packet.' He tore the wrapping open to disclose a finely embroidered pair of silken gloves. 'These are for you, sweetheart.'

Maisie's instant reaction was to gasp with delight. 'Oh they'm lovely, Daniel! They'm beautiful!'

He smiled patronizingly. 'This is why business is important to me, my sweetheart. Because business is what gives me the money to buy you presents like these.'

A glint of calculation entered his eyes, and he told her huskily, 'And here's something else which means far more than any pair of gloves.'

He took a second paper-wrapped object from his pocket and pushed it into her hands. 'Open it and take a close look.'

She hastily unwrapped the paper and stared bemusedly at the small intricately carved object that it contained. 'It's a bloody wooden spoon.'

He suppressed a snort of irritation, and smiled. 'It's a love spoon, my darling. It's what we Welshmen carve ourselves and give to the girls we truly love. You see those entwined hearts, and all those flowers. Well I've spent hours and hours designing and carving them for you. They're the proof of my true love for you.'

'Ohhh, Daniel!' She breathed in delight, and followed immediately with eager questions. 'Does this spoon mean that we'em betrothed now? That we'em to be married?'

After a momentary hesitation he told her, 'That's what it means in my country, sweetheart. But for the time being I want you to keep our betrothal a secret for you and I alone to share, while we prepare for our future lives together. You must wear the spoon hidden between your breasts, so that I'll know that you always have something of me next to your heart.'

Before she could voice another question he bent and, cupping her face with his hands, kissed her hard on the mouth. Then was gone, leaving her sitting gazing at the spoon and gloves with gloating satisfaction.

'Just wait while I tell the girls, and see the looks on their faces when they hears about this. They'll be sick jealous, so they will. Sick jealous!'

FORTY

It was mid-afternoon and the taverns were emptying as their customers headed down the Unicorn Hill towards the 'Pound'. The hedged and fenced meadow was owned by the parish and was normally used to impound strayed or confiscated animals, but today it was the site of the bull-baiting match.

On the green the fiddlers were still playing and men, women, girls and boys bowed and curtseyed, dipped, turned, swayed and skipped through the intricate measures of the country dances. But here also the throngs of spectators were noticeably diminishing as the age-old spectacle of the savage combat between dogs and bull exerted its attraction.

Eugene Sinclair stood sulkily watching Amy and her two friends partnering a trio of young men. The current dance ended and, flushed and smiling, the girls came back to him. He took Amy's arm and led her a little distance from her friends.

'Amy, we have to go to the Pound now,' he told her sharply. 'The bull-baiting is starting shortly so you can't waste any more time prancing about with these bumpkins.'

Amy tossed her head and snapped indignantly, 'I can waste whatever time I want to waste prancing about with these bumpkins, as you choose to call my friends!'

'What's the matter with you today?' he demanded irritably. 'I've chosen to spend time with you, and you virtually ignore me. You leave me standing here by myself while you giggle with your empty-headed workmates, and demean yourself by acting the coquette with a succession of ignorant, unwashed peasants.'

Amy's temper flared. 'Don't you try telling me what I must do or not do! You might think yourself to be Lord Muck, but I'm not one of your skivvies; and it's we ignorant peasants who do the work which keeps you and your kind living idle on the fat of this land. So you can just bugger off, and leave me be! Don't try to speak to me ever again. I want nothing more to do with you.'

Cheeks red with anger she flounced back to her friends, who

had been surreptitiously watching the heated exchange, and announced, 'I've just told him to bugger off for good! The cheeky sod was talking to me as if I was his bloody skivvy! I told him that I'm having nothing more to do with him.'

'You never did that, did you?' Shocked, Lily puffed her cheeks out like a huge red balloon.

'Oh yes I did!' Amy affirmed. 'And I'll do the same to any bloody man, rich or poor, who speaks to me like that!'

'Ohhhh, Amy!' Lily was quite overcome with awe. 'And he's a proper gentleman, as well. How could you dare to do it?'

'But he's not a true gentleman, is he, really?' Maisie Lock's eyes were glinting with satisfaction that Amy had quarrelled with her dandified admirer. She ostentatiously flourished her silk-gloved hands. 'A true gentleman always treats his loved one with proper respect, like my Daniel always treats me.' She shook her head in assumed regret. 'O' course I'm really sorry that Amy's admirer has turned out to be a bad 'un. But if you want my opinion, she's better off doing without such a false-hearted, stuck-up bugger.'

'No, Maisie, I don't believe that I do want your opinion,' Amy snapped tartly. 'I'm well able to make up my own mind on anything I choose to do without anybody else's opinion. Thank you very much all the same!'

With a final long sullen glare at Amy, Eugene Sinclair swung around and stalked away from the green.

Down in the small, compact enclosure of the Pound a second May Day Committee was debating the procedure and rules for this afternoon's bull-baiting. Unlike the Committee on the green this was a strictly male grouping, representing a broad spectrum of the parish's population: needle masters, farmers, innkeepers, shopkeepers, artisans and labourers.

By unanimous vote a referee, the Berrod, had already been appointed. Now the discussion centred on the correct length of rope used to tie the bull to the large post in the centre of the greensward.

'I say twenty-five yards,' said Samuel Thomas, needle master.

'I say ten yards,' reckoned Herbert Willis, innkeeper.

'I say ten yards is too short,' offered Richard Bint, needle pointer.

'That's right! Ten yards don't give our dogs a fair crack,' agreed Jacky Whittaker, Legger.

'And I say let the Berrod decide on the length. He's the expert here,' suggested Charles Scambler, baker and flour merchant.

Berrod George Wells, a short, stocky ex-cavalryman, flourished the sabre he had carried through the battles of Vitoria and Waterloo to emphasize his judgement.

'I've had a good look at the beast, gentlemen, and without a shadow of a doubt it's a game bull.' He swung to point his sabre tip at Daniel Wynne, who was standing a little to one side of the group. 'I trust you'm not going to dispute me over that, am you, Master Wynne?'

The Welshman smiled and bowed. 'Indeed I'm not, Berrod. My Glendower has been baited previously and is most certainly a game bull.'

'And been baited more than once or twice by the looks on it,' Wells asserted confidently. 'So perhaps you'll tell us how many times?'

'Of course I will, gentlemen. I've no intention of hiding anything from you.' Wynne radiated an honest frankness. 'Glendower has been baited five times. Twice at Ludlow, once each at Leominster, Coventry and Northampton, and has never been pinned.' A note of challenge entered his tone. 'And I am fully confident there is no dog here today that is capable of pinning my champion Welsh Black.' He pulled a weighty coin bag from his pocket, jingling the sovereigns it held. 'And here is my gold to back my words, if anyone cares to make a wager.'

'I hope there's enough in that bag to pay us all out, Master Wynne,' Samuel Thomas accepted the challenge. 'Because you'll find that we've got plenty of Redditch bulldogs that can eat both your champion Welsh Black and a bloody Welsh Dragon as well for their breakfasts.'

Laughter and applause greeted his words, and Wynne bowed to the needle master. 'Then you and I, sir, will perhaps be making our personal wager in due course.'

'No perhaps about it, you can be sure of it, sir.' Thomas bowed in return, then asked George Wells, 'What's the length of rope to be then, Berrod?'

'Twenty yards!' Wells stated positively.

'That's too long,' Daniel Wynne demurred. 'I believe it should be ten yards, because twenty yards will tire the beast too much for it to hold its own when the Smut comes.'

The Smut came at the end of the baiting by any single dog at one time, and was when all the dogs were simultaneously set on the bull.

'He's got a point there, gentlemen.' Benjamin Sarsons, needle master, nodded sagely. 'We're all true sportsmen here, and want to see fair play, do we not?'

'I'm saying twenty yards because this is a bull that's well accustomed to being baited,' George Wells explained. 'It's become a wise beast that won't be chasing after any dog that turns tail and runs. For that reason it won't be worn out when the Smut comes.'

'George is talking sense, and we oughter do what he says.' Harry James, bricklayer's labourer, loudly voiced his support.

'Well, Master Wynne, do you agree to twenty yards?' Samuel Thomas questioned.

'On one condition.' Wynne was still smiling. 'I propose that instead of the customary fee of five shillings paid to me by the owner of any dog that is put in to bait my bull, the fee must be ten shillings.'

His proposal invoked immediate scowls and exclamations of protest, and he raised his hand.

'Pray hear me out, gentlemen. What I further propose is that the entire sum of these fees be then utilized this very evening to pay for food and liquid refreshment in the Fox and Goose, for all the members of this esteemed committee.'

Scowls became smiles and protests became plaudits.

Samuel Thomas waved old Jimmy Grier to come to him, and Daniel Wynne signalled to Shanko Mawr sitting on horseback at the gated entrance of the meadow, who then rode off.

Tom Potts was also at the entrance gate, as part of his duties to attend such events. He had earlier seen Maisie Lock rejoin her friends up on the green, and had found Daniel Wynne and Shanko Mawr were already there when he arrived. His suspicions that both of the Welshmen were somehow involved in the deaths of Rose Brent and Irish Joe had inexorably strengthened, but as yet he could think of no way to further any investigations.

Now he was concentrating on close observation of the stream of people coming into the meadow, many of whom were already loud and rowdy with drink. He spotted Eugene Sinclair coming down the hill on foot, and noted the scowl on his face.

'What's angered you, Sinclair?' he mused, and hope sprang up. 'Has Amy sent you packing, I wonder?'

Then another incomer took his attention. A neatly clothed youth, whose thin features were heavily pitted with smallpox scars.

Tom searched his stored memory of information garnered personally and from his employer, Joseph Blackwell, since his appointment as Parish Constable.

Remembrance came swiftly, and Tom accepted that for this day at least he must concentrate on this youth rather than his suspicions of the two Welshmen.

'William Elkin! Suspected pickpocket! Father hanged for robbery on the highway. Mother transported for life to Botany Bay. Brother serving hard labour in Warwick Jail. Both sisters working as prostitutes in Birmingham.'

When Elkin passed into the meadow, Tom strolled casually after him, keeping as distant as he could without losing sight of the youth in the seething crowd. He knew that Elkin would not be operating alone. There would be accomplices here to act as decoys, receivers of any loot, blockers of pursuit should the alarm be raised. Tom desperately wanted to identify Elkin's accomplices before the actual bull-baiting commenced, because it would be then that the gang would strike, when excitement and distraction were at their height and with the crowd frantically jostling and pushing for vantage.

For a brief instant Tom considered whether he should arrest Elkin straight away, but realized that if he did so the gang would almost certainly create an uproar that he was arresting an innocent youth and so turn the crowd against himself. Tom knew from bitter experience that the rougher elements present would welcome such a golden opportunity to attack the representative of hated tyrannical authority that was the Parish Constable.

'No! I'll have to wait and catch the buggers in the act. Then the crowd will be on my side.' He smiled wryly to himself. 'Hopefully.'

'Make way! Make way!'

The shouts went up as Shanko Mawr rode back into the meadow leading the big black bull by a short rope from its nose ring.

The Berrod measured out another twenty-yard length of rope, tied one end of it around both the bull's horns and secured the other end to the big iron ring driven deep into the foot-thick post in the centre of the meadow.

Jimmy Grier rang his bell and announced, 'Oyez. Oyez. Oyez. By order of the Committee, each dog will be allowed four minutes to get the pin. The Berrod will keep the time. All those who want to match their dogs against this game bull must pay ten shillings to its owner, Master Daniel Wynne.'

'We only wants to bait the bloody bull, not buy the bugger!' one dog owner bawled indignantly, and shouts of agreement came from half a dozen more.

Jimmy Grier rang his bell until the shouts ceased, and then continued. 'The tether rope is twenty yards long, and the committee wishes to make it known that anybody what comes into the bull's

range except for the handler of the dog what's fighting will be fined
for interfering with the match. If they'm killed by the bull then
their family 'ull have to pay the fine.'

Hoots of derision and catcalls greeted this announcement. Grier
cackled with laughter and gave a two-fingered salute in reply.

The crowd's attention now centred on the bull and there were
many comments about its long, curved, deliberately sharpened horns.

'If you got one o' them up your jacksy, you'd never be able to
sit down again.'

'I'd like it to stick both of 'um up my bloody woman's jacksy,
because she won't never let me get into it these days.'

'I pity the dogs having to go up against that pair o' javelins!'

William Elkin was still moving slowly through the throng.
Because of his height advantage Tom was able to remain on the
fringes and still keep the youth in view. Elkin finally came to a
standstill by the side of a middle-aged man dressed in the black
clerical clothing and wide-brimmed, low-crowned hat favoured by
Dissenter Preachers.

Tom changed his position until he could see the middle-aged
man's face, and hissed with satisfaction as he recognized another
criminal who had been pointed out to him a year previously by
Joseph Blackwell.

'Gloucester Jack! Ticket-of-leave convict returned from trans-
portation. Used to be a pickpocket when he was younger, then
turned to foot-padding. Those two must be working together today.
But are there others here with them?'

Elkin moved on again but Tom's instinct impelled him to stay
where he was and observe Gloucester Jack.

Eugene Sinclair and Martin Cooke had joined company with Daniel
Wynne and the group of Committee men. Many women, girls and
young children had also come on to the meadow, but by established custom they were clustered on a raised bank away from
the crowd of men and youths around the central post. Between
the two groupings a temporary stall had been erected and was
doing brisk business selling cheap gin, rum and brandy.

Daniel Wynne was receiving match fees and passing the money
into the stout leather bag slung over Shanko Mawr's shoulder.
Martin Cooke was watching and seized an opportunity to mutter
anxiously in Wynne's ear.

'I pray to God that your bull does the business today, or I'm
ruined!'

'Don't worry, there's not a dog alive that can pin my Glendower.' Wynne grinned confidently.

Martin Cooke returned to Eugene Sinclair, who asked casually, 'Are you and your cousin acting together in standing the bets, Cooke?'

'No, but I shall be backing his bull,' Cooke said sombrely, and could not stop himself adding, 'And I pray to God that we win.'

Sinclair smiled bleakly. 'Everyone here is offering up that same prayer, Cooke, including myself.'

The Berrod was busily issuing numbered brass tokens to the handlers of the dogs, who would take their individual turns at the bull when their randomly picked number was called.

The dogs were fine specimens of bulldogs, uniformly tall-legged, with barrel chests, heavily muscled shoulders and thick short muzzles. They were trained to clamp their sharp fangs on to the bull's muzzle, cheek, eyepiece or even its tongue and keep that grip until the bull, driven half mad by agonizing pain, would bring itself toppling to the ground in its frantic efforts to free itself from its tormentor. This was known as 'pinning', and the dog ruled to be the best pinner was the one who downed the bull in the shortest time.

The handlers and dogs gathered in a group and waited for their individual summons. Throughout the crowd wagers were being made, odds haggled, prospects loudly discussed, and the air itself seemed charged with excitement.

Daniel Wynne received the final fee; the Berrod issued the final brass token, and took his station as referee directly in front of the Committee.

Jimmy Grier rang his bell. 'Oyez. The Honourable Chairman of the Committee, Samuel Thomas Esquire, will now select the first number. Can we have the best of order?'

Thomas had a bag of brass tokens, and without looking he reached into it and pulled one out, which he handed to the Berrod.

'Number seven!' Wells bellowed.

The crowd parted to let the designated handler through, and when Samuel Thomas saw who it was he cursed disgustedly.

'Goddamn it! It's me own dog! I was hoping a few others might go before him and tire the bull a bit.'

'Oh, it's bad luck indeed, Master Thomas. I don't think your dog stands any chance of getting a pin with the bull so fresh,' Benjamin Sarsons, needle master, sympathized with consummate falsity, but couldn't resist a sneer. 'But then, gentlemen, I've never known

Master Thomas to have much success with any of his dogs, not even when the bull's been half dead on its feet.'

Samuel Thomas scowled and challenged, 'I've got ten sovereigns which says that my dog 'ull still do better than your mangy cur, Master Sarsons.'

'I'll match your ten sovereigns, Master Thomas. Usual rules, of course. If there's any dispute then the Berrod has the final say so.'

'Agreed!' Thomas grunted sourly.

Eugene Sinclair turned to Martin Cooke and Daniel Wynne and hissed contemptuously, 'I trust our personal wagers will not be for such small sums, gentlemen? I'm ready to back my dog to pin your bull for two hundred sovs.'

'Taken,' Wynne agreed instantly.

'How about you, Cooke? You say you have a fancy for the bull. Will you back it against my dog for the same amount?'

Martin Cooke hesitated, biting his lips uncertainly. Then he drew a long breath and nodded. 'Very well, two hundred it is.'

The Berrod brandished his sabre and shouted to the dog handler, 'Four minutes and your time is up. Release your dog!'

The handler slipped the leash. 'Go on! Go on, Slaps, sic the bugger! Sic him!'

The crowd hushed in tense expectancy.

The bull pawed the ground and lowered its wickedly sharpened horns almost to its hooves. Quivering with excitement the dog charged and leapt, and with a single flick of its head the bull hurled the dog high into the air.

The crowd roared, the dog cartwheeled down and thumped back onto the earth. As it scrambled upright the bull's charge thudded into it. The impact sent the dog rolling over and over, squealing in terror as the bull came again, divots of turf flying from under its hooves. The tethering rope brought the bull to a sudden halt and the dog scrabbled desperately to escape between the legs of the nearest onlookers, who kicked and jeered at it for its cowardice.

Puce-faced with rage, Samuel Thomas bellowed at his dog handler, 'Catch that bloody useless thing and hang it!'

'Hang it?' the hapless man quavered nervously. 'Hang it where, Master?'

'From the nearest bloody tree, you thick-yedded bleeder!' Thomas shook his fists in threat. 'And if it aren't hanging dead in two shakes of a rabbit's arse, then I'll bloody hang you!'

The crowd howled with enjoyment as the blanched-faced handler scrambled his way through them and chased after the fleeing dog.

'Dammee, Master Thomas, if I was as bad a judge of a dog as you are, I'd hang myself from that same branch,' Sinclair jeered derisively.

While wagers were being settled and money changed hands, Daniel Wynne issued some instructions to Jimmy Grier.

The old man rang his bell and the crowd quietened expectantly.

'Oyez. Master Daniel Wynne wishes to advise the men of Redditch to stick to making their fine needles, and leave the sport of bull-baiting well alone. He trusts that they can now see that none of their Redditch curs will stand any chance against his brave Glendower . . .'

Growls of angry resentment and defiance came from a score of throats.

Samuel Thomas handed another brass token to George Wells, who bellowed, 'Number fourteen come forward.'

A young needle pointer stepped into the arena to shouts of encouragement, and several other pointers hurried to place their bets. Shanko Mawr took their money and charcoal-pencilled their names and amounts wagered in a ledger.

'Release your dog!' Wells ordered.

The young pointer grinned confidently, and slipped the leash. 'Get him, Billyho. Tear his snout off!'

The dog moved slowly, ears back, snarling fangs glistening. The bull was motionless by the post, almost as if it were lulled by the sudden silence which had fallen over the meadow. The dog rushed, the bull's horns lowered and thrust, the dog dodged sideways, and ran in a circle around the post, then leapt at the bull. Dodging the thrusting horns, circling and repeating the process once, twice, three times, four times more.

'Pretty play! Pretty play!' the supporters yelled in praise, and its grinning handler taunted Daniel Wynne.

'Your bull is too slow to catch my dog, Taffy! You'll be paying us out in a few seconds.'

Daniel Wynne only smiled and made no reply, and the next instant the dog was impaled upon a horn, its howls of agony rising into a crescendo, then dying away to a final whimper as it slid off the horn and lay twitching in its death throes.

The bull savagely pounded upon the limp bleeding corpse until the Berrod ran in to distract it away, enabling the dog's handler to retrieve his animal.

Groans of angry disappointment greeted the bull's victory.

Daniel Wynne rubbed salt into the figurative wounds by lifting his hat and bowing in all directions, shouting triumphantly, 'I warned you, didn't I, gentlemen? My bull is invincible.'

'Number eight, come forward!' the Berrod ordered, and another dog was brought into the central space.

Angered by Wynne's taunting, more men pressed forward to take up his offered odds, and Shanko Mawr was hard pressed to record the various wagers.

'Number thirteen!'

'Number eleven!'

'Number ten!'

'Number three!'

Dog after dog was brought forward. The bull's shoulders and flanks became bloodied by tearing fangs but dog after dog failed to pin and was dragged away, some punctured, some crippled, a few twitching in their death throes.

Still in his vantage point Tom had kept his attention centred upon Gloucester Jack, and now his vigil was rewarded. Two men, one elderly and frail, wearing the Dissenter clerical garb and walking with the aid of a stick, the other younger, burly bodied and dandified, came to stand briefly at Gloucester Jack's side and, when all the attention was centred on the baiting, exchanged words with him before moving away. 'That's all of them,' Tom decided. 'The old man will be the receiver and the younger one and Gloucester Jack will act as decoys and blockers.'

The afternoon was passing. Wagers were being won and lost, large sums of money changing hands. Tempers becoming heated, winning bets cheered, losing bets cursed, atavistic bloodlust constantly vented in the roaring voices of men and the high-pitched shrieking of women and children.

Confident that all the gang was now here, Tom slowly circled around the fringes of the crowd, keeping the old man in his sight.

Up on the green the dancing was still going on, but now the dancers were many fewer in number, comprising only that minority of men, women, youths and girls for whom the bull-baiting held little or no attraction; but even among that minority there were still those who wanted to be in the Pound Meadow.

'I'm fed up with this now. Let's go down to the Pound,' Maisie Lock urged her two friends as a dance ended.

'No, I'm not going down there,' Amy refused flatly. 'I've no interest in watching animals being tormented to death.'

'Oh come on, Amy. They'm only dumb beasts without any souls. They don't feel any torments. Not like we does, anyway,' Maisie protested.

'That's as maybe, but I still don't want to go down there,' Amy restated stubbornly.

'Nor I don't,' Lily Fowkes declared. 'I wants to stay here. That chap over there has asked me to partner him for the next dance.'

'Phooo!' Maisie tossed her head in scorn. 'I wouldn't be seen dead partnering a bloody ugly milksop like him. I only partners proper men. Gentlemen, like my Daniel.'

'That's why you'm so desperate to get down to the Pound, aren't it?' Lily instantly counter-attacked. 'You knows the minute that Taffy is away from you, he's chasing after other women, aren't he? He comes sniffing around me and Amy every chance he gets when your back's turned. Either of us could have him courting us in a trice if we wanted to.'

'Don't you bring me into this, Lily Fowkes!' Amy flared angrily. 'I'm not like you who can't get a sweetheart and has to go making eyes at everything in britches.'

'Well just come down with me for the walk, Amy. You don't have to stay long,' Maisie pleaded.

'Look at the time.' Amy pointed to the clock on the tower of the chapel. 'We've got to be back at work in twenty minutes.'

'Yes we have, or me Dad 'ull go mad else.' Lily added her support to Amy.

'You two might have to be back in twenty minutes, but I don't need to worry about being back at work dead on time,' Maisie informed them loftily.

'Don't talk so sarft!' Lily reproved her. 'You'd be in a right mess if me Dad handed you your sack.'

'No I shan't.' Maisie could not bear to keep her secret a moment longer. 'Because Daniel is going to marry me very soon. We got betrothed this very afternoon.' She patted her firm breasts. 'And I've got his love spoon here, next to me heart.'

Her listeners gaped in shocked astonishment, and she laughed delightedly.

'There now, that's put the cat amongst the pigeons, aren't it just! I'm going to slip down to the Pound now to have a drink wi' my Daniel. Tell the Gaffer I've had to run down to the tollgate wi' some medicine that the doctor's just give me to take to me granddad, that the doctor says me granddad's got to sup this very minute. I'll see you in about an hour.'

Smiling triumphantly, she walked away, leaving her friends gazing wonderingly after her.

FORTY-ONE

In the fetid alley Martha Standard knocked on the door of the terraced cottage, from behind which the whimpering cries of infant children sounded in chorus.

The door opened, expelling a gust of dank, foul-smelling air.

'Come in, come in, it's lovely to see you both,' Hattie Manders' worn-featured, gaunt-bodied mother invited joyfully. 'I said to my man that I was hoping you might come today. But then I thought that Master Daws hadn't give you the time off when you didn't come.'

As she stepped into the small room, which at first glance was furnished solely with ragged, snot-nosed small children and babies, Martha explained, 'Well when we got here the procession was just about to start, and Hattie had set her mind on going along with it, so we did. And then after that there was dancing on the green, and Hattie's been looking forward to it so much that I hadn't got the heart to drag her from it.' She went on, 'But she can stay here tonight with you, and she needn't get back to the farm afore noon-time tomorrow.'

'You can stay as well, if you wants to, Martha. You'll be more than welcome. The kids can bodge up in bed to make room for you.'

'No, I can't stay, Mrs Manders, thank you all the same,' Martha hastily declined. 'I've only popped in to drop Hattie off safely. I've got to go and get the horse and cart and fetch my master home from the bull-baiting. He'll be too drunk to drive it himself.'

The other woman grimaced. 'And my old man 'ull be in the same state wi'out a doubt. Still, fair play to him. He give me the house-keep money afore he went to the bull bait, so I can't begrudge him his bit o' pleasure, can I? There's a good many buggers in this town who spends all the housekeep money on drink, and gives their women naught but hard words and black eyes.'

'Tarra, Mrs Manders, and I'll see you tomorrow, Hattie. Now make sure you'm back at the farm by noontime, or the Master 'ull be taking his belt to you else.'

Martha exited and made her way back to the centre of the town where John Daws had stabled his horse and cart.

Maisie Lock pushed through to the forefront of the women and children on the raised bank and was able to see Daniel Wynne. During a momentary lessening of the crowd's noise she waved frantically and shouted to him at the top of her voice. He looked straight at her, but then turned away without acknowledging her greeting.

''Tis no use you skrawking at your man, my duck. No bloke pays any mind to us lot when the baiting's going on,' a woman at her side sympathized. 'You'll need to wait until it's over and done with. Then he might pay you some mind and be tender to you.'

There was no tender thought for any woman in Daniel Wynne's mind, as yet another time-failed dog was dragged yelping and struggling from the arena. All Wynne's attention was focussed on Eugene Sinclair, whose dog was now the next and last to be entered against the bull.

'I've already wagered two hundred sovs on my dog, Wynne; are you brave enough to accept my staking a further hundred?' Sinclair challenged.

'Of course I am. There is no possibility of me having to pay out,' Wynne stated confidently.

'Take a good look at your beast.' Sinclair smiled. 'It's in very poor fettle, and I'll swallow my own turds if that last dog hasn't done for its right eye.'

Despite his outward show of confidence, Daniel Wynne was uneasily aware of the condition of his bull. It stood visibly swaying, with lowered head and heaving flanks, froths of sweat mingling with the blood flowing copiously from its torn wounds.

From his position next to Wynne, Shanko Mawr had overheard what Sinclair said. He intervened, speaking in the Welsh tongue.

'I reckon the bastard is right, Brother-in-law. It looks to me that Glendower's right eye has gone. If his dog is any good at all it'll come in on the blind side and make the pin.'

'I've enquired about his dog.' Wynne winked slyly. 'It's a young one and it's never been put to the baiting before. It's got no chance.'

'Number six, come forward,' the Berrod ordered, and informed the crowd, 'This is the final dog, and the last chance to make your bets.'

A sandy-haired, tough-looking man dressed like a needle pointer led the dog into the circle and the crowd buzzed with excitement.

'It's Ritchie Bint, and Gripper.'

'I'll have some o' that.'

'And I 'ull!'

'And me!'

Men scurried to cluster around Shanko Mawr, clamouring to bet on Gripper. The most famous bulldog in the locality, it had pinned every bull it had been pitted against during the preceding four years.

'That isn't your dog, Sinclair,' Daniel Wynne accused. 'It's owned by Ritchie Bint.'

The other man pulled a sheet of paper from his pocket and held it up in front of Wynne's eyes. 'I bought Gripper from Bint three days ago; here's the bill of sale. I am its present owner, and this bill of sale is the proof of that. Ritchie Bint is merely serving as my handler today.' He folded the paper and pushed it back into his pocket, then smiled. 'If you'll excuse me I'll go and place my further bet with your man.'

He sauntered away, leaving Daniel Wynne thinking hard. When all the bets had been placed he asked Shanko Mawr, 'What do you think our chances are?'

Mawr shook his shaggy head. 'Not good. Not good at all. That bloody dog is a champion pinner.'

'How do I stand if Glendower is pinned?'

'There's not enough in the bag to pay them off. You'll be lucky to get out of here alive, and me with you.'

Desperate to gain time in which to think, Wynne stepped forward and shouted, 'Hold hard! I want my bull freshened first.'

The Berrod frowned at having his authority countermanded. 'By rule the bull can only be freshened when it's time for the Smut. And that'll be after this final dog has had its run.'

Wynne turned and appealed to the Committee members. 'You Redditch men have always had a reputation for fair play, gentlemen. Eighteen dogs have had a turn at my bull, and this next one makes a total of nineteen. You know as well as I that generally a bull is baited by only a dozen or so dogs. Surely you won't begrudge my bull being freshened after taking so many dogs on.'

Sinclair immediately objected. 'The traditional rule must be adhered to, gentlemen. The bull can only be freshened when the last dog has had its run.'

Samuel Thomas, still smarting at Sinclair's previous gibe, sided with Daniel Wynne. 'I think Master Wynne has a point, gentlemen. It's only fair play to let his beast be sluiced down and watered after having so many dogs set at it.'

Other members of the Committee who had staked money on Gripper spoke against Thomas, and a heated argument erupted.

Meanwhile, Martha Standard had tethered the horse and cart to the Pound fence and had come up onto the raised bank. Peering down at the seething noisy crowd of men and youths, she sought for her master, John Daws.

Tom Potts' hands were trembling with nervous tension. While he had been watching, William Elkin and Gloucester Jack had both passed the old man several times, momentarily pressing close to him as if forced to by the proximity of the crowd. Tom was certain that in those brief moments pickpocketed loot had been passed over. He was desperately trying to gather his courage, while the prospect of violent confrontation was as always shortening his breath, drying his mouth and throat, churning his stomach.

'Ah, there you are, you old bugger.' Martha Standard sighted her employer, and smiled resignedly. 'And you're as drunk as a bob-owler by the looks of you.'

She asked the woman next to her. 'What's happening now? Have all the dogs had a run at the bull?'

'No, there's still Ritchie Bint's dog, Gripper, to have its go. But from the looks of it the Committee am having high words about summat or other, so that's why we'em having to wait, I expect.' She pointed to the group of disputing men in the centre of the circle.

Martha's gaze locked on one of the group, and she drew a sharp-hissed breath, telling herself, 'It's him again! And it is him, aren't it? I don't know though. One second I thinks it's him, and the next second I aren't sure!'

The disputants moved, and she lost her clear view of his features as the man changed position.

'I needs to speak to him,' she decided. 'I needs to be face to face with him, and tell him that I knows who he is. That's the only way that I'll be able to be sure. But what shall I do when I am sure?'

She spotted the top hat, head and shoulders of Tom Potts above the outer fringes of the crowd, and sighed with relief. 'I can tell the constable, can't I? I can tell Master Potts and he'll arrest him and question him about Rosie, won't he?'

Daniel Wynne had won his argument and buckets of water were being fetched and dashed over the bull, reviving it so much that it began to bellow and charge at the bucket bearers. But as the blood, frothed sweat and dirt was washed from the bull's head and body, Wynne's spirits plummeted. The bull's right eye had been virtually torn from the socket, and a loose flapping skein of ripped hide appeared to be semi-masking the sight of its left eye.

While the majority attention was centred on the freshening of the bull, Shanko Mawr whispered sibilantly in Wynne's ear. Wynne visibly tensed and, after a pause, nodded assent.

The Berrod shouted at Wynne, 'Your beast is well freshened, Master Wynne. The last dog must have his run at it now.'

Wynne nodded. 'Bring it on, Master Wells.'

To a roar of cheering Ritchie Bint brought Gripper to the forefront and paraded it before its supporters while Shanko Mawr used a hooked stick to lead the bull by the nose-ring back to its station at the central post.

The inner circle re-established its boundary and as Shanko Mawr came to rejoin the Committee grouping he exchanged a brief glance with Daniel Wynne, and that glance carried a silent message.

'Where be you going?'

'You can't come in here!'

'There's no fuckin' wenches allowed!'

Indignant protests assailed Martha Standard as she pushed and wriggled through the throng of men and youths. A hand grabbed her arm, and she twisted her head and bit down hard on a finger.

'Oww! You fuckin' bitch!'

She pulled free and with one final push and wriggle broke through to the clear circle and ran towards the group of Committee men. Pointing her hand she shrieked shrilly, 'It is you, aren't it? You'm Rosie's sweetheart! I knows you now. I remember seeing you with her. I'm going to tell the constable about you, so I am.'

The man she pointed at stared back at her in wide-eyed shock, but in that same instant the Berrod's arm clamped round her neck, choking off her shouts, and she felt herself being lifted and literally thrown back against the circle of spectators.

'Get rid o' this cheeky cow! Her's taking the piss coming in here like this. Her's breaking all the rules!' Wells bawled in fury.

Brutal hands seized her and she was buffeted through the throng and hurled bodily from it. She thudded face first onto the ground, and blood poured as her nose smashed from the force of the impact. She lay sobbing in agony and several women came running to her side, lifting her and bearing her back towards the raised bank.

'Bastards! All men are bastards!'

'There was no call to do that to the poor little wench!'

'We'll tend to you, my duck!'

John Daws emerged from the crowd and stumbled drunkenly in pursuit, shouting, 'Wait for me! Wait for me!'

Tom had seen what had occurred and immediately started around the crowd to go to the girl. But as he was moving he saw that aid had already reached her. He turned and hurried back to his initial position, and his impelling instinct was that he must now make the attempt to capture the gang of pickpockets without further delay.

Some of the men near him were laughing and he overheard snatches of their talk.

'What was her shouting at the Committee?'

'Summat about one of them being a sweetheart.'

'Ahrr, I heard that bit. Her reckoned that her was going to tell on him. Which one of 'um was it?'

'I don't know. I thought her called him Ross, or summat like that.'

Tom's heart pounded. 'Ross? Rose? Rosie? Did she mean Rose Brent?'

He stared hard at the Committee group. Even at a distance he could make out that both Daniel Wynne and Shanko Mawr looked tense and strained, and his heartbeat became a thundering drum roll. 'Was she pointing at either of those two? Either of them could be the guilty man!'

He looked across at the raised bank and saw that to its side John Daws, with the help of some women, was placing Martha Standard into a cart, and even as he watched Daws mounted the cart and drove it out of the Pound meadow and away.

'I can go to the farm and talk to Martha tomorrow. But for the present I've got more than enough on my plate to deal with,' he decided. 'But which one of this gang do I go for first?'

'Release your dog, Bint!' the Berrod shouted and the crowd roared as Gripper, with sharp white fangs glistening in a snarl, head and body crouching low, zigzagged towards the bull. The bull snorted, pawed the slippery muddied turf and jerked its head from side to side trying to keep the dog in sight with its sole good eye.

A bystander handed Ritchie Bint a long thin bamboo pole which he hefted and balanced in both hands.

Gripper suddenly hurled itself at the bull, and the next instant was tossed up into the air. The crowd howled, Ritchie Bint darted to slip the pole under the falling body, and the dog slid down it into Bint's cradling arms.

Bint laughed and shouted triumphantly, 'Landed soft as a feather, and not a scratch on him!'

The dog barked excitedly and Bint cuffed its head and ordered sharply, 'Quieten down, you daft bastard, and do what you'm meant to do! Get the black bugger on his blind side this time!'

He set the dog down to face the bull, and the crowd hushed expectantly. The dog began to snake forwards and suddenly a furious brawl erupted in a section of the crowd, and fiercely struggling men spilled into the arena.

'Pickpockets! Pickpockets!' The cry was taken up, drowning out Tom's own shouts as he tried to force his way through milling bodies.

'Make way! Make way in the King's name!'

Then high-pitched howls of panic penetrated the din.

'The bull's loose! The bull's loose! The bull's loose!'

There was an instant stampede in all directions, men knocking other men to the ground and trampling over them in frantic flight as the maddened uncontrollable juggernaut of animal bone and muscle rampaged through the terror-stricken mob.

Within scant seconds Tom found himself battered down onto his hands and knees by the side of the thick central post.

'What the hell am I doing here? Am I hurt?'

He could feel no acutely stabbing pains, so grasped the post and tentatively pulled himself upright to stare at the scene around him.

All around the Pound people were scaling the fences and hedgerows to escape from the charging bull, while scattered across the turf sprawled at least a dozen groaning men and youths knocked down and injured in the pandemonium.

Although severely shaken, Tom was able to think clearly, but his thoughts brought him no comfort.

'What a mess I've made of this,' he chided himself angrily. 'I should have taken Elkin into custody the moment I set eyes on him. The whole gang will be legging it away from here by now. What a damned useless mawkin I am!'

He saw his top hat and staff on the ground a little way off and retrieved them, his initial anger now being rapidly overshadowed by bitter self-disgust and recrimination.

'It was my own cowardice that stopped me from tackling the gang when I'd identified them, wasn't it? I'm not worthy to be called my father's son. The poor man would be turning in his grave from shame if he had seen me behave as lily-livered as I did today ... As I do on every other day, truth be told!'

He saw the Committee men gathered on the other side of the closed gate and ran to join them. A heated argument was raging between Eugene Sinclair and the Berrod.

'The bull must be brought back to the post and my dog must have its run at it,' Sinclair claimed.

'That can't be done,' George Wells insisted. 'It's against the rules. No bull can be run at again once it's broke its tether and gone gallivanting around. It tires the beast and makes it so fuddled that it's unfair for it to be baited again on that same day.'

'But what about my wagers?' Sinclair's voice rose furiously.

'All wagers on your dog are null and void and the stakes must be returned,' Samuel Thomas declared. 'That's the rule we follows in Redditch, Sinclair, and you must like it or lump it!'

He saw that Tom had come to join them, and swung to accuse him. 'What the hell was you playing at, Constable Potts? There was a bloody pickpocket at work and you failed to spot him. The bugger's got away now, aren't he?'

'I know him and one of his gang, Master Thomas, and I'll be able to recognize two others. I was trying to get through the crowd to arrest them when the bull broke loose and I was knocked down in the panic.'

'Well, get after them now then,' Thomas urged. 'They can't have got far.'

'They'll most certainly have horses hidden nearby. Then they'll split up and travel in different directions and there are dozens of tracks they can use,' Tom pointed out. 'My best course of action is to have the magistrates issue warrants and wanted notices for the two whom I know and raise the hue and cry for them.'

Samuel Thomas was forced to accept that this was the only useful course of action to take, and grunted, 'Make sure that you does that then.'

A little distance from the group Daniel Wynne and Shanko Mawr had been talking with the handlers of some of the uninjured dogs, and now Wynne came to inform the Committee, 'We're going to use the dogs to corner my bull, and then my man and myself will rope and nose-ring him.'

'I trust that you'll be using a better quality rope than the one you used to tie it to the post,' Sinclair sneered venomously.

'What do you mean by that?' Wynne frowned.

'Well, having the tether rope snap when it did was a very fortunate escape for you, was it not? It's saved you a deal of money. My dog would have pinned your bull without a shadow of a doubt.'

Wynne smiled grimly. 'Have you forgotten that the tether rope was supplied by the Berrod here? Are you implying that Master Wells might have deliberately tampered with it in order to let the bull break free at that exact moment?'

Wells' features reddened with indignant fury and he growled menacingly, 'Any man who accuses me of cheating had better be ready to get his jaw broke, even though he might belong to some high-and-mighty gentry family.'

'For shame, gentlemen, this is not the time to squabble among ourselves. There are men lying injured who need our help.' Unnoticed by the others the curate, John Clayton, had been listening close by. 'I've sent word for any available doctor to come down here. Now I would suggest that while Master Wynne and his helpers deal with the bull, the rest of us do whatever we can to aid the injured.'

There was a general murmur of assent.

The bull was on the far side of the field and George Wells shouted, 'Come on then, lads. Bring the dogs and let's try and keep the bugger bottled up over there.'

Whooping and cheering, their dogs barking excitedly, the trapping party streamed through the gate. Other men and women had now gathered ready to help the injured.

Clayton announced, 'We'll make a start. Only move those who can safely be lifted. Leave the others lying until the doctors have seen them, but ensure that they can breathe without choking and try to staunch any blood loss . . . And if any of you should find any articles that have been dropped, would you please bring them to me to return to the owners. I'm confident the finders will be rewarded, if not on this earth, then undoubtedly in Heaven.'

Martin Cooke came to Tom and said, 'Let's you and I work together, Master Potts.'

As they entered the meadow side by side Cooke remarked, 'Truth to tell I'm glad to have the opportunity to do something to help. I feel guilty that I wasn't able to aid that poor girl who was so roughly handled earlier.'

Tom's attention focussed immediately. 'Did you happen to see who she was pointing at, or hear what she said? Only I've heard that she mentioned the name Ross, or maybe Rose, and accused the man of being a sweetheart. I can't help but wonder if it might have something to do with Rose Brent.'

The other man shook his head. 'I've no idea who it might have something to do with. I was deep in conversation when the girl began shouting, and only caught sight of the Berrod grabbing her and throwing her into the crowd. But perhaps you may be able to find out who she is, and go and talk to her yourself.'

'Oh, I know her, and where she lives. It's just a matter of being able to find the time to go and see her. Which after what's happened here won't be until tomorrow noontime at the very soonest, because I'll have to spend most of the morning explaining my failure to catch any pickpockets to Joseph Blackwell.'

'Well I wish you luck with him. I wouldn't have your job for any price.' Cooke smiled sympathetically.

'Most of the time if I had any choice in the matter, neither would I have my job,' Tom admitted ruefully as he bent over the nearest groaning victim.

FORTY-TWO

The darkness of the night was split only by wide scattered occasional flickers of lightning followed by grumblings of thunder. The belt of storm clouds travelled slowly up from the southwest, heralding their arrival with spasmodic flurries of raindrops which gradually developed into a continuous heavy downpour.

In the farmhouse kitchen in the dim flickering light of a solitary candle Martha Standard sat huddled on a low stool holding a cold wet rag to her smashed nose in a fruitless endeavour to lessen its painful throbbing.

From the bedroom above her head the long shuddering drunken snores of John Daws were a constant accompaniment to the distant rolls of thunder. But his discordant noises did not intrude upon Martha's thoughts. She was too engrossed to take heed of anything other than her utter determination that tomorrow she would act.

'At first light. At first light I'm going up to Redditch to tell Tom Potts about that man. It is him! I'm sure of it now. At first light, I'm going up to see Tom Potts.'

The rain slackened and virtually ceased as the horseman reined in at the bottom of the track which led off the lane and up to Daws' farmhouse. He dismounted and tied the reins to a hedge branch, then moved cautiously forwards on foot. As he neared the black shapes of the house and outbuildings he could distinguish the dim glow of candlelight in a downstairs window.

He flattened himself against the wall of a brick outhouse which stretched to within a couple of yards of the lighted window and slowly edged nearer to his goal.

When he reached the end of the outhouse wall he stood considering his next move.

A frantically barking sheepdog came hurtling out of the darkness and the man's heart missed a beat as shock struck through him. He ran away from the house and the dog followed in noisy pursuit, snapping at his ankles and becoming entangled with his pumping legs, bringing them both tumbling to the ground. But now the man reacted with adrenaline-fuelled speed, scissor-gripping the dog's body with his legs, locking his hands around its narrow neck, digging his thumbs deep into the collared throat and, with a sudden grunting twisting jerk, breaking the neck of the wriggling furry body.

The sudden eruption of barking caused Martha involuntarily to jerk her hand, sending an excruciating shaft of pain lancing through her head.

'Ohhhhh, look what you'se made me do, you bloody dog!' she groaned angrily. 'I forgot to shut you in the bloody shed, didn't I, and you'll be racketing around and making a bloody nuisance of yourself all night if I don't put you in now.'

Moving very carefully she rose from the stool and went to lift a whale-oil lantern from its hanging nail. She lit the wick using the candle and wrapped a shawl around her head and shoulders, then went outside calling, 'Spot? Spot? Where are you, boy? Come here! Come here, Spot!'

She walked slowly, swinging the lantern beam from side to side of the wet track way, and all the time calling, 'Come here, Spot. Good boy, Spot! Come here now!'

There came a gusting of wind and the downpouring of rain recommenced.

'Oh, damn it, I'll not stay out here and catch me death o' cold for the sake of that bloody dog.'

As she turned back towards the house, a black figure confronted her, and her scream was cut short as arms and hands clamped her chest and throat in a vice-like grip which slowly, inexorably, crushed the life-giving oxygen from her lungs.

FORTY-THREE

I t was not yet full dawn when the ringing of the lock-up bells roused Tom Potts from his bed. Still in his night-shirt and nightcap he drowsily padded on bare feet to creak open the front door. The sight of his caller shocked him.

'Amy! What is it? What are you doing here?''

'It's Maisie, Tom. She still hasn't come back.' Amy Danks' face was pale and anxious.

'Come back? Come back from where?'

'From the Pound.'

'From the Pound? But nobody's down in the Pound.' Tom was desperately trying to clear his sleep-fuddled brain. 'By the time I left there it was empty. Everybody had gone.'

'Was she hurt?' Amy questioned anxiously. 'There was people hurt down there, wasn't there?'

'Some men and lads were hurt. None of them very badly, thank God! But none of the women or girls came to any harm.' Tom recognized how distressed Amy was, and invited her gently, 'You'd best come inside and sit down. Just give me a few moments to get dressed and to wake up properly, then you can tell me the whole story about Maisie.'

'There's little to tell.' Amy shook her head as she stepped inside. 'She just said that she was going down to the Pound to have a quick drink with her Welshman.'

Her words drove all thought of getting dressed from Tom's mind. 'Her Welshman?' he echoed.

'Yes, he's the drover named Daniel Wynne. She said that they'd got betrothed that very afternoon and were to marry very soon.' A note of scornful disparagement entered Amy's voice. 'She was swanking about in the silk gloves he gave her. He hadn't given her a pledge ring though. But she said he'd given her a love spoon and she was wearing it next to her heart! She didn't show it us though.'

The nuggets of information merged with all of Tom's previous suspicions to become a thundering avalanche in his mind.

Welsh love spoons! Wearing it next to her heart! Promise to

marry very soon! Gifts of fashionable, expensive silken articles of clothing! Rose Brent, Irish Tessy at Worcester, the drowned girl at Bewdley! And now Maisie Lock! Surely there were too many similarities between one or another of them for it to be merely a chain of unrelated coincidence.

'What do you think, Tom?'

Tom was so deep in thought that Amy was forced to repeat her question before it penetrated his consciousness.

'Tom! What do you think?'

To soothe her anxiety he hastily sought to reassure her. 'I think that she more than likely has spent the night with Daniel Wynne. But to put your mind at rest I'll go and speak with him myself just as soon as I'm dressed. You go back to the Fox and take some breakfast now, and I'll come and see you as soon as I find out where Maisie is.'

He ushered her through the door, telling her confidently, 'Now try not to worry, my dear; I'm positive Maisie is well and happy. She'll more than likely be back within the hour trying to make you and Lily jealous by telling you what a wonderful night she's spent.'

As the door closed, however, Tom's confident smile metamorphosed into a concerned frown. He hurriedly washed and dressed, snatched up his constable's staff and satchel and exited the lock-up.

Joseph Blackwell pushed his half-eaten breakfast platter to one side and stared sourly at his early-morning caller.

'I've already received a full account of the events of yesterday, Constable Potts. So if you've come with excuses as to why you failed to capture the pickpockets, then you may spare me from hearing them.'

'I have come to tell you of the pickpocket gang, sir, but more importantly I'm also here to ask you for the immediate loan of a horse.'

'For what reason?'

'Another young woman from this locality appears to have gone missing, and I want to make urgent enquiries concerning her.'

'You'd best give me a full explanation.' Interest sparked in Blackwell's voice and he took his customary posture, leaning forward with his chin resting on steepled forefingers, his shrewd eyes locked on Tom's face.

Tom related all he had been told by Amy Danks, and the older man listened intently until Tom fell silent, then stated confidently,

'You believe that her disappearance may be connected in some way with the deaths of Rose Brent and the man known as Irish Joe.'

'Indeed I do, sir,' Tom confirmed without hesitation. 'And I also believe that there are other women who have been killed by the same hands.'

'And can you name who those hands belong to?'

'I can't prove it at this time, sir, but I strongly suspect that two Welsh drovers are implicated in all these deaths. They are Daniel Wynne and his man who is nicknamed Shanko Mawr, which means "Big Shanko" in the Welsh tongue.'

Blackwell nodded and, seemingly at a tangent, asked, 'What about the pickpockets yesterday?'

Well used to the interrogative methods of his employer, Tom was not disconcerted by this change of direction. 'There were four of them in the gang as far as I could ascertain. William Elkin, Gloucester Jack and two accomplices, both of whom I'll be able to recognize at sight.'

'How much did they manage to steal?'

'According to the complaints made to me they stole a deal of money, valuable fob watches, silver snuff boxes and a great many silken kerchiefs.' Tom shook his head in doubt. 'But in all truth, sir, I believe that many of those victims were only hiding from their creditors what they claimed to have been stolen.'

'As always, Constable, as always.' Blackwell smiled with grim amusement. 'Can anyone identify the actual individual who robbed them? How about the fellow who grabbed the pickpocket?'

Again Tom shook his head. 'That was Henry Bayliss, and the man he took to be the pickpocket and began fighting with was his own brother, George Bayliss. Both of them were drunk out of their minds.'

'Well, it's of no importance.' Blackwell snorted dismissively. 'I shall just call up my usual witnesses when these scum are laid by the heels. I'll have the magistrates issue warrants today for Elkin and Gloucester Jack, and arrange for the printing of the wanted notices. Now, with your permission, I would like to continue with my breakfast in peace. You'd best go round to my stables and tell my groom he is to loan you my riding mare. Good day to you, Constable.'

It was mid-morning when Tom rode into the New Wharf at Tardebigge and sought out Martin Cooke in his office. He noted that the other man appeared drawn-featured and weary and asked, 'Are you unwell, Master Cooke?'

Cooke grimaced. 'I slept badly last night. There were a lot of things on my mind. I have a great deal of worrisome concerns at this time.'

'Is there any way in which I can be of assistance to you?' Tom liked this ruggedly handsome man and his offer was sincerely made.

Cooke sighed heavily and shook his head. 'No, Master Potts. But I thank you for your kindness. Now what is it you want of me?'

Tom had already decided that he must act with discretion. 'Oh, nothing of importance. I was passing and thought that I'd enquire as to the condition of Master Wynne's bull. There is much interest in the town concerning the beast. Is it in your paddock?'

'Not now. It was there overnight but Daniel told me that he and his man would be setting out for his farm in Wales at dawn this morning, and the beast had gone before I came to work. I've not seen either of them however since they left the Pound meadow yesterday.'

'I've journeyed several times through Wales myself when my father was in the army,' Tom mused. 'I might well have unknowingly passed your cousin's farm.'

'I doubt it,' Cooke demurred smilingly. 'He lives close to a small village on the western side of the Cambrian Mountains. A place called Pontrhydfendigaid. There's very little foreign traffic passing through it, I do assure you.'

'Now I'm going to surprise you, Master Cooke. I've actually visited the ruins of the Strata Florida Abbey not above a mile from the centre of Pontrhydfendigaid.'

'Good God!' Cooke exclaimed in surprise. 'My cousin's farm lies only half a mile south from those ruins.'

'Well, I'll not disturb you further, Master Cooke.' Tom moved to the office door. 'I have to go to Worcester on official business.'

'I'll see you off; I need a breath of fresh air.' Cooke accompanied Tom outside and as Tom mounted and prepared to leave remarked casually, 'If you make good speed you might well overtake my cousin. He's going back to Wales via Worcester and Leominster, and he'll not travel fast with the bull in the condition it is.'

'I'll keep an eye out for him then. Good day to you.' Tom turned his mount and moved off, and when he was passing out of the wharf entrance Cooke shouted after him.

'Master Potts, if you should happen to overtake my cousin, would you please remind him from me that he is to tell his wife I've ordered the cloth she wanted, and will forward it to her as soon as I receive it.'

The words hit Tom like a physical blow. 'Wife! Daniel Wynne is married!'

He waved back to Cooke and continued on to the roadway with his conviction of Daniel Wynne's involvement in Rose Brent's death hardening rapidly.

'Now I have a likely motive. He killed Rose because she was pregnant, and he feared that his wife would find out. And it could well be that he killed the girl at Bewdley for the same reason. And Maisie Lock? What has he done to poor Maisie Lock?'

Tom began feverishly estimating approximate times and distances.

It appeared that Daniel Wynne had left the wharf at dawn, around the hour of six a.m. It was now just turned ten a.m, so Tom was some four hours behind him. After the ordeal of the baiting, the bull would be in poor condition, so it probably would not be driven at any speed much above two miles an hour.

'From Tardebigge to Bromsgrove is three miles. Bromsgrove to Droitwich, six miles. Droitwich to Worcester, six miles. So Wynne could be eight or nine miles in front of me. Perhaps just coming into Droitwich? This is a strong, fit horse, and should cover eight or nine miles an hour at a sustainable pace. By the time I reach Droitwich, Wynne might not be more than two miles ahead of me, and within a further half hour I could be looking into his face.'

Suffused with the grim determination to confront and arrest Daniel Wynne, no matter the odds, Tom spurred his mount into a fast canter towards Droitwich.

FORTY-FOUR

As Tom Potts was leaving the Tardebigge Wharf, some miles away across the countryside Hattie Manders came running down the track towards John Daws' farmhouse, her ill-fitting hob-nailed boots splashing through the muddy puddles left by the heavy overnight rainstorms. She rounded the final curve of the narrow track and came to a stumbling halt, eyes widening in shock at the scene before her.

Part of the front walls and thatched roof of the farmhouse had collapsed and wisps of steamy smoke spiralled upwards from the fire-blackened rubble.

'Martha?' the child called plaintively. 'Master Daws? Spot?'

Only the soughing of the wind answered her calls.

She took fearful, hesitant steps forwards, calling repeatedly, 'Martha? Am you here, Martha? Martha? Where am you, Martha?'

Sudden terror shuddered through her and the overpowering impulsion to seek refuge in her mother's arms dominated all other instincts. She took flight, screaming at the top of her voice.

'Mammmm! Mammmmm! Mammmmm!'

FORTY-FIVE

The turnpike road linking Bromsgrove, Droitwich and Worcester was a busy transit route and traffic of all kinds was plentiful: dashing mail coaches, huge lumbering stage-wagons, farm carts, private carriages and pony-traps. Besides those, waddling strings of cackling geese, flocks of bleating sheep, small herds of lowing cattle, keening drovers and barking dogs made their way along the road, alongside trudging artisans, labourers, pedlars, tinkers, soldiers, tramps, women and girls, men and boys enveloped in talk and noise.

The difficulty for Tom was that two men and a solitary bull attracted little or no attention within this swirling throng. Several times he reined in to ask, 'Have you passed two men driving a black bull?' only to be answered with shrugs and shaking heads.

He entered the ancient town of Droitwich and dismounted briefly, watering his horse at the public trough, rubbing his aching legs and sore buttocks, admitting ruefully to himself, 'Dear God, you're a bloody terrible rider, Tom Potts. A sack of potatoes could sit on a horse more gracefully than you.'

He remounted and rode on, leaving Droitwich behind. Three miles further as he breasted a sharp rise in the road he sighted on the reverse slope some thirty yards before him two animals tethered to a hitching rail outside a roadside tavern. A saddled horse and a black bull. He rose closer until he was near enough to confirm the bull's identity from the fresh wounds on its head and flanks. Then he reined in his mount and sat staring at the animals, his heart thudding, mouth drying as mingled elation and apprehension flooded through his mind.

'I've got them. But only the one horse? Who's riding it?'

The image of the huge-bodied Shanko Mawr, and the athletic physique of Daniel Wynne, rose forebodingly in his mind. His hand went to the crowned staff tied to the saddle pommel.

'If there's trouble I'll need to use this, because I stand no chance with my fists against either of them.'

As always the prospect of violent confrontation was filling him with dread, and he had to struggle against the urge to go past the tavern and gallop on into Worcester to seek assistance from Henry Vickery, the Head Constable. He marshalled all his determination.

'No, I'll not shame my father's memory by shirking my rightful duty.'

He kneed his horse up to the rail and dismounted. He tethered the beast, took the staff, drew in a long deep breath and nerved himself to walk through the open tavern door. But even as he took the first step the shaggy-headed Shanko Mawr emerged from within and demanded with a scowl, 'What are you doing here, Englishman?'

Tom swallowed hard. He topped the other man by an inch in height, but the Welshman was twice as broad and maybe three times as strong.

'I'm looking for Daniel Wynne.'

'Why?'

'I need to speak with him.' Now that the actual moment of confrontation had come Tom found that his determination enabled him to mask his fear and to keep his voice firm. 'Now where is he? I'm asking in the King's name, so you'll be wise to answer truthfully.'

'And I'm asking in the name of Shanko Mawr, why are you looking for the bastard?' The huge man's yellowed teeth bared in a threatening snarl.

'Just tell me where he is,' Tom reiterated.

'Go fuck yourself!' Mawr growled and sent Tom stumbling sideways with a casual swipe of his massively thick arm before walking back towards his horse.

Tom recovered his balance and went after him. 'Hold hard, Mawr. I'm ordering you in the King's name, hold hard.'

The Welshman turned and they stood face to face only inches apart.

'Now, where is Daniel Wynne?' Tom demanded.

'Fuck off, you Sais pig!' Mawr hawked and spat a gob of spittle and phlegm straight into Tom's face.

White-hot fury flamed through Tom's brain. He stepped back a pace and swung his staff with all his strength. The lead-weighted, carved crown thudded into the side of Shanko Mawr's head, and as his eyes rolled upwards, he swayed from side to side once, twice, three times, four times, then slowly crumpled to the ground.

Tom stood staring bemusedly down at the stunned Welshman. 'I can't believe I did that!'

'Dammee, Constable! That was a neat stroke.' A grinning, scarlet-coated army officer rode up to Tom's side. 'I could use a man like you in my regiment.'

Tom was struggling to collect his scattered thoughts.

'What's this fellow done?' The officer asked.

'I'm not really sure,' Tom was forced to confess.

The officer laughed uproariously.

Shanko Mawr stirred, and Tom was forced to make a quick decision. He took his manacles and chains from his saddle-bag and requested, 'Would you please help me to secure this man on to that horse, sir? I ask this in the King's name.'

'How can I refuse you, Constable, when I hold His Majesty's commission?'

The officer shouted to the squad of redcoats halted on the road. 'Get this fellow on to that horse and tie him tight.'

Within brief seconds Shanko Mawr was slung face downwards over his horse's saddle with hands and feet manacled and chained together under the beast's belly.

'There now, that should hold the brute.' The officer saluted Tom. 'Good day to you, Constable.'

'Many thanks, sir. I'm truly grateful to you.'

Tom stood watching the soldiers march away towards Worcester, and couldn't help but wish that they were going instead towards Redditch.

Using a length of rope he extended Mawr's horse's reins and attached them to the pommel of his own saddle. Then he did the same thing to secure the bull's nose-ring rope to the pommel of Mawr's saddle. Wondering worriedly as he did so, 'What in Hell's name will I do with this man now? And what do I do about searching further for Wynne and Maisie Lock? And what am I to do with this bloody bull?'

FORTY-SIX

'Oh my God! What's the matter, child? What's happened?' Elly Manders shrieked in alarm as her gasping, sobbing daughter burst through the door.

'It's burned and fell down, Mam! It's burned and fell down,' the child choked out.

'What's burned and fell down?'

'The house!'

'What bloody house?' the mother snapped impatiently.

'The one where I works!' the child wailed.

Elly Manders' gaunt features twisted in anger and she shouted, 'Has you been playing with the fire again, you little sod? How many times has I told you not to? I'll bloody well skin you alive!' She stepped forwards, hand raised in threat.

'No, it warn't me! I never didn't never touch no fire!' the girl denied desperately. 'I never! I never! The house was fell down when I got there. Honest it was, Mam! Honest!'

The woman realized that her child was telling the truth and demanded, 'Where's Master Daws and Martha?'

'They warn't there! I shouted for 'um, but they never come.'

'Oh my God!' The possible implications of that information immediately galvanized the girl's mother. She snatched up her shawl and told Hattie, 'You stay here and look after the little 'uns. I'll not be long.'

'Where's you going, Mam?' the girl asked anxiously.

'I'm going to tell the constable to go over to Master Daws' place and see what's happened to him and Martha. Now you look to the little 'uns.'

With her shawl wrapped round her head and shoulders Elly Manders ran from the house.

FORTY-SEVEN

I t was past ten o'clock, the sun had long set and the half moon was lighting the sky when Tom and his small cavalcade finally reached the gate of the Pound meadow.

He wearily dismounted, untied the bull's lead rope from Mawr's saddle pommel and led it into the meadow to release it to graze. As he barred and padlocked the gate nervous tension once more exerted its grip.

'That's the easy part done with, but now how do I get Shanko Mawr safely locked into a cell?'

Several times during the long slow-moving trek back to Redditch the huge Welshman had struggled to free himself, roaring threats and abuse at Tom, causing both the horses to buck and rear in fright, and nearly pitching Tom from the saddle.

'Listen to me, Master Mawr,' Tom said now. 'You are going to be kept in a cell this night. And you will be given food, drink and blankets enough to lie warmly. On condition that you cause me no trouble.'

'Trouble is it? Well you listen to me, you Sais bastard,' Mawr growled. 'You've cracked me head, arrested me for nothing, and treated me like an animal. We've a score to settle, you and me. Some day, God willing, I'll show you what trouble is.'

'I've arrested you on suspicion of murder, Master Mawr,' Tom told him. 'And the score to be settled is between you and the law of this land.'

'Murder?' Mawr bellowed in disbelief. 'Murder? Are you fuckin' mad? Murder?'

'That's what I said. And for the sake of your immortal soul you should tell me where Daniel Wynne has gone, and what's happened to Maisie Lock.'

'Never mind fuckin' Wynne and his fuckin' whore. Who am I supposed to have murdered?' Mawr bellowed.

'Rose Brent and the man known as Irish Joe,' Tom answered as he remounted his horse.

'Well I know neither of them. And as God is my witness, I've not murdered no one.' There was real desperation in Mawr's voice. 'I swear on the grave of my mother and father, and the graves of their mothers and fathers before them, I've not murdered no one! May God strike me dead this instant if I'm lying!'

Tom kneed his mount and moved off, and as the rope pulled Mawr's horse into movement the Welshman began to pray fervently in his own language, his voice loud and sonorous.

Tom turned in his saddle and asked, 'Where is Daniel Wynne? Has he got that girl, Maisie Lock, with him?'

He repeated the question twice more before the Welshman stopped praying and told him, 'I don't know where he is, I swear to you that I don't. We parted company when we'd put Glendower in the Tardebigge paddock after the baiting yesterday. He said he'd catch up with me on the road.' Mawr paused, and then spat out venomously, 'He does this all the time. Going off and shagging his whores while I do his work for him and earn him his gold. I hate the rotten bastard, and I curse the day he married my sister!'

'Did he go to meet up with Maisie Lock this time?' Tom pressed.

'He could have. Or he might have gone to see the whore he keeps in Worcester.'

'What's her name? The one in Worcester?' Excited anticipation pulsed through Tom. 'Is it Bridie Quinn?'

'I don't know what she's calling herself. Whores change their names all the time, don't they?'

Tom posed another question: 'This woman in Worcester. She's the same one who was living with the Leggers at the Tardebigge tunnel, isn't she? The one they called Irish Tessy?'

'Irish Tessy from the tunnel? No, it's not her. I saw Wynne with the whore in Worcester twice or three times. She has a likeness to Tessy, so perhaps they're kin.'

This answer shocked Tom into silence. He reined to a halt at the foot of the Unicorn Hill, and sat in silence, head bent, asking himself over and over again, 'Have I been barking up the wrong tree all this time?'

Long minutes passed as Tom desperately tried to make sense of what was now a confusion of theories, until Shanko Mawr finally asked plaintively, 'Are you going to keep me chained upside-down across this bloody horse all night? Me head's pounding fit to burst. I swear before God that I've never murdered no one. And I swear that I've never met this Rose Brent or Irish Joe. And I'll go as quiet as any lamb into the cell, if you'll just let me stand up and let the blood drain from me head before it blinds me eyes.'

Mawr's voice held a ring of truth, and a sense of disquiet struck through Tom's mind. 'Am I wrong about this man? Could he be innocent?'

He kicked his mount into movement, telling Mawr, 'We'll be back at the lock-up shortly. Then you'll be able to rest your head.'

Despite the late hour the sounds of hammers on metal resounded from the alleys and courts and lights still burned in the workshops and factories as men, women and children toiled to earn back the wages forfeited by their May Day holiday.

At the lock-up candlelight glowed through the window leads of his mother's room and to avoid alarming her by entering the building without warning, Tom called up to her window.

It opened and Charles Bromley's head poked from it.

'Well met, Thomas, my boy; I'm keeping your Mamma company. What's that you have with you?'

'He's a prisoner. Would you please come down and assist me, Master Bromley?'

'Gladly, my boy, I'll be down directly. And I've an urgent message for you as well. From Joseph Blackwell, Esquire, no less. He sent word to say that you are to report to him the very instant you are returned here, no matter what the hour may be.'

Bromley's head withdrew and the window closed.

'Dammit!' Tom sighed glumly. 'I was looking forward to having a rest and something to eat. Well Blackwell will just have to wait until I get this fellow safely tucked away.'

To Tom's heartfelt relief Shanko Mawr proved as good as his word and went quietly into a cell, where Tom brought him a jug of cider, bread, cheese and a couple of onions.

Deciding to wait to satisfy his own sharp hunger pangs until the business of the day was done with, Tom locked Shanko Mawr's cell door and led both the horses across the green to the Red House stables. The groom took them from him and he was then ushered into Joseph Blackwell's study, where the news he received from his employer utterly destroyed his appetite for any food whatsoever.

FORTY-EIGHT

Early morning, Wednesday May 3rd

Tom had spent a night of broken sleep and troubled dreams and the dark rain-threatening clouds blanketing the sky were in keeping with his sombre mood as he walked up the track to Daws' farmhouse.

'You've took your time coming.' Joseph Blackwell's manservant was muffled in a coat and numerous shawls and greeted him sourly. 'I've been here all night long, so I have, and I aren't had a wink o' bloody sleep, nor a bite to ate, nor a sup of beer.'

'Where are the farm animals?' Tom asked.

'The neighbours shifted 'um all yesterday evening, and all the tools and farm gear as well to stop any thieving. And I wish they'd shifted me with the rest! I'm bloody sick to death o' being stuck here.'

'Well I'm here now, so you can be on your way,' Tom snapped irritably.

'Oh no, I can't.' The other man glowered. 'Me master told me that I got to stay and help you search through this bloody lot.' He gestured towards the heap of fire-damaged, rain-soaked rubble, thatch and timber that was once the front half of the house.

'You can tell your master that I've arranged for someone to come and help me so I don't need you here. Go and get some rest,' Tom said quietly, his irritation tempered by recognition of the other man's fatigue.

The manservant's glower changed instantly to a grin. 'Why thank you kindly, Master Potts. I'll be on me way then.'

Almost as an afterthought as he was leaving he pointed to a piece of canvas sheeting amongst the rubble.

'I put that there to cover what looks like somebody's foot sticking out. You'd best take a look at it. Good day to you.'

Tom bent and lifted the canvas sheet and grimaced in recognition. The twisted half-charred flesh and bones protruding from beneath the wreckage were the remains of a human foot. Slowly and carefully, using his bare hands, digging ever deeper and wider he removed wet ashes, remnants of thatch, wooden roof spars and floorboards until he had uncovered a naked corpse. The lower limbs and torso were charred, and the upper body and head badly damaged by fire. But the torrential rain that had fallen on May Day night had extinguished the flames in time to preserve just sufficient of the facial features for Tom to identify Martha Standard.

'Oh, God forgive me!' For long minutes he stayed crouched, his intense pity for the girl coupling with a discomfiting self-blame. 'Poor Martha, I should have come to see you straight away. Then this might not have happened.'

'But what did happen?' a voice deep within his mind questioned. 'Did she die by accident? Or was she murdered? Could this be one or other of the Welshmen's work? Or perhaps both of them together?'

He shrugged disconsolately. 'If the bodies are in this state there's little chance of discovering whether or not it was the fire or human hands that killed them. If the skulls and bones are fractured, or the internal organs damaged and torn, then it could have been falling beams or the heat which caused the injuries.'

'Tom! Have you found something?' John Clayton's stentorian voice broke Tom's train of thought, and he stood upright to greet his friend who was driving a horse-drawn cart.

'I have Martha Standard here, John. Doubtless we'll shortly be finding John Daws as well.'

The cart lurched to a halt and Clayton got down from his seat. 'Well I've brought two coffins, and some picks and shovels.'

He looked with concern at Tom's filthy hands and clothing. 'I'm sorry that I didn't get here earlier. I hope you'll forgive my tardiness.'

'It's of no matter.' Tom waved aside the apology. 'Soap and water will soon set my skin and clothes to rights. Come, we shall lay poor Martha in her coffin and then try to find John Daws.'

They unloaded both coffins and gently laid Martha in one of them.

It took a further hour of painstaking searching to find another corpse. But this time what met their sight was a black-charred, shrivelled figure postured in a grotesque image of a fighting boxer. They were forced to break its locked joints in order to fit it into the narrow coffin.

'Why should Daws be so much more charred than Martha Standard?' John Clayton mused aloud.

Tom hardly hesitated before answering with some degree of confidence, 'There were the remains of thatch, roof spars and floor-boards lying on top of Martha, and only thatch and roof spars on top of Daws. So I think that he was upstairs and Martha was downstairs when the fire started.

'I'm assuming that by the time the fire had burned through enough of the floorboards and joists for them to collapse down on to Martha, the thatch had already fallen and the rain was beginning to douse the flames. Hence the reason why Martha is still just about recognizable, unlike this one.'

'You're a very clever fellow, Tom. I'd not have reasoned this out so readily,' Clayton complimented admiringly. 'So what do you think might have started the fire in the first place?'

'Perhaps Daws was stupid drunk and knocked his candle over. Perhaps he was smoking in his bed and fell asleep. Perhaps a bolt of lightning struck the thatch and set it alight.' Tom shrugged unhappily. 'I doubt that we'll ever know the truth of it, John. Anyway we'd best get these two back to the lock-up. I've rigged up the tarpaulin in the back yard to shelter them from the rain.'

A pattering of raindrops threatened the onset of another downpour and Clayton grimaced up at the lowering clouds. 'We're due a soaking before we reach Redditch, I fear.'

They loaded the coffins on to the cart and Clayton got up on to the seat and lifted the reins, but Tom hung back, staring thoughtfully at the ramshackle outbuildings and sheds.

'Come on, Tom, jump up. There's ample room for both of us on this seat so you've no need to go afoot,' Clayton urged.

Tom shook his head. 'You go on, John. I want to stay here a while longer and take a further look around the place.'

'Very well, I'll manage them myself.' Clayton smiled.

When the cart had disappeared from view Tom went through the outhouses and sheds and what remained of the farmhouse, ruefully admitting to himself, 'I don't really know what I'm looking for. But I'll keep on looking anyway.'

He exited from the last shed and started on the circuit again. It was raining steadily now. One hour, two hours passed and still he continued the same circuit, farmhouse to outhouse, to shed, to outhouse, to shed, to farmhouse, peering into every nook and cranny, bending to shift soggy charred clutches of thatch, bricks, rubble of mortar and clay, and half-burned timbers. His clothing became saturated, with rain squelching in his boots and dripping from the brim of his top hat, his body chilled and clammy.

Finally Tom grudgingly accepted the futility of searching any longer, and decided to go back to Redditch. He was trudging despondently away from the farm when his attention was caught by a clamouring of harsh discordant cries from a raucously squabbling murder of crows that were hopping and flapping about a large clump of nettles in the ditch to one side of the track.

On impulse he stepped towards the clump and the crows scattered in a frantic beating of wings to disclose a dead sheepdog lying within the tall weeds.

Abandoned unburied dead dogs were commonplace. Tom turned away and walked on. Then turned again and went back to the animal, scathingly asking himself as he did so, 'Haven't you wasted enough time already, you damned fool? What in hell's name do you expect to hear from the tongue of a dead dog?'

He bent and peered closely at the animal. The crows had pecked out its eyes and torn rents in its hide, but Tom's gaze was fixed on the angle of head to body. He took hold of the tail and pulled the dog from the nettles, then carefully explored its neck with probing fingers.

'Twisted round until it snapped clean through! It would need strong hands to do that,' he decided, and noting the small brass disc attached to the collar he read the words engraved on both its faces: 'Spot. John Daws. Bentley Lower Farm.'

He unbuckled the collar and stood turning it over and over in his hands as he mentally explored the possible connotations of this discovery.

Theory inexorably strengthened to firm conviction.

'The dog must have been barking and got its neck snapped to shut it up. Then the killer dealt with Martha and Daws and set fire to the house. But how can that be proven?'

A sudden inspiration made him catch his breath. 'My God! I'm such a bloody dullard at times!'

He set out at a run towards Redditch.

FORTY-NINE

The Red House
Late evening, Wednesday May 3rd

'You've done what?' Joseph Blackwell shouted in incredulous anger, and jumped up from his desk chair so violently that he tipped it over. 'Opened the bodies without waiting for the order for a post-mortem? Have you gone insane, Potts? If my Lord Aston comes to hear of this he'll have your guts for garters! And mine as well, damn and blast your eyes!'

Tom had never before witnessed such a furious outburst from this quietly spoken, unemotional man. He swallowed hard and fought to keep his nerve.

'With respect, sir, I couldn't waste time waiting for the result of an official post-mortem, or for the verdict of a Coroner's Court. I believe that young Maisie Lock's life is gravely imperilled. That's if she hasn't been killed already.'

Tom lifted the two wooden buckets he was carrying and placed them on the desk top.

'Look for yourself, sir. Here is the proof that Martha Standard was dead before the fire was started.' He tapped one bucket. 'These are Martha Standard's lungs.' He tapped the second bucket. 'These are the lungs of the corpse whom I believe to be John Daws. I've partially dissected one of each pair so that you can see the proof of what I say.'

Blackwell frowned and gestured for Tom to display the buckets' contents.

Tom lifted a partially dissected lung in each hand and held them nearer the light of the oil lamp.

'Please note, sir, this lung is from Martha Standard's corpse. Its interior tissues are still dark pink in colour, and hold no foreign bodies. But this lung taken from the other corpse is impregnated with numerous particles of soot, which were drawn into it by continuing respiration while the fire was burning and the air laden with thick smoke. There is no soot in Martha Standard's lungs because she was not breathing any smoke into them. When the fire was burning, she was already dead!'

He fell silent and the other man came around the desk to bend close and peer at the lumps of flesh.

After what seemed to Tom's strained nerves endless aeons of time, Joseph Blackwell straightened and said curtly, 'You will tell no one that you have dissected the bodies. Now how do you propose to continue in your investigations?'

Tom's shoulders sagged with relief, and he answered immediately. 'I think, sir, that Shanko Mawr needs to answer questions about his whereabouts during the night of May Day.'

'Very well.' Blackwell's thin lips curved for a fraction in a grim smile. 'But remember, as always we share the kudos of success; you alone will take the blame of failure. Now take your buckets and go, Constable Potts.'

Tom wasted no time before questioning Shanko Mawr about his whereabouts on the night of May Day.

The Welshman asserted that he had spent the entire evening drinking at the Cherry Tree tavern and had also slept there until dawn of the following day.

'Terry Wilkes charged me a bloody shilling for the use of a blanket and mattress full of fleas and bedbugs. If I hadn't been blind drunk on his rotgut gin I'd not have got a wink of sleep all night. You can go and ask the shylock Sais bastard, if you don't believe me.'

'I will ask him, Master Mawr. You may be sure of that.'

FIFTY

Mid-morning, Thursday May 4th

When Tom came out of the Cherry Tree tavern he vented a hiss of frustration.

'Damn it! I'm still getting nowhere!'

Terry Wilkes, the landlord, had positively verified Shanko Mawr's alibi.

Tom briefly pondered his next move, and decided to go to the wharf and inform Martin Cooke that Shanko Mawr was in custody.

'You've arrested Shanko? On suspicion of murdering Rose Brent and Irish Joe?' Cooke's ruggedly handsome face contorted in shocked disbelief. 'And my cousin Daniel? What of him?'

'Nothing yet. I've not been able to find him. I'm very concerned for the safety of a young girl who has disappeared. She was having a love affair with your cousin, who failed to tell her that he was already married. The last time her friends spoke with her, she told them that she was going to meet your cousin and would then return to them within the hour. That was on May Day afternoon and they've not seen her since.

'I'm very anxious to talk to your cousin concerning the girl's whereabouts. I also intend to arrest him on suspicion of being impli-cated in the deaths of Rose Brent and Irish Joe.'

Cooke jumped up from his chair and began to pace agitatedly around the confined space of the room, shaking his head and muttering to himself.

Standing with his back against the office door Tom felt constrained to tell Cooke, 'I must emphasize, Master Cooke, that at present both Mawr and your cousin are still only under suspicion. They may well be able to produce proven evidence which will clear them of any guilt.'

Still pacing, Cooke muttered distractedly, 'Murdering Rose Brent and Irish Joe? That can't be! Daniel is like a dear brother to me! He's not a bad man, no matter what some might say! So what if he beats his wife and his whores? Whores are there to be beaten, and it's a husband's lawful right to chastise his wife! It's not his fault that he was born with a quick temper . . . But murder? No! I can't believe it! He was falsely accused once before! Daniel was only a boy when little Bronny Williams fell down into the quarry . . . He said it was an accident, and everyone but a couple of the parish scandal-mongers believed him. He would never throw a small child down into a quarry, no matter what else he's capable of when roused to anger!'

He suddenly sank down into the chair, hands covering his face, shoulders heaving as he emitted a series of shuddering groans.

Shocked by this dramatic reaction to his words, Tom bit back the eager questions that sprang to his lips, and forced himself to wait silently until Cooke slowly regained some semblance of control, lowering his hands and drawing deep breaths.

Tom then asked quietly, 'The child you spoke of, Bronny Williams? Where and when was your cousin accused of throwing her down into a quarry?'

Cooke frowned sullenly. 'I've no wish to discuss the matter. The accusation was judged to be false, and that's an end to it.' He rose to his feet and told Tom, 'I've a deal of work to be doing, Master Potts, so I must ask you to leave now. I would greatly appreciate you letting me know if and when you arrest my cousin. Because I will immediately attest to his good character, and do all that I can to help him.'

Tom realized that he would get nothing more from the man at this time, and agreed. 'I'll inform you, Master Cooke, and I truly hope that our next meeting will not bring any further distress to you.'

Trudging back to Redditch, Tom was turning over and over again in his mind what Cooke had said about Daniel Wynne beating women, and the child that had died in the quarry. A sense of foreboding increasingly gripped him.

'A trail of violence and death follows behind Daniel Wynne. Has Maisie Lock become part of that trail yet?'

When he reached the green he stood opposite the Fox and Goose, dreading to go inside and tell Amy that he had no news of her friend; and worse still that Daniel Wynne was married, and a woman-beater. Finally he quailed at the prospect.

'I'll just go and check the lock-up first. I need to see to Shanko Mawr's food and have him empty his slop bucket. I'll come back and see Amy a little later.'

He walked quickly on and had almost reached the lock-up when his mother's bedroom window was flung open, and her screech assailed his ears.

'You've come sneaking back at last, have you? Creeping back like the wretched cur dog that you are!'

He sighed wearily. 'There's no need to shout so loud, Mother. I can still hear perfectly well what is being said when you moderate your tone.'

'I've had nothing but aggravation all day long, and it's all your fault, you bad selfish beast! Dear God! If ever a poor tragic woman suffered, then that poor tragic woman is me! My heart is palpitating like a shivering leaf and I'm near to death!'

'I'm coming up to see you, Mother; try and calm yourself.' Tom unlocked the front door and went inside.

He took only three steps along the passageway and Shanko Mawr's furious bellowing dinned into his ears.

'That mad old bitch upstairs has chucked a pot o' piss over me! Opened the hatch and chucked a pot of piss over me, she did! I'll break her fuckin' neck when I get me hands on her!'

'What?' Tom was taken aback and opened the cell door hatch.

Shanko Mawr thrust his head against the square opening. 'Smell me! Smell the stink on me! That mad old bitch did this! Smell me, damn you!'

Tom bent towards the grimy, hairy face framed in the square hatchway and tentatively sniffed. The acrid stench of dried urine filled his nostrils, and he could only ask feebly, 'Why, Master Mawr? Why did she do it?'

In a high-pitched screech scarcely muffled by the intervening floorboards his mother gave him the answer.

'To shut up his heathen-tongued caterwauling, that's why! He was making enough rattle to wake the dead! He was driving me to an early grave with the awful row he was making!'

'I was singing hymns. Giving praises to my God,' Mawr asserted indignantly. 'It's that mad old bitch who's the heathen, not me. I'm an Elder of the Bethesda Chapel, and honoured in my village for being a true Christian.'

His reddened eyes glared upwards and he roared furiously, 'Can you hear me up there, you mad old bitch! I'll smite you with the righteous arm of the Lord! I'll drown you in your own stinking piss!'

'Just come up here and try it, you Welsh turd!' Widow Potts screeched defiantly. 'I'll break your thick skull any day of the week! Just come up here and try it!'

The door bells clanged furiously.

'Dear God, give me strength!' Tom begged silently, closed the hatch and went to answer the bells' summons.

When he saw the caller his heart thudded rapidly. 'Amy! I was coming to see you as soon as I'd done here.'

Rosy cheeks glowing with excitement, Amy poured out a torrent of words. 'She's come back, Tom. Not an hour since. I couldn't get over here to tell you before, because I've been having a devil of a row with Tommy Fowkes! He says he's going to give her the sack for bunking off from work, and I told him that if he did I'd go with her. Then he said I was a saucy—'

'Please Amy, hold hard for a moment,' Tom interrupted. 'Are you saying that Maisie has come back?'

'Are you deliberately acting stupid?' she demanded indignantly. 'I've just told you she has, haven't I?'

'And how is she?' Tom asked eagerly.

'She's spitting feathers! That rotten Welsh bugger has done the dirty on her. Left her high and dry, so he has.'

Tom stepped from the doorway and, taking Amy's arm, pulled her with him across the green.

She shouted in shocked protest and struggled to pull free, but he kept a tight grip on her arm and told her firmly, 'Don't say another word, Amy. I need to hear Maisie's story from Maisie's lips. So just come along quietly.'

Her eyes widened and she stopped tugging against his grip. After a few more paces she smiled.

'I've never before seen you behave so masterful, Tom. It's like you've got fire in your belly at last. What was you eating for breakfast?'

'Brimstone and treacle,' he quipped, then sobered abruptly. 'Now listen to me carefully, Amy. I'm investigating some very serious crimes, and it may well be that Maisie can give me information

which will be of great use to me. So I don't want you interrupting
when I'm talking with her.'

Amy instantly sprang to her friend's defence.

'Maisie won't know nothing about any crimes. She might be a
mouthy cow, but she's as honest and decent as the day is long.'

'I don't doubt that, but you must keep silent while I'm talking
to her. I mean it!'

Amy's blue eyes twinkled as she giggled delightedly. 'Oh I will,
Tom, I promise you. I do like it when you're being so manly and
masterful.'

'I'm beginning to savour it myself.' He chuckled.

In the attic bedroom of the Fox and Goose Maisie Lock's tearstained
face evoked Tom's immediate pity and he told her gently, 'I'm sorry
to come pestering you, Maisie, but it's very important that we talk.
Do you know where Daniel Wynne is?'

Her features reddened with fury and she stormed, 'No! I aren't
seen the rotten bastard since May Day night. I got drunk and passed
out, and when I woke up on Tuesday morning he wasn't there!'

'Wasn't where?' Tom queried.

'In the bloody bed!'

'Where was the bed?'

'In the bloody bedroom! Where else would it be?' she shouted
exasperatedly.

Tom's own exasperation was mounting, but he managed to keep
his voice low and gentle.

'I need to know where you stayed with him that night, Maisie.
It's very important, I do assure you.'

'In the Turks Head alehouse close by Bromsgrove. But just guess
what the bastard did?'

Tom sighed wearily. 'I'm beyond guessing, Maisie. You'll have
to tell me.'

'Well, when I woke up in the morning he'd gone. Well I thought
he'd gone to the privy, and then I thought he'd perhaps gone down
town on a bit o' business. But he never come back at all, did he,
the bastard!'

'But why have you not returned here before now?' Tom wanted to
know.

'Because when he didn't come back I hadn't got enough money
to pay the reckoning. So the bloody landlord and his cow of a
missus took me boots and clothes from me, then give me a stinking
old gown to wear and made me work off the rest of what was owed.

I didn't finish doing the skivvying 'til first thing this morning. Then they give me back me clothes and I came back here. And now bloody old Fatty Fowkes is threatening to give me the sack for missing me work here.'

'Don't you worry about that, Maisie. I'll not let him give you the sack. Trust me, I won't!' Amy declared forcefully.

'Did Daniel ever speak of his family, or his home?' Tom was curious to know.

'He told me that he was living with a woman back in Wales. But he said it wasn't a lawful wedding, because they'd only "jumped the broomstick" like the tinkers do. He said now he'd got me he was going to send her away because she was a sluttish trollop and he couldn't trust her as far as he could throw her. He promised me that he'd wed me in a church, so it would be a proper lawful wedding.' She flared up in anger once more. 'The lying rotten bastard! If he comes near me again I'll bloody well kill him, I take my oath I will!'

'Tell me, did he ever raise his hand to you, or threaten you in any way?'

Maisie shook her head, and her features twisted in distress. 'No, he never did. He always used me tenderly. He was nicer and kinder to me than any man I've ever known. That's what makes finding out what a rotten lying bastard he is so hard to bear!'

Tom decided that he would not add to her unhappiness by telling her that Daniel Wynne was lawfully married and still living with his wife and children.

'Thank you for talking to me, Maisie. I'll leave you in peace now.'

He left the room in a quandary. 'Wynne always used her tenderly? Was kinder and nicer to her than any other man she'd ever known? That's totally at odds with Martin Cooke's account of him being an inveterate woman-beater. And what time did he sneak out from the pub, I wonder?'

Amy hurried after him. 'Tom, hold fast a moment, I want to tell you about Eugene Sinclair.'

He looked down at her pretty rosy face and a poignant sadness swept over him as he waited in dread for her to tell him she was going to marry Sinclair.

She stared keenly at him, and as if she had read his thoughts she smiled and shook her head. 'No, Tom! It's not what you might be thinking it is. I just wanted to tell you that I've sent Sinclair packing, and told him never to come near to me again.'

Tom gasped with relief so intense that he felt his knees go weak.

Amy giggled delightedly as she saw his reaction. 'I've missed our walks and talks, Tom. Really missed them. So shall we keep company together again?'

'Oh Amy, of course we shall,' he blurted eagerly. 'You've just made me the happiest man in Creation. Truly you have.'

She reached up, pulled his head down towards her, and standing on tiptoe planted a kiss on his lips.

'Dear Tom, you might be woeful plain to look at, but you're still the sweetest man I've ever known.'

'Amy? Be that you up there, Amy?' Tommy Fowkes bawled from the bottom of the narrow staircase which led up to the attics.

'Yes it is,' she shouted back.

'Well you and that hussy had better get down here this instant and do some work, or I'll sack the pair of you else.'

'We're coming directly, Master Fowkes.' Amy's eyes danced mischievously and she whispered as she moved back into the room, 'I told you that I can twist Tommy Fowkes round my little finger, didn't I?'

'As you can with me,' Tom murmured happily as he went downstairs.

Walking across the green, Tom felt like dancing for joy.

'This has to be the best day of my life. I'm not going to risk losing Amy again. I'm going to ask her to marry me the very next chance I get. And if she says yes, I'll have the banns called on the very next Sunday. I'll be released from being the constable come next March and then I'll find work which will enable me to properly support a wife and family!'

Back in the lock-up his thoughts turned to the apparent contradiction between Maisie Lock's account of how gently Wynne had treated her and Martin Cooke's description of him as an inveterate woman-beater.

He went to Shanko Mawr's cell and was greatly relieved to find Mawr had calmed down.

'I'll take you to the pump and give you soap and towel, Master Mawr. Then I'll bring you food and drink.'

When they were in the rear yard he waited until Mawr had finished washing and was drying himself before asking casually, 'I've been told that Daniel Wynne is heavy-handed with women, and beats your sister. Is that why you don't like him?'

Mawr grinned derisively. 'Wynne's heavy-handed with women and beats my sister! Whoever told you that is talking out of their arse. My sister would shoot any man who even dared raise his voice to her. Oh, she knows that Wynne's a womanizer, but so long as he's good to her and the kids she don't give a damn about his whoring and the bastard kids he fathers. No, Daniel Wynne might be a slave to his prick but he don't knock women around. In truth he loves them all too much, be they sluts or saints.

'Why I don't like him is because he's a lazy bastard, and he only pays pennies to me and the other lads who earns him the sovereigns he spends like water on his own bloody pleasures!'

'What about Bronny Williams, the girl who died in the quarry some years past? Wasn't he accused of throwing her down into it?'

'Wynne? Accused of chucking little Bronny down the quarry? That's a load of bollocks! Nobody knows how little Bronny came to fall into the quarry, but me and Wynne was away with the droving in England when she did.' The huge man scowled angrily. 'Who the fuck's been telling you these tales?'

Before Tom could reply Mawr asserted confidently, 'Hold on now! It's Martin Cooke, aren't it? Him and Wynne might act like loving cousins but deep down they hates each other. Cooke believes that Wynne has shagged his missus. And Wynne is bitter because when they was kids Cooke used to bully him something awful and he still bears the grudge for it.'

'How do you know this?'

'Because I've heard them having high words about it when they've been drunk.'

'And is it true?' Tom was very thoughtful. 'Has Wynne had a relationship with Cooke's wife?'

The huge man chuckled grimly. 'I don't know, but he might well have . . . By all accounts Cooke's missus is a bit flighty, and Wynne 'ull shag any woman who's got a pulse. But he don't beat them. It's Cooke who's the woman-beater, not Daniel Wynne.'

FIFTY-ONE

It was late afternoon and while Tom had been serving warrants and summonses, his mind had been filled with ever-increasing doubts. Now as he was slowly walking back up the Unicorn Hill he reluctantly accepted the situation.

'Because of some unlikely coincidences of Welsh love spoons and the like I've been leaping to unproven conclusions!'

He considered the arguments against those conclusions: 'Assuming that Shanko Mawr has told me the truth about his sister knowing all about her husband's whoring and not giving a damn for it, then Daniel Wynne has no necessity to commit murder to keep that whoring hidden from her.

'Did Wynne kill in a fit of fury, or driven by a maniacal compulsion? Well Maisie Lock and Shanko Mawr, who both have reason to hate him, insist that he is and has always been soft and gentle with women.

'Martin Cooke is the only one who claims that Wynne is violent with women, and it appears that he could be driven to lie by his belief that Wynne has cuckolded him.

'And I've not one iota of proven evidence that implicates Wynne or Mawr in any of these deaths.'

Tom sighed ruefully.

'I've made a damned fool of myself by arresting Shanko Mawr. All I can do now is release him with my sincerest apologies.'

As he reached the crossroads Joseph Blackwell's manservant came running.

'Master Potts! Master Potts! My master says that you're to come to him directly, no matter what you might be busy at. And you'd best hurry because my master aren't in the best o' tempers.'

He turned and ran back towards the Red House, and Tom lolloped clumsily after him.

Tethered outside the house were a sweat-lathered, mud-caked horse and an opulent carriage and pair with a liveried coachman. Tom recognized the carriage as being the Lord Aston's and experienced a premonition of impending troubles.

His premonition was confirmed when he was ushered into the drawing room to find Lord Aston and his fellow magistrate, the Reverend Timmins, seated in company with Joseph Blackwell and a travel-stained, stubble-chinned Daniel Wynne.

The magistrates were clad alike in the black full-skirted coats, breeches and stockings of their calling, white short-queued tie-wigs perched upon their heads. There the similarity ended, because Reverend Timmins was as woefully pasty-faced and meagre-bodied as the Lord Aston was purple-faced and fat.

'Do I have your permission, my Lord, to conduct these proceedings?' Blackwell requested, but not waiting for the other man's assent frowned sternly at Tom and ordered, 'Constable Potts, let us hear your explanation for the arrest of Master Shanko Mawr, and for the impounding of Master Daniel Wynne's bull and horse.'

Tom's heart was palpitating with apprehension. He swallowed hard in a vain attempt to moisten his dry mouth.

'Damn your eyes! Let's have no more of this deliberate prevarication! Let us be hearing from you, you damned clown!' Lord Aston bellowed furiously.

'My Lord.' Blackwell directed a look of pained reproach at his superior.

'Well, make him get a move on, Blackwell. I've much urgent business to attend to this day,' Aston blustered.

'As your Lordship wishes,' Blackwell answered smoothly, and frowned at Tom, but his right eye flicked in a wink, as if to reassure Tom that he possessed one ally in this hostile gathering.

'Come now, Potts, let us be hearing your explanation without further delay.'

Tom fought down the overwhelming temptation to make excuses for his actions, and admitted quietly, 'I was wrong to arrest Shanko Mawr. I suspected him of committing a crime, but have since realized that he is innocent. In fact I was on my way to release him when Master Blackwell's servant accosted me.'

Tom thought he detected a congratulatory gleam in Joseph Blackwell's eyes. Daniel Wynne's expression was impassive.

'Do you have any questions to put to Constable Potts, sir?' Blackwell invited the Welshman.

Wynne shook his head. 'I am satisfied with his explanation, sir.'

'I'm gratified to hear that, sir.' Blackwell smiled bleakly, and bowed his head to Aston. 'Then this matter is concluded and we are done here, my Lord.'

Wynne coughed and raised his eyebrows quizzically.

'As I was saying,' Blackwell continued smoothly. 'This matter is concluded but for authorizing the sum of twenty guineas compensation to be paid by this parish to Daniel Wynne, Esquire, for the inconvenience and expense he has suffered as a result of the wrongful impoundment of his animals and the loss of Master Mawr's services.'

'Paid by the parish?' Lord Aston shouted angrily. 'The ratepayers of this parish cannot be penalized for the stupidity of its damned clown of a constable. Any compensation must come out of Potts' own pockets.'

'Indeed so, my Lord,' Blackwell agreed. 'What I propose is that I will advance Master Wynne the sum of compensation from the parish coffer, and will dock it from the monthly fees that Constable Potts will be receiving from the parish. Also of course, Constable Potts will have to reimburse myself for the cost of stabling and feed for Master Wynne's horse since Tuesday. That will be an added three shillings.'

As Tom stood listening all his dreams of enjoying early marital bliss with Amy came tumbling down into ruins.

'Twenty guineas! Twenty guineas! That's near to ten months' fees. How can I afford to marry Amy with such a debt hanging over me?'

'Constable Potts, you will release Master Mawr immediately, then go down to the Pound with him. Master Wynne will be bringing the horses,' Blackwell instructed.

Tom could only bow in depressed acquiescence.

Shanko Mawr offered no recriminations and accepted Tom's apologies with good grace, telling him, 'You've fed, drunk and bedded me very well, Master Potts. To tell truth, I've enjoyed having a little rest from working. But I can't say that I enjoyed meeting your old mam.'

They waited at the gate of the Pound meadow for Daniel Wynne to arrive with the two horses, and when he did he and Mawr spoke in Welsh for several minutes. Then they went into the Pound to secure the bull to Mawr's saddle with a long rope.

As they returned through the gate Daniel Wynne reined in briefly and grinned at Tom.

'Shanko has told me of your conversation with my cousin Martin, Constable Potts, and I bear no ill will towards you for harbouring suspicions of me as a result of the lies he told you. But I assure you that I've never met Rose Brent or Irish Joe. I fully admit that I'm a seducer of women. I never beat or murder them, however.'

'I believe you, and offer sincere apologies for my wrongful suspicions, Master Wynne,' Tom replied truthfully. 'But I despise you for the callous manner in which you seduce and then abandon silly young girls such as Maisie Lock. You're contemptible!'

Wynne scowled and Tom tensed himself for trouble but the other man said nothing and moved on.

As the Welshmen rode away Tom padlocked the gate, then leaned against its bars mulling over the totally unexpected developments of this eventful day.

To his own surprise he discovered that as he resigned himself to the depressing fact of his error and the punitive debt he had acquired as a result, he gradually began to discern that there were some positive aspects to this present situation.

'At least those two major suspects can now be disregarded. I'm also now convinced that it was Rose Brent's killer who Martha Standard confronted at the bull-baiting, and he was standing among the Committee men and their companions. What do I already know about the killer?

'That he has the strength to crush into insensibility a powerfully built roughneck like Irish Joe, and to snap a dog's neck with his bare hands. He's attractive enough to have a pretty girl like Rosie fall in love and want to marry him, and has a gentlemanly manner. He apparently has freedom of movement and time to travel around the parish and beyond without attracting undue attention or challenge. So he is not taken for a suspicious stranger and could be living in the parish.

'He was known to canal-shanty dwellers Irish Joe and Irish Tessy, and must be both respectable and wealthy if they thought it possible and profitable to hold the threat of blackmail over his head. Who among those men confronted by Martha Standard best fits these criteria?'

Tom thought long and hard, until he reached a personally unwelcome conclusion.

'Martin Cooke best fits these criteria! The man who saved me from drowning!' Tom sighed regretfully. 'Yet he's also the man who lied to shield Jacky Whittaker, and again to blacken Daniel Wynne's character; and according to Shanko Mawr, he mistreats women. He didn't shrink from shooting that rioter either, did he? So he is capable of extreme violence. I think he must now be placed at the top of my list of suspects. I needs must search for evidence against him.' Tom grimaced unhappily.

'It's needle in the haystack time again, and I'm in desperate need of a magnet . . . or a bloody miracle!'

FIFTY-TWO

Song birds fluted in the trees, sparrows squabbled noisily in the hedgerows and the sun-warmed air was heavy with the scents of nature. In the paupers' section of the Old Monks graveyard, Tom Potts laid a posy of wild flowers upon the raw, red clay mound of Martha Standard's grave and murmured apologetically, 'I'm sorry, Martha, I'm still no nearer finding the evidence I need to bring your murderer to justice. But I swear by all that I hold dear that I'll not rest until you're avenged.'

During the past weeks Tom had spent every hour he could sifting through the wreckage and outbuildings of Daws' farm. Tramping its environs, questioning neighbouring farmers, stopping people travelling the lanes to enquire if they had seen or noticed anyone behaving suspiciously in the days and nights prior to the fire. All his efforts had been fruitless, however, and at times his ever-mounting frustration had momentarily tempted him to go and confront Martin Cooke face to face with an accusation.

For several nights Tom had mounted a covert moonlight watch on Cooke's large house, and found its shuttered windows, padlocked gate and high spiked walls more reminiscent of a fortress than a home, the only sign of life within the building an occasional shifting gleam of lamplight through an ill-fitting shutter.

'Does he have servants?' Tom wondered on the first night's vigil, and noting the overgrown, neglected grounds, he took it for granted that Cooke didn't employ a gardener.

The next day Tom had made discreet enquiries in the neighbourhood of Cooke's home, and discovered that it was rumoured that Cooke's wife was an invalid being cared for by a resident nurse, but no one really knew anything for certain.

Now, standing looking down at Martha Standard's grave, what was weighing heavily on Tom's mind was the fear that behind Martin Cooke's attractive physical façade and pleasant manner there might lurk a menacing murderous beast. A beast who might kill again if Tom's present lack of success in finding evidence continued.

He heard sounds behind him and turned to find John

Clayton and an elderly white-haired, mutton-chop-whiskered man approaching.

'I thought I might find you here, Tom.' John Clayton smiled. 'Allow me to introduce Sir Roderick Mackinnon. May I present Constable Thomas Potts, Sir Roderick?'

'I'm honoured, Sir Roderick.' Tom bowed.

'The honour is mine, Constable Potts.' Mackinnon returned the salutation, and gabbled hastily. 'Forgive me for not exchanging further polite pleasantries but I'm in urgent need of your services and have no time to waste. I have very good reason for fearing that my niece, Edwina Cooke, may have been seriously harmed by her husband, Martin Cooke, who is the Wharf Superintendent of the Birmingham and Worcester Canal Company. Cooke dismissed his housekeeper, a Mrs Chesney, from his service some days since, and she came to tell me about how brutishly he has been behaving towards my niece.

'Chesney told me that he beats my poor niece as if she were a dog, and continually drugs her with tincture of opium and suchlike potions. Chesney says that he is behaving like a madman . . .'

Tom's jaw dropped in absolute astonishment at how this opportunity to further his own investigations into Cooke had so amazingly presented itself.

'Dammee, sir! Are you ill?' Mackinnon demanded.

Tom recovered himself sufficiently to stammer, 'No, sir. Please continue.'

After a moment of dubious regard the older man went on to relate how his niece's parents, who were too ill and frail to travel, had had no communication with their daughter for many months, and how his own efforts to see her had been blocked by Martin Cooke.

'But Cooke has woefully underestimated me, Constable Potts.' A hint of boasting coloured Mackinnon's recital as he produced a ribbon-wrapped roll of paper and brandished it under Tom's nose. 'I have influential friends and through their good offices have this very morning obtained this warrant from my Lord Aston to enter my niece's home by force if necessary and ascertain her circumstances. My Lord Aston instructs that you are to aid me in achieving these ends.'

As he listened Tom was inwardly marvelling, 'This is a miracle. A bloody miracle!'

He bowed. 'I'm at your disposal, Sir Roderick.'

'I shall be accompanying you, Tom,' John Clayton put in. 'My

Lord Aston wants me there as his observer. We'll make the journey to the house in Sir Roderick's carriage.'

'I'll need to call into the lock-up and collect my staff and satchel. It will only mean a moment or two of delay.' Tom's excitement was rising fast. 'I would suggest that we go first to the New Wharf at Tardebigge; Master Cooke may well be at his office there. I'm told he spends many Sundays at work.'

'No, the boss aren't been at work for days.' The aged watchman of the New Wharf glanced around him as if fearing there might be others listening and, dropping his voice to a conspiratorial whisper, informed his three visitors, 'Just between you, me and the gatepost, the boss has been acting a bit queer of late.'

'How so?' John Clayton queried.

'Well, he's always been a good-natured master to work for. Not a man to lose his rag without good reason. But of late he flies off the handle for nothing. He don't pay no mind to what folks tries to tell him neither. It's like hisself is here, but his mind is somewhere else entirely, if you gets my meaning. Just between you, me and the gatepost, I reckon that he's losing his marbles. My old dad was the same when he started to go doolally tap, if you knows what I means.' He winked slyly, and tapped his head with his gnarled fingers.

'That will be all, my man.' Mackinnon handed the watchman a coin and told Tom and John Clayton, 'We must make haste to Martley House, gentlemen. I confess I'm in fear of what may await us there.'

The coachman halted the carriage in front of the chained and padlocked gates. The house shutters were closed, no smoke wafted from its tall chimneys, and the only movements and sounds in the overgrown, unkempt grounds came from buzzing, fluttering insects, bird flights and songs.

Tom alighted and tugged the bell pull. During the next few minutes while Mackinnon fidgeted restlessly, he tugged it several times more but no one answered the summons.

Mackinnon finally ordered irritably, 'Break the chain, Constable; we're authorized to use any necessary means to gain entry.'

Tom examined the chain and padlock and knew that his staff would be useless as a tool against the thick links and huge lock.

'We need a sledge hammer and chisels or heavy-duty files to get this chain off, sir.'

'God dammit, you fool! Why didn't you think to bring them with you?' Mackinnon demanded furiously.

Before Tom could answer, John Clayton sprang to his defence and sternly reproved the irate old man. 'Oh come now, Sir Roderick, you are unjust. You said to me that the gates were chained and padlocked when you called here previously. So either you or myself should have thought of this and brought those tools with us. Constable Potts cannot be blamed for our failure to do so. We're the thoughtless fools, not he.'

After a moment or two Mackinnon grudgingly accepted the reproof.

'Perhaps you're not at fault, Constable. Now can either of you suggest where we might soonest obtain such tools?'

'The nearest smithy is up at Astwood Bank on top of the Ridgeway there.' Clayton pointed at the far-stretching wooded high ground. 'I know of a shortcut to it. We'll not be long away, Tom.'

The carriage rattled off.

Tom was watching it disappear round a bend when a faint wailing cry turned his attention to the house, and the breath caught in his throat.

A shutter on one of the upstairs windows was partially opened and in the split second as Tom focussed his gaze it closed.

'Did I imagine that?' he asked himself. 'Was it a trick of the light distorting my sight? A play of cloud shadows? A sudden gust of wind perhaps?'

There was no wind, the sky was cloudless, and Tom knew that his eyesight was very good.

'Was that a cry for help from someone in the house?'

The possibility disturbed him greatly, and on impulse he decided, 'I'll go up there and knock on the door.'

He regarded the long rusty spikes crowning the high gates and quailed at the prospect of climbing over them.

'I'm not limber enough. I'll end up spiking myself.'

He hesitated for long seconds, then in angry self-disgust at his own cowardice he threw his staff, satchel and top hat over the gates and began clumsily to scale the bars.

By the time he reached the ground on the other side he was sweating profusely, his hands bleeding from cuts and scrapes, his entire body trembling. But he retrieved his kit and strode on towards the house.

Tom was mounting the steps of the portico when the front door swung open and Martin Cooke stepped out, the long-barrelled pistol in his right hand pointing unwaveringly at Tom's head.

'Oh my God!' Tom gasped in fright and came to an abrupt halt.

Cooke was clad only in shirt, breeches and boots. His face was pallid and heavily stubbled, his eyes sunken, and Tom could smell the mingled stenches of strong liquor, excreta and urine exuding from his mouth and soiled clothing.

'Lay down your staff and satchel, Master Potts, and do it gently, or I'll kill you.' Cooke's voice was hoarse, but controlled and even.

Tom obeyed.

'Discard your hat and coat also, Master Potts. I want to be sure that you're not concealing a weapon.'

Tom removed his coat and hat and laid them down. Struggling to appear calm he told the other man, 'You've no need to present that pistol at me, Master Cooke. I've not come to do you any harm.'

'And I intend you no harm, Master Potts. But if you make any move against me, you're a dead man.' He stepped to one side. 'Keep your hands joined behind your head. Go into the house.'

Coming from the brightness of the day into the shadowed gloom of the entrance hall filled Tom with a sense of impending doom, and he battled his rising panic, knowing that if he was to have any chance of surviving he must think clearly.

An unearthly wailing cry shattered the silence and Tom started visibly in shock.

'Don't be alarmed, Master Potts.' Cooke said from the doorway. 'My wife is somewhat restless today. I've no more laudanum left to ease her sufferings. Mercifully she will very soon be at peace forever.'

Tom's mind was abruptly invaded by the images of the dead bodies of Rose Brent and Martha Standard, and a fierce anger overlaid his fear. He swallowed hard, turned to face the other man and challenged, 'Why so, Master Cooke? Are you going to murder her like you murdered poor Rose Brent and Martha Standard? Don't deny your guilt, because I have certain proof of it.'

The raised pistol quivered violently and Tom thought death was upon him. But then to his utter astonishment he heard Cooke exclaiming admiringly, 'By God, Master Potts! You really are as sharp-witted as I've heard some people claim you to be. Although it must be said that many more in number regard you as a doltish clown. Tell me now, how did you come to suspect that they were murdered, and to fix the blame on me?'

Completely taken aback by this apparent confession of guilt, Tom haltingly listed the many reasons.

Cooke listened intently until Tom was done and then began to relate in a conversational tone, 'I didn't wish to kill any of them, you know, Master Potts. Rose Brent's death was an accident. I told her that I didn't wish to see her any more and she physically attacked me. I was forced to restrain her and unfortunately under-estimated my own strength. When I released my grip I found that she was dead. I placed her in the canal so that it would be thought she'd drowned by accident.

'A short while after that unhappy evening, Irish Joe tried to blackmail me, claiming that he'd witnessed what had happened. I'd no choice other than to dispose of him.'

He fell silent, and Tom pressed cautiously, 'Rose Brent's death was a tragic accident indeed, Master Cooke. Was it the same with Martha Standard and John Daws?'

Cooke shook his head with seeming regret. 'Sadly no. Standard had recognized me as her friend's lover. So I was forced to silence her. When I found Daws snoring drunk in his bed I was briefly tempted to leave him sleeping, because I reasoned that he might be blamed for the girl's death. But after a little more thought I decided it would be kinder for him to die in a drunken stupor and be spared the awful torments of being wrongfully hanged for murder.'

By now Tom was firmly convinced that Cooke was most definitely insane, and was nerving himself to spring at the man to try to overpower him.

A wailing cry echoed from the floor above, and Cooke stepped into the hallway, shouting, 'Be quiet, you bitch. I'll deal with you presently.'

Tom hurled himself forwards.

The pistol exploded.

Bodies impacted violently, collided against the door jamb and crashed to the floor, Tom uppermost lying akimbo across Cooke.

He reared up on to his knees, frantically flailing his fists into the other man's face, until abruptly the realization came that Cooke was motionless, blood pulsing from a long gash on the side of his head.

Tom rushed to snatch up his satchel, spilling the manacles out from it and using them to secure Cooke's hands and feet. Cooke groaned and twitched and Tom slumped with his back against the wall, body trembling as the rush of adrenaline drained from his muscles. He was physically spent, but mentally exultant.

'Rosie! Martha! John Daws! You'll be avenged now. You'll be avenged!'

FIFTY-THREE

Morning, Thursday June 1st

T he gloriously sunny weather harmonized perfectly with Tom's mood as he walked through the door of the Red House. The last ten days had been a feast of plaudits from all and sundry.

Martin Cooke was in Worcester jail awaiting trial for murder. His wife Edwina was safe in the loving care of her family, and was reported to be slowly recovering from the years of torment and abuse she had been subjected to by her husband.

The seal on Tom's happiness was that he and Amy were now formally betrothed. They planned to marry in March of the next year, when Tom's stint as constable would be finished, and he would be free to obtain employment lucrative enough for him to support a wife and family.

'And today is payment of fees day. Only another nine to come, and I'll be a free man,' he thought contentedly as he entered the study.

The coins chinked as Joseph Blackwell counted them out on to the desk. 'One pound, eighteen shillings and fourpence, Master Potts. Payment in full for services rendered as constable of this parish for the month of May in the year of Our Lord, 1827.'

'Thank you, sir.' Tom reached for the money only to be stopped by Blackwell's hand.

'Hold hard, Master Potts. This month I have to deduct three shillings for my stabling and feeding of Daniel Wynne's horse.'

'Very well, sir,' Tom accepted philosophically.

Blackwell removed the sum. 'My Lord Aston has instructed me to tell you that from next month onwards four shillings will be docked from your fees every month until the debt of the twenty guineas you owe the parish coffer is cleared.' He smiled bleakly. 'The loss of one shilling per week will not cause you any undue hardship, I'm sure.'

Tom was very pleasantly surprised at the small amount being deducted. 'No indeed it will not, sir. And after next March I'm sure that I'll be well able to afford to increase the weekly amount.'

'How so?' Blackwell enquired.

'Well, sir, as you know my term as constable will be finished at the end of March, 1828, and I'll be enabled to find more lucrative employment.'

The other man sighed and told Tom regretfully, 'I'm truly sorry Master Potts, but my Lord Aston is adamant that you will continue in the post of constable until the debt is fully paid.'

'But that's ridiculous!' Tom protested hotly. 'He can't force me to remain as constable after March if I can raise the twenty guineas somehow or other.'

Blackwell shook his head. 'I regret that my Lord Aston is adamant that the debt is to be paid off at one shilling weekly, and that the Vestry has fully acceded to his wish. Accordingly the parish cannot under any circumstances accept any greater sum than that amount as the weekly repayment. It's a sad fact of life, Master Potts, that my Lord Aston wields absolute power in this parish and thus can commit you to the debtors' prison with a mere stroke of his pen. Surely it is better for you to remain in the post of constable, rather than spend years rotting away in prison.'

'But at that rate it'll take me years to clear the debt.'

'Four hundred and twenty weeks to be precise. A total of eight years and one month,' Blackwell stated pedantically.

'But dammit, sir! I'm to be married in March next year. How can I support a wife and family in reasonable comfort on a constable's earnings?' Despair was overwhelming Tom.

A smile quirked at the corners of Blackwell's mouth.

'Quite easily, I would presume. The Mackinnon family informs me that they have established a fund for you as a reward for your rescue of Edwina Cooke. Starting from tomorrow the sum of twelve guineas a month will be paid into an account in your name in the Midlands Shires Bank. Should you pre-decease your wife, she will continue to receive that sum until her own demise. What say you to that, Master Potts?'

It took Tom some time to fully appreciate all the connotations of this almost incredible news, and he stood motionless, head bent, frowning with concentration.

Joseph Blackwell waited patiently for a reply.

At last Tom lifted his head and beamed happily. 'Well, sir, it seems that for the next eight years and one month my future wife's full marital title will be Mistress Constable Thomas Potts.'

'And a very fine title it is indeed, Master Constable Thomas Potts.' Blackwell chuckled dryly.